T0290435

Investigating the Kennedy Assassination
Volume 2

Why Was Kennedy Killed?

Michael J. Deeb and
Robert Lockwood Mills

Investigating the
Kennedy Assassination
Volume 2

Why Was Kennedy Killed?

**HISTRIA
FICTION**

Histria Fiction

Las Vegas ◊ Chicago ◊ Palm Beach

Published in the United States of America by

Histria Books
7181 N. Hualapai Way, Ste. 130-86
Las Vegas, NV 89166 USA
HistriaBooks.com

Histria Fiction is an imprint of Histria Books dedicated to outstanding works of fiction. Titles published under the imprints of Histria Books are distributed worldwide.

Library of Congress Control Number: 2024933253

ISBN 978-1-59211-390-3 (hardcover)
ISBN 978-1-59211-416-0 (eBook)

"A man does what he must – in spite of personal consequences, in spite of obstacles and dangers and pressures – and that is the basis of all human activity."

— John F. Kennedy, Profiles in Courage

Preface

Kennedy's presidential campaign and his inaugural address established him as a traditional Cold War warrior. But his behavior after he took office put him at odds with the national security establishment of his own administration.

By the end of October 1963, members of the national security establishment saw JFK rejecting their moves to turn the Cold War into a 'hot war.' Instead, they saw him making moves to come to an understanding with the Soviets and their Communist satellite countries.

Entering November, they knew he was communicating secretly with Khrushchev with the intention of ending the Cold War, and they saw him making overtures to Castro with the intention of normalizing relations with Cuba

In addition, Kennedy's peace agenda included limiting the Cold War covert activities of the CIA, negotiating a disarmament agreement with Russia, reducing the amount spent annually for defense, and sharing the exploration of space with the Soviet Union.

Probably the final straw was JFK's October 1963 executive order 263 calling for the complete withdrawal of American forces from Vietnam as soon as he won re-election in 1964.

The elites of the national security establishment and those of the military-industrial complex found themselves in agreement that Kennedy's peace agenda posed a serious threat to the security and the economy of the United States. They feared that he would continue to pursue this agenda if re-elected, as expected, to a second four year term.

Allen Dulles, who JFK fired as director of the Central Intelligence Agency, said of President Kennedy,

"We could not permit another cripple to occupy the White House."

Outside of the national security establishment, other elites were fearful of a second Kennedy term too. JFK had issued NSAM 11110 in the fall of 1963 to replace the Federal-Reserve-issued money with silver-backed currency, the cam-

paign against the Mafia and organized crime in the labor unions was gaining traction, the oil depletion allowance was under review, and the administration had
become an advocate for Black American civil rights.

A second term could cement these policies in place. In the summer of 1962,
Santos Trafficante, the Mafia Don of Miami, told an FBI informant, *"No Jose. You
don't understand me. Kennedy is not going to make it to the election. He is going to be
hit."*

Harper Woods, Michigan

Michael Burke returned to his home in Harper Woods from his downtown Detroit law office early one evening in June 1979. He was a dark-haired six-footer of Irish decent. He had graduated from Boston College in 1957, and thereafter worked in Washington, D.C. for the FBI and then as a staffer for the House Judiciary Committee.

His three kids were just out of school for the year. Susan, the eldest, was studying accounting at the University of Detroit. Ann had just finished her senior year at Bishop Gallagher High School. Jackie, the youngest, was going into her junior year at the same school.

"Hi Dad," Jackie greeted. "What's up?"

"Nothing all that exciting," he responded. "How about you?"

"I slept in today and just lay around the house after," Jackie told him. "But I baby sit tonight."

"Where's Mom?" he asked.

"I think she's in the basement doing laundry."

Mike put down his briefcase and went down the stairs. Marilyn was transferring wet clothes from the washer to the dryer.

"Hey, sweetheart." he said. "You about ready for a glass of wine?"

"You bet," Marilyn answered. "Why don't you pour us each a glass and get out some cheese and crackers?"

Mike gave his wife a hug and a kiss.

"Sure. Will you be long?"

"Not if you stop interrupting my work. I'm Just about finished here. Be right up."

"I didn't realize a hug was such a problem. I just wanted to get a kiss and a quick feel."

"Yeah, I know the kind of feel you wanted. Maybe later, big fella.' If you're lucky, that is."

"Promises, all I get are promises," he said, chuckling.

The Burkes had moved to this Detroit suburb twelve years earlier when Mike took a job with Circuit Judge Harold Ryan as his court clerk. The two men had met in Washington, D.C. the summer of 1967, when they worked for the House Judiciary Committee investigating the Kennedy assassination. That fall, Ryan was elected to a seat on the circuit bench in Wayne County, Michigan and asked Mike to be his clerk.

During his tenure as clerk, Mike earned a law degree from the University of Detroit. After Judge Ryan had taken retirement two years ago, Mike went to work with a Detroit law firm. His wife Marilyn worked as an elementary teacher with the Harper Woods Public Schools.

Mike poured the wine, loosened his tie, kicked off his shoes and set up a plate of their favorite cheese on the living room coffee table. Then he waited.

Marilyn wasn't long. She sat next to him on the couch.

"Whew! That's a good job done," she sighed. "What kind of wine did you open for us?"

"I thought we might try some chilled Sauvignon Blanc tonight."

Marilyn took a sip. "It's a bit dry, but tasty," she judged. "How was your day?"

"Somewhat exciting, actually," Mike responded. "At least the office staff was excited."

"By what?"

"They were impressed and excited because I received a call from a member of the United States House of Representatives."

"Who'd be calling you, and why?"

"Congresswoman Lindy Boggs of Louisiana called."

"OK, big shot," Marilyn taunted. "Why was she calling you?"

"She wants to hire me, that's why."

"I hate it when you drag things out Michael," Marilyn declared. "All right, I'll play your game. I hardly think she needs a lawyer to represent her in Circuit Court here in Detroit. So what does she want you to do for her?"

"She was so impressed with the report Harold and I prepared for the Judiciary Committee back in 1967, she wants me to head up another Kennedy assassination investigation."

"Oh, my God!" she exclaimed. "It's coming back to haunt us."

Mike laughed. "I suppose you could look at it that way. But I'm just seeing her as another client who needs my services."

"You got shot the last time you worked on this issue. Remember?" she snapped. "You could've been killed."

"I remember very well, sweetheart," Mike responded. "I still have the scar on my arm from the bullet."

"And I have the emotional scars from the FBI harassment the girls and I had to endure. Remember that Michael?"

"Yes, I do, dear."

"Do you really need clients that badly, Michael?"

"Actually, yes," Mike admitted. "I've been with the firm two years this August. If it weren't for the work the partners send my way and court appointments, I'd have had a hard time justifying my office space, much less making a living. Your teacher's salary has been a Godsend. So, Boggs' offer would give us a real boost."

"I suppose," Marilyn agreed. "With Ann headed to Michigan State this fall, we'll have two of the kids in college. What exactly is her offer?"

"Basically, she'll pay my hourly rate plus expenses."

"And what does the Congresswoman get for her money?"

"She wants someone to take a look at why Kennedy was killed' maybe who did it, too."

"I thought the Church Committee looked into this a couple of years ago."

"Not really," Mike informed her. "Actually, that investigation looked into the CIA and their shadow government activities. You're thinking of the House Select Committee on Assassinations. That group decided that the Kennedy assassination was probably a conspiracy, but didn't look into who killed him, or why he was killed either.

"Congresswoman Boggs' husband Hale was a member of the Warren Commission. Before he was killed in a plane crash, he was very critical of its Report. He believed the assassination was a conspiracy and suspected that government people were involved in it. He was impressed with the report Harold and I completed for the House Judiciary, and his widow wants us to take another look at the evidence."

"Did you agree to do it?"

"No, I didn't," Mike told his wife. "Since the job would require some travel and some possible danger, I wanted to talk it over with you first."

"Thank you for that," Marilyn said. "Have you talked with Harold about it, yet?"

"Funny you should ask that," Mike responded. "It occurred to me that he might be interested in helping, now that he is retired from the bench."

"How much travel do you think this job would involve?"

"I really don't know, sweetheart. Not much more than the last time, I would guess. Why don't we have Harold and Lillian over and talk about the possibilities. What do you think?"

"Michael," Marilyn began, "I don't see any problem with your taking on this job. As you say, it's just another client asking you to do something. But if it truly becomes dangerous or keeps you away too much, I want you to promise me that you will back off. Are you willing to do that?"

"I think so. Yes, I can do that, sweetheart. But I would like to talk it over with Harold, too.

"Now, what's for supper?"

"Mac 'n cheese," Marilyn teased.

"No really. What's for supper?"

"Tonight the chef has prepared blueberry pancakes."

"I was hoping for meatloaf."

"You're the one who insisted last Saturday that we go to that u-pick place in Macomb County and pick blueberries. You wanted blueberries, so we got blueberries; a ton of them. Now we've got to eat up the darn things or they'll rot."

"I suppose," Mike admitted.

"Michael," Marilyn continued, "I'll not throw out perfectly good food."

"Enough already," Mike protested. "Blueberry pancakes it is."

After supper, Mike and Marilyn were enjoying their coffee. "I've got to admit, those pancakes were real tasty."

"I think I know what I'm doing around a stove."

"Honey, you're the greatest," Mike assured his wife.

"And don't you forget it, buster."

St. Clair Shores, Michigan

Lillian Ryan picked up the phone.

"Hello, this is the Ryan residence. How can I help you?"

"Is this Lillian Ryan?" someone on the other end of the line asked.

"Yes, it is. How can I help you?"

Lillian was always cautious talking with people she did not know. Her husband, Harold, had held public office for many years. As a result, he had attracted all kinds of weird calls. So she had acquired an unlisted number for their home phone.

How did this person get our number? she wondered.

"You probably don't remember, dear," the caller began, "but twenty-five years ago, you and Harold were guests at a dinner party I held at my Washington home."

Holy smokes! Twenty-five years ago, and I'm supposed to remember this person?

"This is Lindy Boggs, dear. How are you?"

"Well I'll be darned," Lillian remarked. "I must confess, I didn't remember your voice, but now that you mention it, I do remember visiting your home back when Harold was in Congress. I was so sorry to read of Hale's death a few years back. Harold thought so highly of him."

"I remember the flowers and Mass card you sent back then. It was most thoughtful of you. Believe me when I tell you, Hale thought highly of Harold as well."

Lillian responded, "Harold will be glad to hear that. He told me you had taken Hale's seat and had run successfully in your own right since. Good for you. He says you are an important and strong voice in Congress."

"I try, sweetie," Lindy said. "Before I talk to Harold, I wanted to ask you something."

"Sure," Lillian said, pausing.

"I want Harold to do some more investigating on the Kennedy assassination," she began. "I read that report he and Michael Burke completed back in 1967 for the House Judiciary and think it's a first-class piece of work. Too bad it was deep-sixed by Ford.

"Hale always regretted signing off on the Warren Commission Report," Boggs continued. "He thought all along the killing was a conspiracy, but he caved in to President Johnson and signed the damned thing. He was also livid about the harassment Mike Burke and his family got from those FBI goons. Now the House Committee on Assassinations has released its report. Once again, they didn't finish the job and stopped short of finding out why he was killed or who might have been involved."

"I want that rock turned over, once and for all," Lindy declared. "Is Harold up to looking into that?"

"What do you mean, up to it?"

"I don't want to suggest it if he's gone 'round the bend' or is suffering some serious disability, don't you know."

"Truth be told, Lindy," Lillian snapped, "I'm the one on the verge of going 'round the bend.' Since he retired from the bench, he's been hanging around the house and driving me crazy."

Both ladies erupted in laughter.

"Believe me, he would love the challenge," Lillian assured the Congresswoman. "And I would love getting my life back."

More laughter erupted.

"Would you like to talk with him right now?"

"Sure, put him on."

It took a few minutes for Harold to put down his Detroit News and pick up the phone.

"Hello," he said. "This is Harold Ryan."

"How the dickens are you, sweetie?" Lindy Boggs greeted.

Harold responded, "Is it my imagination, or is this Lindy Boggs, the gentle woman from Louisiana?"

"Don't get smart with me, Harold Ryan," Boggs snapped. "I'm anything but gentle; and you know it."

"That's what I hear, Lindy," Harold admitted. "I was long gone from Congress before you could roast my tail feathers in a House debate."

"I never would have done that to you, sweetie," Lindy assured him.

"Sure," Harold bantered. "And I have a bridge across the St. Clair River I want to sell you. What can I do for you, young lady?"

"I want to go after these Washington elites who keep playing games with the Kennedy assassination. Pisses me off that everyone is still tiptoeing around the heart of the matter. You and your buddy Burke pretty clearly identified the killing as a conspiracy back in 1967. And our House Assassination Committee investigation, after spending millions of dollars, could only get the balls to say the killing was 'probably' the result of a conspiracy. Can you believe it?"

"I read the report, Lindy," Harold told her. "With all the evidence at their disposal, inserting that word 'probably' upset me, too. What do you want to do about it?"

"I want you and Burke to get back in the saddle, Harold," she responded. "I want you two to come to D.C. and reopen your investigation. This time I want you to focus on why President Kennedy was killed and who most probably was involved in the conspiracy to kill him."

"Hot damn, Lindy," Harold exclaimed. "A powerful House committee with a lot of money and a large staff backed off that issue and you want an old retired judge and a young attorney, neither of whom have any standing, to tackle the question of the century?"

"Yes."

"You don't want a lot, do you?"

"I want you here to give it a shot," Lindy shot back. "Will you do that for me and for Hale? He felt that signing off on the Warren Commission Report was the worst act of his public life."

Harold thought he had a way out. "I would need Burke to work with me, and he's struggling to build a practice here in Detroit. I doubt if he could get away."

"I already talked to him, and he's on board with it."

"There is one other thing, though. After all the years I spent away from home in public office, I promised Lillian that my wandering was over. I doubt if she'd go along with this."

"I already cleared it with her, Harold."

"Damn! Did I just hear a door slam?" Harold exclaimed. "You trapped me, Lindy Boggs. No wonder they call you the dragon lady in Washington. I didn't have a chance, did I?"

"Nope, you didn't sweetie," Boggs admitted. "I wanted you on this and I usually get what I want. So stop your whining. I got some money together to pay you and Burke and to cover your expenses. Just get your butt down here and get to work. After you talk with Burke, call my office and talk with Mable. She'll be your contact person on this project and will arrange for your flight and local housing."

"You talk as though this is a done deal, Lindy," Harold complained.

"It is, my friend. Burke will call you this evening. Get with him. I expect you two to be here the first of next week. Bring your pajamas, toothbrush, clean underwear and reading glasses, Harold. I don't pay for any lollygagging or sightseeing. You'll be busy. Say bye-bye to Lillian for me, sweetie."

The line went dead.

"Son-of-a-gun. I've been had."

Harper Woods

Later that week, Harold and Lillian joined the Burkes for supper. This time, Marilyn had fixed meatloaf.

"Hi you two," Harold greeted as he gave Marilyn a hug. Then, he shook his old clerk's hand.

"I haven't seen much of you lately, Mike."

"You forget that young lawyers have to hustle for clients. We can't sit around having martini lunches an' such, like you retired judges."

"Doesn't he wish," Lillian joined in. "For the first time in 20 years, I've got him to myself. With all the chores I have for him, he has no time for extended lunches with other judges."

"Lillian won't even let me met my old friends for morning coffee at McDonald's."

Marilyn joined in the fun. "How is it mowing your own grass, cleaning out the garage and such, Harold?"

"I have an entirely new appreciation for what Lillian has been doing most of our married life, believe me."

"Poor baby," Lillian teased.

"How about I pour a glass of wine, you?" Mike asked.

"We'll have whatever you and Marilyn are having, Mike," Lillian decided.

"See," Harold quipped. "I can't even order my own drink."

Over dinner, Mike brought up the job offer from Congresswoman Boggs.

"I served with Hale Boggs in the House," Harold told everyone. "We got along real well. Sounds like what the Congresswoman wants is a natural extension of the report we did for the Judiciary committee twelve years ago. I like it. What do you think of her offer, Mike?"

"Well," Mike began, "her public statements have identified her as a serious critic of the Warren Commission as well as the FBI Report. Beyond that, I don't know if she has formed any other opinions. But she wants us to look into why JFK was killed and who might have done it, if it wasn't Oswald."

"The mystery of the century," Lillian added.

"Does she know you're talking to Harold about this, Michael?" Marilyn asked.

"Yes, she does," Harold interrupted. "She called me Wednesday and told me she had already brought Mike on board.

"And here I thought we invited you Ryan's over so Mike could talk you into joining him on this investigation."

"I just wanted to sample your excellent meatloaf, Marilyn," Harold chuckled.

Lillian challenged Mike. "Are you just trying to get Harold out of doing his chores, Mike?"

"Not at all, Lillian," Mike assured her. "If I have him back home on weekends, can he join me on this adventure? Please?"

"Hello you two," Harold interrupted. "Can I join this conversation?"

"No," Lillian insisted. "If I can have him Saturdays and Sundays, you can have him Monday through Friday."

"You two are out of order," Harold banged his spoon on the table.

"You're not on the bench now, Judge," Lillian reminded him, laughing. "You can put your gavel away. Besides you have no authority in this court."

"And I suppose you're the judge and jury in this case," Harold complained.

"Oh all right, you crybaby," Lillian ruled. "You can go off and chase ghosts with your old buddy, Mike."

"I'm so relieved that I have your permission," Harold said.

"Now that we have that settled, how about a real drink, Harold?" Mike asked.

Washington, D.C.

"We believe and the facts strongly suggest that President John F. Kennedy was assassinated as the direct result of a conspiracy although, the persons responsible for such an act cannot be identified."

— Statement of, The House Select Committee to investigate the Kennedy and King Assassinations: House Resolution 1540. September 15, 1978.

Harold Ryan and Michael Burke were seated in a conference room when their host came into the room. They both stood.

"Gentlemen," Congresswoman Boggs said. "Welcome to Washington. I hope your journey here was pleasant. Good to see you again, Harold. It's been a long time." Without hesitation, Harold stepped forward and gave the wife of his old colleague, a hug.

"Good to see you too, Congresswoman," Harold assured her.

"You know better than that Harold. I'm 'Lindy' to you and to this young fellow, Burke. Take a seat you two."

Boggs began the meeting.

"I have asked Mable to join us. She will be your contact person in this office and take notes of our meetings. I hope you don't mind."

"Not at all, ma'am," Mike agreed.

"Michael Burke," Boggs said. "You worked too long for a House committee. You are to address me as 'Lindy.' Is that clear to you, young man?"

"Sorry. Old habits are difficult to break, I'm afraid."

"I hope you'll break this one, young man.

"Let's get started then," Boggs continued. "When the House is in session, I may have to run out in order to vote on something or other. I hope you will excuse me. It will be no reflection on the topic we're discussing at the time."

"I remember such calls during my time in the House, Lindy. Do what you have to do. We'll understand."

"I mailed you each a copy of the summary report of the House Committee on Assassinations. I hope you have had a chance to review it."

"Yes, we have," Mike revealed. "In fact, we discussed it on the plane ride down."

"What did you think of it, overall?"

Harold spoke first. "This was my second look at it. I still couldn't help feeling that the leadership of the Committee pulled the plug too soon. They had a good staff of investigators who had momentum going and a handle on the dynamic of the scene in Dallas; then, they just stopped. Like kissing your sister; not satisfying for anyone."

"I agree with Harold, ma'am," Mike added. "The Committee members seemed to be right on the verge of a breakthrough when they stopped, and closed the door."

"That expresses my feelings on the matter, exactly. And that is why you're here, gentlemen," the Congresswoman reminded them. "You're going to open that door. And the three of us are going through it even if we have to drag every member of the House with us, kicking and screaming."

"Speaking of kicking and screaming, Lindy," Harold asked, "Why would anyone cooperate with us? The Committee on Assassinations worked for two years and finally concluded what over 70% of Americans already believed, that a conspiracy was involved in the killing of John F. Kennedy. Few Americans believe Oswald acted alone, if at all."

Harold continued. "Now, we two outsiders come along and openly criticize the Committee on Assassinations for not going further with the evidence they had. Mike and I don't have standing, nor do we have subpoena powers. There is not even a House committee behind us. So, even the lowest clerk knows we can be told to take a hike and not suffer serious consequences."

"I think you're mistaken, Harold," Boggs said. "You will be acknowledged as members of my staff, both of you. You will have credentials and a charge from my subcommittee. From Burke's office in Michigan and my offices here the three of us will conduct our investigation, with help from Mable and Burke's clerical staff.

We will not act with a great deal of fanfare. But we will shed a new and very bright light on this conspiracy."

Harold added. "Twelve years ago, I believe Mike and I wrote our report to the House Judiciary on the Kennedy Assassination in that same vein."

"That's why I welcomed you two here today," Boggs revealed.

"You are lawyers here, gentlemen. As such you will follow the evidence as we look to see why he was killed. That might just lead us to discover who was involved in the conspiracy to kill John F. Kennedy, President of the United States on November twenty-second, 1963 and why."

"Harold and I are here to work with you toward that end, ma'am," Mike assured her.

"I believe you, young man," Boggs assured him. "As your reading of the report revealed, the Committee on Assassinations found that Kennedy was probably killed as a result of a conspiracy. Further, they concluded that the Warren Commission's and the FBI's investigations into the possibility of such a conspiracy was seriously flawed.

"All three reports refused to acknowledge any evidence which might shed light on why the president was assassinated and by whom.

"We shall not make that error, I assure you," Boggs asserted. "Instead, we will identify those who seriously opposed JFK's policies and the elites who would benefit from their reversal. So, I want you to look into the possibility that President Kennedy was set up for assassination. In short, I want you to ask and answer the question, was the assassination a true coup d'état?

"Are we on the same page, gentlemen?" Boggs asked. "Are you with me on this?"

"Yes ma'am," Mike answered with a smile on his face.

Harold nodded in agreement.

***

Mike and Harold were still in Bogg's conference room going over the documents used by the House Select Committee on Assassinations.

Burke slammed down a handful of papers. "Where in hell do we start on this thing?" he exclaimed.

"My eyes are getting tired of plowing through all of this legalese. It feels as though I'm back on the bench." Harold complained. "I get it. This investigation concluded that the nation of John F. Kennedy was probably a conspiracy. They stopped with that. Now where do we go?"

"I remember a quote from Oliver Wendell Holmes. He said a conspiracy was "…a partnership in criminal purpose."

Harold picked up that thought. "He was talking about two or more conspirators joining to accomplish a criminal act."

"Exactly," Burke agreed. "But is the criminal act we're looking into one where two or more shooters were organized to achieve a limited objective; that is, the killing of Kennedy? Or was the objective of our conspiracy the accomplishment of a full-blown coup d'état?"

"That's an interesting question," Harold thought out loud. "As an undergraduate student, I recall studying the legal implications of the Lincoln assassination. Back in 1865, it was claimed that Booth and his co-conspirators attempted to kill not only Lincoln but the Vice President and the Secretary of State as well.

"That would have made the Majority Leader of the Senate, President of the United States. That Senator was a big dealer in smuggled cotton. Who knows? Had they been successful, the South might have gained its independence after all."

"But Kennedy was the only target in the Dallas assassination," Burke reminded Harold.

"That's right, Harold said. "So, why don't we look at the possibility that the assassination of JFK was a coup d'état, and not simply the act of an angry Mafia Don, a few rogue CIA operatives or a crazed nut as the FBI claimed."

"You're getting me all excited here, my man," Mike told his old boss. "First though, let's see if the killing and the aftermath of the assassination contain all the elements of a coup."

"Good." Harold slammed his hand on the table in front of him. "We're off to the Library of Congress. We ought to find what we need there, don't you think?"

"Sounds too simple, Harold."

"Sometimes it's the simple things that lead to answers and solutions."

"Where did you get so smart?" Burke teased.

"You aren't the only lawyer in this room educated by the Jesuits, ya know."

"Oh ya," Burke chuckled. "I forgot."

***

On their way out, they stopped and checked in with Mable.

"We're headed to the Library of Congress." Harold told her. "Do you have a contract person over there?"

"As a matter of fact we do," Mable told him. "In the research room, check in with Irene Gohsman. I'll have told her to expect you by the time you get there. She's a peach. Anything special you want to research?"

Harold told Mable what they were looking for.

"By the time you get there, Irene will probably have tons of stuff for you to review."

Sure enough, by the time they arrived, Irene had piled periodicals and books on a table in a quiet corner.

"This should keep you busy for a while, gentlemen," she told them, smiling. "There's plenty more material where this came from, too. If you have any questions don't hesitate to tell me. We close at five."

"Thanks Irene," Mike said.

"I used to do research in here for the Judiciary committee, and I sometimes browsed in here on my lunch breaks," Mike told Harold. "But I never realized how deep their collections were."

Harold got himself settled and commented. "That's the last time I make such a broad request of Mable. It'll take us more than just this afternoon to plow through all this stuff."

"That's probably why Irene smiled when she told us what their closing time is," Burke responded with a sigh. "So, I guess we had better get at it, then."

"Let's compare notes in one hour, Mike."

"That sounds good to me."

It wasn't even an hour later when Mike stood up and stretched. "I don't know about you Harold, but I'm going blind here."

"I don't need to hear about your eyesight, Mike," Harold snapped. "I'm tired too. Right now I want to know if you found anything useful."

"Look at my list, Harold. During the past twenty-five years, every coup in Central or South America the Middle East and the Far East had military involvement as a common element. In every case, the military took over the state-run media, captured the statehouse and suspended the legislature. There's nothing there of use to us. What did you find?"

"Not much of use, Mike. But one of the volumes Irene put in my stack is a work by a fellow named Edward Luttwalk. Interestingly enough, his book is called: *Coup d'État: A Practical Handbook*. It was originally published by Penguin Press ten years ago in England and was just published here this year by Harvard Press.

"According to the table of contents, Luttwalk lays out all the pre requisites and elements of a true coup. And from his introductory comments, it would appear that we have in this book a guide for our investigation.

"I suggest we ask Irene if we can check this book out and have Mable order us a couple of copies this afternoon for overnight delivery. Then we can compare the killing of Kennedy and the aftermath with Luttwak's elements of a coup."

"In the meantime, Harold," Mike suggested, "while we're waiting for the book, let's list every step that was taken by LBJ following the killing of President Kennedy."

"What kind of steps do you have in mind?" Harold asked.

"I'm talking about the takeover of power by Lyndon Johnson and his people. We would start from the moment Johnson was sworn in on Air Force One and then identify all the steps Johnson took to consolidate power in the days that followed."

"I see what you mean. But let's do that tonight," Harold suggested. "Right now, I'm brain dead. I need a nap, and after that, a cocktail and a good meal before we tackle anything."

"What's with a nap?" Mike asked. "When did you start taking afternoon naps, Judge?"

"After I retired from the bench, that's when, Burke," Harold snapped.

"Oh ya, I forget."

***

Burke and Ryan had been given rooms in the Willard Hotel on Connecticut Ave., a stately place with a storied history. It had been established by the Willard brothers in the 1850s. Lincoln stayed there awaiting his first inauguration. In 1861, the failed Peace Commission met there as well. During the Civil War, it had housed a hotbed of intrigue, conspiracy, and was a center of government corruption. It was also a great place to have a good meal.

It was also considered the most luxurious hotel in Washington back then, with baths and lavatories on each floor. One hundred-plus years later, despite a need for renovation, it was still a fine place to stay while in the District.

While Harold took his nap, Mike relaxed in his room to read Luttwak's book. He hadn't gone far when he began to take notes as well. By the time Harold rang his room around 6 PM, Burke had filled a good part of a legal-sized pad of paper.

The two investigators met in the hotel dining room.

"Feel rested, Judge?"

"You bet. Nothing like a good nap in the afternoon to get the mind and body prepared for the rest of the day," Harold informed his partner. "You'll find out in a few years."

"Maybe I will. But right now, I can't afford such a luxury," Mike complained. "If I'm not working on some client's case, I'm doing chores at home. How do you manage?"

"That's the beauty of retirement," Harold whispered conspiratorially. "I play the age card to get out of all sorts of chores."

"It really works?"

Harold chuckled. "Sometimes it does. I'm afraid Lillian is on to my tricks, though. Often the best I can do is put off a chore until after the nap and before the evening cocktail. My wife is not all that gullible, I'm afraid.

"Tell me, Mike," Harold asked, "did you get in a snooze while I napped?"

"Nope I didn't. I don't want to start forming any bad habits. In fact, I read Luttwak's book and took some notes for our meeting tonight."

"Wonderful. When you were my court clerk, I could always depend on you to keep one step ahead of me. It's good to see things haven't changed. Let's order drinks and talk about it."

Both men ordered a Manhattan. Their waiter brought some freshly baked bread warm from the oven some and butter as well.

"What's with the three cherries in your drink, Howard?"

"Joe Yager started me on that habit. I expect he still puts three in his drink, too. You remember Joe?"

"Oh sure," Mike told him. "Joe and Cathy have been friends of ours ever since that first campaign back in 'sixty-seven. If I'm not mistaken, Joe is about ready to retire from teaching at Dearborn Community College. His boy Eric is in college just like my daughter Susan. She's at the University of Detroit. I think his daughter is still in high school like my daughter Jackie."

"Your eldest attends U. of D., doesn't she?"

"That's right. Susan is an accounting major. She might go on to law school. We'll see. Ann is going to attend Michigan State in the fall. I don't know what major she'll pursue; my guess is retailing or marketing.

"I don't think many freshmen students actually know," Mike continued.

"As I recall, your youngest is a year, two at most behind her, isn't she?"

"You recall correctly, Harold. We'll have three in college for at least one or two years."

"Phew!" Harold exclaimed. "I'm happy that stuff is behind Lillian and me."

"It's a rite of passage, Harold," Mike reminded him. "You can't send your kids into the world without that piece of paper. High school is not enough anymore."

"Susan had thought of becoming a dental hygienist. So, when she was a sophomore in high school, we got her a job in a dentist's office. She soon changed her mind about that career choice. She now manages the accounts of the dental office she works for. She's a natural at it, enjoys the bookkeeping and even is very good at collecting past due accounts.

"I just hope my other daughters find a fit that comfortable."

"Amen to that," Harold said, holding up his glass as in a toast. "Now, tell me a bit about the reading you did while I napped."

Just then, their meal was delivered to the table. Mike had the house special, pork chops. Harold stayed with his favorite, prime rib, medium rare. All conversation stopped while the two hungry men dug in.

Both men were too busy enjoying their food to talk much.

"Can I get you gentlemen some coffee?" their waiter asked while he cleared the empty plates.

They both welcomed a cup.

"Whew!" Harold said, relaxing into his comfortable high-back chair. "That was so good. Did you enjoy your pork chops?"

"Yes, I did. They were very tasty. I order them when I get the chance because Marilyn seldom serves them at home."

"Prime rib is a bit rich for our budget, too," Harold revealed. "Since I retired from the bench no lawyers are buying me fancy lunches any more, either. So I intend to take advantage of our expense account opportunity."

Mike raised his cup toward his partner. "Here's to expense accounts, Harold."

The men clicked their cups. "Hear, hear," they intoned.

***

Back in the sixth-floor conference room, Mike spread his notes out on the large table in the center of the room.

"What did you come up with, Mike?" Harold asked, leaning over the table.

"Nothing earthshaking, actually," Mike admitted. "But let's start with the six questions normally asked in any criminal investigation," Mike suggested.

"You mean the 'what, where, when, who, how and why?'"

"Right," Mike answered. "Of those four questions you identified only three were addressed by the FBI and the Warren Commission. You and I also looked into the 'what' back in '67."

"We did," Harold recalled. "As a result of our investigation, we flatly disagreed with those two government reports. In our report to the Judiciary Committee back then, we decided that Oswald was not the only shooter. In fact, we concluded that there was probably a well-planned conspiracy in operation to kill the president on November twenty-second, 1963.

"Now, I suggest that if we are ever to identify who was involved, we must first take a look at the 'why' and the 'how.'"

"Makes sense," Harold agreed. "Where should we start?"

"Lindy Boggs mentioned that she knew some insiders who helped the Church Committee with information. I think we need to ask her to set up a meeting for us with one or more of them."

"There are a few others who have publicly disagreed with the, Warren Commission, the FBI Report and the House Select Committee on Assassinations Report. They might talk with us, too." Mike suggested.

"I hope so," Harold agreed. "Let's contact Mable first thing. In the meantime, I'll take your notes and go over them tonight. How's that sound?"

"Good. While you're doing that, I'd like to call home. I might catch one or two of the girls before they go out tonight."

Harper Woods

Mike was surprised; his home phone was not busy when he called.

"Hi, sweetheart," Mike greeted his wife. "How's everything?"

"Hello yourself, big guy," Marilyn responded. "We're all fine; and you?"

"We're losing our eyesight plowing through tons of documents. Otherwise, all is well. We're probably going to be home by the end of the week. Boggs promised to get us a meeting with one or more insiders. Hopefully, they can get us to better understand the why of the assassination."

Marilyn responded quickly. "I thought that it has been already decided that the Mafia and the CIA were behind the whole thing; and maybe LBJ too."

"Hold on, dear. None of that has ever been proven. Garrison's court evidence aside, he never proved anything; nor did Oliver Stone in his movie '*JFK.*' Both guys made a lot of accusations and were entertaining. But at the end of the day there was a lot of smoke and little fire."

"So you're looking for the fire."

"You got it, dear," Mike said, "And so far, we ain't found much more than more smoke."

"Remember," Marilyn said sternly, "while you're looking for the fire, you promised no heroics. I don't want you or us getting burned; promise?"

"Yes dear," Mike assured her. "No heroics. Are any of the girls home?"

"Sue has a date with a handsome dude named Anthony who drives a black Trans-Am. Ann is out with a bunch of girls, but Jackie just got home from her job at the Sweet Shop."

"Let me talk with her, will ya'?"

"Hi Dad. How's the big investigation going?"

"Fine, thank you. You mother did not report having any tires slashed. Did you find any dead cats on the porch?"

"Not that we noticed, Dad. I guess you haven't ruffled enough feathers in Washington yet."

Mike chuckled. "Give me time, my dear. There's always hope."

"I can hardly wait," she responded with a chuckle of her own. "When will you get home?"

"Probably by this weekend."

"Sweet! See you then, Dad; love you."

"Love you too, sweetheart."

Mike finished talking with his wife, turned on the TV to catch the late news and got ready for bed.

Representative Boggs' Office

"We could not permit another cripple to occupy the White House."

— Allen Dulles, April 1964.

As soon as they had finished breakfast, Harold called their contact person in the Boggs congressional office.

"Hi Mabel," Harold greeted. "Lindy mentioned she could put us in touch with people who could help us with information not generally known. Are you the one to do that?"

"I don't think so, Congressman. This request is one Representative Boggs will probably have to handle herself," Mable told him. "Some of these contacts were real sensitive. I don't even have any of their names in my file. And I know the she will want to discuss this matter with you directly. So, why don't you come into the office? The Congresswoman should be here about 9 AM. Will that work for you, Congressman Ryan?"

"Yes it will, Mable," Harold assured her. "Thank you. Burke and I will see you at nine."

***

The three met in the Congresswoman's conference room.

"What is it you need?" Rep. Boggs asked.

"We need to check out some information about Allen Dulles; things he said off the record," Harold told the Congresswoman.

"And you need someone to verify or dismiss such things?"

"Exactly," Mike said. "Your source will not have to reveal anything damning to Mr. Dulles, only tell us if what we have uncovered is accurate, or at least has some foundation in fact."

"There is a fellow who might assist you," Boggs revealed. "He was of deputy rank, close to the top at the CIA. He might give you a hand. I'll call him this morning. Where can I reach you?"

"Just tell Mable, ma'am," Mike suggested.

"Look here, young fella," the Congresswoman replied. "I told you when we first met to call me 'Lindy.' If you're going to keep this formal nonsense going, I'm going to have to call your mother."

"I wouldn't want you to do that, Lindy," Mike pleaded. "But to answer your question, we're going to spend some time at the Library of Congress this morning. We'll check in with Mable at noon. By the way, we plan to head back to Michigan Friday."

"Good to know," she told Harold and Mike, "I'll have word for you by noon."

***

After lunch, Mike and Harold sat in a small conference room at the Willard.

A man sat across the table from them. Like most high level Washington bureaucrats, he was dressed in a three-piece suit. His gray hair was thinning and he wore a mustache. "How can I help you gentlemen?"

Harold began. "How do we address you, sir?" he asked.

"Why don't you just call me, 'George'?"

"All right, George," Mike said. "The other day I was digging through some documents at the Library of Congress. This one file was associated with the Warren Commission deliberations. In this document Allen Dulles was quoted as saying, 'We could not permit another cripple in the White House.' To your knowledge, did Mr. Dulles ever say this?"

"Yes, I was present when he said exactly that."

"What was the occasion?" Harold asked.

"Several of us were at his home in Georgetown one evening. We were finishing up our second drink before dinner and one of those present asked a question about how the Commission was coming along. Mr. Dulles just said, 'You know, we could not permit another cripple in the White House.' I was very surprised at the comment. But the others just went on as though nothing new or startling had just been revealed."

"He was referring about John Kennedy, wasn't he?"

"Oh, yes. There was no doubt about that."

"Who were the other cripples in the White House?"

"Historians have been very open about the governance problems Wilson had during his second term, after he had a severe stroke. The loss of the United Nations vote in the Senate is often blamed on his stroke. The loss of Central Europe to the Soviets is often blamed on the diminished capacity of FDR at the Yalta Conference. FDR reacted poorly to Russian moves in that region just before his death. And the heart attack Ike suffered in Denver after his second election victory has been cited as being responsible for the weak US response to the Hungarian revolution. We might have missed a chance then to snatch Hungary from behind the Iron Curtain."

"But Kennedy was considered athletic and intellectually brilliant. How could he have been a cripple?" Mike protested.

"You are evidently unaware of all the medications Kennedy was taking daily. Let me give you a quick rundown. I assure you that you can check what I tell you with a little research.

"To begin with, according to his mother's notes, John Kennedy was a rather sickly young man. In 1937 his doctors began giving him steroids to help control the chronic colitis he suffered. As a Congressman visiting England in 1947 he was hospitalized and diagnosed with Addison's disease. On the ship bringing him home, he was bedridden and so sick that the last rites of the Catholic Church were administered. He was given a year to live.

"By 1955 he had had two failed back operations and thereafter had to be given cortisone injections daily by his personal physician, Dr. Janet Travell. JFK was also taking three types of medication for chronic diarrhea. Of course, this was in addition to the steroids he was taking for the colitis."

"Holy crap," Mike exclaimed. "Who would believe this?"

"He fooled a lot of people, Mr. Burke. During the 1960 campaign for the nomination, Johnson's team claimed that Kennedy had Addison's Disease.

"This was loudly denied by Kennedy and his staff. Then JFK's media people bombarded the press and TV with stuff that he was a healthy and athletic young man. His smiling face with those capped front teeth was everywhere in the press and on TV.

"It didn't hurt this image either that it seemed every woman in America wanted to jump into the sack with him. For his part, it seemed he was trying to accommodate most of them.

"J. Edgar Hoover had an extensive file on JFK's sexual adventures, too; and Kennedy knew it. Despite that, President Kennedy was even bedding Judith Campbell the mistress of the don of Chicago's Giancana crime family. Phone records of the White House switchboard show that she called him often and visited him there as well. Many in Washington, Hoover in particular, felt that this behavior was reckless and posed a security threat to the United States."

Harold had been quietly listening. "I was in Congress for all of his term," he revealed. "Beyond his back trouble, the physical problems you mentioned were not widely known. But I did hear rumors about the sexual stuff."

"One more thing on the health issue," their informant said. "Dr. Max Johnson visited the White House and even accompanied the president on his trip to Vienna in June 1961. This physician has since had his license taken away. But for a time he served what were known as the rich and famous and was often called 'Dr. Feel-Good.' We had information that he gave JFK injections of amphetamines."

"How would you know such things?" Mike asked, still incredulous at the revelations.

"Mr. Burke. It was and still is important for our government to know such things about every world leader, even our own. Kennedy's need for all this daily medication might lead you to understand why any sensible person would worry about him. But Dulles called him a 'cripple' because of the decisions he made while taking all that medication. Even a cursory review of history shows that physically impaired leaders often do not make good decisions. With that in mind, you might understand why many in high places were concerned about the decisions Kennedy made while under the influence of all those drugs."

"Which of his decisions would such people considered real problems for the United States?" Harold asked.

"I suggest that the Bay of Pigs would qualify as a fiasco and very damaging to both the image and the future of the United States."

"Why begin with that episode?" Mike asked.

"We should begin with that episode because it was the first foreign policy test for the Kennedy administration," George quickly answered. "It was the first important opportunity the new administration had to work with the holdovers from the Eisenhower days...Dulles, Hoover, and the military leaders.

"The new president and his advisors were a blank slate, you see. This would be his first opportunity to demonstrate his decision-making ability and to show if he had a spine of steel or jelly when the chips were down and the going became difficult.

"Remember," George continued, "a plan to support an invasion of Cuba to depose Castro was ready to go when JFK's was sworn into office in 1961. So he and his advisors had to deal with it immediately.

"In fact, during the presidential campaign the previous fall, Kennedy had roasted Eisenhower and Nixon for allowing Castro to take over Cuba and establish a Communist stronghold just ninety miles off our shore. JFK also strongly criticized them for not taking aggressive action against Castro after the takeover. Poor Nixon couldn't say anything during the debates about the planned invasion to oust Castro. He had run the top-secret operation from the White House himself, so he just had to take the abuse from Kennedy.

"Secretly, Eisenhower had approved these plans to overthrow Castro. Toward that end, and well before the fall election of 1960, Cuban exiles had been trained and equipment gathered for an invasion of Cuba. The plan called for armed Cuban nationals to be landed at the port of Trinidad. Once that port and the nearby airfield had been captured, a new Cuban government would be declared and quickly recognized by the United States. Massive US military aide would follow and Castro would be ousted greeted by a supportive Cuban population."

"This was not Kennedy's project. It was a plan approved by his predecessor. But after all his strong talk during the presidential campaign, it appeared that it would earn Kennedy's support. Anyway, it was an opportunity for JFK to put up or shut up."

"Seems ta' me he put up, as you say," Mike offered. "JFK allowed the invasion to go forward, didn't he?"

"Correct, Mr. Burke. He did, but only after he ordered some key changes."

"What were those?" Harold asked.

"His advisors wanted to appear tough, and be seen as doing something to remove Castro. But they also feared turning word opinion against Kennedy and alarming the Soviet Union. So, first, his people changed the invasion site from Trinidad to the more secluded Bay of Pigs. Second, they reduced the number of planes involved in pre-invasion air strikes against Castro's small air fleet from 26 to 6, and limited air strikes to one night attack. Third, they required the off-loading of the invasion force to be done in darkness. Fourth, all American ships were ordered to be at least fifty miles away from the Cuban coast. And last, they cautioned that the president would not allow any support of the invasion force by American off-shore forces or air strikes by our planes.

"Admiral Burke told the president that these changes reduced the chances of success to 'at best' fifty- fifty."

"How did the changes affect the actual results?" Harold asked.

"Two of them critically destroyed any chance for success," George told them. "First, the Bay of Pigs site had no port facility and the nearby airfield was too short for the invader's planes to land. It was also closer to Castro's troops stationed in Havana. In addition, should the beachhead be compromised, there was no escape, because the landing site was separated from the nearby mountains by a swamp. All the invaders would be killed or captured.

"The primary reason for failure, according to the Cuban Study Group appointed by Kennedy in the aftermath, was the failure to destroy the small Cuban air force. One of Kennedy's advisors, McGeorge Bundy canceled the air strike scheduled to precede the invasion.

"Castro's planes were sitting ducks parked wing to wing at a nearby airfield. But with the air strike canceled, the two jet fighter planes and his B-26 bombers were unharmed. Subsequently, these planes destroyed the invasion fleet's B-26 airplanes, strafed the troops on the beach and destroyed their supply ships offshore as well.

"As a disaster became apparent, a meeting was held with the president. Present were Admiral Burke, General Lemnitzer, Richard Bissell, General Cabell, Dean Rusk and Bobby Kennedy. Faced with defeat the president refused to support the invasion with our forces standing offshore or even to rescue the invaders.

"Bobby Kennedy said, 'All you bright fellows have gotten the president into this.' Those present then knew that this would be the spin the Kennedy team would put on this failure.

"But the greater disaster was the effect Kennedy's performance had on that blank slate I mentioned. He completely lost the trust of the military and the CIA. And it only got worse as his people began to look for scapegoats to blame for the disaster."

"Wait a minute," Mike protested. "The public was told that he was poorly advised and that the project failed because it was badly planned. As proof, General Charles Cabell was fired and Allen Dulles was forced to retire."

"All of that's true, Mr. Burke. Those moves were made. That's also when Kennedy's team floated the story that JFK was so angry he intended to shatter the CIA into a thousand pieces.

"That was all political damage control. It only deepened the anger and the distrust of those involved in the invasion and coup attempt. But the negative effects went way beyond that. Now, important career decision-makers throughout government felt they would be thrown to the dogs, and their careers ruined, anytime the Kennedys felt the need to sacrifice them in the service of their political agenda."

"Did Kennedy give any reason for the changes he made to the invasion plan?" Harold asked.

"As part of the damage control operation, he met with President Eisenhower at Camp David. He told Ike that he insisted on the changes because he didn't want the United States linked with the invasion and coup attempt for fear of world opinion and the Soviet Union reaction.

"Ike told him that there was no way we could have avoided being identified with the invasion and coup attempt. Since we were going to be blamed anyway, it was better to have won than lost. 'Success was always better than failure,' Ike lectured. 'But,' Kennedy insisted, 'there was the Soviet response in Berlin to consider.'

At this point, we're told Ike became somewhat angry. He told Kennedy that whether the invasion had been successful or not, the Soviets would react only in their own best interests. 'Remember,' he insisted, 'they would have moved on Berlin in the past if they had thought they could get away with it. They only respected strength. At the Bay of Pigs we had only shown vacillation instead of resolve.'"

"You see, gentlemen," George continued, "JFK's team and his leadership style set a tone of fear for what was to come. It set the context, the prism as it were, through which what followed was viewed. And what happened next only added fuel to the fire of fear and anger."

"What would that have been?" Mike asked.

"It was the June 1961 Summit meeting with Khrushchev in Vienna."

"That was a public relations victory, wasn't it?" Mike asked.

"Oh yes," George replied. "Our handsome athletic president and his beautiful wife conquered Vienna and the whole of Europe. At the same time, the dumpy old and crude Russian leader was mocked. The public fawned over America's magnificent couple. From a public relations perspective it was great.

"But behind the scenes our President was taken to the woodshed. Khrushchev blindsided him with his gruff bully style. To top it all off, when Kennedy suggested the two nations explore space together and share technology to do so, the Soviet leader blew him off."

"Kennedy's suggestion sounds like a good deal for the Soviets. After all, we beat them to the moon." Mike protested.

"It would seem so, Mr. Burke. But the Soviet leader blew this suggestion off for two reasons. First, he believed Russian scientists were far ahead of the US in booster development at that time. Second, he did not trust Kennedy after the Bay of Pigs fiasco.

"This was the trip on which Kennedy brought along Dr. Feel-good and his shots of amphetamines."

"OK," Mike interrupted. "I'm looking through the prism of the Cuban disaster. Why was the Vienna conference considered so bad from our perspective?"

"It was a disaster because JFK was offering to share our technology with our enemies, the Soviet Union. He appeared to be more concerned with trying to get them to like us than with the defense of the United States. Our people present carried the message back that Kennedy had come off as weak and vacillating, and had been pushed around during private exchanges with Khrushchev.

"Also remember, gentlemen, we were still in a very intense Cold War with these people, and here comes a liberal upstart with the power to weaken us. He failed his first test of leadership during the Bay of Pigs matter and now he was giving away our secrets. What would be next?

"The impression our people brought back to Washington was that Khrushchev looked our young vibrant president in the eye and found him weak. On the other side of the table, this young vibrant president looked Khrushchev in the eye and ran back to Doctor Feel-good for another shot of amphetamines."

"You can imagine the anxiety our people felt over what the next Kennedy disaster might bring."

"Was it long in coming?" Mike asked.

"Not long at all, Mr. Burke. The American media called it The Cuban Missile Crisis."

Harold asked, "Why do you call that a disaster, George?"

"A discussion of that will have to be put off for another time, Mr. Ryan. Right now, I have to get to a meeting I could not cancel when Lindy asked me to meet with you. I also understand that you are leaving town at the end of this week."

"Yes, that's true," Harold confirmed. "Will you be able to meet with us in the meantime?"

"Today is Wednesday," he answered. "I can make some time early Friday morning. In the meantime I suggest you read up on a few issues which impact your area of interest. I have listed a few I think you should look at as well as three National Security Action Memorandums, 55, 56 and 57. I will also leave a copy of the report of the Cuban Study Group for you to read. I'll contact the Congresswoman with the time I can meet with you Friday."

George stood, and before he left said, "I hope I've been of some help to you."

Harold stood, too and shook George's hand. "Yes sir, you have been. Thank you for your time."

Mike and Harold watched their informant leave the room.

"This guy was so down on Kennedy, He could have been JFK hater back then."

"Mike my boy," Harold said. "A lot of people hated Kennedy back then. Keep in mind that you and I are not here to evaluate Kennedy's performance or motives. We're here to find out why he was killed and then who might have done it.

"This guy can help us with that. He is a fellow who knows where a lot of bodies are buried in this town. I for one will delay my flight until late Friday, if we can meet with him again. How do you feel about it?"

"I'm with you Harold," Mike agreed. "Look at this list he left for us. It's pretty extensive. I think we'll be spending a good deal of time at the Library of Congress between now and then, too. But first I have to get something off my chest."

"What's that?" Harold asked.

"George is very knowledgeable, I agree. But his account of the Kennedy White House sounded like a paranoid rant. He came across to me as an extreme right-wing partisan."

"It does seem that way. Mike. And as far as the assassination is concerned, that's precisely the point," Harold replied. "George's thinking probably mirrors that of potential assassins."

Burke winced. "Wait a minute. What if he's twisting the facts? I loved JFK. It's hard for me to picture him as a tool of the Soviets."

"Look, Mike. Remember what I just told you. We're not here to decide JFK's historical legacy. That's for historians to determine. If the men who killed JFK felt the same way George obviously feels toward him, then saving the country from Soviet domination could easily have been sufficient motivation for the assassination.

"Lindy Boggs hired us to find out who killed Kennedy, not to provide a report card on his presidency."

"You're right, Harold. I guess my Irish-Catholic pride got the better of me."

"I'm an Irish-Catholic, too, Mike. Maybe I'm just older than you."

"OK, Father Time. You win. Now let's get to work. We should start with our library angel, Irene. She probably can put her hands on all sorts of reading material. But let's split this list up first. Any of the topics have special interest for you?"

"I was in Congress during all the TFX controversy. So I'll take that one," Harold suggested. "The silver-certificate order Kennedy issued always fascinated me. Give me that one, too. Since I'm covering the fighter plane contract, it makes sense that I take Roswell Gilpatrick's talk explaining what was behind the award."

"All right, Mike said. "That leaves me to look into the rest of the list: Kennedy's proposal to share space technology with the Soviets, the Cuban Missile Crisis, his order to withdraw troops from Vietnam, and the Nuclear Test Ban Treaty."

***

Harold called Irene Gohsman at the Library of Congress and told her what they were interested in. By the time they arrived there she had a table piled high with material for them to review.

"That ought to keep you busy for a while," she said with a smile. "Let me know if you need anything else."

Mike and Harold went to work. Before long, Mike took a chair beside his partner.

"Take a look at this, Harold. I found this article by Tom Sinson, an American reporter for a foreign paper. He wrote it after having lunch with Allen Dulles in April 1964. That was while Dulles was serving on the Warren Commission."

"Let me take a look at it," Harold asked. "Give me a minute."

When he had finished reading it, he said, "During their lunch, Dulles made the same comment to this guy Sinson that our informant mentioned this morning."

"*We couldn't permit another cripple in the White House.*"

"Interesting, huh," Mike said.

"Yes it is," Harold commented. "In this article Sinson even gets into the drugs Kennedy needed. Sinson also supports George's contention that JFK brought Dr. Max Jacobson with him to Vienna in June of 1961 when the president had his conference with Khrushchev. He says that doctor feel-good gave Kennedy shots of methamphetamines, (uppers) before his meetings with the Soviet leader."

"That confirms what our informant George, told us about JFK's medications, too. It's always good to have a second source for stuff like this." Mike added.

"Sinson got all this information from Dulles?"

"Apparently he did," Mike observed. "It seemed odd to me that Dulles would be so free with such comments. But then I came across some information in Fletcher Prouty's book about the CIA, *The Secret Team*. He revealed that Dulles would occasionally entertain his favorite journalists for lunch in his private offices and sometimes give them classified information."

"That could explain it, Mike," Harold suggested. "Probably liked to impress them,"

"Mike concluded, "On the assumption that Kennedy suffered constant back pain and had to deal with colitis and Addison's too, I can understand why he needed all that medication on a daily basis. It is amazing to me that he could act so normal, vibrant in fact."

"Remember the old saying, 'There are no secrets in Washington." Harold said. "I was in Congress then and I was unaware of the extent of his physical problems. Dulles and the others may have disagreed with Kennedy's agenda and his decisions, but in my view JFK performed heroically under the circumstances."

Harold then asked the key question. "How would you connect Dulles' cripple comment to the assassination?"

"It appears to me that there are two important elements contained in the Dulles statement," Mike postulated. "First, the use of the word 'we' suggests multiple people held the same view and therefore a conspiracy was in place or in the making. Second, in light of what happened in Dallas, the comment 'we could not permit' suggests his complicity in a plan to eliminate JFK, or at least that Dulles knew such a plan was already in place."

"Now we're getting somewhere," Harold said. "We have two independent sources for this statement. So, I think we can consider the Dulles 'cripple' comment an accurate one.

"So, do you think we're dealing with a coup d'état?" Harold asked.

"Either that or," Mike interjected, "it's just a coincidence that according to the FBI, an unhappy nut just happened to get a job working in a tall building that just happened to put him a perfect position to shoot the President of the United States?"

"Michael, me lad," Harold joked, "In all my years on the bench and hearing the many claims of coincidences by defense attorneys, I can honestly say, there are very few coincidences; certainly not the possibilities you just mentioned anyway. The parade route for Kennedy hadn't even been chosen when Oswald got his job in that tall building.

"But hold up here. We're getting ahead of ourselves," Harold cautioned. "We have more homework to do before our meeting Friday with George. We'll get back to the 'who' later."

"You're right," Mike agreed. "Let's not forget the thought we just shared, though."

"Right. Before you get back to your stack of stuff, I've got something to show you."

***

"By that pleased look on your face I'd say you found a $50 dollar bill in one of these books"

"Not hardly, Mike. But I did find those three National Security Action Memoranda George suggested we look at."

"Were these memos signed by Kennedy after the Bay of Pigs failure and before the announcement of the TFX contract award?"

"That's very good, partner. It appears you've done a bit of digging yourself."

"Hey, Harold," Mike kidded, "I'm not just the pretty face here, ya' know."

"Spare me, please."

***

Harold began to present the result of his research.

"President Kennedy's confidence in his Joint Chiefs of Staff had not recovered from the misleading briefings he had received as a presidential candidate. During his fall election campaign, the military briefings they provided had led him to believe the Soviet Union was far ahead of the United States in both nuclear and conventional weapons.

"After he won that election, he discovered that far from being behind, the United States possessed a substantial lead in both categories. His lack of trust in the information and advice he was given was made worse by the misleading information they provided him on the lead-up to the Bay of Pigs disaster in April 1961.

"So, in June of that year he brought in a military advisor who was outside of the current military hierarchy. On this occasion, he made General Maxwell Taylor a member of his foreign policy inner circle. Taylor's first assignment was to serve as a member of the Cuba Study Group to analyze the Bay of Pigs failure.

"On the heels of that assignment, the president used Taylor to assist him develop a revolutionary approach on how the United States designed operated and controlled Cold War covert operations.

"That's certainly a mouth full, Harold," Mike declared. "Want to translate that for me?"

"Simply put," Harold explained. "Kennedy was beginning his effort to control the activities of the Central Intelligence Agency."

"Can you be a little more specific, Judge?"

"Sure. In late June 1961, the president issued three National Security Advisory Memorandums: NSAM 55, 56, and 57. The first of these was the blockbuster.

"In NSAM 55, the president informed the Joint Chiefs of Staff that in future they were responsible for all activities dealing with the Cold War as though it was a declared conflict; a hot war."

"Even clandestine operations?" Mike asked.

"Yes," Harold answered, "especially covert operations. According to Colonel Fletcher Prouty, who presented and explained the NSAM 55 to General Lemmitzer, Chairman of the Joint Chiefs of Staff, they were directed to usurp control of paramilitary ops from the CIA.

"In effect, President Kennedy was putting all CIA covert operations worldwide under the control of the military. In addition, as the president's principal military advisor responsible both for initiating advice to him and for responding to requests for advice, he expected, in the future all advice to come to him directly from the JCS, unfiltered."

"It would seem, Harold," Mike surmised. "That he didn't want the Joint Chiefs to consult with the CIA or the State Department before they gave him advice."

"President Kennedy was actually referring back to the original need expressed by President Truman over a decade earlier. Truman wanted information and advice sent him unfiltered. Kennedy wanted the same thing.

"Neither man wanted covert operations hidden from them, either." Harold said.

"It sounds as though Kennedy was starting his effort to shatter the CIA into a thousand pieces as he was reported to have vowed after the Bay of Pigs failure." Mike said.

"It would appear so, Mike," Harold agreed. "The third of the three NSAMs was interesting as well."

"How so?"

"NSAM 57 was addressed to the Defense Department, the State Department and the CIA. It was titled, '*Responsibility for Paramilitary Operations.*' Basically it required that all paramilitary operations had to be reviewed by the Strategic Resources Group. That group would assign the operation to the department or individual best suited to carry it out."

"That certainly cuts the CIA out of taking the initiative on any covert operation." Mike observed.

"There's more, Mike," Harold cautioned. "Anytime covert operations might require large numbers of people, equipment and/or military experience, primary responsibility would rest with the Defense Department."

"Seems ta' me Harold," Mike decided. "That, according to this memorandum, the CIA adventure in Vietnam should be the responsibility of the Defense Department."

"You're right, my man," Harold informed Mike. "The most important covert operation of all in play at the time was the activity of our Special Forces in Vietnam which was then under the operational control of the CIA.

"Because of NSAM 57, control of these paramilitary forces would be switched to the Defense Department in 1962 under the code name '*Operation Switchback.*'

"Nevertheless, Kennedy continued to be uncomfortable with the Joint Chiefs of Staff under General Lemmitzer. So, effective October first, 1962, he replaced Lemmitzer with General Maxwell Taylor."

"It appears that the president was tightening the screws, Harold." Mike said.

"I think so too. He simply didn't trust Lemmitzer. So he appointed a man he did trust. In this case, Kennedy appointed a man who had helped him write the orders Lemmitzer did not want to enforce.

"With Taylor as Chairman of the JCS, it would appear that those memoranda would at last be implemented." Mike suggested. "But from what I've read they were slow about doing it."

"Things often take time in Washington, Mike," Harold reminded him. "Even so, back in 1961, Kennedy took another step at the same time the memoranda were issued." Harold added.

"In July of that year, he announced his intention to create the Defense Intelligence Agency (DIA). That August, Secretary of Defense McNamara did just that. This was another clear attempt to begin circumventing the activities of the CIA."

"Wasn't Allen Dulles dismissed as the Director of the CIA around this time, too?" Mike asked.

"You're right," Harold said. "Let's see. Here it is. Allen Dulles Director of the CIA since 1954, along with Deputy Director Richard M. Bissell Jr and Deputy Director General Charles Cabell resigned their positions effective November twenty-ninth, 1961."

"I'll bet the folks at the CIA heard another shoe dropping with that announcement." Mike commented.

"I'm sure they did, Mike. As I recall, there was quite a stir created in D.C. when that happened. John McCone, a fellow with no government, military or intelligence gathering background was appointed to replace Dulles."

"Another decision to downgrade of the CIA's influence in Washington, ya' think?"

"In contrast to the power and influence possessed and exercised by Dulles, it was definitely viewed as a signal from Kennedy that the CIA had been pushed outside the loop and thus reduced in power."

"Another shoe dropped by Kennedy."

"Let me assure you, Mike," Harold agreed. "It was noticed around town, too.

"During this time Kennedy resisted suggested increases to our military presence in Vietnam. In the fall of 1961, the JCS urged him to allow sending sixteen thousand troops there. He refused."

'Let me get something into the discussion, Harold," Mike insisted. "While all this was going on back in Washington, the Vietnam problem was percolating. That area of the world had been of major interest to the CIA ever since 1945.

"Back then, a power vacuum had been created there with the defeat of the Japanese. The old OSS, predecessor to the CIA, had supplied Ho Che Min with arms and funds in the Vietnamese fight against our common WWII enemy, the Japanese. After the war, and the division of the country into North and South Vietnam, a guerilla war of liberation was begun by the Communist North. Our government supported the non-communist South.

"By 1960, we had several thousand advisors in South Vietnam. Since 1945, we had given two to three billion dollars in economic support and military equipment to the South Vietnamese government too. In fact, by 1960, over five thousand helicopters had been lost in military action and 62 American military advisors had been killed.

"In a televised interview with Walter Cronkite on September second, 1963, President Kennedy said:

"I don't think that unless a greater effort is made by the government [South Vietnamese] to win popular support that the war can be won out there. In the final analysis, it is their war. They are the ones who have to win it or lose it."

"In the fall of 1963, General Maxwell Taylor and Secretary of Defense McNamara gave recommendations to the president after returning from a fact-finding trip to Vietnam. The result of that report and his consultation with the president was National Security Advisory Memorandum 263 issued October eleventh, 1963.

"The two key actions directed by President Kennedy in this executive order were:

The withdrawal of one thousand US personnel by the end of 1963.

The withdrawal of all US personnel by the end of 1965.

"This constituted the basis of Kennedy's policy regarding our involvement in Vietnam going forward. According to what I read, this was a clear signal that Kennedy meant to disengage the American military and CIA from Vietnam."

"I remember when that word leaked out," Harold said. "It was quite a bombshell; and was headline news in Washington."

Mike was somewhat frustrated. "If you already know all this stuff why am I knocking myself out reading 'till my eyes are red?"

"Easy, Mike. I know some of it from my time in Washington, but not as much as you've told me. Besides, you're putting a lot of this stuff into context, filling gaps and helping us build a better understanding of why Kennedy was killed."

"Are you pulling my chain, judge?" Mike asked.

"Not at all, my friend. But I wasn't the only one in Washington during the Kennedy years. You were working for the FBI in the Washington office when Kennedy took office and then the House Judiciary Committee right after weren't you? Didn't you hear any of this, or the stuff about Kennedy's physical problems, or his sex life?"

"I must have too busy rushing home to change diapers, walking the floor with our first child who seemed to have colic all the time and helping Marilyn prepare for our second child. I was just happy that my first born was healthy and kept me from being drafted."

Harold agreed. "I suppose that wouldn't give you much time to listen to rumors over a beer after work an' such. Right now, I'm just tired and red eyed like you. Let's call it a day, OK?

"Nap time is it, judge."

"You got that right young fella. We can meet again around five-thirty in our conference room at the Willard. Then I'll tell you about the TFX contract and the announcement of reduction ordered in defense spending. These were two more bricks in the hate Kennedy wall that was going up."

"I think I'll take a nap today, too." Mike chuckled.

"Be good for you; you'll see."

Willard Hotel

The two men were in the hotel conference room.

"Did you have a good nap, Judge?" Mike asked.

"I surely did, Mike," Harold reported. "How about you? I don't suppose you shut your eyes at all."

"Not for a minute," Mike insisted. "I did call home though, and then took a refreshing shower."

"Since you're so fresh then, why don't you start? Tell me about Kennedy's proposal to share our data and jointly explore space with the Soviets."

"Sure," Mike said. "We're going through these issues sort of haphazardly. We need to remember that they are not in any cohesive order yet."

"We'll bring them all together after we meet with our friend George tomorrow, all right?"

"Makes sense to me. Now let's get on with the sharing stuff with the Soviets. You recall that in June 1961, Kennedy proposed to Khrushchev at their Vienna meeting that the two country's share technology and jointly pursue the exploration of space. The Soviet leader turned JFK down cold.

"Before Kennedy could make any progress on this private proposal to the Soviets, they threw another bomb at the new president. We called it the Cuban Missile Crisis.

"Nonetheless, Kennedy continued to push the idea. He suggested it again during his UN speech on September twentieth, 1963. He said the United States would put off our announced plans to get to the moon ahead of the Soviets in favor of space cooperation with our Cold War opponents.

"His proposal was greeted with a positive response throughout the world. Such support for the idea prompted a reluctant but positive reaction from the Soviets.

"Then JFK went even further. On November twelfth, 1963 he issued National Security Memorandum 271, directing NASA to take the initiative and develop a program of cooperation with their Soviet counterparts for the purpose of sharing space technology, and to pursue joint future space exploration. Kennedy told James Webb, NASA Director, that he wanted a progress report by December fifteenth, 1963.

"Another memorandum dated the same day directed the CIA to provide the Soviets with all the information we had gathered about UFOs. He demanded a progress report on this issue by February first, 1964. At this time JFK also told the CIA Director about Memorandum 271, directing NASA to share space technology and future space exploration efforts with the Soviets.

"This was not greeted very positively by our military, the folks at the Department of Defense or the CIA. Some considered this another reason to prevent JFK from getting a second four years in office, somehow."

"I had no idea this was happening," Harold admitted. "My committee assignments in Congress back then kept me pretty busy. I was struggling just to keep up with them. I had no time for space issues. Besides, I don't recall that much publicity was given that stuff."

"It wasn't, Harold," Mike told him. "The entire initiative began so close to the assassination that I suspect it sort of flew under the radar. Then, with the change of administrations, it was all rescinded. And JFK's offer to share was simply shelved by President Johnson."

Harold continued to probe. "With the Cold War still very hot, I'll bet the powers that be were not pleased with Kennedy's sharing initiative."

"It was explosive when considered along with other events. Those include JFK's comment that he intended to destroy the CIA during his second term, the award of the TFX fighter plane contract in 1962, and Gilpatrick's April 1963 speech on preparing for peace."

"Now that you bring it up," Harold responded, "let me tell you a few things about the TFX fighter plane contract award."

"First, I want to let you know that I made a dinner reservation for seven o'clock. Can you get through that issue in forty minutes?" Mike asked.

"I think so. But fasten your seat belt, Michael. There's a lot to absorb on this issue."

"In that case, give me a minute to run to the men's room."

"Get to it, young man, you're burning daylight here."

Harold organized his papers while Mike was out of the room.

Mike returned quickly. "Okay, Harold. Fire away."

"During the final year of the Eisenhower administration, Congress authorized four billion dollars for the development and production of a new tactical jet fighter plane. It was referred to as the TFX contract.

"The selection of the builder process was completed before the November 1960 presidential election. The Source Selection Board had decided to recommend that the award of the contract should go to Boeing. It was planned that Nixon would announce it after he won that election. But when the unexpected happened and Kennedy won, the announcement of the award was delayed until the new administration was in place.

"Robert McNamara, the Kennedy administration's Secretary of Defense demanded a new review of the competing contracts. He added another two billion or so dollars from funds set aside for the Navy, thus creating the largest defense contract ever to be awarded in peacetime.

"Kennedy asked Secretary of the Treasury Goldberg to be involved in the decision. His role was to assure that the money was spent in a politically smart way."

"What the hell did that mean?" Mike asked.

"Goldberg's job was to see to it that these billions of dollars were spent in such a way that the Democratic Party would be strengthened; that Kennedy would win the presidential election of 1964 and with it, win a Democratic majority in the Senate and the House of Representatives."

Mike pressed one, "And how would they do that with a fighter plane contract?"

"A team of Labor Department analysts set up headquarters in a suite of offices at the Pentagon. On the walls of these rooms were maps of the United States by state and others by county. Some maps were colored one way to show all the counties won by Nixon in the 1960 election. On another map a different color was used to show the counties won by Kennedy.

"Also, county by county, the Labor Department analysts charted the dollar impact if the TFX award went to Boeing. Another group of analysts charted the resulting dollar impact in each county if the contract went to General Dynamics/Grumman.

Mike interrupted. "Didn't it count that one design might produce a plane better suited for landing on an Air Force runway but not on a Navy aircraft carrier?"

"It didn't count one bit," Harold told Mike. "Instead, the contract award was used to direct money into political districts believed important to the re-election of John Kennedy."

"So what happened, Harold?"

"On November twenty-fourth, 1962, two years after Kennedy was elected, McNamara announced he was ready to announce a decision. The Source Selection Board had given him its recommendation; it was Boeing once again. Goldberg's people had given him the results of their political/economic impact study as well.

"The night before the formal announcement, the Secretary of the Air Force told people at a dinner gathering that Boeing would be given the contract."

"Well?"

"McNamara ignored the Source Selection Board and went with Goldberg's study that determined the Democratic Party would get the most benefit from the award if it went to General Dynamics/Grumman. So, he awarded that company the almost 6.5 billion dollar contract to build the TFX."

"Then what?" Mike probed.

"All hell broke loose, that's what." Harold told him.

"McNamara said he awarded the contract to General Dynamics because that company had planned to build one type of plane for both the Air Force and the Navy as he had requested. But Boeing, he charged, intended to build a plane for the Navy that was different than the one built for the Air Force.

"In the Senate hearings that followed, Admiral Burke answered this rationale. 'Well ya. As any fool can see, a plane that has to land on a moving platform at sea needs to be different from one designed to land on the ground.' And, so the public debate went on for months. No one in the administration ever mentioned Goldberg's role in all of this. But, with all the personnel working on his political/economic impact study prior to the award, it had been impossible to keep it a secret.

"With this award, a new order, 'the Kennedy Way', became obvious to everyone: government bureaucrats, members of the military/industrial hierarchy and the elites of the nation. It was: the political needs of the Kennedy administration would trump defense considerations and the needs of the armed services."

Mike added, "Maybe George will verify that when we meet with him tomorrow. You also mentioned McNamara's deputy, Roswell Gilpatrick. What role did he play in all of this?"

"In April 1963, the TFX controversy was still raging. He gave a speech at a banker's convention in Boston. The title of his speech was, 'The Impact of the Changing Defense Program on the United States Economy.' He was speaking for the administration and intended what he said for a wider audience than just the bankers.

"Among the things he said were two comments he made that rocked the military/industrial folks and the elites of the private sector, who were already upset with the TFX contract award.

"He said that the administration intended to use defense contracts to give work 'where it can be done effectively and efficiently, to depressed areas.' It was assumed that he was applying the new Kennedy political criteria of spending defense dollars where votes were needed by the administration.

"He went on to declare, 'I have not the slightest doubt that our economy could adjust to a decline in defense spending.'

"These remarks even surprised Democrats like me who served in Congress. So, the real message of the TFX award was to brush off the military elites and the traditional way the feds did business with the military/industrial complex and instead use defense funds, however reduced, to benefit the president's political base."

Mike asked. "Would you say then, that this brought many of the powerful elites in the private sector to join their military and government counterparts together to agree that Kennedy must not win a second term?"

"I would think so, Mike."

"I know we're jumping back and forth chronologically, but in 1961, after the Bay of Pigs failure, JFK's weak performance at the Vienna meeting with Khrushchev, and his handling of the dust-up over Berlin further alarmed Cold War hawks. It appeared to be so alarming, that Dean Acheson, who was advising Kennedy at the time, went on the warpath. He was quoted as saying,

"*Gentlemen, you might as well face it,*" he said. "*This nation is without (foreign policy) leadership.*"

"William Bundy, a member of Kennedy's staff believed that Acheson held Kennedy in contempt and saw the president as weak and, "*…not worth my while to be advising.*"

"In July 1962, it seemed that the United States and Russia were on the verge of war over Berlin. Kennedy was being publicly attacked at home for his apparent ambivalence, pressured by his own military leaders to act aggressively and doubted by the Soviets for his supposed weakness. Just to give his speech on the subject broadcast to a worldwide audience, he had to take extra doses of steroids to combat the strain.

"He concluded his speech by saying, 'we seek peace – but we shall not surrender.'

"JFK's speech seemed to calm the storm at home and convince the Soviets of his resolve. But when the East German government built a wall to keep their people from escaping to the West, the debate resumed in the United States. Kennedy believed the wall was better than a war. Once again, Dean Acheson, President de Gaulle of France and our military disagreed.

"But evidently, Khrushchev had had enough of brinkmanship. He signaled at his Communist Party congress that it seemed to him the West was beginning to understand Russia's problems. It appeared that the Berlin crisis was over.

"However, Kennedy's problems with his military and the hawks in the United States were not. Instead, difficulty on the foreign policy front was only beginning for the administration.

"The problems in Southeast Asia, and in particular Vietnam, were just simmering on the back burner. They were made worse by the October 1962 Cuban Missile Crisis and the internal turmoil over the resumed negotiations with Russia for a nuclear test ban treaty."

***

At this point, Harold interrupted. "Hold on, Mike. It's time for our dinner reservation and I'm a hungry fella here. Let's get into this other stuff later."

"That's fine with me. I'm hungry too."

When the waiter brought their cocktails, they ordered their dinner.

"I'll have the T-bone steak tonight," Mike told the waiter. "Medium rare, I think."

"That sounds good to me, too." Harold said. "I'll have the same. But, I don't want mine too red."

The waiter told him. "Then I'll bring it to the table cooked rare, sir. You can take a look and send it back for a minute or two more on the grill if it is too red."

"That's the ticket. Medium rare it is, then."

"What happened to your usual order of prime rib?"

"I just thought I'd try something else. I never get a T-bone steak at home either." Harold laughed.

The two men sipped their drinks while spreading butter on slices of warm bread.

"It'll be good to get home tomorrow," Mike said. I think it would be a good idea to involve the wives in our project?"

"It worked pretty well to have Marilyn on board for our 1967 Report," Harold reminded him. "Let's ask 'em."

"We could take them out to dinner Sunday evening; maybe at our favorite Chinese place, The Golden Buddha?" Mike suggested.

"That sounds good to me, unless they want to go somewhere else." Harold chuckled.

"Oh, ya. In case they don't want to go somewhere else. Why didn't I think of that?"

"You haven't been married long enough."

***

After the plates were cleared the two men talked over coffee.

"Where was I, Harold?"

"You were talking about the increasing staccato of foreign policy challenges facing the Kennedy administration after the Bay of Pigs disaster in the spring of 1961, the Cuban Missile Crisis of October 1962 and the negotiations over a test ban on nuclear testing in the atmosphere."

"Right.

"I'll leave the discussion about the October 1962 Cuban Missile Crisis for our talk with George tomorrow. But, the nuclear test ban treaty of 1963 is an interesting example of the increasing tension within the Kennedy administration."

"Khrushchev signaled to the United States and Great Britain that he was ready to resume talks that had stalled during the Eisenhower years over inspections and verification. In July 1963, representatives of the three nuclear powers met in Moscow.

"The result was an agreement to ban all nuclear testing in the atmosphere and in the ocean. Monitoring, a sticking point to an agreement in the past, was resolved, too.

"Even agreeing to talk with the Russians on this subject was opposed by our military, the intelligence community and other Cold War hawks. During the first year of the Kennedy administration, JFK had declined to test in the atmosphere because Khrushchev had promised not to do so if we didn't.

"Our JCS warned Kennedy not to trust the Russians. Instead, they recommended he resume testing lest the Soviets break their promise and catch up to us in developing bombs with greater destructive force than we believed they had, or for that matter than we had. But JFK did not want to be the one to initiate another round of testing in the atmosphere. So, he refused to resume testing.

"Of course, he was accused openly of being weak and possibly a closet communist. He paid no attention. An agreement was reached with the Russians that summer.

"The limited Test Ban Treaty was signed and ratified, during all of this internal bickering. In fact, in the fall of 1963 a big bi-partisan majority in the Senate supported it. And, it was hugely popular throughout the world.

"But, from what I read, the treaty was not popular among our military or with the elites of the CIA either. They seemed to have been convinced that Kennedy was weak and was selling out our country.

"So, I think all of this is worth a mention when we talk with George tomorrow."

"Did you ever read the novel, *Seven Days in May*, Mike?" Harold asked.

"No, I didn't. Why do you bring that up now?"

"It was a novel about the reaction of our military to such a treaty with the Russians."

"And?"

"In the movie that was made based upon the book, Burt Lancaster played the military general who tried to conduct a coup d'état against a liberal president. His character was an Air Force general who was actually a thinly veiled General Curtis LeMay. Fredrick March played the liberal president. The plot was barely foiled. It was a very well written story, a well-done movie and very believable.

"As I recall, JFK thought so much of the script, he left the White house for a weekend to allow the movie people complete access for filming in the building."

"Are you suggesting some kind of parallel here, Harold?"

"Ya got to read the book."

"While we're home let's rent the video." Mike suggested.

***

The following morning Burke and Ryan met with George.

"Thank you for changing our meeting place, gentlemen," he told them. "One can't be too careful in this town."

"Something about 'there are no secrets in Washington'?" Harold asked.

"Exactly, Congressman." George agreed. When we ended our last discussion, I recall, you were asking about the Cuban Missile Crisis, Mr. Burke. Is that correct?"

"Yes I did, but you had to leave."

"The first three years of the Kennedy administration were full of foreign policy challenges. After the talks in Vienna between President Kennedy and Premier Khrushchev, there was a year of relative calm.

"But during the summer of 1962, we received intelligence that the Russians were building missile launching sites in Cuba. Of course, after verification, this information was passed up the line to the President and his advisors.

"They insisted that we were mistaken."

Harold asked, "How would the president's people know that?"

"It appears that they had been given repeated assurances by the Russians that our intelligence was wrong. Therefore, the Kennedy's assumed we were mistaken and their Russian informants were truthful."

"How did you know they were lying?" Burke asked.

"It is our business to know such things, Mr. Burke." George reminded him. "Our people urged the president to order an overflight to verify our information. We were told by the administration that the Russians would never lie about such a thing. So, the request for a U-2 overflight was refused.

"We got our information to Senator Keating of New York. He made a very public fuss over our information and eventually enough pressure was applied so that a flight was authorized. It clearly showed launch site preparations in Cuba. So it was verified, the Russians had lied to the President of the United States."

"Then what happened?" Burke asked.

"Both countries went to the brink of nuclear war, that's what, Mr. Burke. Kennedy and his people had not forgotten the Bay of Pigs package they had been sold eighteen months earlier. They didn't believe the information we gave them.

"Their doubt was understandable," George continued, "But it was a grave mistake not to verify with an overflight when we first told them. By the time they did discover the Russian's deception, the sites were almost ready for the installation of the missiles.

"By then, the options Kennedy had available to him were reduced and the United States was closer to an all-out war."

"Then what?"

"Everything went public with Ambassador Stevenson's exposure of the Russian deception at the United Nations. Remember, we didn't have the 'Hot Line' available then, so direct contact with President Kennedy's counterpart in Russia was not possible. With their lies as a backdrop, it was difficult to fathom just what the Russians would do now that we knew of their deception and also knew that we were very upset.

"What options were on the table?" Harold asked.

"The Joint Chiefs wanted to bomb the sites and invade Cuba. Remember, they wanted to invade Cuba when the Bay of Pigs blew up in our faces. Now, it was worse because Russians were crawling all over the place with weapons of an undisclosed nature. But they argued; best to get it over and done with once and for all.

"Kennedy rejected this option immediately," George added. "He wanted to hear of other possibilities."

"Is that when the idea of a blockade was mentioned?"

"Yes, it was. But the navy people pointed out that such a step would be difficult even with our large naval capability. Also, they added, a blockade was an act of war."

At this point, Harold said. "I was serving in Congress at that time. My colleagues and I did not want a nuclear war over the issue of the missiles. But we didn't want those missiles in Cuba either. How was it resolved?"

"It appeared that a secret line of communication was established through some intermediaries. Then President Kennedy and Chairman Khrushchev reached an agreement, largely kept secret.

"We got what we demanded and the Russians got what they wanted. War was avoided."

Burke spoke up, "I recall Secretary of State Rusk saying in an interview something like "We were eyeball to eyeball and the other fellow blinked."

"I recall that boast, too." George said. "That was for public consumption. But it wasn't like that at all."

"Everyone knows now that we agreed to remove our missiles from Turkey and Italy in exchange for the Russian removal of theirs from Cuba." Harold said.

"That's true congressman," George agreed. "But there was more. The president pledged never to invade Cuba or support subversive activity against the Castro regime.

"The Joint Chiefs were angry. This was the second time Kennedy had passed up an opportunity of overthrowing the Castro regime; the first time being his refusal to send our military into Cuba in support of the Bay of Pigs invasion.

"We had also passed up an opportunity of a direct face-off with Russia over a legitimate issue; national security. And, in addition, we had promised never to overthrow a communist regime ninety miles off our coast."

"How did Kennedy react to their opposition?" Burke asked.

"By all reports, he was very calm. He asked for their estimate of Russian casualties that would have resulted from a thermo-nuclear exchange. They told him they figured that about 140 million people would die in that country and their satellites. He then asked what their estimate of American casualties would be. They estimated that about forty million of our citizens would die in the exchange.

"Our reports indicate that he appeared to become angry only when they told him that this casualty ratio was acceptable. He left the room without further comment."

"I lived in Maryland at that time." Burke said. "My wife, my children and I would all have died if they had had their way."

"Never-the-less, Mr. Burke," George continued. "Remember what many believed led to this confrontation. The weakness Kennedy showed at the Bay of Pigs and at the Vienna meetings encouraged Khrushchev to insert missiles in Cuba. We believed that he decided to test Kennedy in such a way that his country could both neutralize the missiles in Turkey and forestall a future invasion of Cuba.

"The Joint chiefs of Staff figured that Khrushchev won and Kennedy lost."

"But, Kennedy was wildly applauded worldwide for his actions." Burke protested.

"That's true," George agreed, "But, the facts are, the Russians pushed and Kennedy backed down. Again!

"You asked me about the impact his decisions had on the military/industrial elites, the CIA, Cold War Hawks, diplomats and others concerned about our national security. At every turn, they saw President Kennedy backing off and thus, they felt, weakening our position in the world. Some were even beginning to see him as a traitor.

"Most all of the elites in the groups I mentioned feared what a second Kennedy administration would bring."

"Before you leave, can we get your thoughts on the reaction of the elite money people to Executive Order 1110?"

"It's interesting, Congressman Ryan that you would pick that executive order of all those that caused controversy. Why are you so interested in that one?" George asked.

"It fascinates me and it is important to our investigation I believe because it is so often ignored when the Kennedy Agenda is being discussed. Our reading and the information you have provided has explained much of the fall-out for the other pieces of the JFK agenda; but not this one."

"Put that way, I can see why you want to spend some time discussing the reaction to it. Let me start with just what his executive order did. By issuing this order Kennedy in effect destroyed the Federal Reserve System.

"Since 1913, the United States monetary system relies solely on the issuance of Federal Reserve interest bearing notes to serve as money.

"Kennedy attempted to change that. His Executive Order 1110 authorized and directed the Treasury department to issue four billion dollars in silver certificates into circulation in two- and five-dollar denominations. These would be an interest-free and debt-free currency backed by silver reserves currently held in the US Treasury. These notes would eventually replace the Federal Reserve bills currently in circulation."

Harold interrupted, "I read that he gave a speech on November twelfth, 1963 at Columbia University in which he said,

"*The high office of the President has been used to foment a plot to destroy American's freedom and before I leave office, I must inform the citizen of his plight.*"

"I recall studying about the fight between Jefferson and Hamilton over this issue."

"Correct, Mr. Burke," George said. "And, the Second Bank was killed by President Andrew Jackson some years later. Our current Federal Reserve Bank system was authorized by Congress in 1913. It still operates under that charter."

Harold joined the conversation. "Back in the Middle Ages, goldsmiths rented out space in their vaults to individuals and merchants to store their gold or silver. The goldsmiths gave these depositors a certificate that showed the amount of precious metal stored. These certificates were then used by the depositors to conduct business.

"Over time, the goldsmiths realized that the precious metals in their vaults were not withdrawn very frequently and never entirely. Some deposits would be withdrawn, but the large majority of the deposits never moved. So, they began to issue multiple certificates for the metals on deposit. Such certificates began to exceed the value of the metal on deposit thus creating money (certificates) from nothing. Then they lent these certificates to depositors creating debt and charged them interest on top of that, too. Thus, was born the banking system."

"That's correct Congressman." George concluded.

"Now we have the Federal Reserve system doing much the same thing. They print money and lend it to our government for distribution. This creates debt and they charge the government interest to boot. It is estimated that the Federal Reserve earns a trillion dollars per year tax free for the owners of the Federal Reserve stock.

"Who owns the Federal Reserve? The Rothschilds of London and Berlin own stock; and so do the Lazard Brothers of Paris; Israel Moses Seif of Italy; Goldman, Sachs and the Rockefeller families of New York. These families own the Federal Reserve.

"Let me make another point," George continued. "Who do you think is responsible for all the ups and downs of the marketplace if not the Federal Reserve? When dollars they print chase goods, prices go up, business seeks to expand to satisfy the demand and borrow money to do so.

"The Fed then restricts the amount of money in circulation ostensibly to control rising inflation. Prices tumble and the ability to pay back the loans goes down as well. Assets and stocks are then at rock bottom prices available to be bought cheaply. Historically, guess who buys them?

"If you're wondering how the stockholders of the Federal Reserve reacted to Kennedy's executive order, let me tell you their outrage could be heard 'round the world. In time, you see, Kennedy's Silver Certificates would have run the Federal Reserve notes out of the market. By November, the Treasury was about to print ten- and twenty-dollar notes as well. But then Kennedy was killed in Dallas.

"Within days of his murder, Johnson ordered the Secretary of Treasury Dillon to immediately take all silver certificates out of circulation."

"Did you have information that would lead one to believe that any of these money elites were involved in the Kennedy assassination?" Mike asked.

"People have killed others for a lot less, Mr. Burke. What would you do to protect a trillion dollars of tax free income per year?"

"George, do you have time for one more question?" Burke asked.

"What would that be?"

"The final report of the U.S. House of Representatives Select Committee on Assassinations stated rather bluntly that the Secret Service …"was deficient in the performance of its duties.

"In fact, they went further and decided that escort security was …"uniquely insecure."

"Do you have a question, Mr. Burke?" George asked with a smile.

"Sorry, of course I have. Do you agree with the conclusion of the House Committee on Assassinations?"

"It should not take a two-year congressional investigation for fair minded people to recognize that Secret Service agents in charge of the Dallas leg of Kennedy's Texas trip fell down on the job. Most of us in Washington knew of their failure shortly after the assassination. I can think of several failures off the top of my head.

"What would those be?" Harold asked.

"First: When asked when they were asked to approve this parade route, the Secret Service people should have never given its approval especially when a safer and more often used route along Main Street was easily available. The route they approved required a sharp right turn to get on to Houston and another very sharp left turn to the left to get on to Elm. Both turns seriously violated parade protocol and actually set up Kennedy for the assassin's shots.

'Second: There was no attempt to monitor windows in the tall buildings along the parade route. Explanations of being shorthanded are without foundation since additional help offered by the Dallas Police Department, the Dallas Sheriff's office, the local FBI and the military were turned down by the Secret Service people in charge of the Dallas parade.

"Next: Even the overpass directly ahead of the presidential limo was lined with people contrary to regulations.

"Also: Motorcycle policemen flanked the presidential limo in Houston but were ordered back from the limo by the Secret Service in Dallas.

"And: Agents who attempted to ride on the rear of the Kennedy limo were ordered off by Agent Roberts at Love Field.

"In addition: Most of the agents assigned to the Kennedy detail in Dallas partied until almost dawn in direct violation of service protocol. Not one was disciplined.

"Finally: And, perhaps most importantly, the driver of Kennedy's limo, Agent Greer, directly violated an order from his superior, Agent Kellerman, to pull out of line and accelerate the vehicle. Instead, he put his foot on the limo's brake and turned to look at Kennedy who had already been wounded twice. Greer only accelerated after he saw Kennedy react to the fatal head wound.

"These omissions made the assassination possible. So, in my view, their admonition fell far too short of laying proper responsibility on the Secret Service. People in the Secret Service were culpable, not just negligent.

"Gentlemen," George concluded. "I have to leave it at that for now."

"You have been most helpful, George," Harold assured him.

"Absolutely," Burke added.

"Have a safe trip home, gentlemen."

Detroit City Airport

The two investigators walked into the small terminal to wait for their bags.

"Hi guys," Marilyn said as she walked up to her husband. She gave him a warm kiss and a hug. Lillian Ryan gave Harold a hug, too.

"I'll have to travel with Mike more often," Harold said in surprise. "This is the warmest greeting home I've received in a while."

"We just thought one car was better than two to pick up our weary travelers," Lillian said.

"Besides, we decided to take you two out for dinner on the way home," Marilyn added. "What do ya' think a' them apples, fellas?"

Mike laughed, "That takes care of one of our plans, eh Harold?"

As they walked to the car, Lillian asked, "What plan was that, dear?"

"Mike and I were going to ask you two out for dinner tomorrow."

Marilyn quipped, "You can still do that, Harold."

The two ladies ushered their men into the back seat, and off they went.

"This really is a treat. We don't even have to drive," Harold said.

"Where are we headed, ladies?" Mike asked.

"That's all part of the surprise, my man. Be patient, you'll see," Marilyn said.

Before they knew it, Marilyn pulled the car up to the sidewalk by their favorite Chinese restaurant, The Golden Buddha.

"My favorite place," Mike said. "Thanks, gals."

"Mine too," His wife said.

Inside, it took a minute to adjust to the dim light. But quickly they saw that already seated were Joe and Cathy Yager.

"Well, this is a pleasant surprise," Harold said, shaking Joe's hand.

"We thought that too when Marilyn called. It has been a while, hasn't it."

"Good to see you Cathy," Mike said as he gave her a hug.

"No Manhattans served here, boys," Lillian warned them. "So, I guess it's hot tea all around."

Once they were served their tea, Mike and Harold brought everyone up to date on their investigation.

"How is it you two get to have all the fun?" Joe asked.

"You want to join in, Joe?"

"What do you have in mind?"

"Tell you what," Mike said. "Why don't you listen as we talk about what we still need to do? You jump in whenever you think you might lend a hand. OK?"

"When we were putting together the first report back in '67, Marilyn helped by making appointments and working with us on the final report," Harold reminded everyone.

Mike picked up things at this point. "We have a person in Congresswoman Boggs' office named Mable and a contact person at the Library of Congress named Irene Gohsman. They have both been great.

"We have a few more interviews to complete before we return to Washington. Then we'll need help organizing all our information and interview material into a report."

Harold turned to his wife and Marilyn. "On the final report, we were hoping you would help once again, Marilyn, and that this time Lillian might join in that effort."

"It depends," Lillian answered.

"On what?" Harold asked.

"Did they really listen to you back then, Marilyn? Or were you just a pretty face serving them coffee and cake?" Lillian asked Mike's wife.

"I must say, Lillian," Marilyn said. "Much of the organization and language of the report was actually mine; at least I can say it was ours."

"It sounds to me as though you have it covered, guys," Joe said.

"Not entirely," Harold objected. "When you get into material sometimes you lose focus. We could use a couple of editors. You think you and Cathy would be willing to go over our work before we present it to Congresswoman Boggs?"

"Would it require traveling to Washington, D.C., Harold?" Cathy asked.

"You'll do all your work at home. Any trip to the nation's capital would be for sightseeing and on your own dime."

"I was afraid of that," Joe complained.

"I suppose we're stuck in this town, too," Lillian added.

"You are unless you can finagle an invite from the Congresswoman to one of her parties."

"I might work on that," Lillian said.

"Fine, then," Harold said. "When do you think we'll have something for the Yagers to review, Mike?"

"Probably in a couple of weeks."

After the food was delivered, Lillian asked Howard, "How many times did you have prime rib for dinner while you were in Washington, dear?"

"How many evenings did we eat at the Willard Hotel dining room, Mike?"

"This is Friday and we arrived Monday. So, we ate there four times."

"One evening I joined Mike to have their pork chops. So, I had my favorite prime rib three times."

Joe asked, "Is that the same Willard Hotel that was so famous during the Civil War?"

"According to their literature it is," Mike answered. "It is nowhere as new as most of the other hotels in D.C., but we had great service and the food was super. I'd stay there again anytime."

"If the walls could speak, the tales that place would tell," Joe told everyone. "As I recall, Lincoln stayed there awaiting his first inauguration. And the Peace Conference was held there at the same time, trying to work out a deal to keep the Southern states in the Union.

"I read that more money changed hands under the table there doing government business during the Civil War than anywhere else in Washington."

"That might still be true, Joe," Harold said. "But I didn't see any evidence of that when I served in Congress a few years ago."

"At least no one approached you with a packet of money?" Marilyn asked.

"I guess I wasn't important enough, Marilyn."

Detroit

In Mike's downtown office, a gentleman approached the receptionist and handed her his business card.

"I'll tell Mr. Burke that you're here, Mr. Prouty."

"Thank you."

"Can I get you some coffee while you're waiting, sir?"

"No thank you. I'm fine."

Both Harold and Mike came into the waiting room.

"Colonel Prouty, good morning," Mike said, shaking his guest's hand.

Harold shook Prouty's hand as well and then led the way to their conference room.

"Congresswoman Boggs told me you two were working on a project of some importance to her. she and her late husband were close to the Kennedys as I recall."

"Yes, that's correct," Harold told Prouty. "The Select Committee on Assassinations concluded that the killing of JFK was a conspiracy. Her late husband believed that as well. Currently, she is unhappy that the committee members didn't get into why he was killed or even look into who might have been party to the conspiracy."

"So, she brought you two to Washington to pursue the 'why' and the 'who' of the Kennedy assassination?" Prouty asked them.

"That's right," Mike said.

"How can I be of help, gentlemen?"

Harold told him, "Both of us have read your 1974 book, *The Secret Team: the CIA and its Allies*. We found it a concise and a clear guide to the problem Kennedy encountered with the national security community after he took office."

"Thank you," Prouty said. "Before you start your questions though, allow me to give you some background. "

"Certainly," Burke allowed.

"Just a few months after being sworn in, President Truman disbanded the wartime OSS. He thought there was no need for clandestine activities during peacetime. All their intelligence gathering and analysis responsibilities were transferred to the departments of State and War.

"But very soon the new president faced a very aggressive Soviet Union. Berlin, Central Europe, the Balkan countries, Turkey and Iran were under virtual attack by our former ally. President Truman did not hesitate to confront the Russians very aggressively.

"And it became obvious to him that his administration needed a more coordinated intelligence gathering and analysis effort. So in 1946, the president set up the Central Intelligence Group. This body would be supervised by the secretaries of State, War and Navy and headed by a Director of Central Intelligence.

"To further cement that relationship, and thus control the new effort, Truman directed that funds for the CIG were to be obtained from the Departments of State, War and Navy rather than directly from Congress.

"By doing this, Truman wanted to prevent this new intelligence agency from engaging in clandestine operations without the express direction and authority of the Secretaries and the White House. He intended this CIG to be the quiet intelligence arm of the president. He never intended it to be an autonomous agency or one active in clandestine operations."

"What exactly was this new agency supposed to do, Colonel?" Burke asked.

"It was intended to coordinate and analyze intelligence as a first line of defense."

"Weren't agents of this new CIA supposed to gather intelligence?" Harold asked.

"No, Congressman Ryan, they were not. Their people were to only coordinate and analyze information gathered from other government agencies. Obtaining information in the field might come later. The National Security Act of 1947 further identified their role. Small covert operations were now allowed within a new organization called the Office of Policy Coordination and supervised by a National Security Council.

"President Truman wanted his Central Intelligence Agency to be the 'quiet intelligence arm of the President.'"

"Our current CIA is hardly quiet, Colonel," Mike joked.

"I'd have to agree with you on that, Mr. Burke," Prouty chuckled.

"The Korean War changed everything. The unexpected invasion of South Korea made it obvious that the existing system of intelligence gathering, coordination and analysis had proven to be inadequate. In that atmosphere, the Central Intelligence Agency grew enormously during the conflict. It grew from less than two dozen employees and a few million dollars of budget to over one hundred agents and a 100-million-dollar budget.

"Allen Dulles was appointed director in October 1952. By the time the fighting in Korea stopped in 1954, the agency had taken control of bases both in the United States and on foreign soil, along with enormous surplus war supplies and equipment.

"By 1955, the CIA had become the largest and most active peacetime operational force in the country. In fact, over the years, Allen Dulles had very cleverly inserted CIA personnel in most every department of the federal government, especially at Defense and State.

"By this time too, the CIA had an annual appropriation from Congress independent of any governmental department. And their resources, their activities, the number of employees, personnel files and their budget had all become highly classified; even from the president and his people."

Burke asked, "Was there any attempt to rein in their influence before Kennedy announced that he intended to 'scatter them to the winds?'"

"Remember, Mr. Burke," Prouty continued, "President Eisenhower came into office just before the end of the Korean War. He was unaware that the CIA had grown so far beyond what was authorized by Congress.

"So, he and his advisors were not even aware that there was a problem. By 1961, the CIA was virtually beyond the control of anyone in the Executive Branch, even the president."

"What demonstrated that conclusion, Colonel?" Harold asked.

"Why do you think the 1960 Paris Summit meeting between President Eisenhower and Premier Khrushchev was canceled?"

"It was well publicized that a U-2 flight downed in the Soviet Union caused such an international uproar that it destroyed the summit," Harold said.

"That is exactly what happened, Congressman," Colonel Prouty told him. "What you might not know is that prior to the summit, the president had specifically ordered that no such flights be conducted. Nevertheless, the CIA ordered such a flight and then caused the plane to crash on Soviet soil."

"You're saying that the CIA ordered that flight against the president's express orders and then caused it to crash just to sabotage the Paris Summit conference?"

"Now you have it, Mr. Burke. That's what I mean when I say that the CIA was out of control. Remember, this all happened in May of 1960. Eisenhower term was about over. So, to answer your earlier question, nothing was done by President Eisenhower in the aftermath to rein in or punish such conduct."

"And Allen Dulles remained as director of the CIA."

"That's right, Mr. Burke. The lame duck Eisenhower administration took no steps to rein in the power of the CIA."

"Why would Dulles disobey a direct order from the president and do such a thing, Colonel?" Harold asked.

"Dulles ordered it done because he did not want Eisenhower to come to an agreement with the Soviet Premier. Eisenhower had suffered a heart attack late in his first term, and after that Dulles feared that Eisenhower was crippled and no longer the Cold War warrior he had once been.

"Dulles didn't want Eisenhower to end the Cold War. Dulles wanted to win the Cold War."

"And John Kennedy kept Allen Dulles as director of the CIA."

"That's true. He did."

"Early in the first year of his first term, the Bay of Pigs fiasco made Kennedy aware of the problem that Eisenhower had passed on to him. Kennedy began aggressively to do something about it. Earlier, former President Truman had recognized the danger but the intelligence needs of the Korean War prevented him from taking any firm action to stop the growth and power of the CIA.

"In December 1963, Truman wrote an op-ed piece warning of the danger he saw in allowing the CIA to continue operating their shadow government. It wasn't given much press. But In that piece he said that the CIA was out of everyone's control."

Washington, D.C.

Congresswoman Boggs told her secretary "Get me Lillian Ryan on the phone, please."

"That would be Congressman Harold Ryan's wife?"

"You got it. The one and only Mrs. Ryan."

"Right away, ma'am."

It wasn't long before Lillian Ryan was on the other line.

"Sweetie," Boggs began. "How are you, dear?"

"I'm fine, Lindy," Lillian told her. "Harold's not here right now. As a matter of fact, he's at Burke's office interviewing Colonel Prouty as we speak."

"I was aware of that," Boggs told her. "But, I wanted to talk with you anyway."

What could she want with me, for heaven's sake? Lillian wondered.

"Could you and Burke's wife get away for a few days?"

"I suppose so, Lindy. But why would we do that?"

"I need you to come to Washington to interview Madeline Brown."

"Isn't she the gal who was supposed to have been President Johnson's mistress?"

"The very one," Boggs told Lillian. "She's going to be in D.C. next week for a few days and has agreed to meet with you and Burke's wife. What's her name, Marilyn?"

"Yes, it is. Why would you want us to talk with her, anyway?"

"As you remembered, she is reported to have been President Johnson's mistress over a period of years. I understand that she has some interesting things to reveal about Johnson before he became president. For the purposes of the study Harold and Mike are conducting, I think it would be worth our while to hear what the lady has to say."

"I can understand that. But why do you want the two of us to talk with her? You could chat with her, couldn't you?"

"She seems willing to talk now that Lyndon is dead. Still though, she is still a bit nervous. It appears, like most Texans, she remembers that people who threatened LBJ's political career disappeared or died under mysterious circumstances.

"I could do the interview, but I want her to feel comfortable enough to spill whatever she knows; not hold anything back, as it were. After talking with her on the phone yesterday, I believe you two will stand the best chance of getting her to open up.

"Will you do it, Lillian?" Boggs asked.

Lillian was quick to respond. "It's been almost fifteen years since I've been in D.C. I'd love to see what you birds in Congress have done to the ol' town since Harold was there. So, I'm fine with flying down; how about Marilyn?"

"I've already talked with her, dearie," Boggs revealed. "She's on board, too."

Lillian chuckled. "You certainly cover all your bases, don't you, Lindy?"

"You have to around this town, or you get run over, don't ya' know. I'll get Mable on the line. She'll make travel arrangements for your flight. She has already reserved rooms at the Willard for the two of you, too. You'll find they have a superior dining room."

"Pretty sure of yourself, weren't you Lindy?" Lillian said.

"No place for the meek in this town, dear," Congresswoman Boggs replied. "I gotta run. See you soon."

Detroit

Harold changed the subject. "Colonel Prouty, do you agree with the Select Committee that there was a conspiracy to murder John F. Kennedy?"

"I do, absolutely, Mr. Ryan. Over 70% of the American adult population came to that same conclusion shortly after the 1964 publication of the Warren Report. Only Congress thought it necessary to confirm that belief thirteen years later when it authorized a two-year-long investigation."

"In your writing, Colonel, you made it quite clear that the failure to protect the president in Dallas lay squarely on the shoulders of the Secret Service. Both the members of the Warren Commission and the members of the House Committee on Assassinations agreed that the Service did not provide adequate protection. Why did you feel that way?" Harold Ryan asked.

"I don't have any inside information to offer, Congressman. But I do have a good deal of experience with presidential tours, which include parades. I was not involved in making arrangements for President Kennedy's Texas trip, but I do know what security procedures must be in place to protect a president in such an environment. After the assassination, I did take a look at the security arrangements in Dallas."

"What did you notice?" Mike asked.

"The most glaring problem with the pre-parade preparations was the route chosen for the presidential motorcade. Look at this map. You can clearly see that the route chosen required that the president's vehicle be slowed to ten miles per hour or less in order to make the sharp right turn from Main on to Houston, heading toward the multi-storied Book Depository Building.

"If that wasn't bad enough, the president's limo had to stay at low speed to make a second very sharp turn, this time to the left on to Elm, then to head toward an unsecured overpass and leave behind tall, unsecured buildings.

"Like the School Book Depository building?" Burke interjected.

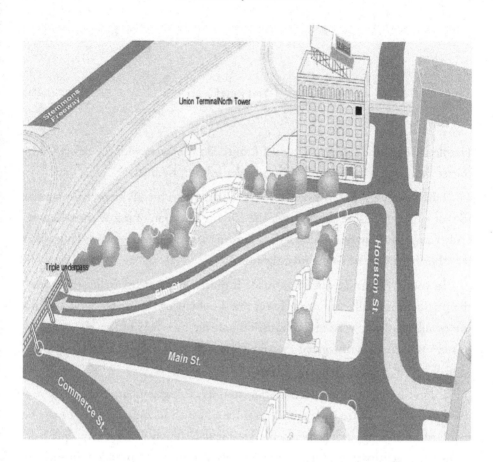

"Exactly, Mr. Burke," Prouty agreed.

Harold wondered aloud, "This was a parade during lunch hour, though. Wouldn't the president have wanted the people in the crowd to see him up close?"

"At the other Texas cities where the president toured, safety trumped campaigning each time, Congressman."

"But the Secret Service people in charge of the Dallas parade approved the route, didn't they?" Burke asked.

"As I recall, Mr. Sorrels said he approved that route in order to maintain a tight travel schedule between Love Airport and the Trade Mart lunch site. Staying on Main Street might have cost another five minutes. How important is five minutes to avoid putting the President of the United States in a kill zone?

"And remember," Prouty insisted, "long-standing parade procedure demanded that the presidential vehicle travel at a speed of 42 miles per hour at all times. That speed could have been maintained had they chosen the Main Street route, as Kennedy's people wanted.

"But the Secret Service agent in charge of the Dallas trip, Forrest Sorrels and his superiors in Washington violated this basic parade requirement. For Kennedy's vehicle to be required to slow to ten miles per hour while moving by multi-storied buildings and headed toward an overpass crowded with people, set him up for exactly what happened."

"What else did you notice, Colonel?" Harold asked.

"For both the president and vice president to be out of Washington at the same time is hardly ever done. To be traveling together and in the same motorcade is definitely against security procedures. It certainly defied common sense as well.

"Another breach was the lack of building security," Prouty continued. "It is procedure to have all the windows of multi-storied buildings along a presidential parade route closed, sealed and under surveillance; none of this was done at all in Dallas."

"Wes Lawson, the agent in charge of the Dallas visit, testified before the Warren Commission that he was shorthanded that day," Harold said.

"He may have been, Congressman," Prouty responded. "Then why was assistance of trained personnel offered by Sheriff Craig turned down? Why was the help of the 112th Military Intelligence Group stationed at Fort Sam Houston refused? Forty men from this unit had been used for security purposes during the San Antonio parade earlier on this trip; why not in Dallas, as they were offered?"

Prouty went on. "It's also customary to have motorcycle police flanking the presidential car, too. Four on each side of the president's limo were offered, but the Secret Service reduced the number to four, total. At Love Field, the mounted units still allowed in the parade were ordered by Secret Service Agent Lawson to follow the president's limo, instead of flanking it as was customary."

"Why would he do that, Colonel?" Burke asked.

"He testified that President Kennedy requested it because JFK wanted to be as exposed to the public as possible."

"So, Kennedy told them to back off normal parade security measures?" Harold asked, surprised.

"That's what Agent Lawson claimed. But it has since been verified that the president did not tell them any such thing," Prouty revealed. "In fact, there is ample evidence that Kennedy always cooperated fully with all standard procedures and that he never objected or overruled security arrangements made by Secret Service personnel.

"In addition to moving the motorcycle escort, there were no agents riding on the rear of the president's limo either. In fact at Love Field, Secret Service Agent Roberts ordered one of his Secret Service colleagues, agent Henry Rybka, not to assume that customary security position on the rear of the president's vehicle.

"Kennedy's military aide, General Clifton, who normally rode in the front seat of the presidential limo, was removed from that position by Secret Service Agent Lawson at Love Field and sent to a vehicle in the rear of the parade. He was told that President Kennedy wanted more exposure to the crowd and had ordered the move. JFK never gave that order.

"The bottom line is that the President of the United States was placed in a 'kill zone', fully exposed."

"Purposely, Colonel?"

"It would appear so, Congressman Ryan."

Mike Burke added, "That's probably why the Warren Commission concluded that the Secret Service did not do a proper job in Dallas."

"That's correct, Mike," Harold added. "And the Select Committee on Assassinations came to a similar conclusion. As stated in their report, it read:

"*The Secret Service was deficient in the performance of its duties.*"

"I believe that this language was overly kind, Congressman Ryan. Also, remember what happened following the first shot," Prouty went on. "The driver of President Kennedy's limo, Agent Greer, is clearly shown on film turning to look at the stricken president.

"Instead of speeding away from the scene as is demanded by procedure and his training, he actually is seen to stop the vehicle. Then, film shows him turning to look at the president again. It wasn't until after the president is struck in the head and killed that Greer pulls out of line and speeds away.

"Sitting next to him was Agent Kellerman. His sworn duty was to cover the president's body at the first sign of danger. Instead he sat there ramrod straight until the third shot had been fired.

"If the driver, Greer had reacted properly after he heard the first 'pop' or even after he turned for the first time and saw the president in obvious distress, the shooters would have had a much more difficult target. Those few seconds Agent Greer paused, probably made the difference between a wounded John Kennedy and a dead one.

"Two cars behind, Agent Youngblood was on top of the vice president before the second shot was fired, according to Mrs. Johnson. And his limo driver accelerated terrifically fast according to her testimony. What a difference!"

"The way you put it, Colonel," Harold said, "the conduct of the Secret Service Dallas detail on November twenty-second, 1963 has to be considered extremely lax and disturbing."

"Along that same line," Burke added, "Dallas Chief of Police Curry told me back in 1967 that contrary to Service regulations, the entire Kennedy detail was out drinking until at least closing time at the Fort Worth Press Club, and after that many of them went to an afterhours bar called 'The Cellar' where they stayed until dawn.

"Curry also said that the manager of The Cellar told him that after the assassination, he received a call from the White House asking him not to say anything about the Secret Service guys drinking there. The manager told Curry that none of his people said anything, but that the agents in his place were 'bombed' from drinking 190-proof alcohol.

"While there, they had a big laugh, he reported, about having left a couple of local firemen guarding the president and First Lady, who were sleeping back at the Hotel Texas."

"In contrast," Prouty told them," not one member of Vice President Johnson's Secret Service detail went out on the town drinking that night. In contrast, all those men were in their rooms as regulations demanded."

"That I didn't know, Colonel," Harold said.

"I've often thought it strange that all the members of Johnson's detail obeyed regulations, while all the members of the Kennedy detail broke the rules," Prouty confessed.

"It does seem curious, doesn't it?" Burke added.

"Were the agents who partied until the morning of the president's assassination ever disciplined?" Harold asked.

"No, they were not," Prouty revealed. "In fact, the Chief of the Secret Service, James J. Rowley, testified to the Warren Commission that he did not even reprimand them. When asked why a clear violation of Secret Service conduct rules was not punished, he said:

"Well, I thought that in light of history, to place a stigma on them by punishing them at that time, from which inevitably the public would conclude that they were responsible for the assassination of the president – I didn't think that was fair and that they did not deserve that, with the family and children."

"I can't understand that line of reasoning," Harold commented.

"I agree. There is no way to sugar-coat it. In my opinion, gentlemen, President Kennedy was set up."

"Are you suggesting a coup d'état was carried out on November twenty-second, 1963, Colonel?" Burke asked.

Harper Woods

Mike walked into the house from the garage.

"Anyone home?" he shouted.

"I'm in the living room, Dad," Ann shouted back.

"Hi, kiddo. Where's your mom?"

"It's Monday, so she's at choir practice."

"Oh ya. How was your day?"

"Fine, actually. I drove Jackie to her job at the Sweet Shop and then went to my singing lesson."

"Is your Beetle behaving?"

"Sure, she's not a problem, Dad. I caught myself in time and got some gas, unlike someone else I know."

"You mean you were down to the reserve gallon, and didn't forget, like I did."

"You got it, Dad," she told him. "I don't think I'll ever forget your running out of gas on the expressway about ten years ago. You made us walk up the embankment, climb the fence and trudge over to Bill Knight's house to get a ride to a gas station."

"Didn't hurt you to get in a good walk, did it?" Mike told her. "By the way, when did my old VW graduate from being an 'it' to becoming a 'she'?" Mike teased.

"We girls bonded with your old car when you made Susan and me take our drivers tests in it. Remember our nightly sessions at the high school parking lot trying to learn how to manage a stick shift and the what ya' call it; the pedal between the gas and the brake?"

"That's called a clutch, dear."

"Oh, ya. All I remember is stalling the car out half a dozen times each time we went out there practicing before I got the hang of it. Not a fun time."

"You passed your driver's test, didn't you?"

"I think the policeman just felt sorry for me. He's the one who taught me how to parallel park, remember."

"You do a nice job of it, too.

"By the way," Mike continued, "are you getting a job this summer?"

"For now, I'm picking up Jackie's babysitting jobs since she began working at the Sweet Shop. They might hire me there too. I'm babysitting one of her jobs tonight instead of going to choir practice at St. Peter's."

"Just remember, my dear," Mike told her, "you need to salt away some money for school next year. Spending money does not just grow on trees, ya' know."

Ann didn't hesitate to tell her father, "Don't forget that new invention called a credit card, Dad."

Mike responded with equal speed, "And don't you forget that ya' have to pay that bill each month, too."

"That's why children have parents," Ann chuckled on her way out of the room.

"Oh my," Mike moaned.

Detroit

The next morning, Mike and Harold met with Colonel Prouty once again.

"If you don't mind, gentlemen," Prouty said, "at this point, I'd like to take our discussion back to the CIA."

"One more question about the Secret Service while we're on the subject?" Harold asked.

"Certainly, Congressman," Prouty answered. "What is it?"

"Back in 1967, when Mike and I investigated the assassination for the Judiciary Committee, we interviewed several witnesses who claimed to have run into Secret Service personnel on the Grassy Knoll. Remember that, Mike?"

"Yes I do Harold," Mike responded. "As I recall, witnesses reported to me that they saw a puff of smoke or heard a shot from the area of the fence on the Grassy Knoll. And when they attempted to investigate, they were turned away by men in suits who had Secret Service credentials.

"But, in his Warren Commission testimony, the Dallas Secret Service man in charge of the president's visit said that all his agents were involved in the parade or were at the Trade Mart. He testified that none of them were on the ground at the Grassy Knoll or in any of the buildings along the parade route."

"So what is your question, Congressman?" Prouty asked again.

"Do you have any information about how men posing as Secret Service agents would have gotten the legitimate credentials witnesses swore they saw?"

"I think I have some information on that subject that will help focus your investigation," Prouty told them. "And this also brings us right back to the role of the CIA in all of this.

"Back in 1963, the Technical Services Division of the CIA somehow took over the printing of documents for the Secret Service. This included all gate passes, security passes, emblems for presidential vehicles, and most importantly to your investigation, authentic credentials for Secret Service agents assigned to the White

House detail. This CIA department was headed by a Dr. Sidney Gottlieb, who answered to Richard Helms. It was sometimes referred to as the 'department of dirty tricks.' It just so happened that after the assassination of President Kennedy, the Treasury Department took over printing Secret Service credentials and passes."

"Are you suggesting," Burke asked. "That it is possible that the CIA was responsible for printing legitimate credentials for fake Secret Service agents; the ones our witnesses said they encountered on the Grassy Knoll?"

"It is certainly possible, Mr. Burke." Prouty responded. "And since immediately after the assassination, the Secret Service resumed the responsibility for all such printing, it seems very likely that the CIA did just that."

"You remember Mike," Harold interjected, "our confidential informant, George, told us this very thing last week in D.C."

"Right, I remember," Burke agreed.

"At this point I want to emphasize the importance of President Truman's comments made in December of 1963, shortly after the assassination. In an interview for Plain Speaking, he was asked by the reporter, Merle Miller:

"How do you feel about the CIA now, Mr. President?" Miller asked.

Truman responded,

"I decided to set up a special organization charged with the collection of all intelligence reports from every available source, and to have those reports reach me as president without department 'treatment' or interpretations.

"I wanted and needed the information in its 'natural raw' state and in as comprehensive a volume as it was practical for me to make full use of it."

"But for some time, I have been disturbed by the way the CIA has been diverted from its original assignment. It has become an operational and at times a policy-making arm of the government

"I never had any thought that when I set up the CIA that it would be injected into peacetime cloak and dagger operations.

"I therefore, would like to see the CIA be restored to its original assignment as the intelligence arm of the president, and its operational duties be terminated or properly used elsewhere."

Harper Woods

Marilyn Burke came into her house around 9 o'clock. Mike was watching a shoot 'em up on television.

"Hi there," Mike greeted. "Have a good rehearsal tonight?"

Marilyn kicked off her shoes and sat beside her husband.

"We have fun at these rehearsals, so it's always good. How about you? Did you find the food I left for you in the fridge?"

"Yep. The pot roast was tasty. I heated it up and buttered a piece of bread. I especially enjoyed that bowl of chocolate pudding. It was all neat stuff. Thank you."

"How are your interviews going?"

"Really good. This Colonel Prouty is a treasure trove of information. He is going to be a great help."

"Remember when you and Harold suggest that Lillian and I lend a hand?"

"Yes, I do. What about it?"

"Well, it appears that we are going to be more involved than any of us imagined."

"What is that supposed to mean?"

"I got a call from Congresswoman Boggs today requesting that I fly to D.C. to interview Madeline Brown."

"Well, I'll be," Mike exclaimed. "That Lindy Boggs is a real mover and shaker. No wonder she is such a powerful member of Congress. Did you accept her request?"

"You know her," Marilyn chuckled. "She's got you roped in before you can say much of anything. She's already gotten our flight booked and rooms reserved for us at the Willard Hotel where you stayed."

"You said 'us.' Who else is involved?"

"Lillian Ryan is going, too."

"When is this supposed to happen?"

"You know Boggs," Marilyn reminded her husband. "We're off to Washington next week."

"Excited?" Mike asked.

"Sure am. I haven't been there in years. Lillian is a good natured gal, too. She and I should have fun. I think I'll stay over for a few days and visit my folks. Do you mind?"

"Of course not. It's too good an opportunity to pass up a visit with your parents. They will absolutely love it, I'm sure."

"I was thinking of taking Ann," Marilyn continued. "You know, have my folks pick her up and then I can join them after my job is completed. What do you think?"

"I don't think it's a good idea, actually," Mike cautioned.

"This is not a family trip, sweetheart. Besides, Ann is needed here to drive Jackie around and find a job for herself so she can earn some college spending money. Your folks can come here and visit with the kids anytime they want. I hope you suggest that very thing when you see them."

"I suppose you're right," Marilyn decided. "When did you become so wise?"

"Hanging around you, I guess." Mike said as he moved his arm around his wife.

"What do you think you're doing?"

"I've missed you lately."

"Do you have designs on me, mister?"

"Absolutely miss; I do."

Their kiss went on and on. All the while Mike was fumbling with the buttons on his wife's blouse.

She pulled back some. "You seem to be out of practice there, buster. It'll be dawn before you get down to business." She took over. Soon Mike was fondling his wife and working on her slacks. They paused long enough to make it to their bedroom.

Detroit

The next morning everyone was back in Mike's law office conference room. He and Harold were eager to continue working with Colonel Prouty. Today though, they had invited Joe Yager to sit in. They thought that Joe might bring some fresh insights to their interview.

When approached on this yesterday, Colonel Prouty had agreed to the addition.

"Good morning gentlemen," Prouty began. "This will be my last day with you here in Detroit, since I have to be in Washington tomorrow. During our time today, I suggest I cover two actions taken by President Kennedy that I believe are very critical to your investigation. I was intimately involved with both of them."

"The floor is yours, Colonel," Mike assured him.

"First let me give you a bit of background just to remind you:

"Kennedy had been in office only a few months when he and his team had to deal with the CIA planned invasion of Castro's Cuba. And,

1. "The president had been assured that the landing of the CIA trained invaders on a Cuban beach would be welcomed by enthusiastic Cubans. An uprising against Castro was predicted.

2. "Once ashore the force would quickly be able to establish a revolutionary government, be recognized by the United States and thereby eligible to receive military support.

3. "The result would be that the Castro regime would fall with the overwhelming support of the Cuban people.

"None of this proved to be the case. The invaders were not able to establish a beachhead, nor were they welcomed by an uprising of the Cuban populace. So, it quickly became apparent that the invasion would fail without massive American military intervention.

"To salvage this situation, Kennedy was urged by both his military and CIA advisors to allow our military to intervene.

"The President felt he had been misled; lied to, actually, and thus placed in a no- win position by the CIA. They had set this up in hopes that he would begin a full scale invasion of Cuba just to salvage the initial landing. He refused to take the bait and instead denied our military permission to support the CIA sponsored Cuban exile invasion of their homeland.

"This would be the first time since Allen Dulles was appointed director of the CIA by President Eisenhower in 1952, that an operation of the CIA had been stymied by a president.

"Thus, Kennedy earned the anger of the Cuban exile community, who felt he had betrayed them, and of the CIA leadership who had promised our support to the exiles. The military leaders of the United States were also angry that the President of the United States would allow a Communist presence to remain in Cuba only ninety-five miles from our eastern shore when it could have been eliminated.

"It was not a good start for the new president. But it alerted him to the problem he had with a rogue CIA and its supporters in the Pentagon. He realized that the intelligence the CIA had provided was tainted to support the outcomes they wanted. Therefore, going forward, he could not trust the advice they gave him. He decided to take action.

"First, he brought retired General of the Army Maxwell Taylor into the White House as a presidential advisor. Then, in June of 1961, he issued three National Security Action Memorandums, numbers 55, 56, and 57. It was my responsibility to give the Chairman of the Joint Chiefs of Staff, General Lemnitzer, a briefing on these executive orders. "

"Did you help write them, Colonel?" Joe asked.

"No, I did not, Mr. Yager," he responded. "General Maxwell Taylor did. But I did explain to the chairman that it was at the president's direction that the Joint Chiefs take on this new responsibility. In Memorandum 55, President Kennedy clearly directed:

"I wish to inform the Joint Chiefs of Staff as follows with regard to my views of their relations to me in Cold War Operations (*covert operations*):

I regard the Joint Chiefs of Staff as my principal military adviser, with responsibility for initiating advice to me and for responding to requests for advice. I expect their advice to come to me direct and unfiltered.

The Joint Chiefs of Staff have a responsibility for the defense of the nation in the Cold War similar to that which they have in conventional hostilities."

"It occurs to me, Colonel," Harold interjected, "that the president had given his Joint Chiefs of Staff a new responsibility, namely of initiation and oversight in Cold War operations. Do you see it that way?"

"Without doubt, Congressman," Prouty responded. "As I explained it to General Lemnitzer, the language of the memorandum made that intention of the president very clear."

"Did this clip the wings of the CIA in regard to clandestine operations?" Mike asked.

"It was only the opening gun, Mr. Burke," Prouty revealed. "Remember, at this time the CIA had operations going on all over the world. They had stockpiles of military assets stored at bases everywhere as well. In Vietnam alone they had almost fifteen thousand people running their operation there.

"A single presidential directive would not shut down all their active covert operations and return the agency to intelligence gathering and analysis as they were originally charged to accomplish. It would take a determined president time to accomplish that reversal. It was clear that Kennedy believed he could accomplish that task during his second term."

"Did he have anyone in particular he believed could handle that task?" Joe asked.

"The rumor mill suggested that he would move his brother Bobby in as director after the 1964 election. He needed a tough as nails person, a take-no-prisoners kind of administrator over there; someone he trusted. Robert Kennedy was that kind of person, so I think that is exactly what he would have done."

"If this was only the opening gun in Kennedy's war on the CIA, what was next?" Harold inquired.

"President Kennedy announced in September that Allen Dulles would retire on November twenty-ninth, 1961, and that John McCone would be the new director of the CIA. Everyone knew it was a firing, but Dulles was ushered out with great fanfare amid smiles and the award of medals of appreciation from a grateful nation."

"As I remember," Harold said, "Mr. McCone was regarded around Washington as an interim director; that Kennedy was waiting to be reelected before he really began the reorganization of the CIA. Is that what you guys over at the Pentagon thought?"

"You hit the nail on the head, Congressman. With Dulles not operating behind his back, Kennedy intended to take on the other hot items simmering on his international relations agenda."

"What were those, Colonel?" Mike asked.

"They were Cuba and Southeast Asia, Mr. Burke," Prouty revealed.

"Cuba appeared the most pressing. Kennedy was still smarting from the embarrassing debacle of the Bay of Pigs. He publicly took personal responsibility for the mess but at the same time he seemed determined to destroy the Castro government; but, in his own way."

"Are you suggesting that at the same time he was trying to limit the covert operations of the CIA, he was using their clandestine capabilities to undermine the Castro government?" Mike asked.

"That is exactly what happened. Kennedy promised the Cuban-American exiles that he would do whatever was necessary to overthrow Castro.

"Bases for operations were set up all over Florida. Millions were spent recruiting and training guerilla forces. At the same time, an international effort was made to cripple the Cuban economy. Cuban shipping and port facilities were attacked by Cuban exiles with the support of the CIA.

"Wealthy Americans even became involved. They provided well equipped attack boats to raid Cuba. Under the direction of Robert Kennedy, millions of dollars were allocated to the effort.

"Great enthusiasm was generated for this secret operation within the Cuban-American exile community. Kennedy seemed to be honestly determined that Castro's Communist government would fall. After all, he had promised just that. The people of the exile community were excited. They could taste victory.

At this point Burke interrupted. "Nikita Khrushchev threw a monkey wrench into the works and everything changed, didn't it?"

"You've been doing your homework, Mr. Burke," Prouty complimented.

"I'm not just a pretty face around here, ya' know."

"Of course, you're correct. We now know that Khrushchev suspected that Kennedy was up to something, an invasion of Cuba possibly. So, he pressured Castro to accept the secret insertion of Russian missiles, air-defense systems and support troops into Cuba.

"The Cuban exile groups were passed intelligence from their Cuba contacts about what the Russians were doing in Cuba. They passed that information on to their CIA handlers.

"But the administration was very reluctant to believe the intelligence for two reasons. First, they had been misled by the CIA before: remember the Bay of Pigs disaster. Second, they distrusted the information because they had been assured by the Russians that no such thing was happening.

"As you know, eventually the installations were photographed and the Russian lies were discovered. The Cuban Missile Crisis was suddenly the world's hot item, and both nations appeared to be moving toward nuclear war.

"It was in this atmosphere the Joint Chiefs suggested to President Kennedy that they be authorized to launch a pre-emptory nuclear strike on Russia. He walked out of the meeting after they assured him that 'only' forty million Americans would be killed in the resulting Russian retaliation.

"As you know, that disaster was averted and the Russian missiles were removed. In exchange, we removed our Jupiter missiles from Turkey. General Curtis LeMay told Kennedy that he considered this the worst defeat the United States had ever suffered. Those views were shared by others in the Pentagon.

"Kennedy believed that avoiding nuclear war was more important, so he went forward with the agreement. What wasn't well known was that Kennedy also promised Khrushchev that the United States would not attempt an invasion of Cuba or support any anti-Castro activity either.

"As a result, Kennedy ordered an end to all the anti-Cuba activities he had supported of the CIA and Cuban exile groups. The Coast Guard impounded the Cuban operated attack vessels, the Cuban support money dried up, their supply chain shut down and their Florida bases closed. The CIA operatives were told to stand down as well.

"Of course, the Cuban-American community and their CIA handlers were outraged, and they blamed President Kennedy. They all felt he had lied to them and that his promises to Khrushchev had destroyed any chance they had for returning to a Communist-free Cuba."

***

At this point, Harold suggested that they break for lunch. The four men drove to Joe Muir's seafood restaurant.

"Seafood for lunch?" Prouty asked.

"Best place in downtown Detroit, Colonel," Harold told him. "Power lunches are held in this place every day. Food's not bad either."

"Good to know, Congressman," Prouty told him.

Washington, D.C.

"Lindy," one of Congresswoman Boggs' secretaries said, "I just got a call from Mr. Burke. He and Congressman Ryan have set up some appointments here in D.C. the same week you scheduled their wives to be in town. He suggested that they share accommodations with their spouses since they'll be here at the same time. Do you see any problem with that?"

"That Burke is a crafty fellow," Boggs said. "He's arranging a little time away from the kids for him and his wife all on the public dime. Hell's bells, no I don't mind.

"Actually, they'll be saving me money doing it that way. My only concern is the wives might object to having the men butt in on their Washington adventure. Go ahead though, Mable. Set it up the way Mr. Burke suggested. We'll let them sort it out."

"While you're at it, put them on the invitation list for the party I'm having that weekend. That'll save me the cost of another meal for the lot a' them," she said, chuckling. "Besides, they probably would enjoy attending a Washington party."

"Yes ma'am," Mable said.

St. Clair Shores

Harold was enjoying a cocktail and Lillian was sipping a glass of wine. They were sharing crackers and cheese as well.

"So, you're all set to take off for D.C. next week?" Harold asked.

"Yes, I am. But what's this I hear about you and Burke busting into our getaway to the big city?"

"Burke told me he informed Mable, our contact at Boggs' office, that we have appointments in D.C. the same week you gals are scheduled to be in town."

"I understand that part," Lillian said. "But how did that get to you and I rooming together?"

"I was told that he suggested that such an arrangement might save the Congresswoman money; they agreed. That's how I heard that it happened, anyway."

"Can't get away from you, can I, sweetheart?" Lillian kidded her husband.

"Do you want to, dear?" Harold asked.

"Not entirely," Lillian informed Harold. "But it seemed like it might have been a good break; a temporary one that is. Would that have been a problem for you?"

"Not at all, dear. Want me to fix a cracker for you?"

"Yes, please. "

"Are we done with this discussion?" Harold asked.

"I think so." Lillian said with a smile.

"What's for supper?"

"I haven't decided," Lillian answered.

"Then I think I'll freshen up my drink while you're thinking about it." Harold told his wife.

Washington, D.C.

"After today, those Irish Mafia bastard Kennedys will never em-
barrass me again – that's no threat – that's a promise."

— Vice President Lyndon Baines Johnson: November 22, 1963. Dallas, Texas.

The Willard Hotel had a quiet coffee shop on the main floor. Marilyn Burke and
Lillian Ryan were seated in a private booth waiting for their guest, Madeleine
Brown.

She was only a few minutes late when a hotel employee brought her to their
booth.

"Good morning gals," she said. "I'm Madeleine Brown."

Lillian and Marilyn turned and greeted their guest.

"You're both from Michigan I take it," Madeleine said.

"Born and bred." Lillian revealed.

"I'm a Marylander myself, Marilyn said. "Were you born in Texas, Madeleine?"

"Sure was; in the Dallas area actually. I wasn't long out a' high school that I
married and had a child. But my husband turned out to be a drunk. So, we di-
vorced. I love most everything about Texas. But Dallas is my favorite."

"From what I read, Texas weather is too extreme for my taste," Lillian told her.

"Actually, the state is so damned big you can pretty much pick your climate,"
Madeleine said with a chuckle. "My experience has taught me that it's the men ya'
haf ta' be careful of, not the weather."

All three ladies laughed at that comment.

"On the subject a' men ta' be careful of, Congresswoman Boggs tells me you
have an interest in my old buddy, Lyndon. That right?"

"Right," Marilyn said. "I hear that you knew him pretty well."

"I guess you could say that. I jumped into and out a' bed more times with that man than I could rightly count. I know I wasn't the only gal he lassoed neither. He was the horniest man I ever met. Just the same, we had some good times together."

"Did you have any bad times with President Johnson, Madeleine?"

"Oh, sure," she responded. "He wasn't too pleased when I got pregnant. He gave me the cold shoulder for a time. But he paid for everything. It hurt me though that he would not recognize our son as his. But I understood. Jus' tha' same it hurt – a lot, too."

Marilyn plunged ahead. "Excuse me for asking, but were you sure your son was Johnson's child?"

"It's all right, sweetie," Madeleine assured her. "I've been asked that question lots a' times.

"My boy was Lyndon's. Ya see, I wasn't beddin' anybody but him for some time. He insisted on that. So, I knew it was his. Later in life, my son looked the spittin' image of his daddy. But once I told Lyndon I was expecting, he avoided me like I was a rattlesnake coiled an' ready to strike.

"Either a' you ladies been pregnant?"

"Oh yes, and more than once, Madeleine," Lillian assured her.

"Three times for me," Marilyn added.

"Then you remember how lonely the experience can be. And, as you get the big belly, how ugly you feel and how you need your man's assurances and support."

"Sure do," Marilyn answered.

"It seemed pretty important to me at the time, too," Lillian agreed.

"I didn't get any a' that; certainly not from Lyndon, my baby's daddy."

"You went back to him, just the same, didn't you?" Lillian reminded her.

"I had no place else to go, ya see. Besides, I had these foolish illusions that he might bond with our boy and that he'd see ta' it that we became a family. He only had two girls with Lady Bird, ya know; and a pretty cold bed ta' boot.

"So, as foolish as it was, I went back to his bed. He took good care of my boy an' me though. He had an attorney, Jesse Ragsdale give us a nice house, expense money, even a nanny. I knew it all came from Lyndon. So, I can't fault him on that. After a while, though, I realized that all I was ever going to be was one of his Texas squeezes.

"It must have been hard to accept that," Lillian asked.

"No, it wasn't," Madeleine told them. "In Texas, it was clear to everyone that I belonged to Lyndon. I had no place to go, ya' see. I either accepted that or I'd a' ended up like so many others who got in Lyndon's way – dead maybe."

"Even though he's dead now," Marilyn asked. "Do you still feel threatened?"

"No, not that way. But I've been discredited by the Texas media just tha' same. Ya' know, they ran stories dismissing me as a loose and scorned woman who was jus' trying ta' get some money from the LBJ estate. His widow has done a pretty thorough job a' that."

"Would you take some money to shut up?"

"Probably," Madeleine confessed. "No one pays any attention to what I have to say about LBJ and the killing of Kennedy anyway."

"We will, Madeleine," Lillian assured her. "Believe me, we will."

"That's so sweet a' you, dearie; truly sweet, indeed."

"So," Marilyn began, "what can you tell us about LBJ and the Kennedy assassination?"

"For starters," Brown began, "Ya' gotta remember that I can't prove any a' this. LBJ just told me stuff from time to time. Some of it I just chalked up ta' bragging like men do. But once in a while, he'd speak in a real serious deep voice an' have a certain look about him, an' I'd know he was tellin' me God's gospel truth as best he knew it.

"Like back in 1960, he told me a story about what happened at the Democratic National Convention in Los Angles. Lyndon wanted the nomination for president but as it turned out, he didn't have the convention votes to get it. Seems the Yankee Democrats in his party up north didn't like him much.

"Lyndon told me that H. L. Hunt met with Joe Kennedy to try to work out something."

"Who is this Hunt person?" Marilyn asked.

"He's a big shot oil billionaire from Texas. Hunt wanted Kennedy to accept LBJ as his running mate on the ticket. Hunt wanted LBJ as vice president just in case something happened to JFK, ya' see.

"Later on Lyndon also told me that Hoover had some dirt on JFK's secret sex life but promised to keep it a secret if Kennedy accepted Lyndon on the ticket. Despite that threat, Robert Kennedy still didn't want LBJ as the vice presidential candidate. But JFK and their father overruled Bobby."

"Do you think any of that's true, Madeleine?" Lillian asked.

"Well, I'll tell ya' girls," Madeleine responded with a smirk. "I don't know about you and your men, but I got so I could tell pretty darn well when Lyndon was jus' bragging, telling me the truth or leadin' me astray with a tall one.

"Know what I mean?"

"Gotch ya', Madeleine," Marilyn Burke said.

"So, you're telling us that Johnson told you these things were true?"

"Exactly," Brown insisted. "But still, ya' got ta' remember I have no proof this stuff actually happened or that what he told me was true."

"Did he tell you anything else?"

"As a matter of fact, he did," Brown responded.

"I remember one time I was with Lyndon. He was feeling especially depressed. I think it was during the summer of '63 or maybe the fall. Lyndon went on about he knew Bobby Kennedy was feeding the Life magazine people information about him.

"He was convinced that the Kennedys were out to get him indicted for taking bribes for something or other while he was still a Senator. I recall he said it was about takin' some federal subsidy money for crops supposedly planted but never were, if that makes any sense. He also mentioned that he hadn't paid the taxes due for a gift of a TV station's stock he was given in exchange for helping a Texas construction company get millions of dollars to build a dam in Texas.

"He was sure that the Kennedys were trying to ruin him politically so they could drop him from the ticket in 1964. He was afraid that he might even go to jail over this thing.

"Anyway, he said he be damned if he'd let them get away with that. He seemed to really hate the Kennedy brothers."

"Another time, it was the morning of November twenty-second, 1963. Lyndon called me and sounded very agitated. Out a' the blue he said, *"Those God damned Irish Mafia bastard Kennedys will never embarrass me again. That's a promise, not a threat."*

"Wait a minute, Madeleine," Lillian said. "I thought you said in some article I read that he told you that at a party you attended the night before the assassination."

"Oh, ya," Brown responded. "I attended a party at Clint Murchison's house the evening of November twenty-first. Lyndon might have said it then. One of those two times fer' sure though."

"Later on the morning of November twenty-second, I was driving out of town alone. I stopped for lunch and heard the news of the assassination. I called a TV producer I knew and asked if it was really true.

"Yep, they got the bastard," he told me.

"On Sunday I saw a picture in the newspaper of LBJ taking the oath of office. The article said he was on Air Force One. Mrs. Kennedy was standing by his side and that Texas congressman Albert Thomas was at the far end of the photo grinning like a Cheshire cat."

"After Johnson became president, did you continue seeing him?" Lillian asked.

"Oh yes," Madeleine revealed. "The same guy who had arranged our meetings in the past, Jesse Kellan, continued to do so. Lyndon kept a room at the Driskoll Hotel in Dallas, Room 254 even after he became president. Kellan arranged for me to meet Lyndon there on December thirty-first, 1963 after he paid a visit to a New Year's Eve party held at the hotel.

"Later that night we were laying' in bed jus' talking. I told him that people in Texas were saying he had had something to do with Kennedy's murder. He exploded; scared me near ta' death. He jumped out a' the bed in a rage and stormed around the room."

"It was Texas oil and those CIA renegade intelligence bastards in Washington who done it," he shouted.

"Did he ever bring that up again, Madeleine?" Marilyn Burke asked.

"We met for the last time at the Shamrock Hotel in Houston back in 1969. It was sort a' different, cause' we talked for the longest time, almost two hours. He was in one of his depressions, a deep one.

"He was out of the White House by then a' course and felt neglected. I think his biggest fear was that he might be blamed for the Vietnam conflict an' all those boys being killed.

"Anyway, that day, he went on an' on about the Kennedy assassination. He said he thought Oswald didn't do it alone; maybe not at all. He insisted that he only went along with that publicly to help the nation get over the trauma of the killing and to prevent people from blaming the Soviets an' maybe causin' a big war. Then, he said something I'll never forget."

"What was that?" Marilyn asked.

"He told me that he really was sure that the CIA had something to do with the killing.

"Just listening to him ramble on that day, I believe he was actually afraid they might have done the same to him if he hadn't let them and the military have their way in Vietnam. In fact, he said to me that, right after becoming president, he told to the military big wigs:

"I'll let you have your war in Vietnam."

"Then, the strangest thing happened. After a while of us jus' sittin' there all quiet, an' not sayin' anything more, he stood, gave me a hug, and left the room."

"Was that it for you two?" asked Lillian. "You had no more contacts of any sort?"

"Yep, that was it. The next time I got a call from Jesse Kellan wasn't to arrange another meeting. This time he called to tell me that Lyndon had died."

Willard Hotel

The Burkes were just waking up. Marilyn stretched and Michael reached over and pulled her close.

"Making love in a hotel room is much more fun than at home," Mike said. "Don't you think?"

Marilyn snuggled her bare body closer. "It does seem deliciously sinful, actually. I love it."

Mike's hand moved on his wife's warm body.

"Oh my," Marilyn said. "Don't you dare stop what you're doing, Michael Burke."

"It's my pleasure, madam." He assured her as he touched her moist center, "I'm here to serve."

She could feel her husband's arousal. He was ready for her. As she turned in his arms, she looked over his shoulder and noticed the clock on the bed stand.

"Oh, my Lord," she said sitting up. "I have to meet Lillian in fifteen minutes for breakfast and a day on the town."

"She'll wait a few minutes, won't she?" Mike urged trying to pull his wife back into his arms.

"Is that all I am to you mister; a quick lay in the sack?"

"Right now, yes," Mike admitted.

Marilyn stretched on top of her husband and gave him a quick peck on the lips before she escaped from his arms, jumped off the bed and ran into their bathroom.

"I'm dying here," Mike shouted after her.

"Later," Marilyn said as she turned on the shower.

"Promises," Mike shouted after her. "All I get are promises."

"Poor baby; so neglected," Marilyn shouted as she stepped into the shower.

"You got that right," Mike shouted back.

***

Right after breakfast, Harold and Mike met in their customary hotel conference room. They decided to get organized before the afternoon meeting with their informant, George.

"Coffee, Mike?" Harold asked.

"Thanks, but I'm coffee'd out. Pour yourself some, though."

Harold did and joined Mike at the conference room table.

"First, I think we ought to go over this week's schedule," Mike began. "We have three interviews set up for this week, correct?"

"Right," Harold confirmed. "We have a session with George this afternoon in this conference room. Tomorrow morning, we drive up to Philadelphia to meet with Gaeton Fonzi for lunch."

"That's correct, Harold. And on Thursday we meet with Jerry Bruno here in Washington," Mike added.

"Aren't we going to meet with Secret Service agents, William Greer, Roy Kellerman and Emory Roberts?" Harold asked.

"Just our luck Roberts passed away in 1973." Mike complained.

"Can't have everything, Michael me boy. We'll make do with what we have."

"We'll have to, Harold. I'll ask Mable to set up appointments with the Secret Service guys who were in charge of the parade in Dallas; agents Sorrels and Lawson, too."

"Don't forget Kellerman and Greer, Mike," Harold reminded him. "I for sure want to talk to those guys."

"Sure. For now though, let's lay out our interview with George," Mike suggested. "According to my notes from our last meeting with him, he wanted us to look into a series of executive orders Kennedy issued in 1962."

"Correct," Mike agreed. "I have it right here; NSAM numbers 55, 56 and 57."

"We covered those with Colonel Prouty when we interviewed him back in Detroit, Mike. All we need from George this afternoon is verification of the purpose those executive orders were to serve."

"We might be able to reveal just how the CIA leadership felt about Kennedy's attempt to clip their wings." Mike added.

"Fine," Harold agreed, "Add that question to our list."

"What about Kennedy's secret correspondence with Khrushchev?" Mike asked.

"Do you mean we should discuss with George the content of their communications? Or do we want to know how CIA and State felt about Kennedy using his press secretary, Salinger, and a KGB agent assigned to the Russian Washington embassy to communicate with his Russian counterpart?"

"All of the above," Mike responded.

"Oh yes," Harold decided. "Kennedy used some back-channel method to begin discussions with Castro on normalizing relations between our two countries. George should know about that too."

"How about the topic of disarmament?" Mike reminded his partner. "Let's not forget McNamara's aide giving a speech in 1963 about reducing the defense budget and its impact on the economy."

"I seem to recall that Khrushchev had expressed some interest in disarmament when he suggested that talks on a nuclear test ban be reopened," Harold remembered. "George could probably take the entire afternoon talking on any one of these topics."

"We shall see, won't we?" Harold said.

Meeting with George

As in the past, their informant showed up right on time.

"Good afternoon, gentlemen," he began. "Welcome back to our nation's capital. I'll have to leave by five o'clock this evening. But you probably want to get away from here early enough to clean up and meet your wives for cocktails and dinner anyway."

"That's very clever, George," Harold admitted.

"You mean my telling you that I know your wives are in town?"

"Exactly," Harold agreed.

"A small indulgence I could not resist. I hope you are not angry. It is an old habit to know as much as possible about the people you are doing business with. If you are offended, I could leave."

"I'm just surprised, not offended," Harold said. "Certainly no harm has been done."

"And none is intended, I assure you, Congressman."

Mike entered the conversation. "My colleague's memory has somewhat diminished about how some overzealous FBI agents fired on us when we were in Dallas back in 1967 when we were investigating the JFK assassination.

"But I haven't forgotten that my wife's automobile tires were slashed. She received calls during the night while I was out of town. And my children were frightened at my home in Maryland by finding a dead cat on our doorstep. Mr. Hoover's people were sending a message to us back then.

"You just sent us a message too, didn't you, George?"

"Do you think I should leave, Mr. Burke?"

Mike was quiet for a moment. "Just because you know that our wives are in town, and probably much more, doesn't negate the fact that you have a great deal of information that Harold and I need.

"So, no, I don't think you should leave, George," Mike decided. "But my Irish temper is up right now, so I think I'll let my colleague begin our conversation today while I cool down."

"Where would you like to begin, Congressman?" George asked.

"We've had some recent conversations about the National Security Memorandums. You suggested we take a look at numbers 55, 56 and 57. So we know what they ordered and why Kennedy issued them. But we don't know much about how they were perceived in Defense, State and in particular at the CIA. Could you address that?"

"Yes, I can," George began. "I must compliment you gentlemen. You could not have contacted a more knowledgeable person than Colonel Prouty to brief you on them. He was the one charged by General Taylor and the president with the responsibility to brief General Lyman Lemnitzer, Chairman of the Joint Chiefs."

"Holy shit!" Mike exclaimed. Red faced, Mike almost shouted, "Are you giving us another message, George?"

George looked directly at Mike. "You bet your ass, I am my hotheaded Irishman. I felt the need to remind you that talking with you is no trivial matter for me. It's not just a chance for me to take a break from the office. I took a great risk when I gave information to the people on the Committee on Assassinations. I did so then in the hope that they would use it to blow the lid off the Kennedy assassination. They chose not to do so.

"Congresswoman Boggs assured me that you two might just be the ones to finally do it. Reading the report you produced back in 1967 convinced me that she may be correct. I hope I am not mistaken a second time.

"If you think I'm the only one who knows about whom you see and why, you are mistaken or very naive. The agency has plants in every Congressional office. How do you think you got that job offer years ago to work for the Judiciary Committee, Mr. Burke? Hoover's deputy Bill Sullivan got it for you so he would have a mole among that committee's staffers."

"Hold it there. Sullivan never contacted me for information when I was working there," Mike protested.

"You are naïve, Mr. Burke. He didn't have to," George chuckled. "He had others. In fact, each time you two had a draft of your report typed up, he got a copy before you even did. Besides, Hoover had a member of the committee, Congressman Ford, keeping him informed.

"Understand something, gentlemen. Every time I meet with you, my life is on the line. Yes, I'm sending you a message, Mr. Burke. The message is: take what we are doing here very seriously because what we do here could get me killed; you too for that matter.

"A year ago a retired high ranking CIA agent reportedly died of a heart attack. His name was David Sanchez Morales. He had built a fortress of a home in Arizona near the Mexican border. When asked why he took such security precautions, he replied that he didn't fear his Mexican neighbors, he feared his own (CIA) people.

"Why was he concerned? Because he knew too much; and he knew it. Unfortunately alcohol loosened his tongue occasionally. One night in Phoenix, he was drinking with friends. He drank a lot on that occasion. He said something that I believe cost him his life."

"What did he say, George?" Harold asked.

"In a drunken rage over something another person said about John Kennedy, Morales brought up the Bay of Pigs disaster, the Cuban Missile Crisis settlement, the subsequent betrayal of the Cuban exiles and his hatred for John Kennedy. At the end of his rant he said: *Well, we took care of that son of a bitch, didn't we?*"

"Somewhere or other I read that Morales was an important CIA covert agent. I'm pretty sure he was involved in serious stuff around the world, like assassinations," Mike offered.

"We don't need to get into that, Mr. Burke," George cautioned. "Suffice it to say, it is unlikely he died of a heart attack. Also keep in mind, his death last year was almost fifteen years after President Kennedy was killed. So, the issue is still evidently very important to some very powerful people.

"Now that you understand the reason for my messages, gentlemen, do you wish to call it a day and return to Michigan with your wives?"

"Speaking for myself, George," Harold answered, "I'd like you to tell us the effect President Kennedy's attempt to limit the covert activities of the CIA actually had on that agency.

"What do you think, Mike?" Harold asked his partner. "You want to go on with this or go home?"

"I think we should go on, Harold," Mike decided.

"Very well, gentlemen. But, before I get into that allow me to digress a bit. Let me set the scene as it were.

"World War II ended in 1945. Immediately, the Soviet Union took control of Central Europe and showed every sign of taking over Greece and Iran as well. In the Far East, Manchuria, parts of Japan and Korea were absorbed within their post-war empire too.

"The United States was the only nation capable of stopping Russia's aggressive advance. But we had disarmed quickly after the war ended and our people wanted a return to the serenity of the prewar situation. The media called the Truman policy toward Russia's post-war aggressive behavior the 'Cold War.'

"In any war, the governments involved must determine a policy; that is, what they are fighting for. Only after their policy is identified can the strategy and the tactics used to win be identified.

"Unlike 'hot' wars, we had no experience with 'cold' contests. We were an all-or- nothing type of people who, when an evil was identified, were unwilling to sort of oppose it. In our past we went for victory and had been willing to do whatever was necessary to gain that victory. So, this time, we argued among ourselves about the strategies and tactics we should use as we strove to win this new type of contest, this 'Cold War' with Russia.

"Should we negotiate and give up trying to gain a traditional win? Should we just accommodate and learn to live with one another? Or should we use our military superiority and simply destroy our adversary as demanded by traditional warfare?"

Harold commented, "Over dinner and drinks my colleagues in Congress used to argue about that very thing."

"I assure you, Congressman," George told him, "the conversations held within the administration during the Kennedy administration were not just idle banter over drinks among friends. What I will reveal to you is more serious than that.

"I have prepared a chronology of significant events that might help guide our discussion."

George took some materials from his briefcase and gave each man a copy.

"After you look this over we can discuss any one of the events I have listed."

Mike looked through the pages of the report he had been given. "Thank you, George," Mike told him. "This should be a great help."

Report Prepared for the Bogg Investigation

Foreign Policy Events of Significance

1. Presidential Campaign of 1960.

George interrupted their reading. "You'll notice, gentlemen that I began by listing Senator Kennedy's presidential campaign as an event of significance. I did so because I believe it important that you be reminded that during his campaign he created the image of himself as a Cold War hawk. This was an image he failed to live up to as president in the opinion of his administration's hawks.

"The other items and events I've listed should be familiar to you, too. And we should still discuss their impact within the Kennedy administration."

Harold and Mike returned to their review of the document.

2. Bay of Pigs Invasion. 4/61

3. Vienna Summit Conference. 6/61

4. NSAMs 55, 56, & 57 Issued. 6/61

5. Preemptive Nuclear Strike Proposal Rejected. 7/61

6. Proposal of JCS to Increase Number of Troops in Vietnam Denied. 7/61

5. Berlin Crisis. 8/61

6. Anti-Castro Buildup in SE United States Began. 8/61

7. Allan Dulles Retired. 11/61

8. Speech: There Will Not Be an American Solution to Every World Problem.

9. Laos Coalition Government Agreement. 4/62

10. TFX Decision Announced. 4/62

11. Nuclear Test Ban Negotiation Completed. 9/62

12. Cuban Missile Crisis. 10/62

13. Reversal of Support for Cuban Exile Anti-Castro Activity. 11/62

14. Back Door Communication with Khrushchev continued. 11/62

15. A 10% Annual Reduction of Defense Spending Ordered. 3/63

16. Fifty-two Military Bases Ordered Closed in US & Abroad. 3/63

17. JFK Contacts with Castro Begin. 4/63

18. Desirability of Peace Speech. 4/63

19. Announcement of Intention to Seek a Peaceful Solution in Vietnam. 5/63

20. UN Speech: Offering to Share Space Info & Exploration with Soviets. 9/63

21. NSAM 9 Issued Ordering NSA to Share Our Space Data with Soviets. 9/63

22. NSAM 263 Issued Ordering US Personnel Withdrawal from Vietnam. 10/63

"There are possibly other issues you may wish to discuss, but these are the ones I am prepared to discuss with you."

***

"In addition, there are also some domestic policy matters in which President Kennedy was involved that aroused the ire of many important elites in the United States. I have listed the most prominent of those in this discussion guide as well."

Domestic Issues of Significance

1. Justice Department's War on the Mafia Begun. 4/6

2. Hoover Told He Must Retire at Age 74. 4/61

3. JFK's Interest in the Reduction of the Oil Depletion Allowance. 4/61

4. Steel Price Increase Issue. 4/62

5. TFX Decision Announced. 4/62

6. Support of African-Americans in Civil Rights Controversies. 5/62

7. Defense Spending Reduction Impact on Domestic Economy. 3/63

8. Signed NSAM 11110 to Issue $4.3 Billion in Silver Certificates. 6/63

9. Continuing Justice Department Effort to Destroy the Mafia. 7/63

Assured that they had finished reviewing his document, George asked, "Do you have any you wish to add, gentlemen?"

Mike responded first. "Your list is very complete, George," he said. "Just off-hand, I can't think of anything I would add. How about you, Harold?"

"There is one I would add," Harold offered. "I believe the NSAM 11110 ordering the issuance of four billion dollars in silver certificates is significant enough to be included."

"I can see that," George agreed. "Let's pencil that in. We did discuss that the last time we met. So, unless you have more on that, Congressman, I suggest we move on."

"And I think the TFX controversy could be on both lists, actually, "Harold added.

"You're right, Congressman. Let's pencil that in as well.

"Before we begin, though," George interrupted, "Could I trouble you for a cup of that coffee I see brewing over there?"

"Of course," Mike said. "I'll freshen up mine, too." In a few minutes, all three men were sipping on their hot drinks.

"Now then, gentlemen. Any more comments before I go down the list?"

There were none.

"Before I begin, let me digress for a bit and remind you of a bit of history.

"World War II ended in 1945. Immediately, the Soviet Union took control of Central Europe, Yugoslavia and Albania, also the Baltic States, and showed every sign of taking over Greece, Iran and Turkey too. In the Far East, Manchuria, parts of Japan and Korea were absorbed within their post-war empire, as well.

"The United States was the only force in the world capable of stopping their aggressive advance. But, we had disarmed quickly and our people wanted a return to 'normalcy', that is, to a peaceful world. The media called the Truman administration policies toward the Soviet Union's post-war aggressive behavior the 'Cold War.'

"To fight any war, though, government policy must be formulated. Only after this step is completed can the strategy and the tactics used to win it be identified. Unlike 'hot' wars though, we had no experience with such 'cold' contests.

"We were an all or nothing kind of people. If the World War with Germany and Japan had told us anything, it had driven the lesson home that it was not wise to make deals with evil governments. After all, they tried to enslave free people like us. Those kinds of governments were the enemy of freedom and therefore had to be destroyed, not accommodated. To use that strategy was considered appeasement, even traitorous.

"So, how in the post-war world of 1945 and beyond could we justify negotiating with and accommodating the new bully on the block: the Soviet Union? They were evil, weren't they? Therefore we argued among ourselves about the strategies and tactics we should use as we struggled with the advance of Communism around the world.

"Should we negotiate and give up trying to win? Should we just accommodate and learn to live with them? Or should we use our economic power to bring our adversaries into line? Failing that, should we use our military superiority and simply destroy these evil governments, as demanded by traditional warfare?

"Unable to reach a mutually agreeable understanding with his Soviet counterpart through negotiation, President Truman had to spend American lives in Korea in order to stop the expansion of the Soviet empire there.

"But at the same time, he denied the use of our superior military weapons to win that hot war. Our military leaders wanted to punish the Communist Chinese for using their army in Korea against ours. But that would have widened the war and maybe brought the Soviet Union into it. Truman prevented our 'winning' that hot war, to keep it controlled. He even fired the popular General Douglas MacArthur over the issue. Following the firing, a strong public debate resulted and the general public took positions supporting one man or the other, Truman or MacArthur.

"Truman's successor, President Eisenhower, negotiated a settlement to that contest. A former General of the Army, he was not against using our military strength. But he did not resist using diplomacy either to reach an understanding with the Soviet Union, our enemy. In 1960 he went to a summit meeting with Premier Khrushchev in Paris to try and negotiate a settlement of the Cold War. He wanted to end the Cold War through accommodation and diplomacy, not win it through warfare.

"Allan Dulles, Director of the CIA sabotaged that meeting. He wanted the United States to win the Cold War. He poisoned the summit by disobeying a presidential directive and ordering an overflight of the Soviet Union which his CIA allowed to be discovered.

"President Eisenhower backed off for the remainder of his term and then retired to his home at Gettysburg.

"Early in his administration, President Kennedy was forced to accept blame for authorizing the failed attempt to overthrow the Castro regime in Cuba.

"He recognized this situation too late, as a trap laid by his military and CIA advisors to gain his approval to use our military forces in support of the coup. Instead, he refused to rescue the stranded Bay of Pigs invasion force. Following this debacle, he was tested again and again by these hawks in his own administration.

"For example, he refused his military advisors' request that they be allowed to commit our armed forces stationed in Europe to a conflict over access to Berlin. Once again he chose to negotiate a settlement with the Soviet Union.

"In Laos he agreed to the creation of a coalition government there that included Communists, instead of committing ground troops to support our side in that country's civil war.

"And in October 1962, instead of war he negotiated a settlement with Premier Khrushchev over the Russian insertion of missiles into Cuba. This happened to be another instance wherein he resisted advice from his military advisors that he order an invasion of Cuba and authorize the use of our nuclear missiles against the Soviet Union. Instead, he used the strategy of negotiation with the tactic of accommodation to end the confrontation.

"Clearly, President Kennedy was holding firm to a strategy of using negotiation to achieve the Cold War goal (policy) of peace. He was making it clear time and again that he wanted to end this Cold War through accommodation, not win it by destroying our adversaries.

"Despite the tough Cold War words in his speeches, he continued to send messages that he wanted to win a lasting peace, even if it meant accommodating the enemy (Communist) regimes around the world.

"In September 1961, he said:

"It is therefore our intention to challenge the Soviet Union, not to an arms race, but to a peace race, to advance together step by step, stage by stage, until general complete disarmament has been achieved."

"As time went on his strategy of choice was peaceful accommodation, not armed confrontation. His hawkish critics noticed. It became clear that most of the security establishment members of his administration did not support this strategy. It was as though his administration was at war with itself."

"When did the hawks in his administration decide that his strategies and the tactics he was using posed a danger for the United States?" Harold asked.

George responded quickly. "Candidate Kennedy burst upon the national scene as a Cold War hawk. During his campaign for the presidency, he claimed that we were behind the Soviet Union in missiles and in general military preparedness. In particular he criticized the Eisenhower administration for allowing a Communist takeover of Cuba, a country only ninety miles off our shores.

"He was especially critical of his opponent, Vice President Nixon, who was part of the administration that tolerated this situation. After the election, he found out that the so called 'missile gap' he had claimed was the other way around. The United States was far ahead of the Soviets. The same was true, he discovered, with general military preparedness. He had simply been misled by the military/intelligence briefings provided him as a candidate."

"But his opponent, Nixon, knew his claims were bogus, didn't he?" Harold asked.

"Of course, he did," George admitted. "But he couldn't prove it to the public without revealing information to our enemies about how far advanced the United States really was. That was highly classified information. So he had to keep quiet, not answer Kennedy's claims, and just take the public criticism.

"After his election victory, Kennedy also discovered that far from tolerating Castro's Communist Cuba, Eisenhower had authorized Vice President Nixon to head up the planning for a coup d'état in Cuba. Support for the invasion by US trained and supplied exiles was well underway and about to be launched shortly after his March 1961 inauguration.

"In that setting the new president's leadership style was on display for the first time. The national security members of the administration were old hands, having worked with Eisenhower and some with Truman. In short, they were not new to the game.

"But they were new to the Kennedy style of decision making. With Kennedy's predecessors, once an issue had been thrashed out and a decision reached, it would be etched in stone. The people charged with carrying out what had been decided knew they could take it to the bank.

"But the Kennedy style was shockingly different. What course of action might be decided after one discussion might be changed after the next. His military and intelligence advisors soon learned that what they thought was a decision was more like a definite maybe.

"In the aftermath of the failed coup d'état, President Kennedy authorized an investigation to tell him why the invasion had not succeeded. The primary reason, reported by the Cuban Study Group, was that Castro's small air force had destroyed the invaders on the beachhead and their supply ships and thus destroyed any chance for success."

"I thought the president had authorized strikes on the Cuban air force," Mike said.

"He clearly did, Mr. Burke," George replied. "on the afternoon before the landing, the president, after much discussion, decided to allow an air strike against the small Cuban air force. But that same night, just before that raid was to launch, presidential advisor McGeorge Bundy called off the strike.

"One of those 'definite maybes' doomed the invasion?" Harold suggested.

"It would appear so, Congressman," George agreed. "The Cuba Study Group appointed by Kennedy came to that conclusion."

"Still, Kennedy was convinced he had been misled about the entire project and that he was actually set up by the CIA to authorize a United States invasion of Cuba. He was so upset with their leadership people over this that he is reported to have said he would break the agency into a thousand pieces. He also said that he could no longer trust his military advisors either.

"Later, in July 1961, the president was presented with a proposal by the Joint Chiefs of Staff. This particular suggestion asked the president to authorize a peremptory nuclear strike on the Soviet Union. Allan Dulles, the CIA director, supported this proposal.

"The Joint Chiefs assured the president that the United States would only suffer an acceptable forty million casualties as a result of the Russian retaliatory strike.

"On this occasion, President Kennedy did not hesitate. He refused authorization and ended all discussion. After the meeting he told Secretary of State Dean Rusk: *And we call ourselves the human race.*"

"But the president was not through with Castro's Cuba. That same summer, the president signaled a tough line toward Castro's Cuba. He pledged that he would do all that was necessary to free Cuba of Castro and his Communist government.

"Toward that end, he appointed Robert Kennedy to supervise a massive buildup of anti-Castro activity. No money was spared and CIA operatives were all over Florida assisting the buildup. The CIA became the largest employer in South Florida.

"The Cuban exile community in Florida was excited with the prospect of a return to a Cuba free of Communism.

"Economic attacks on the Cuban economy were devised to put pressure on their trading and supply partners. Joined with raids on their ports and shipping coming from Florida bases, the Cuban economy began to falter. Kennedy appeared to be the ultimate war hawk of old; delivering on his promise.

"It was within this atmosphere that Allan Dulles was 'retired' along with other CIA leaders who had led the president into authorizing the Bay of Pigs disaster."

"And then the Missile Crisis erupted in the fall of 1962," Mike interjected.

"Exactly, Mr. Burke," George agreed.

"You gentlemen know the particulars of the crisis and its settlement. You may not know that Kennedy's agreement with Khrushchev hit the national security community like a thunderbolt. They were outraged and feared what the future held with this president.

"General Curtis LeMay told Kennedy that he considered the settlement the worst defeat in United States history."

"But it kept the world from possible nuclear war, didn't it?" Harold said.

"It appeared so, Congressman," George agreed. "But it seemed obvious to the members of our national security community that when the chips were down,

Kennedy had blinked, not Khrushchev, and given away the store in the process. So they concluded that they could not trust Kennedy to properly protect and defend the interests of the United States as he had promised.

"They came to the conclusion that in in a crisis he would not push back and use our strength in defense of this country. Instead he would betray our principles and trash the oath he took to protect and defend, just to accommodate our enemies and thus avoid conflict."

"So, he was considered weak, was he?" Mike surmised.

"Exactly, Mr. Burke. Kennedy had been reinforcing that image with other actions. After the Bay of Pigs matter, he had vetoed another Joint Chiefs proposal to send sixteen thousand combat trained soldiers to Vietnam. And in November 1961, he refused another proposal to allow half that many to be sent. He expressed his view on the matter when he said: *"People of this country do not want me to use troops to topple a Communist government ninety miles off our coast. How can I ask them to send troops to overthrow a Communist regime nine thousand miles away?"*

"Nevertheless, the military had changed the role of such forces in Vietnam to one of combat, without notifying President Kennedy.

"At the same time, Kennedy had come to distrust his own State Department people. So, after the Cuban Missile Crisis he hesitated communicating with Soviet Premier Khrushchev through normal diplomatic channels. Instead he had Press Secretary Pierre Salinger hand deliver his personal messages to a KGB officer assigned to the Russian embassy for delivery to the Soviet Premier.

"Likewise, Kennedy's attempts at normalizing relations with Castro's Cuba did not go through our State Department. Instead, he used unofficial messengers.

"It began with the Cuban ambassador to the United Nations, Carlos Lechuga. Our ambassador, Adlai Stevenson and he talked unofficially about the possibility of normalizing relations between the two nations. Mr. Stevenson told the Cuban ambassador that normal relations between the two countries could be restored if:

1. Cuba ceased being an agent of Soviet policy.

2. Cuba stopped its subversion of other American republics.

3. Castro restored his people's constitutional rights.

Then William Attwood, an old classmate of Kennedy's, held talks with a Castro representative. This was followed by ABC News reporter Lisa Howard flying to Havana to interview Castro in April 1963. She also carried a personal message to Castro from Kennedy.

"Kennedy gave an additional signal in a Miami speech four days before he was killed. He said then that: *Every nation is free to shape its own economic institutions in accordance with its own national needs.*"

"He continued in that speech to say that the only thing that divided Cuba from the United States diplomatically was: "*... a small band of conspirators... in an effort dictated by an external power to subvert the other American republics. This and this alone divides us. As long as this is true, nothing is possible; without it, everything is possible.*"

"In October 1963, a French journalist, Jean Daniel, met personally with President Kennedy. They talked of the president's wish to normalize relations with the Cuban government. When Daniel left he wrote in his journal:

"*When I left the Oval Office I had the impression that I was a messenger for peace. I was convinced that Kennedy wanted rapprochement.*"

"Daniel did meet with Castro and he did give him the Kennedy peace message. At that time, Castro responded with a peace message of his own. It seemed to Daniel that something very positive had been triggered.

"The date of this meeting was November twenty-second, 1963. It was during their meeting that they were told Kennedy had been killed in Dallas.

"On this same day a CIA operative gave Rolando Cubela, a high ranking member of Castro's regime, a lethal hypodermic needle hidden inside a writing pen. This attempt to assassinate Castro was contrary to orders given by President Kennedy to end all such attempts on Castro's life.

"Later, Castro sent President Johnson the peace message he had intended for Kennedy. There was no reply from the new American president."

Mike Burke said, "So, it would appear that once again, using the strategy of accommodation to achieve peace between nations had been thwarted."

"Exactly, Mr. Burke," George said. "You see, it was believed at Langley that President Kennedy was determined to reach an accommodation with Castro, if not before, certainly after his reelection. And, given his popularity at the time the public was expected to welcome it."

"Was timing important on this matter, George?" Harold asked.

"Definitely it was," George replied. "CIA wiretaps verified that some positive agreement was imminent. It was feared that a peaceful settlement with Castro would be viewed very favorably by the American public and would just add to Kennedy's world-wide reputation as a peacemaker. His reelection would certainly be assured in that case."

"It appears that Kennedy's peace moves with Castro were happening at the same time that he was exchanging his secret backdoor messages with Khrushchev. And his October 1963 Executive Order 263 concerning withdrawal from Vietnam happened during this time as well," Mike reminded the others.

"That's true, Mr. Burke," George said. "All of these initiatives were coming to a head in late 1963. And remember, in addition, the president had sent a directive to Secretary of Defense Robert McNamara the previous spring to close over fifty military bases and reduce the military budget by ten percent for the coming fiscal year."

"The Kennedy Peace Agenda was picking up momentum, wasn't it?" Harold suggested.

"Yes it was, Congressman. It was like the beginning of an avalanche picking up speed and mass as it moved down a mountainside, crushing everything in its path."

"And the hawks of President Kennedy's administration saw themselves watching it rumble toward them, destroying any chance they had of winning the Cold War."

"I imagine the elites of the banking and industrial leaders of our country viewed a Kennedy settlement of the Cold War as destructive to their interests as well," Mike added.

"Once again, you've hit the nail on the head, Mr. Burke. Beyond the immediate impact, give John Kennedy another four years as president and his peace strategy would shatter the Cold War justification for big military spending. The lid would certainly be firmly on that coffin if Bobby Kennedy were to succeed him in the Oval Office after John's second term."

"So we're back to somehow preventing a second term for John Kennedy," Harold surmised.

"It would seem so," George admitted. "At this point I think it timely that I tell you about what was going on in the background within the Kennedy administration.

"What would that be, George?" Harold asked.

"You gentlemen have not asked about what the vice president was doing while all this was going on."

"I thought he was sort of ignored by President Kennedy and his circle. You know, sent to represent the United States at State funerals around the world, and fact- finding missions outside the country," Mike suggested.

"You're right on both counts, Mr. Burke. But Lyndon Johnson was not being ignored by the administration's Cold War hawks; believe me he wasn't.

"It is true that following the Bay of Pigs disaster in the spring of 1861, the vice president was not included in any important Oval Office discussion on foreign policy. He certainly was excluded from John Kennedy's inner circle of advisors. But he was definitely a supporter of the Cold War agenda espoused by the administration's most avid hawks. He made sure they knew it, too.

"So, while President Kennedy would tell Kenny O'Donnell and Ted Sorensen that he could not pull out of Vietnam until he was reelected, *"So we had better make damned sure that I am elected,"* he told them.

"Lyndon Johnson was assuring the national security hawks that he supported their Cold War agenda of winning through global confrontation with the Communists. He was assuring them that they had a hawk in the wings, just waiting to become Commander in Chief.

"They in turn gave him the latest intelligence and military briefings as though he were already president. On one occasion he went to Vietnam on a fact-finding mission for President Kennedy. He went at the request of President Kennedy, but when he got there he acted on behalf of our military and CIA to convince Vietnamese President Diem to formally request we send troops to help him with the civil war in his country. Such a request was contrary to the wishes of President Kennedy, but reinforced the wishes of the national security establishment hawks."

"Did he get the request for troops from President Diem?" Harold asked.

"He did."

Burke then asked, "Was the word also spread of his opposition to sharing space with the Soviets; his opposition to lowering or eliminating the oil depletion allowance; his stance against issuing silver certificates to replace the Federal Reserve System; his resistance to a reduced military budget; his support for a strong CIA; and his support for his friend, J. Edgar Hoover?"

"Yes. That was all part of the shadow government agenda that Lyndon had created right under Kennedy's nose. In short, Lyndon firmly established himself as the man who would restore the status quo, 1960." George concluded.

"But the word around Washington," Harold interjected, "was that Bobby Baker, then under indictment, would implicate Lyndon and get the vice president indicted, too. As a result Lyndon Johnson would be dropped from the Kennedy ticket before the Democratic Convention. That would end his political career as well as his plan to become president. It might have even landed him in jail."

"Right, Congressman, you're correct. That was the word around town. There was even an article about that possibility in the Dallas Morning Herald of November twenty-second, 1963. Vice President Nixon was cited as the source of that information," George said. "Quick action was necessary."

"It all makes sense, doesn't it, Mike?" Harold decided. "You can't have a coup d'état without an acceptable replacement ready to step in."

"And what better situation would there be than to have the vice president just two cars behind the sitting president in the parade and thus on the spot to be sworn in as the new president?" Mike added.

"Well, gentlemen, before I go, there is one more thing I'd like to share with you.

"By now you are aware that President Johnson's NSAM 273 of November twenty-sixth, 1963 has been sealed from the public. All the public was told about the escalation of the Vietnam Conflict was that it was an extension of the Kennedy policy. On the surface that might appear to be the case.

"However, a closer review would suggest that it was not," George concluded.

"We read Kennedy's NSAM 263 and concluded that he was determined to withdraw United States personnel from Vietnam by the end of 1965 at the very latest," Harold remembered.

"That's true, Congressman," George agreed. "But NSAM 273, while not rolling that timetable back, signaled a determination to win the Vietnamese civil war by all means necessary. General Maxwell Taylor said that NSAM 273 directed us to win the war with whatever means necessary. That was not the intent of Kennedy's earlier order.

"Thank you very much, George," Mike said. "You have helped clarify many issues."

"Right," Harold added. "This investigation is such a minefield, and so much has been hidden away, I can't tell you how helpful you have been."

"You're welcome, gentlemen, George said. "Is there anything else you need to ask me?"

"Yes, I have a question," Mike told him. "We have been led to believe that a CIA unit under the direction of Mr. Helms printed all the passes and identification material for President Kennedy's White House detail during that trip. Is that true?"

"I assume you got that information from Colonel Prouty," George told them. "But to answer your question; yes, that is true, Mr. Burke."

"One thing more, while we're at it, George," Harold began. "Once he became president, did Lyndon Johnson ever attempt to limit the size of the CIA or the scope of the Agency's activities, as Kennedy had tried?"

"Not once, in any way, Congressman," George answered. "Nor did his successors, Richard Nixon or Gerald Ford show any interest in doing that."

Mike concluded, "It appears that Lyndon Johnson, Richard Nixon and Gerald Ford had learned an important lesson from the Kennedy assassination; lay off the CIA."

"You might remember that Lyndon Johnson told intimates that he thought the CIA was somehow involved in the president's murder. So, your point is well taken, Mr. Burke," George said.

The men stood and shook hands. Then George turned and left.

***

"Before we get ready for dinner," Harold suggested, "let's go over a few things while this afternoon's discussion is fresh in our minds."

"Good idea," Mike agreed. "Too bad we can't actually prove most of what he told us this afternoon."

"I don't think we're expected to, Mike," Harold responded. "Besides, with so many assassination witnesses dead and the millions of pages of information hidden away by executive order, how can we?"

"So, we state situations, give information and raise questions that should lead to logical conclusions," Mike concluded.

"Exactly, Mike," Harold said.

"Did being a judge make you so smart?" Mike asked.

"Well, ya!" Harold chuckled.

Willard Hotel

"Did you say that we're meeting the Ryan's at seven o'clock for dinner here in the hotel?" Marilyn asked.

Mike was sitting in the high back chair by the bed with a beer in his hand.

"Yep," he responded. "Harold wanted to take a nap. So, we made reservations for that time."

Marilyn kicked off her shoes and flopped down on the king size bed.

"I'm walked and shopped out," she said. "I bet we visited every monument and went in every shop there is downtown Washington. Any wine in that cooler where you got your beer?"

Mike got up and looked into the room's beverage cooler. "You have a choice. You feel like Pinot Grigio or White Zin?"

"Open a White Zin this time, please."

Mike poured the wine into a room glass and brought it over to his wife. He sat on the bed beside her and finished his beer. Then he ran his hand up her leg.

"You have something in mind there, big fella?"

"You got that right, sunshine," he assured her as he began to slip off her panty hose. Marilyn set her tumbler of wine on the bed table and turned to help her husband.

Later, they lay alongside one another.

"See what you missed this morning, little lady?"

"Makes what we just did all the more delicious, don't you think?"

"True, but," Mike protested, "we could have had both."

"You always were a glutton," Marilyn teased as she turned toward her husband. Then she smiled and ran her hand down his torso. "Speaking of that, it appears that you're ready for another helping."

"Right again, sunshine."

The Willard Dining Room

Entering the large ornate room, Marilyn saw Lillian and Harold Ryan already seated.

Lillian greeted them. "I'd almost given up on you tonight. I just called you room to see if we had the wrong time, or something."

"It was the 'or something' that held us up, Lillian," Marilyn whispered.

Mike saw that Harold already had a Manhattan sitting on the table in front of him. "I see you're one drink ahead of me already, Harold."

"I may be slow, but I know what I want and when I want it," Harold kidded back.

"How many cherries in you Manhattan tonight, partner?" Mike asked.

"The usual three, of course," Harold responded. "They don't charge any more for an additional cherry or two. I might just as well take advantage."

"Have a good nap, Judge?"

"Yes, I did thank you. And you?"

Marilyn had heard their exchange and waited to hear Mike's answer to Harold's question.

"As a matter of fact, I did get some sack time. I agree with you, Judge, it can be very refreshing. Where is that waiter? I want a drink some time tonight, too."

Later, after their meal, they were relaxing over coffee. The four talked of the Boggs study.

"How did your interview with Madeleine Brown go, Lillian?" Mike asked.

"I found Madeleine Brown very charming," she answered. "She was pretty open about her long term affair with Lyndon Johnson."

"As I recall, the Texas press pretty much doubted that story." Harold said.

Marilyn said, "She was rather open about that too. Right up front she said she could not prove anything she told us. But you know, I had the feeling she had it right when she claimed to know when Johnson was telling her the truth and when he wasn't."

"I did too, Marilyn," Lillian agreed.

"Did she say anything startling?" Harold asked.

"Frankly, most everything she told us was new to me," Lillian said. "So, it was all sort of startling."

"I was most impressed with the photo of the son she claimed Lyndon Johnson fathered. It really got my attention."

"Why was that?" Mike asked.

"It startled me because it was the photo of a man who was the spitting image of Lyndon Johnson. Her son could have been his twin at a younger age. You don't need a paternity test to prove it as far as I'm concerned; just one look at the photo told it all."

Lillian agreed. "Once I saw that photograph, I was inclined to give the other stuff she told us more credence," she told the others.

"In that case, I'm more interested in reading your notes," Mike assured them.

"Oh, thank you so much," Marilyn snapped. "I feel ever so much better knowing you think we did an acceptable job."

"You're welcome." Mike replied laughing.

"How are you two coming with your interviews?" Marilyn asked.

"Really well, don't you think, Mike?" Harold stated.

"Today's visit with our confidential informant was outstanding. I could hardly keep up with taking notes as he talked; really heavy stuff."

"Are you ready to begin laying out a report?" Marilyn wondered.

"I think we need to complete a few more of our interviews to get a sense of how the report should look," Mike told them.

"I agree," Harold said. "We have to talk with some Secret Service people who were in Dallas on November twenty-second, Kennedy's aide Ted Sorensen, Gaeton Fonzi, who was one of the investigators for the House Committee on Assassinations, and James Hosty, who worked in the Dallas FBI office at the time of the assassination."

Mike added, "It may be that Fonzi will direct us to one or more people in Florida. The Cuban community there was his special area of investigation for the House Committee."

"Then I think we can sit down and organize our report," Harold concluded.

"There's something else we need to share with you ladies," Mike began. "Our informant today told us that he knew you two were in town with us. He also told us that he knew who we had interviewed in Detroit last week."

"Why did he tell you that?" Lillian asked.

Harold said, "He wanted us to know that what we were doing is no secret. In fact, he told us that the report we put together twelve years ago was shared with the FBI and others even as we were putting it together.

"Remember, Marilyn, when we met with a steno girl from Congressman Conyers' office?"

"Sure, I do," Marilyn recalled. "She took notes of our meetings and typed up drafts for us to review."

"It appears that she was providing those drafts to others, too," Mike said. "Probably Sullivan in the FBI and someone at the CIA were given copies or our drafts right along with us."

"He wanted us to know that our work was being watched," Harold emphasized.

"Do I sense some danger here?" Marilyn asked warily.

"Our informant didn't say that in so many words, Marilyn, but he did say not to take what we are doing lightly and that the CIA people have a long memory and a long reach," Mike told his wife.

"Are we in danger, Harold?" Lillian asked.

"I don't think he would have been meeting with us so openly if we were, dear. But it probably would be wise not to attend Lindy's reception this weekend. Doing something that provocative here in Washington might be taking more of a chance than we need."

"I agree. I think we should head home at the end of the week," Mike suggested.

"The hell with waiting 'til Friday," Marilyn said testily. "I'm worried about our kids alone at home, Michael. Remember what those FBI bastards did the last time you were involved in this stuff? I want you to make arrangements for me to fly home tomorrow, first thing."

"Include me on that trip, Harold," Lillian ordered.

"Very well, dear," Harold promised. I'll call Lindy's people first thing tomorrow."

Boggs' Congressional Office

Mike and Harold met with Congresswoman Boggs the next day in her conference room.

"I don't know what to say about the veiled warning my informant gave you two yesterday. I understand why the ladies decided to head back home. But damn it, I just hate to see this kind of thing happening."

"I looked at my notes before we came over this morning, Lindy," Mike revealed. "Your informant told us how several members of the House Committee on Assassinations were pressured to back off several things, not to look under certain rugs or open various doors. In addition, it appears that budget constraints were brought to bear just when some pretty important issues began to surface. He said that it was a serious morale problem for their staff, as they were forced to prematurely end their investigation."

"When we talk to Gaeton Fonzi later this morning, we intend to ask him if this actually happened." Harold said. "I had the impression that the pressure came from the CIA."

"I talked to Mr. Fonzi yesterday," Lindy Boggs told them. "He is willing to share his experience working for that committee. In fact, if necessary, I'll fly you down there for a face to face talk with him. I have the feeling he has some important things to share."

"We'll see how much we can handle on a conference call, Lindy," Mike assured her.

"Well, Mable has arranged a flight later today for your wives. A car will pick them up at the Willard and take them to the airport. Another car will take them home from the Detroit City Airport. I can't tell you how sorry I am that they have been frightened like this. Damned shame; makes me angry as hell," Lindy Boggs said.

"I've talked to them both and told them the same thing."

"Thanks for understanding, Lindy," Harold told her. "Mike and I have made a commitment to you on this. So, you get off to your work and Mike and I will get on with ours."

"I appreciate that Harold," Boggs told him. "Thank you both." She rose from her chair and left the room.

"You think Marilyn will be all right, Mike?" Harold asked.

"I'm sure of it. She's a tough one, that wife of mine. Even an implied threat like this has fired her up. She wants to help us shine a bright light on these guys once and for all. She's all right, believe me. How is Lillian reacting?"

"She's a trouper," Harold assured his partner. "Like your wife, she wants me to do a job on these creeps."

"Well then," Mike concluded. "Let's get on with it."

***

Mable had put through a call to Gaeton Fonzi in Satellite Beach, Florida. Originally a Philadelphia writer, he had been brought to Washington by Senator Schweiker of Pennsylvania to work as an investigator in 1977. The Senator had successfully lobbied for funds and staff to look into the Kennedy assassination in addition to the committee's other focus, the unlawful covert actions of the CIA and the FBI. So he wanted an investigator of his own to pursue the Kennedy killing, too. Fonzi fit the bill.

Gaeton Fonzi had forged a reputation as an investigative reporter in the Philadelphia area and had published several articles on the Kennedy assassination. Living in Florida now, he was between projects and had some time. So, he accepted an offer to work for a few weeks with Senator Schweiker's subcommittee. That job was followed by two years of work in the Miami area with the Cuban exiles, for what became known as the House Select Committee on Assassinations.

Lindy Boggs told Mike and Harold, "Fonzi left that post when political pressure and budget constraints limited the committee's reach. The committee leadership used that as an excuse to not follow-up on promising leads uncovered by its investigators, or to take on the CIA for its failure to release key documents to the Church Committee."

"You think Fonzi will be able to shed some light on the possible involvement of Cuban exiles in the assassination?" Harold asked Mike.

"That could be, Harold. He worked with the Cubans most involved in the campaign against Castro during the post-Bay of Pigs period. It was between that disaster and the Cuban Missile Crisis eighteen months later that the Kennedy administration funded a massive CIA effort to topple the Castro regime."

"Correct," Harold said. "Everything I've read about the missile crisis settlement leads me to believe that the Cuban exiles were really upset about what Kennedy did to end that crisis, too.

"Remember? As part of that settlement Kennedy promised Khrushchev that the United States would not assist any effort to achieve regime change in Cuba. So, when he cut off all support for the anti-Castro campaign, the Cubans of the exile community in Florida considered this a betrayal," Harold told Mike.

"Lindy said Fonzi became pretty tight with leaders in that community," Mike commented. "And according to the House Committee's report, he spent most of his time talking with the Cuban exiles. If he doesn't know, I doubt if anyone will."

The intercom rang. Mike answered the phone.

"Mable says that Fonzi is on line one, Harold."

The two men each picked up a phone.

"Mr. Fonzi," Harold began." Thank you for talking with us."

"Good morning, gentlemen," he responded. "Congresswoman Boggs asked me to talk with you on a matter of some importance to her. I am happy to do so. Am I talking to former Congressman Ryan and Mr. Michael Burke?"

"Yes, you're correct on both counts," Mike answered.

Fonzi went on. "I've had a chance to read the report you two prepared for the House Judiciary Committee twelve years ago. It was spot on; it only took the rest of Congress over a decade and several hundred thousand dollars to come to the same conclusion. Good job, gentlemen. I was very impressed."

"That's high praise coming from an experienced investigator such as you, Mr. Fonzi," Harold said.

"Too bad Ford and Conyers buried your report. I thought your finding was very persuasive," Fonzi added.

Mike entered the conversation. "As a result of your work for Senator Schweiker, did you solve the crime of the century?"

"Don't I wish, Mr. Burke," Fonzi answered with a hearty laugh. "Frankly, I doubt if it will ever be solved. In my opinion there have been too many documents destroyed, hidden away or altered and too many key witnesses put in the ground since the assassination for that to happen.

"In fact, two years ago, just before they were to testify before the House Select Committee on Assassinations, a good number of people died under suspicious circumstances. This included several FBI officials, Oswald's friend George DeMohrenschildt, retired CIA operative David Morales, anti-Castro and CIA operative William Pawley, Cuban exile leaders Carlos Prio and Manuel Artime, former labor union president Jimmy Hoffa, and Mafia bosses Charles Nicoletti and Johnny Roselli. All of them met unexpected deaths; most of the cases are still unsolved."

"Do you recall if any of the witnesses before the Committee were intimidated by this?" Harold asked.

"I can recall one prominent witness who backed off information he had given the FBI earlier," Fonzi mentioned. "A big player in the Miami hotel business, one Jose Aleman Jr., was also an FBI informant. He had met with Carlos Trafficante in the summer of 1962 to obtain help in getting a loan from the Teamsters Pension Fund. During a conversation with Trafficante in Aleman's Scott-Bryant hotel office in Miami, Aleman predicted that President Kennedy was so popular he would most likely win reelection in 1964. Trafficante responded with, *"No, Jose, you don't understand me. Kennedy's not going to make it to the election. He's going to be hit."*

"Aleman reported this conversation to the Miami FBI in August 1962. He repeated it to me more recently. But in September 1978, testifying before the House Committee on Assassinations, he developed memory problems."

"So, Aleman noticed the sudden rash of witness deaths?"

"That's what I think, Mr. Burke," Fonzi told him. "That's exactly what I think happened."

"What about the Cuban exile community?" Harold began. "Did you come across any connection with members of that group and the assassination of Kennedy?"

"That's a problem for me, Congressman," Fonzi responded.

"How so?"

"Because the plug was pulled on the investigation before my leads in that area were fully pursued. In addition, the word was out among the exile leaders; cooperate and you might end up in jail for tax evasion, or on some other charge. So my sources dried up.

"My best source, Antonio Veciana was convicted of conspiracy to import narcotics. Although he could never be directly associated with narcotics, he was sent to federal prison for 26 months on the testimony of one witness, a dirty one at that. I met with Antonio after his release to find him reluctant to talk because he now feared his parole might be jeopardized.

"I believe he even feared that he would be charged with tax evasion if he was seen to be cooperating. His exposure to that charge was a real possibility. You see, a good deal of money was funneled to him and others by their CIA handlers who had been active in the anti-Castro efforts of the post-Bay of Pigs disaster.

"Veciana and others who led raids on the Cuban mainland and against Cuban shipping feared they would be asked to account for funds (as income) provided to them for their anti-Cuban operation during that eighteen month effort that ended with the Cuban Missile Crisis of October 1962."

"Did he tell you anything related to the Kennedy assassination?" Mike asked.

"Before his drug conviction and before the Kennedy assassination, he had met with his CIA contact, Maurice Bishop, several times in Dallas. On one of those occasions, he found Bishop with a young man. Veciana later saw a November twenty-second, 1963 photograph of this same young man in the newspaper. It was Lee Harvey Oswald."

"So there was a connection between the CIA and Oswald, after all," Mike exclaimed.

"It would seem so, Mr. Burke," Fonzi said. "But as far as I know it's been denied. I recall reading that Richard Helms, then a CIA Deputy Director, testified to that effect before the Warren Commission."

Harold told Fonzi, "Mike and I met in Washington with an insider who told us that Oswald had a '201' file at the CIA."

"What does that indicate?" Fonzi asked.

"We were told that only employees have such a file," Mike revealed.

"I didn't know that, Mr. Burke. So it might not surprise you that another of the House Select Committee's investigators discovered a 201 folder with Oswald's name on it when that investigator was given access to a few CIA file cabinets. He wasn't allowed to read that file, however."

"Mr. Fonzi," Harold interrupted. "Do you believe that any people in the Cuban exile community were involved in the Kennedy assassination?"

"I talked with many exiles that were very big in anti-Castro activity prior to the settlement of the Cuban Missile Crisis. To a person, they remembered being furious with Kennedy over his agreement with Khrushchev to settle that crisis. They felt he had betrayed them; gone back on his promises to them.

"But I never got the sense that they were involved in the assassination or even thought about it. There were not even whispers in that group about taking such an action in anticipation of President Kennedy's visit to Miami in the fall of 1963."

"Do you have any questions of us, Mr. Fonzi?" Harold asked.

"No, Congressman, I don't. But I do want to wish you well with your investigation. Possibly you can shed some light on the Kennedy assassination we investigators for the House Select Committee on Assassinations were not allowed to discover."

"Thanks you for your help," Mike said in parting.

***

Both men sat quietly with their own thoughts for a few moments.

"Impressions, Mike?"

"It wasn't a long interview, but it was very revealing," Mike said.

"I agree," Harold said. "Tell me if you agree with this:

"Fonzi verified the existence of Oswald's CIA employee file and placed him in Dallas with CIA agent David Atlee Phillips, aka Maurice Bishop. He told us of the report from a credible FBI informant that mob boss Carlos Trafficante predicted the killing of Kennedy prior to the actual assassination. And he poured cold water on the suspicion that Cuban exiles might be involved in the assassination.

"Do your notes reveal anything else?"

"No, Harold. I think you've gotten it."

"Where do we go from here, Mike?"

In answer, Mike opened the appointment folder Mable had left on the conference room's table.

"I show you flying to Boston tomorrow for an interview with Ted Sorensen. I'm off to Salisbury, Maryland for a talk with Gerry Bruno. Then back in Detroit, you and I will have a telephone conference call with James Hosty, who just retired from the FBI."

"When do we talk with the surviving members of Kennedy's Secret Service detail?"

"We're to meet back here the week after next for that," Mike concluded.

"You know who I'd really like to talk with?" Harold mused.

"I'll bite, who would you really like to talk with?" Mike probed.

"I'd love to spend some time with Robert McNamara."

"Sure, and I'd like to win the lottery. Fat chance we could ever get an appointment with the current president of the World Bank. And what would you want to question the former Defense Secretary about, Harold?"

"I'd like to know more about Kennedy's order to reduce defense spending and the October eleventh NSAM 263. Was it integral to Kennedy's 'Peace Agenda' or just part of McNamara's drive for efficiency?

"And, in light of the reports I've read saying that Johnson's escalation of involvement in Vietnam, was he really only carrying out what Kennedy intended? I'd like to ask McNamara what exactly he and Kennedy had in mind in Vietnam; withdrawal or escalation. Did they really intend to remove 1,000 American personnel by December thirty-first 1963, and the rest of our people by the end of 1965?

Harold went on. "What really intrigues me is McNamara's jump to the Johnson team and his wholehearted support of the November twenty-sixth NSAM 273, which appears to be the very opposite of Kennedy's October order."

Half-kidding, Mike suggested, "Well heck, ask Lindy to set something up. Maybe lightning will strike and he'll agree to see us."

"What do ya' mean, we? Aren't you the one who thinks this is a wild goose chase?"

"Someone's got ta' watch your back, ya' know."

"Oh, good, Mike! I feel better already. But I'll get over it after a nap this afternoon and a Manhattan cocktail tonight," Harold concluded.

Harvard University

Harold took the early Amtrak train to Boston. A cab took him to the Harvard campus for his meeting with Ted Sorensen. Sorensen had become the chief legislative aide to newly elected Senator John F. Kennedy in 1953. Part of his job was to help write the Senator's speeches and articles. In his autobiography, Sorensen said that he wrote most of the first drafts of each chapter in Kennedy's famous book, *Profiles in Courage*.

Sorensen followed the Senator into the Oval Office in 1961. At first, his primary responsibility was speech writing and the administration's domestic agenda. Eventually though, he joined Kennedy's innermost circle of advisors that included the Secretaries of State, Defense and Treasury as well as Robert Kennedy, the Attorney General and Chairman of the Joint Chiefs of Staff, General Maxwell D. Taylor.

Sorensen resigned his White House post on February 29, 1964 after helping Kennedy's successor, Lyndon Johnson, craft his first State of the Union address. Currently, Sorensen was teaching at the Institute of Politics at Harvard University.

"You may go in, Congressman Ryan," the receptionist told him. "Mr. Sorensen is expecting you. His office is the third on the right."

"Thank you," Harold said. He walked down the corridor as directed.

"Good morning, Congressman," Ted Sorensen greeted with an outstretched hand. "Please take a seat. Would you join me in a cup of coffee?"

"I would appreciate that, Mr. Sorensen; a dash of cream and a teaspoon of sugar will do nicely."

Once Sorensen had refreshed his cup and served Harold his, both men relaxed on opposite sides of a large desk.

"I understand that you're digging into the assassination of my old friend and boss, President Kennedy."

"That's correct," Harold responded. "My colleague Michael Burke and I composed a study for the House Judiciary Committee twelve years ago. We concluded at that time that the assassination was a conspiracy rather than an act of a single person.

"Following the release of the House Select Committee's report on the assassination, Congresswoman Lindy Boggs asked us to take a look at who might have killed the president."

"Lindy asked me to meet with you. I was happy to do so. She told me you were a Michigan Congressman during the Kennedy days. Then I read that you got caught up in one of those redistricting election runoffs. It appears that you narrowly missed reelection back in the summer of 1964 to a fellow Democrat, Congressman Lucian Nedzi."

"That's correct," Harold confirmed.

"But I know more, and would very much like to show off some if you don't mind."

"Go right ahead," Harold urged.

"After you and Burke finished your report in 1967, you won election as a circuit judge in Detroit, and Mr. Burke became your clerk. You're now retired and Burke is practicing law in that city. Have I missed anything, Congressman?"

"Yes, Mr. Sorensen," Harold replied, smiling. "I enjoy a Manhattan cocktail before my dinner and a nap most afternoons."

Smiling, too, Sorensen replied. "Good to know, Congressman. How can I help you today?"

"You worked with John Kennedy for the entire time he was a Senator and during the one thousand days of his presidency; ten years in all. During that time you prepared speeches and articles which expressed his thoughts on various matters. "Outside of his brother Robert, I would say that you were arguably the closest to understanding his thinking on most matters that demanded his attention. Is this fair to say, Mr. Sorensen?"

"I think we can be a little less formal, Harold. Please call me Ted," Sorensen responded. "I would say that you have expressed it accurately. While his speeches contained my words, those words reflected his thinking."

"That's what I thought. Aside from formal speeches, did you also help compose most of his messages?"

"I definitely did, Harold," Sorensen replied quickly. 'I had a hand in writing virtually every Kennedy statement, speech or message that went out of his Senate office and then later, the White House. I came to know President Kennedy's thinking so well that I could very accurately predict any off the cuff response at press conferences and interviews. In fact, whenever I would go over a transcript of his comments later, I seldom came across an answer that contained anything new, nor was I ever surprised by what he had said."

"So, you wrote the speech he gave in Miami during his November 1963 trip, in which he clearly laid out the requirements for our relations with Castro's Cuba to be normalized?" Harold asked.

"Yes, I wrote the address he gave that day."

"Do you believe he would have restored diplomatic relations with Cuba?"

"Harold," Sorensen began, "remembering that time, and the conversations within Kennedy's inner circle on that topic, I can assure you that normal diplomatic relations would probably have been restored between our two countries. At the time of the assassination, it was up to Castro. All he had to do was meet President Kennedy's three requirements."

"What about President Kennedy's secret messages to Soviet Premier Khrushchev? Did you have a hand in crafting those as well?"

"Yes, I helped put those messages together, too," Sorensen admitted. "The Soviet Premier had expressed an interest in disarmament at the time the Nuclear Test Ban Treaty was negotiated. But President Kennedy had to put that discussion off. He needed to take care of one thing at a time.

"Remember, his administration's national security hawks were very suspicious of the Soviets. What they really wanted was to destroy the Soviet empire, not live in peace with it. They were opposed to the Test Ban Treaty. So, the president had to move incrementally.

"But once the Test Ban Treaty had been overwhelmingly ratified by our Senate, he felt emboldened to reach out to the Premier about disarmament. However, he believed our State Department people couldn't be trusted to accurately convey his intentions. He also believed that they would share them with the CIA and the military. He knew how the CIA had sabotaged Eisenhower's 1960 Paris peace talks.

"So, messages to Khrushchev were delivered through Pierre Salinger to a KGB member of the Russian embassy."

"What about the conflict in Laos?"

"The hawks wanted a major military response to the Communist War of Liberation in Laos. The president refused and instead pushed for a diplomatic solution. The debate was intense but at the end of the day, President Kennedy was successful.

"He agreed to the installation of a coalition government in Laos. This was a political compromise with the Communists. This solution was another example of Kennedy's turning his back on an opportunity to confront our enemies, the Communists and instead accommodating them. It was totally unacceptable to the Cold War hawks in his administration."

"His speech on the Berlin Crisis of 1962 was a masterpiece," Harold said. "Did you write that?"

"When you ask that question let me remind you of something, Harold," Sorensen cautioned. "After President Kennedy and I talked, I always wrote a first draft for him to review and edit. We then would work together to polish it. In the last analysis, while President Kennedy may have used my words, he was just using them to convey his thoughts. And, of course, it was always his speech to deliver.

"But to answer your question, yes, I wrote that nationally televised speech just as I wrote the speech he delivered at the Berlin Wall the summer of 1963."

"The Berlin Crisis was another instance wherein the national security folks in his administration opposed his diplomatic approach. They wanted a military response, he didn't. And, as you might remember the crisis was solved without conflict."

"As I recall," Harold said, "Khrushchev backed down on that occasion."

"You could say that, Howard," Sorensen confirmed. "But the Cold War warriors in his administration did not celebrate it as a victory. They instead felt Kennedy had betrayed the United States, because he had bypassed another opportunity to confront the Soviet Union militarily and 'win' the Cold War.

"They simply didn't understand. He wanted to win, too. But he wanted to use the strategy of diplomacy, not war to accomplish the same end."

Harold then asked, "Is it fair to say that virtually two power centers developed within the Kennedy administration? One power center was made up of people who wanted to use diplomacy as the principal strategy to win the Cold War, while the contrary power center was made up of people who wanted to use military might as the primary strategy to win the Cold War; these being the military, the CIA and others at State and at Defense."

"Yes, Harold," Sorensen responded. "The administration was definitely split between those two national security camps. The vice president was firmly in the latter camp and represented a return to the status quo circa 1960.

"President Kennedy represented the peace group. It was feared by the military national security hawks in the second camp that Kennedy would have his way if he won a second term."

"And, President Kennedy appeared to be a shoo-in for the 1964 presidential election," Harold said.

"That's what our polling suggested, Harold. So, if you believe that a leader dangerous to the security of the United States is about to be reelected president for a second term, how do you proceed?"

"A coup d'état?"

"That's a thought, Congressman. Would you like your coffee freshened?"

"Yes, thank you."

"Want me to add a dash of cream and a teaspoon of sugar?"

"That would be perfect."

Once the two men were settled with their coffee, Harold suggested, "Let's shift the discussion to the war in Vietnam."

"I thought you would eventually get there," Sorensen commented.

"Ted, the thorn in our side on this report is the Vietnam issue."

"How so, Harold?"

"The late President Johnson and his people, and in fact many historians have insisted that his Vietnam strategy was simply a continuation of President Kennedy's. They claim that Kennedy's NSAM # 263 was based upon the optimistic appraisal of the fall 1963 situation in Vietnam, as presented to him by Secretary of Defense McNamara and General Maxwell D. Taylor.

"The say that based on their optimism the pull-out required by the NSAM 263 was feasible. But they also insist that it left the door open for escalation should the situation deteriorate in that country.

"They contended that by November twentieth, 1963 the situation had become grave in South Vietnam, especially after the assassination of President Diem. So, at the high-level meeting held in Hawaii the week of the president's assassination, new recommendations were prepared for President Kennedy, recommendations that called for escalation, not withdrawal; in effect, NSAM 273.

"Continuing this scenario, and in accordance with those new recommendations, President Johnson signed NSAM 273 November twenty-sixth, 1963. General Taylor, Chairman of the Joint Chiefs of Staff who had helped write President Kennedy's withdrawal order now said that this new presidential order: '… *makes clear the resolve of the president to ensure victory…to do this we must prepare for whatever level of activity may be required.*'

"Your question is?" Sorensen asked, smiling.

Harold laughed. "Excuse my long winded lead-up, Ted. Burke and I had several long conversations with Colonel Prouty and with a CIA insider. The information they gave us and the reading we have done have led us to believe that President Kennedy was firm in his resolve not to commit American troops to Vietnam. What is you recollection of his intent?"

"President Kennedy was firm in his position," Sorensen began. "I was a party to countless discussions with him on the issue during his presidency. Remember, referring to the Vietnamese, he said in an April 1963 interview with Walter Cronkite of CBS, *"In the final analysis, it is their war. 'They are the ones who will have to win it or lose it."*

"He never changed his opinion on the matter. So, in my view, John F. Kennedy would never have escalated the conflict by introducing American combat troops in Vietnam. My Lord, we went from around sixteen thousand in November 1963, to over 550,000 Americans in South Vietnam, and undertook massive bombing of North Vietnam. And we still couldn't win a military victory there.

"But Johnson kept his promise to the military; they got their war. He also kept his promises to the suppliers of military hardware. Fulfilling those promises came at a steep cost. Aside from the massive national debt he ran up financing the war, he sacrificed a generation of America's young men in the rice paddies of Vietnam and he lost the trust and support of the American people at home."

"So, would he have allowed a Communist takeover of South Vietnam?" Harold asked.

"If the situation there had deteriorated badly between September and November 1963, he might have increased our military equipment and economic aid to the South Vietnamese.

"At the same time he would have pursued a strategy similar to the one he employed in Laos. Instead of military escalation using American troops, he would have employed a diplomatic strategy and striven for the establishment of a coalition government, like Laos.

"Before he left for Texas, he was handed a report of a recent American death in Vietnam. He commented to Assistant Press Secretary Malcomb Kildoff,

"After I come back from Texas, that's going to change. Vietnam is not worth another American life."

"Did he say anything about Vietnam and the 1964 election?"

"Yes, he did," Ted confided. "He believed that he couldn't be seen to get completely out of Vietnam prior to the election. Such action might have made him appear weak on Communism and threaten his reelection. He told Kenny O'Donnell once, in my presence, that we would get out of Vietnam after the election. But he was a realist. So, he added, *"So, we had better make damned sure I'm reelected."*

"In the camp of the national security hawks," Sorensen went on, "the newly sworn in President Johnson told a gathering of military people at a 1963 Christmas reception at the White House, *'Get me elected and you can have your war.'*

Sorensen concluded, "I believe this expression of their contrary positions was very clear. How much different must their positions have been for people to believe that the two men had very different intentions for Vietnam?

"Kennedy wanted to be the president who maintained the peace while keeping us out of wars of liberation. Johnson's shadow government wanted a militarily confrontation with Communism everywhere around the globe, and the imposition of an American dictated peace.

"You can argue semantics and shuffle troop numbers around as Johnson's people did, but how more clearly different could the positions of the two men have been?

"I think that the voters would have chosen John F. Kennedy's route to peace in November 1964. Don't you Harold?"

"Your voter polling data certainly indicated that would have happened, Ted. So, in your opinion, what chance did the national security hawks and Lyndon Johnson have of stopping Kennedy's reelection?"

"There was very little they could have done," Sorensen replied. "This would have been especially the case if the vice president had been dropped from the ticket after being charged with tax evasion and found guilty of corruption charges. The Cold War hawks would have lost their champion in the administration ta' boot."

"Was President Kennedy aware of the shadow government Johnson led?"

"Absolutely, Harold," Ted revealed. "He and Bobby also knew that Johnson and the military Cold War warriors had the support of Hoover and the CIA leadership."

"Do you agree then," Harold asked, "that if Kennedy had lived to be reelected, we would have seen major changes, such as withdrawal from Vietnam, Johnson out of the administration, normalized diplomatic relations with Cuba negotiated, continued reduction of defense spending, aggressive issuance of a silver-based currency, J. Edgar Hoover replaced, and the CIA reorganized?"

"I believe all of those you mentioned would have happened, Harold," Ted responded. "And a few more should be added to that list like continued personal income tax reduction, reduction of the oil depletion allowance, a balanced federal budget, peaceful coexistence with the Soviet Union and the continuation of the war on organized crime.

"The items on both of our lists would have been pursued aggressively under Kennedy's second term agenda."

"That sounds pretty ambitious, Ted," Harold judged.

Sorensen went on. "But all of that changed on November twenty-second, 1963 in Dallas. After that date, not one of the initiatives you or I mentioned was attempted. And, all those agenda items that had begun during the Kennedy administration were formally rescinded or simply allowed to die for lack of support by President Johnson."

"So, the Johnson administration really returned the federal government to the status quo that existed in 1960?"

"Yes, that's basically true. In many ways Johnson and his people did exactly that, with three exceptions."

"What were those, Ted?"

"The massive escalation of our participation in the Vietnamese civil war was the major one, of course. And it was during the Johnson administration that his people increased the federal government's role in attempting to shape society with the War on Poverty programs and the Voting Rights Act. The federal budget ballooned out of balance to support the Vietnam conflict and Johnson's social programs. These were all post-1963."

"During my time in the House, I recall that Johnson had quietly opposed the social programs such as these when he was vice president," Harold said. "What changed?"

"Kennedy had mistakenly thought his vice president would carry the water in Congress for his social programs. But when one program after another failed to win approval in the various Congressional committees, Lyndon would say it failed to gain support because it just wasn't the right time.

"What changed was that Lyndon Johnson was president. As the sponsor of his Great Society, he wanted to be seen as the second coming of Franklin D. Roosevelt's New Deal. So, once he gained the office of president, he sought to create that legacy by the redistribution of the country's wealth to his party's base.

"The idea was to create a dependent class and thus a voter group with a vested interest in keeping him and his political party in power.

"Also, Johnson was so taken with Franklin Delano Roosevelt as a war leader that he thought his place in American history would be secure for all time if he won a war, just as FDR had won World War II.

"It's rather ironic, I think," Sorensen chuckled "that instead, Lyndon Johnson has become virtually hated, even within his own political party. Now, his legacy is as the president who wasted the lives of over 50,000 American young men in Vietnam and billions of dollars of treasury, too."

"Is that what's really behind the insistence of Johnson's people that Vietnam was actually Kennedy's war, not Johnson's?"

"Now you've got it, Harold," Ted smiled.

"Is there anything else you could share with us? What I mean to say, is there anything you might know about the assassination that would help us in our investigation?"

"Nothing specific comes to mind, Harold," Ted responded. "But I recall reading that after he left the Oval Office, Lyndon Johnson said in a television interview that he believed CIA rogues and big oil had been behind the assassination. Before that interview was scheduled to air, though, he called the station and had that particular statement deleted."

"Do you agree with the statement he made?"

"I also recall that Mrs. Kennedy told me privately, not for your use, that she believed Lyndon Johnson had a hand in the assassination."

"What do you think?"

"I've always believed Mrs. Kennedy to be very wise woman."

Salisbury, Maryland

Mike Burke drove from Washington to interview Jerry Bruno at his home in Salisbury. He wanted to ask about the arrangements that had been made for Kennedy's trip to Texas. Bruno had worked as an advance man for the president since the presidential primary days of 1960.

Recently retired, Bruno was very receptive to Mike's request for an interview. In 1971, he had written a book titled *The Advance Man*. Mike made sure to get a copy from the Congressional librarian, Irene Gohsman. He read it before the two men met.

Bruno met Mike at his front door.

"Welcome to my home Mr. Burke," he greeted. "Would you join me in the family room?"

Bruno was balding and a good deal shorter than Mike. A bit pudgy, he had pink cheeks and a middle age paunch.

Once the two men were settled, Mike said, "I just read your book; yesterday, as a matter of fact."

"I only put it together because so many people wanted me to tell them about John F. Kennedy and the November trip to Texas. But you wouldn't be here if my little book answered all your questions, would you now?"

"No, I wouldn't," Mike responded with a smile.

"Excuse me, Mr. Burke," Bruno interrupted. "Where are my manners? My wife has brewed some fresh coffee and set out some rolls. Can I fix you a cup?"

"Black would be nice. And please call me Mike."

"I'll be right back with your java. And call me Jerry."

Once the two men were settled, Mike began the interview by explaining why he and Harold Ryan were investigating the assassination.

"Yes, I'm familiar with the Boggs record. Mrs. Boggs sort of took over her late husband's seat in the House. She has forged quite a reputation for herself, too. From my experience in Washington, she doesn't take any prisoners."

"That's what I have heard, too."

"Anyway, back in 1967, Congressman Ryan and I put together a study for the House Judiciary Committee on the assassination. We concluded back then that Oswald did not act alone. We came to the conclusion that a conspiracy existed to carry out the killing of President Kennedy.

"Just last year the House Select Committee on Assassinations came to the same conclusion. But the members of that committee chose not to speculate on why the president was killed, nor did they comment on who might have been involved in the assassination.

"Congresswoman Boggs wants us to look into why JFK was killed, in the hope it might point to who might have arranged to have it done.

"Can you answer either of those questions?"

"You want to know if I can solve the crime of the century. Wow! Let me assure you, Mike, I was not a big player in the scheme of things back then, nor was I a mouse listening in the corner of the important people of the day. I can share an opinion or two, but nothing concrete, I'm afraid."

"Let me share this with you then," Mike began. "The author of *The Death of a President,* William Manchester, wrote a good deal about the Texas political situation and your work there as the advance man for the Kennedy trip to Texas. He listed four potential meeting places available in Dallas for the president's luncheon the twenty-second of November."

"Right, Mike," Bruno interjected. "I favored the Sheraton-Dallas Hotel, but that was already booked for a woman's organization. Another potential spot was the Market Hall. But that was taken by the Bottlers Association. That left two others, The Woman's Building and the Trade Mart."

Mike consulted his notes, "Right, Jerry. He wrote that you favored the Woman's Hall. Why was that?"

"That place was large enough to accommodate a good-sized crowd and could be easily secured. In addition, it could be accessed by the direct route of Main Street, which route could be easily secured for the president's motorcade."

"What was wrong the Trade Mart location?"

"The primary access to it involved two sharp turns which required the president's limo to slow almost to a stop, twice. And it required his motorcade to drive slowly past several multi-storied buildings. So, the route was a security nightmare.

"In addition, the Trade Mart itself had over a dozen hidden corridors that would have to have been secured.

"Of the two sites, the Woman's Building was the best from a security standpoint."

"Manchester wrote that, on November first, you could have picked the site and didn't. Why didn't you end the argument and pick the more secure site when he says you could have done so?"

Bruno sat quietly for a moment before he answered.

"Let me tell you a bit about the divisive fighting going on within the Democratic Party in Texas. The conservative arm was led by Governor Connally, the liberal wing by US Senator Yarborough. The two and their respective supporters were always looking to somehow damage the position of the other.

"Yarborough got his wish when the president agreed to visit Texas; so as not to be ignored, Connally wanted to control the meeting place for the president's Dallas luncheon. The meeting place Connally wanted was much smaller and more ornate than the Woman's Building and thus more suitable for his big money supporters.

"So, the choice of the site for the November twenty-second luncheon in Dallas became the focal point of the power struggle between the two men. Connally was a pompous ass in my opinion, and I believe he truly hated the idea of New England Ivy League liberals having their way in his state, too.

"Anyway, I was caught between the two camps, so I left it to the White House. Besides, I was sure that the Secret Service would surely nix the Dealey Plaza route to the Trade Mart because it was obviously so difficult to secure. So, what was the bottom line? Kenny O'Donnell threw up his hands in despair. For all I know, the president told him to let Connally have his way. I do know that O'Donnell agreed to let the Texas governor make the choice. The Trade Mart was chosen.

"Maybe if I had chosen the Woman's Building on November first as Manchester suggests I could have, it would have been accepted. But I doubt it. The feuding going on in Texas was too bitter. Connally was going to have his way, or the president could park his tender Yankee ass in Washington; Connally's words, not mine."

"So, you knew how dangerous the Dealey Plaza route to the Trade Mart was?" Harold asked.

"Sure did. I'd done too many of these motorcades not to recognize the problems with that route," Bruno exclaimed. "It's what Lawson and Sorrels found out when they drove that route, believe me. The turns required of the president's vehicle were way out of line with the basic Secret Service rules for motorcade safety. It wasn't just I who thought that, even the Secret Service guys on the ground thought so.

"In fact, earlier in the month before the final decision had been made, Dallas County Sheriff Bill Decker, Forest Sorrels and Winston Lawson of the Secret Service drove the route. Sorrels is reported to have said,

'Hell, we'd be sitting ducks here.'

"The other two men in the car agreed. Despite that, those same Secret Service men reported that either the Maine Street route to the Woman's Building or the Dealey Plaza route to the Trade Mart was acceptable from a security standpoint.

"Winston Lawson was the agent in charge of security for the motorcade. He was the one who actually recommended the Trade Mart location and the use of the Dealey Plaza motorcade route. Figure that one, Mike.

"Lawson was also the Secret Service agent who told the Dallas police he didn't want the customary six motorcycle policemen flanking the president's vehicle. He insisted only four of them would be needed and only two of those positioned at the rear bumpers of the President's limo."

"So, not only did Lawson support using a route he thought would make the president a 'sitting duck', he further exposed the president by reducing vehicle security?"

"You got it, Mike," Bruno said.

Mike asked another question focusing on the route selection subject. "Another thing Manchester wrote had to do with route selection, too. Evidently he had talked earlier with Michael Terina, who was Chief Inspector of the Secret Service.

Manchester reports, Terina told him that whenever a presidential motorcade must slow down for a turn, the entire intersection must have been checked in advance.

'Manchester follows this information by reporting that in Dallas, the two intersections involved in the Dealey Plaza route to the Trade Mart required the president's vehicle to slow to less than ten miles per hour, twice.

"Just the same,' he wrote, 'neither of those intersections was checked in advance. The windows of the multi-story buildings by the two intersections had not been required to be closed or placed under observation during the motorcade either.'"

"Do you think Manchester had it right, Jerry?" Mike asked.

"It has been some time since I read Manchester's book about the Kennedy assassination. But I recall the testimony given by Lawson to the Warren Commission. They asked him why the buildings along the route had not been checked beforehand or placed under observation during the parade, as Secret Service motorcade protocol required. He said that he had not checked the buildings along the motorcade route or arranged to monitor the windows of those buildings during the parade because he didn't have the manpower to do either."

"That seems odd," Mike commented. "Dallas County Sherriff Curry testified to the Warren Commission that Lawson told him the Secret Service had it covered and didn't need any manpower. As a result, Curry had nearly one hundred of his deputies standing in front of his building, just watching the motorcade drive by.

"Back in 1967 when I was in Dallas, I used the FBI offices to conduct interviews for the House Judiciary Committee. The Chief of Station there, Gordon Shanklin told me he offered Lawson FBI agents to help with security. Lawson turned his offer down; said he had it covered."

"You need to know, Mike," Bruno continued, "in contrast, none of these route problems existed during the November twenty-first motorcades in Houston, San Antonio or Fort Worth. All the windows along the parade route in each of those cities had been checked and were under observation during the motorcades.

"Only in Dallas on November twenty-second did the White House Secret Service detail violate long-standing presidential parade protocols."

Mike asked, "Why didn't Secret Service people have the same manpower problem in the other cities as well as Dallas?"

"Does seem strange doesn't it?" Bruno concluded.

Mike and Jerry Bruno ended their conversation.

Standing at the front door, Mike shook Bruno's hand. "Thanks, Jerry," Mike told him. "You really cleared up some things. I appreciate your time."

"Not a problem," Bruno assured him. "If you have any more questions, you have my phone number. Don't hesitate to call."

Boggs' Office

Harold arrived from Union Station, having taken the commuter train from Boston. Evidently a good number of federal employees used it, commuting daily from their homes further north. Today, Harold joined them.

Mike was already in the office.

"Do I smell freshly brewed coffee, Michael me lad?"

"Yep, Judge. You do. To get some, you can either go down the hallway and help yourself, or if you're really foolish, you can ask one of the staff to fetch you one."

"Why foolish?"

"In this office, even Lindy Boggs pours her own coffee, that's why."

"Oh, ya. I forgot the local rules for a moment," Harold admitted.

"Good thing you caught yourself, Harold," Mike chuckled. "Or the staff might have banished you to the file room for the rest of the day."

Harold returned with his coffee and joined Mike at the conference table.

"How was your trip to Boston?"

"Really great," Harold responded. "It was worth the time I took to visit with Ted Sorensen. I went over my notes last night. You can take a look at them later. How was Bruno?"

"He was spot on dealing with the luncheon site selection. The infighting between the liberal and conservative members of the Texas Democratic Party was intense. It appears that Kennedy was caught in the middle of that war. So Bruno was caught up in it too, and in the last analysis had to let Kenny O'Donnell make the call on the luncheon site.

"The fighting got so bad that Senator Yarborough threatened to stay in Washington if too much attention was paid to Connally. The Kennedy people had to be seen not to favor either side. As it turned out, Connally got to make the call on the Dallas luncheon site. It seems that it was sort of his turn to decide something.

"But Bruno's information on the role played by the Secret Service was especially insightful. I'll go over it with you over lunch today.

"By the way," Mike continued. "Mable asked me to have you to talk with her this morning about your request that she arrange an appointment for us with former Defense Secretary Robert McNamara. I think she has news."

"You're just eager to gloat that my request was turned down as you predicted, aren't you?"

"Absolutely," Mike laughed, leaning back in his chair. "Remember, if he turns you down you treat for a meal at the Golden Buddha."

"But if he agrees?" Harold snapped back.

"I know, I know," Mike admitted. "Go and find out, I can't stand it, waiting like this."

Harold returned in short order and sat down.

Mike looked at him, waiting. "Well? What's the story, Judge?"

"Just you remember, Burke, none of those fancy drinks with fruit and a fan sticking out of an orange slice. One cocktail and one entrée is all you get."

The front legs of Mike's chair hit the tile floor with a bang as he leaned forward.

"I knew it!" he said as he slapped the top of the table. "I knew the World Bank president wouldn't see the likes of us; not even a former Congressman, or as a favor for a current Congresswoman."

"It turned out that you were right, smart-aleck," Harold admitted. "McNamara probably wants no part of answering questions about the debacle of the Vietnam Conflict. It's got to give him nightmares as it is.

"I'll bet he knows that had Kennedy lived there would have been no escalation, and we never would have had to suffer the loss of an entire generation of young American men. Along with Johnson's, McNamara's was the face of that defeat."

"Right on, Harold," Mike agreed. "So where do you go from here?"

"I recall Lindy saying she has often had General Maxwell Taylor and his wife as guests in her home. I'll ask her to arrange a meeting for us with him. I believe he lives somewhere around Washington. There's more than one way to skin a cat, don't you know."

"Go for it, partner," Mike encouraged. "Then I want to talk to you about our up-coming interview with James Hosty, the former FBI agent who just retired."

"Right," Harold agreed. "Then we should outline our approach to the former Secret Service agents who screwed up the Kennedy detail in Dallas, Lawson and Sorrels."

"Don't forget Kellerman, who virtually stole JFK's body out of Parkland Hospital at gunpoint before the coroner could perform an autopsy."

"Who's going to take him on, Mike?" Harold asked.

Mike consulted his notes. "He's living in St. Petersburg, Florida. Lawson is living in some kind of retirement home in Lake Taylor, Virginia. Which one do you want to take?"

"I flew to Boston, so why don't you take the flight to St. Petersburg to see Kellerman. I'll rent a car this time and drive over to interview Lawson. Sound good?"

"Sure," Mike answered. "After we spend a week at home, I'll fly direct from Detroit to Florida while you come back here for your interview with Lawson."

Mable came into the room. "I'm going to get a sandwich in the commissary and while I'm there, one for the boss," she told them. "Can I get anything for either of you?"

"That would be very nice, Mable," Mike told her. "Thank you for thinking of us."

"I'd like a ham sandwich and some Jell-O pudding, please," Harold told her.

"How about you, Mike?" Mable asked.

"I'll have an egg salad sandwich and a carton of chocolate milk, please."

Harold harrumphed. "Chocolate milk is not a manly drink ya' know."

"You don't have to drink any."

"Thank the Lord for small favors."

"Don't worry, I'll make up for it tonight and have a second cocktail with supper."

"I would hope so," Harold chuckled.

***

"If you drink too much of that sweet stuff you face will break out, don't ya' know," Harold teased his partner.

"You're just jealous of my smooth complexion, Judge," Mike taunted.

"Ya got me there, young fella. What time is Mable calling Agent Hosty?"

"I have one o'clock on my appointment pad."

Sure enough, the intercom buzzed at a couple of minutes past one. Harold answered.

"James Hosty is on line two, Congressman."

"Good afternoon Mr. Hosty," Harold began. "Harold Ryan here."

"Same to you, Congressman," James Hosty responded. "Is Mike Burke on the other line?"

"Yes, I am Mr. Hosty," Mike told him. "Thank you for visiting with us today."

"I'm told you worked in Jim Sullivan's shop for several years, Mike," Hosty said.

"Yes, I did. Then I got an offer to become a staffer on the House Judiciary Committee. It was a promotion in pay and seemed to offer more stability for my family, so I jumped ship after four years with the Bureau. I see you stuck it out for thirty-one years and just retired."

"Right," Hosty confirmed. "After the Kennedy assassination Hoover transferred me from Dallas to Kansas City, his version of the North Pole. Actually, my family and I enjoyed that city. I worked there until early this year when I retired."

"So, you had the last laugh on the old man," Mike chuckled.

"I suppose you could look at it that way," Hosty said. "Actually, you're right though, since the transfer turned out pretty well for me as well as my family. I never held any grudge. I'm more of a detail guy; not a politician. So going to work each day away from all the politics of a busy big city office like Dallas was not a chore. Since I retired, I sort of miss it, if you want to know the truth."

Harold broke into the conversation. "Speaking of the truth, Mr. Hosty, I have a question."

"Call me Jim, Congressman."

"All right, Jim," Harold continued. "We have uncovered some information about the Mafia that we'd hoped you could help us on."

"Will if I can, Harold."

"We have witnesses who claim that the FBI had information to the effect that a hit was planned on President Kennedy. Could you verify that?"

"Let me answer your question this way, Harold," Hosty began. "Word around the Bureau was that Kansas City was the end of the earth. To some extent that was true. Not much going on there as far as organized crime was concerned. Besides, Mr. Hoover had insisted for a long time that the Mafia did not exist in the United States.

"Anyway, Dallas was a different story. Jim Sullivan's unit did prove that the Mafia operated there. So, the Bureau office there did receive bulletins about organized crime from time to time.

"I remember a bulletin out of Los Vegas. It was back in 1962, I believe. An informant told agents there about a conversation he'd witnessed in New Orleans. It seems that our informant, Edward Becker, was introduced to Carlos Marcello, the Mafia Don who controlled organized crime out of New Orleans. His people operated in Dallas as well.

"Anyway, Becker, who was a promoter, told FBI agents that one evening he was taken to Marcello's place out in the swamps near New Orleans to talk about funding some product or other. After drinking a good deal it appears Marcello said something about his hatred for Bobby Kennedy. Becker said something about how foolish it would be to take out the Attorney General of the United States.

"Marcello responded that he wasn't talking about a hit on Bobby but on the president. He related an old Sicilian story to the effect that if you want to stop a dog from biting you, you don't cut off the tail because the dog will continue to bite you. No, you cut off the head of the dog.

"Becker was sure Marcello was talking about President Kennedy being the person assassinated," Hosty continued.

"Isn't that pretty much what happened, Jim?" Mike asked.

"Of course you're right, Mike," Hosty responded. "Shortly after Johnson took over the Oval Office, he pretty much shut down Robert Kennedy's war on the

Mafia. I could see that from my desk in Dallas, and even later from my remote outpost in Kansas City."

At this point, Harold reentered the conversation. "We also have information that another of your informants told Miami FBI agents about a hit that was planned on President Kennedy before the presidential election of 1964. Do you know anything about that, Jim?"

"In 1962 I was still in Dallas," Hosty began. "So, I was still in the loop. It seems that an informant reported to the Bureau's Miami agents a conversation he'd had with Santos Trafficante.

"Our informant, Jose Aleman Jr., met with Miami's Mafia Don Santos Trafficante, seeking his help in obtaining a loan for his hotel business from Jimmy Hoffa's Teamsters retirement fund. They were in Aleman's office talking of one thing and another, when Aleman said that he expected Kennedy to easily win a second term.

"Aleman reported to the Miami FBI agents that Trafficante said, "*Kennedy's not going to make it to the election. He's going to be hit.*"

"Don't hold me to those exact words, but it's close."

"I see nothing is wrong with your memory, Jim," Harold observed.

"Not hardly, Harold," he chuckled. "Mike, you will remember how we agents were constantly badgered to remember the smallest details. It was almost like having a daily quiz to challenge our memory. I'm still pretty good at recalling stuff."

"Were these two threats on the life of President Kennedy the only ones that came to your attention while you were stationed at the FBI office in Dallas?" Mike asked.

"Now that you ask," Hosty said, "I remember another bulletin that came across my desk from the Bureau office in Washington."

"Was it information about another threat on the life of President Kennedy?" Harold asked.

"Yes, it was, sort of." Hosty said.

"How could a threat be 'sort of'?" Mike asked.

"You can judge for yourself, Mike, "Hosty challenged. "I saw this bulletin in September, but the information was dated as having been received in July 1963.

It appears that on one of our wire taps Jimmy Hoffa was heard to have said to his attorney Frank Ragano, "*The time has come for your friends, Santos Trafficante and Carlos Marcello to get rid of him. Kill that son of a bitch John Kennedy.*"

"So, let me get this information in context, Jim," Harold stated. "Both of these informants shared the threats made against the president in the summer and fall of 1962. Is that correct?"

"Right," Hosty confirmed.

"And you heard an additional reference to a possible hit made in July 1963?"

"Right," Hosty said.

"Did you receive any orders to investigate local organized crime guys or be on the look-out for information about such an eventuality to take place in Dallas?" Harold asked.

"No, I didn't, Congressman. And I would have known if anyone else in the office had. No one did," Hosty admitted.

"So, you're saying that in advance of Kennedy's 1963 trip to Miami, there was no alert sent out?"

"Not that I saw come over the wire."

"Not even in Miami where Santos Trafficante held power?"

"Not a word of warning."

"And when the Dallas trip was in the works, your office didn't sound the alarm, given the reported threats made my Mafia Don Carlos Marcello?"

"Not one, gentlemen."

"Not even after Hoffa was demanding action three months before the president was killed during his visit to Dallas?"

"None that I remember, Mike. There was no warning bulletin or order to be on the alert."

"Do you know if the Secret Service people had been told any of this?"

"Customary procedure dictated that the people of the president's Secret Service detail would be informed. But I can't vouch for it on this occasion.

"But, in November 1963 at a Bureau briefing, Gordon Shanklin, our Special Agent in Charge of the Dallas Bureau, told us that if we came across information about any potential threat to the president to be sure to let the Dallas Secret Service guys know.

"Shanklin also told us that he had sent one of my colleagues, Vince Drain, to tell the Secret Service guys that our forty or so agents were at their disposal during the president's visit to Dallas. Drain reported back that he was told we weren't needed; they had everything covered.

"About the threats that were made, we might assume the Secret Service knew about them, because they took extreme security measures during the president's earlier November visit to Tampa.

"They appeared to have done a fine job of securing the president's visits to Houston, San Antonio and Fort Worth as well. I can't imagine why they dropped the ball so badly in Dallas."

"If you don't mind, Jim, I need to change the subject some."

"Excuse me, Mike. There's one more thing about the Mafia I can share," Hosty said. "In 1970, I was visiting old friends in Dallas and had occasion to have lunch with my old FBI boss there, Gordon Shanklin.

"He and I were shooting the breeze when he asked some questions going back to my time with him in Dallas. He wanted to talk about Oswald and the Kennedy assassination. I think he felt guilty about ordering me to destroy the note from Oswald that resulted in my being reprimanded. I think Gordon knew that he had sort of thrown me under the bus back then, ya' see.

"I wasn't able to add much to what he already knew, but he sure gave me some new information.

"Shanklin told me that the Bureau had a wiretap of a conversation between Jimmy Hoffa and his attorney recorded in July 1963. It was the same one I just told you about."

"That's pretty revealing," Mike said. "I would sure like to have heard more conversations between those people."

"There was one more wiretapped conversation he told me about that would interest you, I'm sure. Years later, in 1969, there was another FBI wiretap, this was one of a Carlos Marcello conversation about Hoffa. The New Orleans Mafia Don, Marcello was recorded as saying about Hoffa, "*I wish that hothead would keep quiet, you know. He's going to get us all in trouble. Someone needs to remind him we did him a favor in Dallas."*

"That comment should put the final lid on the rumor of Mafia involvement, don't you think?" Hosty suggested.

"It would if we could get corroboration for that last wiretap, Jim," Harold said.

"Ask Shanklin. He's in private law practice in Dallas. The Kennedy assassination seems to have become a passion with him. You can tell him I suggested you call."

"Thanks, Jim," Mike said. "We'll do that for sure. If you don't have anything more on the Mafia involvement, I have something else to ask."

"Go right ahead, Mike. You've tapped me out on that topic."

"I'm sure you remember Lee Harvey Oswald," Mike began.

"Oh yeah," Hosty responded. "I remember that asshole. He was the guy I was assigned to keep track of when he arrived in Dallas. The report Mr. Hoover leaked to the press in December 1963 identified Oswald as the lone gunman, totally responsible for the killing of President Kennedy.

"That sure put me in a bad spot, believe me. Once the Bureau study was public, we all had to get in line behind it, of course. Because of that Mr. Hoover's deputy, Bill Sullivan, ordered us to stop investigating any leads associated with the assassination. He even insisted we stop cooperating with local law enforcement on the case. Even the local media were off base. Only Gordon Shanklin, our station chief was allowed to speak with them.

"That's pretty much when I came under a microscope. It was circle the wagons time at the Bureau. I ended up being blamed for losing track of Oswald, reprimanded publicly by Mr. Hoover and sent to the Kansas City office as punishment."

"Do you agree with the Bureau's December 1963 report, Jim? Do you think Oswald was the lone gunman?"

There was dead silence on the phone for a while.

Then Hosty responded, "At the time I did," Hosty said. "As more information came to light about the directionality of the president's wounds I began to doubt it some. But remember guys, I'm a company man.

"I still find it hard to believe the Washington guys at the Bureau would do a poor job investigating the killing of the President of the United States. And since I haven't seen much evidence to the contrary, I'd have to say I still believe the report the Bureau issued back then.

"This interview is the first I've granted in a very long time. I hope I've been of help to you."

"You definitely have, Jim," Mike assured him.

"I have one more question, if you don't mind," Harold mentioned.

"Go right ahead, Congressman," Hosty replied. "I'm retired, don't you know. I have plenty of time."

"In preparation for President Kennedy's visit to Texas, motorcades were planned for Houston, San Antonio and Fort Worth preceding the one in Dallas. During the first three parades FBI agents were involved with the Secret Service in the planning and implementation of motorcade security measures.

"But there were no FBI agents from your Dallas office involved in the Dallas motorcade security force. Why weren't there?"

"That did seem strange at the time, Congressman. Most of us assumed we would have been involved," Hosty began. "Remember, I just told you that Shanklin sent one of our agents tell the Secret Service guys he was willing to lend a hand. No reason was given for their refusal to take his offer."

"That seems strange," Harold declared. "Winston Lawson, who was responsible for the security arrangements for the president's Dallas visit, told the Warren Commission otherwise. He complained that the reason he did not check the multistory buildings around the two intersections at Elm and Houston streets was that he was shorthanded of security personnel."

Hosty added, "At a meeting before the president's visit, Gordon told us that his offer of help included all of the agents in our office, but Sorrels or Lawson, one or the other, said no thanks. He insisted that his guys had it covered. He obviously didn't. Go figure."

Mike added, "That's the second source of similar information. The other one was from Dallas County Sherriff Bill Decker. He testified to the Warren Commission that Sorrels turned down help from his office, too. As a result Decker had over one hundred deputies standing outside his office on Elm Street, just watching the parade go by; doing nothing.

"Possibly the Secret Service guys were just protecting their turf," Hosty offered. "You know, they didn't want to admit they couldn't protect President Kennedy without outside help. It could've been something like that.

Hosty concluded, "I find it hard to believe they were part of a conspiracy to murder the President of the United States. My God, every single agent of the White House security detail was pledged to give his life to protect the president's."

"Whatever, Jim," Mike added. "It's pretty obvious though. Both the Warren Commission and the House Select Committee on Assassinations concluded that the Secret Service fell down on the job in Dallas. They reported that the Secret Service did not properly protect President Kennedy. Both reports blamed the White House detail for Kennedy's death."

"You know, gentlemen," Hosty said, "that happened over ten years ago. Afterwards, I got pretty well beaten up by the Warren Commission and in the press. Even Mr. Hoover sort of threw me under the bus even when I was trying to protect the Bureau and their Report.

"So I've kept a low profile since I was transferred to Kansas City. During the time I've worked in that city, I haven't paid much attention to the assassination of President Kennedy. But are you guys thinking his assassination was an organized coup?"

"We don't know that, Jim," Harold said. "But it does have a lot of the elements of a coup."

"My Lord! I pray to God that it wasn't," Hosty exclaimed.

"That's our prayer too, Jim," Mike added.

***

"Do you want to make the call or me?" Mike asked.

"I think we ought to let Mable make the call," Harold answered. "Shanklin is retired from the Bureau but still in Dallas. He's practicing law there but most of his clients are the result of his government contacts. So, I think a call from Congresswoman Boggs' office will certainly have more impact that from either of us."

"Sounds good to me, Judge," Mike responded.

It wasn't long before the intercom rang. "Mr. Shanklin is on the line, gentlemen."

"What'd I tell you, Mike," Harold bragged. "Lindy has some influence, even with retired agents it appears."

"I always knew you were a smart former Congressman," Mike snapped back.

Harold answered the phone. "Good afternoon. This is Harold Ryan."

"Former Congressman Ryan?" Shanklin asked.

"Yes, that's right."

"Is a former FBI agent named Burke with you?"

"Yes I am, Agent Shanklin," Mike responded. "Thank you for talking with us."

"I haven't agreed to do anything yet, Burke," Shanklin snapped back. "Why should I talk with either of you?"

'Probably because Congresswoman Boggs asked you to," Harold snapped back.

"Look here, you two," Shanklin responded. "I got this call out of the blue from a woman named Mable who told me you were working for Boggs on some wild goose chase about the Kennedy assassination. So, I'll ask you one more time before I hang up; why should I talk with either of you?"

"Tell you what, Agent Shanklin," Mike responded. "I worked for Deputy Director Bill Sullivan in the late fifties and early sixties, and for the House Committee on the Judiciary after that. Harold Ryan served in the House during and right after the Kennedy administration.

"Back in 1967, he and I were charged by the Judiciary Committee chairman, John Conyers to investigate the possibility that President Kennedy was killed as the result of a conspiracy and not as the act of a lone gunman. Back then, I was in Dallas conducting interviews and talked with you. Look up the report for yourself. I'm sure you can get a copy. Lord knows everyone else seems to have one.

"More recently, the House Select Committee on Assassinations released its report. As far as the Kennedy assassination was concerned, the committee agreed with our earlier study and declared the killing was probably the result of a conspiracy. But they refused to get into who might have been a party to that conspiracy to kill President Kennedy.

"That upset Congresswoman Boggs," Mike continued. "So, she asked her husband's old colleague, Harold Ryan and me to look into what that committee had avoided; the why Kennedy was killed and possibly who was involved in that conspiracy."

Harold got into the conversation at this point. "In the course of our investigation we talked with a former colleague of yours, a retired agent named James Hosty. He was most informative. But he suggested we talk with you, because of your time as Chief Agent in charge of the Dallas office and your experience with the FBI's Organized Crime Unit."

"Why the hell did he tell you that?"

Mike answered, "Because he said you might have more information than he did about the possible involvement of the Mafia in the assassination. That's what we want to talk with you about."

"Holy crap!" Shanklin shouted. "Do you two realize that you're playing with fire here?

"No," Mike challenged. "You're the organized crime specialist, Shanklin. Tell us about the fire we're playing with."

"You almost got me to tell you, Burke," Shanklin chortled. "Tell you what. I'll look over that report you two wrote for the House Judiciary and check with the Congresswoman herself. Then I might get back to you. Where are you going to be later today?"

"We can be right here, Mr. Shanklin," Harold told him.

Burke interrupted. "That you might get back to us is pure horseshit, Shanklin. Ryan and I are not playing games here, as Boggs will tell you. So, I expect as a matter of courtesy for you to at least call us back even if you decline to share your precious information."

There was a long pause.

"I'll call you."

Then the line went dead.

Harold looked at Mike. "My Lord, he's a piece of work," Harold said with a laugh. "Think he'll call us back?"

"Actually I don't know, Harold. Lord Almighty, some of these agents were so full of themselves they can't imagine treating anyone outside the Bureau courteously. My guess is that he will eventually talk with us, if for no other reason than to enhance his importance and give his ego a boost."

"Why don't you give Mable a heads-up? Hopefully she can see to it that Lindy is available to take this guy's call."

"If he calls, you mean?"

"I stand corrected; if he calls."

"I need some more coffee. So I'll check with Mable on the way." Mike left the room to talk with Mable.

At the end of the day, there had been no call.

***

The next day the two investigators were to meet with General Maxwell Taylor. A lunch meeting had been arranged by Congresswoman Boggs at the Army-Navy Club. An exclusive downtown Washington club, it boasted one of the best restaurants in the city. It also provided short term housing for both active and retired military personnel who happened to be in Washington.

The general and his wife Linda had a home on Embassy Row in Washington but often met with guests at the Army – Navy Club restaurant.

Harold and Mike met the Congresswoman in the lobby.

"Thanks for meeting me here a few minutes early, gentlemen," Lindy Boggs said in greeting.

"Not a problem, Lindy," Harold said. "We appreciate having the opportunity to meet with the general."

"Maxwell does not tolerate people who are late," Boggs said. "So. let's go up to the dining room right now. I'll bet he's already there."

The elevator operator took them to one of the upper floors. "The dining room is to your left ma'am," he directed.

As they turned down the hallway another uniformed person, a woman this time, met them in front of a closed doorway.

"Do you have a reservation today?" she asked.

Boggs answered. "I'm Congresswoman Boggs. I have a lunch appointment with General Maxwell Taylor."

"Of course," the uniformed officer answered. "The general told us to expect you, ma'am. Please follow me."

They were led down the hallway in the opposite direction of the dining room.

Their guide opened a door to a small room. As soon as the Congresswoman entered the room, General Maxwell Taylor stood up and approached. He was a very trim and handsome man, well over six feet tall.

"Lindy, how are you?" he asked as he gave her a kiss on the cheek. "You remember my wife, Linda."

"Of course, I do, General," Boggs told him as she crossed the room to his wife. They exchanged a kiss on the check as well. "It is good to see you, Linda. I'm sorry you had to miss my last party; something about your son at West Point?" Lindy took the seat alongside Mrs. Taylor.

"Nothing serious, Hap's West Point choir was performing and he had a solo. We couldn't miss it. It was his first, you see."

"I understand completely."

"He accomplished something I never could," the general said. "He can carry a tune. But he was scheduled to sing a solo; we couldn't miss that.

"Now, just whom did you bring to interrogate me, Lindy? I hope they don't get me into hot water."

"This is Congressman Harold Ryan who served with my husband years ago. His companion is Michael Burke, a former aide with the House Judiciary Committee."

"Have a seat, Lindy," he urged. "Gentlemen, please be seated. Allow me to introduce my wife of over fifty years, Linda."

Harold and Mike both stood and greeted Mrs. Taylor.

She told them, "I hope you will not be too hard on my husband. After so many years away from home, I'd hate to lose him again. I hope he is not in too much trouble."

"Hardly, ma'am," Mike assured her. "Congresswoman Boggs asked us to pick up the investigation of the Kennedy assassination where the House Select Committee on Assassinations left off."

"Oh, my," she responded. 'That sounds so mysterious."

Harold continued. "At this stage, we're looking into the opposition President Kennedy encountered because of his foreign policy agenda. General Taylor was a member of the president's inner circle of advisors. He worked with the president most closely on formulating that agenda. So, we asked the Congresswoman if she could set up a meeting for us to visit with the general."

"That doesn't sound too intimidating, Maxwell," she told her husband. "See, you worried for nothing."

Everyone laughed at the prospect of this much decorated hero of WWII, General Maxwell Taylor, and the veteran of many Congressional hearings, being frightened at the prospect of this particular interview.

General Taylor interrupted and suggested, "Let's order our lunch first. We can get into the discussion while it is being fixed." With that he gave a signal and an aide came over to Mrs. Taylor to take her food order. Congresswoman Boggs and the general were consulted next, followed by Harold and Mike.

Once that housekeeping chore was finished, the general returned to the object of their meeting.

"How can I help you gentlemen?" he asked.

Harold began. "It is our understanding, General, that you became President Kennedy's military advisor shortly after the Bay of Pigs disaster and his meeting with Premier Khrushchev in June 1961. As such, he included you in his inner circle of advisors on national security and foreign policy matters. Do I have that correct, sir?"

"Yes. I was privileged to serve President Kennedy as you have said. His premature death was a terrible tragedy for the United States."

"Yes, sir," Harold agreed.

Burke continued. "Our research and interviews have left us to understand that the Chairman of the Joint Chiefs, General Lyman Lemnitzer, and his colleagues on that body did not feel comfortable with Kennedy as commander in chief. Would that be an accurate characterization, sir?"

"That would be a fair assessment, Mr. Burke," the general said. "General Lemnitzer was a hardliner. He was also a leader who believed the Soviets could not be trusted and would only respect strength. You should know that the general held the same view on the matter as did Kennedy's predecessor, President Eisenhower."

Burke continued. "Would it be fair to say, sir, that General Lemnitzer and the other Joint Chiefs thought that Kennedy's willingness to reach an accommodation with the Soviet Union was bound to fail at best, and at worst, put the security of the United States at grave risk?"

"That assessment is also a fair one, Mr. Burke," Taylor said. "But keep in mind, President Kennedy came into office at the peak of the Cold War. A great deal was at stake in our contest with the Soviet Union. Simply put, the Cold War was a contest for the control of the world's human and material resources.

"Those of us interested in the national security of the United States believed that this contest with the Soviets could go either way, you see," Taylor continued.

"Then in 1960, a liberal from the Northeast became Commander in Chief of the most powerful country on earth. Despite his public rhetoric, when the chips were down, he appeared unwilling to use our strength to protect our interests. Instead, he appeared, to the same people, to be determined to weaken the United States and trust that the Soviets were willing to live in peace with us.

"As part of that effort, he ordered a reduction in defense spending, the sharing of our space program information with the Soviets, the reduction of our nuclear arsenal and the complete withdrawal of personnel from the latest hot spot, Vietnam. So the national security folks in the administration were frightened of this peace-seeker."

Harold asked, "What then was your role in all of this, General?"

"I was privileged to be President Kennedy's military and national security advisor, Congressman. I was also to be the bridge between his office the Joint Chiefs and the other national security people in his administration."

Before the conversation could go any further, a food wagon was pushed into the room. Lunch was served.

Harold was brought an open face roast beef sandwich with a side of mashed potatoes and gravy. Burke had baked ham. Each of the ladies had some sort of salad and the general had what looked to Harold like a T-bone steak. Bread, warm from the oven, iced tea and water was provided, too.

Later, over coffee, the conversation resumed when the general said, "Where were we, gentlemen?"

Harold began. "After the Bay of Pigs, President Kennedy supposedly promised to break up the CIA into a thousand pieces. Toward that end, we have been led to believe that the issue of NSAMS 55, 56, and 57 was a move taken to achieve that objective. Did you assist the president and his staff to put these executive orders together before you were appointed to chair the Joint Chiefs of Staff?"

"Yes, I did Congressman Ryan," General Taylor confirmed. "Colonel Prouty explained their purpose to the Joint Chiefs while General Lemnitzer still chaired that body."

"It didn't seem to alter anything, though," Burke suggested. "Did it surprise you that General Lemnitzer simply ignored the military's supervisory role in covert activities that these orders demanded?"

"Not really, Mr. Burke," General Taylor answered without pausing. "Changing bureaucratic behavior is difficult. It takes time. The CIA and the military had developed supportive alliances during and since the Korean War. I was not at all surprised at the foot dragging of the Joint Chiefs on this issue; nor was President Kennedy."

Burke pushed on. "Was Kennedy looking toward his second term to push for compliance?"

"I think that is a fair reading of the situation."

Harold Ryan asked, "May we move on to ask about your role in the growing Vietnam quagmire?"

"Yes, of course, Congressman. None of that is terribly sensitive any longer. What do you need to ask?"

"Were you aware that Vice President Johnson was receiving national security reports that were different from those being provided to President Kennedy?"

"Yes, I was. The vice president's commitment to oppose the spread of Communist governments everywhere in the world was well known within the administration. So, I wasn't surprised the vice president was receiving briefings from Defense, CIA and State. After all, he was only a heartbeat from the Oval Office, as we were all tragically reminded on November twenty-second.

"The vice president's views were hardly a secret either, and quite honestly, they garnered more support than President Kennedy's within those departments of the administration.

"The president had appointed men to head those departments who basically agreed with his approach in dealing with the Communist threat. But he hadn't been in office long enough to alter the attitudes of their support personnel or the overall bureaucracies that made up those departments.

"So, I dare say, Vice President Johnson's position was more strongly supported from virtually top to bottom within each of those departments of President Kennedy's own administration."

Ryan continued, "So, General, when President Kennedy issued NSAM 263 directing the Secretary of Defense to immediately begin the withdrawal of American personnel from Vietnam, it was not regarded with widespread approval within his own administration, was it?"

"No, Congressman, it was not; nor was his order to reduce defense spending by ten percent in the 1964 fiscal year's executive budget. In this mix, we should also consider the dismay and opposition he met when he ordered NASA to begin sharing our space program information with the Soviets, when he pursued the Nuclear Test Ban Treaty, and ordered the closing of military bases.

"All of these steps seemed to initiate a downgrading of our military preparedness at the very time we were being challenged by our Communist enemies all over the world.

"His steps gave every indication to our Cold War hawks that President Kennedy was weakening the United States and thus sacrificing our dominant world position in our struggle with the Soviet Union."

Burke asked, "Our information suggests that members of the CIA hierarchy considered Kennedy's actions treasonous. Would you agree, General?"

General Taylor stiffened in his chair. "Do I think President Kennedy's actions were treasonous?" he snapped back. "Or are you asking me if I recall if there were people in the government who thought Kennedy was pursuing a treasonous path?"

"Please excuse my awkwardly put question, General," Burke apologized. "I did not intend any disrespect. I was asking about the possibility that others in the administration held that view of the President, certainly not you, sir."

"Thank you for that clarification, Mr. Burke. You apology is accepted. To answer your question, though," the General continued, "you might remember that prior to the Japanese attack on Pearl Harbor, Franklin Roosevelt was denied sensitive national security information because Army Intelligence believed the people around him were of questionable character. President Truman was called a traitor in the halls of Congress after he fired General MacArthur. President Eisenhower's desire to reach a detente with the Soviet Union was opposed by the director of the CIA, Allen Dulles."

"Some believe that Dulles sabotaged the Paris summit, dooming Eisenhower's plan," Burke interjected.

"I've heard that rumor, too. I suggest to you gentlemen," Taylor continued, "any president who surrounds himself with only agreeable advisors is in trouble. I assure you President Kennedy did not. He was many things, but traitor was not one of them."

"Sir," Harold went on, "you were in Hawaii with the Secretary of Defense and other cabinet members on November twenty-second, participating in a conference studying the situation in Vietnam. Isn't it true that among the suggestions being prepared for President Kennedy's review was an alteration of his NSAM 263?"

"Yes it was," Taylor said. "The recommendation prepared by our group meeting in Hawaii for Kennedy was given to President Johnson instead. When issued shortly thereafter, it was known as NSAM 273. It is still classified."

"How was it different than NSAM 263?"

"Since it is still classified, I can't go into specific detail about it. But it basically stepped back from ordering a reduction of personnel by a date certain and instead suggested that the president pursue a policy with the best chance of gaining victory in Vietnam."

"So," Burke asked, "the complete withdrawal of American personnel that was ordered by President Kennedy to be completed by the end of 1965, was ignored?"

"It wasn't ignored Mr. Burke, it was avoided in NSAM 273. In this executive order President Johnson declared his intention of seeking a victory in Vietnam by whatever means necessary."

Harold asked, "So in effect, Johnson's 273 replaced Kennedy's 263 NSAM?"

"I believe that is a fair conclusion, Congressman," Taylor responded.

"General," Burke asked, "it appears to me that in October, you supported President Kennedy's executive order withdrawing all American personnel from Vietnam. But in November, you supported President Johnson's order to accelerate our presence there. How could you support such contradictory positions?"

General Taylor stiffened once again. "Mr. Burke," he began, "I have been a military man for over fifty years. As such, I swore to accept and support orders given by my civilian superiors, whether or not I agreed with them.

"I was privileged to serve President Kennedy as a member of his inner advisory group and as Chairman of the Joint Chiefs of Staff. I did not always agree with his search for peaceful coexistence with the Soviet Union. But he was the President of the United States and my boss. So, when all the arguments were heard, the discussion ended and the decision made, I played the role required of me with all the enthusiasm and drive I had in my being.

"I did no less for his successor, President Johnson. He too was the President of the United States, and my boss. So, when he decided to confront the Soviet Union and use our military resources to resist the spread of Communism in Southeast Asia, I obeyed with all the enthusiasm and drive I had in my being.

"Thank you, sir," Burke said.

At this point General Taylor stood. "If there is nothing more, gentlemen, Mrs. Taylor and I will take our leave. Lindy, it is so nice to see you again. I wish you well with your investigation."

Goodbyes were exchanged. Congresswoman Lindy Boggs led Michael Burke and Harold Ryan out of the room and to the elevator.

"Did you get what you wanted?" Boggs asked.

"I think so. Don't you, Mike?" Harold answered.

"He cleared up a couple of cloudy issues for us," Mike said. "But he was careful not to give us any smoking gun."

"Oh, but I think he did, gentlemen," Congresswoman Boggs told them. "Don't you think he clearly distinguished between Kennedy's NSAM 263 and Johnson's NSAM 273?

"Think about what the general told us. Conventional wisdom has it that Johnson was only continuing his predecessor's Vietnam policy. But General Taylor told you today that there was a clear distinction between the Vietnam policies of the two presidents."

"You're right," Burke agreed with enthusiasm. "In his explanation of his role as a military man he as much as told us the difference between the two Vietnam policies embraced by the two presidents."

"Thank you for setting up the meeting, Lindy," Harold said.

They stood on the street waiting for the Congresswoman's car. "Are you fellows any nearer to wrapping up your investigation?" she asked.

Burke said, "We plan to interview three or four members of the Kennedy Secret Service advance team before we leave Washington. Then we'll meet at my offices in Detroit to put together a report for you."

"Don't be surprised though," Harold cautioned. "As we put our report together, we might discover a need to interview someone else."

As she was about to enter her limo, Boggs assured them, "Do what you have to do. Just let me know."

Detroit

Early Monday morning Harold was sipping a cup of hot coffee in Mike's downtown office.

"I see you've gotten yourself settled, Judge," Mike observed. "Where'd the ladies go?"

"Where else? The ladies' room, I expect."

"Why do the female of the species always seem to go to the rest room in pairs?"

"I have no idea and I have no interest in finding out," Harold chuckled. "Life between the sexes is complicated enough. Besides, some things are meant to remain mysteries."

"You're probably right."

Just then, Marilyn and Lillian waked into the conference room.

"Oh look, Marilyn, the boys have coffee already poured for us. Isn't that sweet?"

Harold sheepishly looked up at his wife, stood and walked toward the door.

"Remember dear, two sugars," Lillian reminded him. "Please."

Mike looked at Marilyn. "Ya, I got it; black and unsweetened for you." He followed Harold out of the room. "Yes dear. Remember, I'm sweet enough," Marilyn taunted, smiling at her husband's back.

Once the two couples were settled, Harold asked no one in particular, "I wonder where Joe and Cathy Yager are?"

"Harold," his wife said, "it's only eight forty-five Just because you insist on arriving early to whatever office you're headed, normal office hours for lawyers are still nine to five. They'll be here at nine. I guarantee it."

"Mike. Did the good judge here expect you to report for duty early when you were his clerk?"

"Somebody had to get the coffee started, Lillian," Mike responded.

"Every day, Michael left the house by seven at the latest," Marilyn reported.

"How did you stand it, Michael?" Lillian asked.

"It was a pleasure to spend my day with Judge Ryan," Mike told everyone. "I couldn't wait to get to the court each morning."

Even Harold was laughing now.

Sure enough, just as Lillian had predicted, Joe Yager walked in with the secretaries and paralegals. It was nine in the morning. They were all right on time.

"Where's Cathy, Joe?" Marilyn asked.

"Her brother David had a spell last night. So, she's sort of hand holding today. She sends her regrets."

"I'm so sorry to hear about her brother," Harold said. "I hope it's nothing serious."

"He should be fine, thank you. But Cathy needs to be with him for a few hours. How can I help the cause today?"

"Have a seat, Joe," Mike urged. "There's a stack of papers over there for you, too."

Joe looked through the documents at his place. "Looks like you have one of those new 3M copy machines in this office, Mike. That's pretty slick," he said.

"I'm impressed that you know about that, Joe," Mike told him. "Our machine is very new, the latest in copy-making technology. You seem to be up to date on such things."

"Yes, I am," Joe replied, smiling. "After all, I read the New York Times and Mechanics Illustrated."

Everyone chuckled at that declaration.

"All right everyone," Harold said. "We've had enough of this tomfoolery. It's time to get down to business. Mike and I have not finished our interviews, nor have we organized all the material we've gathered thus far. Just the same, we thought it will be good for us to have the structure of our eventual presentation in mind as we move toward the end of our investigation."

Mike joined in. "Contained in your packet – in fact right on top, is a copy of our report to the House Committee on the Judiciary. The report is twelve years old, but I believe the format is one we could use on the current report for Congresswoman Boggs. After you've read it, we'd like comments on that suggestion."

The room was quiet for a while.

Lillian was the first to respond. "I think it is ideally suited to your current report, Harold."

"Any other thoughts?" Harold asked.

Marilyn was next to speak-up. "Having worked on this old report, I think it organized our thinking very nicely back then. I suggest we try using it now, if for no other reason but to see if it fits our current need."

"I agree with that approach," Lillian said.

"What do you think, Joe? It seems like you're deep in thought over there," Harold observed.

"Looking over this report, Congressman, I'm reminded of my first impression when I last read it. In it, you, Marilyn and Mike did a fine job of presenting your case. The conclusion you reached and the recommendation you made were both slam dunks; obvious to anyone willing to be open-minded on the subject.

"It seemed to me then, and I still think, that it has all the logic of being written by two excellent lawyers and the clarity of being edited by a teacher of English, so that it would be understood by ordinary people.

"I suggest we pursue those twin goals on the Boggs report as well," Joe concluded.

"Come on, Joe," Mike asked. "You didn't say if you thought this format was appropriate for our current report. I'd like to know what you think about that."

Joe smiled a bit. "You noticed that I didn't really answer your question, I see," he responded. "All right, have it your way. I like Marilyn's suggestion just fine.

***

"It appears that's settled," Harold began. "So now I suggest we start with the second page, the charge Congresswoman Boggs gave us."

Mike added, "Since this time we were asked to respond to the Select Committee's second conclusion, I suggest we start with that first, followed by a sentence or two from the Congresswoman herself."

"OK," Marilyn offered. "At the top of page two, put 'Charge.' Below that we give the House Select Committee's 1978 conclusion: *"We believe, and the facts strongly suggest, that President John F. Kennedy was assassinated as the direct result of a conspiracy, although the persons responsible for such an act cannot be identified."* – House Select Committee on Assassinations: September 15, 1978

"Then, on the same page, we should put in some language stating the specific charge Boggs gave you," Marilyn finished.

"How about this language?" Joe asked. "We could state next: 'In reaction to the report of the House Select Committee on Assassinations, Congresswoman Lindy Boggs, said: *"The House Select Committee is to be applauded for their tireless work. However, it is unfortunate that the committee members stopped short of looking into why President Kennedy was murdered. By not doing that, they closed the door on the possibility of discovering who might have been involved in the conspiracy to murder the President of the United States.*

"So, it is my intention to take that investigative step and open that door." July 4, 1979.

Mike liked the language Joe suggested. "Let's go with that for now. As we move through the report, we might have to back up and edit it some. But for now, I think it clearly shows the purpose of our investigation. What do you think, Harold?"

"I agree with you, Mike," Harold quickly added. "Right now, though, I want to suggest that our investigation thus far has revealed several categories we might use as we organize our report. Off the top of my head, these two come to mind:

The Kennedy Peace Agenda and its opponents.

The Kennedy Domestic Agenda and its opponents.

Mike added, "The death threats known to the FBI and the Secret Service prior to the assassination need to be in there somewhere."

"Right," Harold agreed.

"How about including an overview of the whole business about setting up the trip to Dallas?" Lillian asked. "I'd want that to be discussed, too."

"I agree with Lillian," Marilyn said. "That should be a category all by itself."

"Wouldn't all the steps the Feds took to gain control of the evidence immediately after the assassination be important as well?" Joe suggested.

"You have that right, Joe," Harold said.

"But before we go any further," Harold cautioned, "take a minute and look in your packet for the list of items provided us by our Washington informant, George. He gave us a list under the title 'Foreign Policy' and another he titled, 'Domestic Issues.' He used those two lists to guide our discussions with him." Harold held up several sheets of paper.

Foreign Policy Events of Significance

1. Presidential Campaign of 1960.

"Our informant, George, explained this item to us," Mike said. "You'll notice, gentlemen that I began by listing Senator Kennedy's presidential campaign as an event of significance. I did so because I believe it important that you be reminded of the Cold War hawk image he created for himself during his campaign. This was an image he failed to live up to as president, in the opinion of his administration's national security people and his administration's Cold War hawks."

"Then I've listed some important events that occurred and initiatives that were part of President Kennedy's peace agenda," Mike told them.

2. Bay of Pigs Invasion. 4/61

3. Vienna Summit Conference. 6/61

4. NSAMs 55, 56 & 57 Issued. 6/61.

5. Preemptive Nuclear Strike Proposal of JCS Rejected. 7/61

6. Proposal of JCS to Increase Number of Troops in Vietnam Denied. 7/61

7. Berlin Crisis 8/61

8. JFK's Anti–Castro Buildup in SE United States Began: 8/61

9. Allan Dulles forced Retirement. 11/61

11. Speech: "There Will Not Be an American Solution to Every World Problem."

12. Laos Coalition Government Agreement. 4/62

13. TFX Decision Announced. 4/62

14. Nuclear Test Ban Negotiation Completed. 9/62

15. Cuban Missile Crisis. 10/62

16. Reversal of Support for Cuban Exile Anti-Castro Activity. 11/62

17. Back Door Communication with Khrushchev continued. 11/62

18. An Annual 10% Reduction in Defense Spending Ordered. 3/63

19. Fifty-two Military Bases Ordered Closed in US & Abroad. 3/63

20. JFKs Backdoor Contacts with Castro Begin. 4/63

21. Desirability of Peace Speech. 4/63

22. Announcement of Intention to Seek a Peaceful Solution in Vietnam. 5/63

23. UN Speech: Offering to Share Space Info & Exploration with Soviets. 9/63

24. NSAM 9 Issued, Ordering NSA to Share Our Space Data with Soviets. 9/63

25. NSAM 263 Issued, Ordering US Personnel Withdrawal from Vietnam. 10/63

Domestic Issues of Significance

1. Hoover Told He Must Retire at Age 74. 4/61

2. RFK's war on the Mafia Began 4/61

3. JFK's Interest in the Reduction of the Oil Depletion Tax Credit. 4/61

4. Steel Price Increase Controversy. 4/62

5. TFX Decision Based on Political Impact Announced. 4/62

6. Support of African-Americans in Civil Rights Controversies. 5/62

7. Defense Spending Reduction Announced – Impact on Economy. 3/63

8. Signed NSAM 11110 to Issue $4.3 Billion in Silver Certificates. 6/63

9. Kennedy told Mrs. Lincoln he was going to drop Lyndon Johnson. 10/63

After a few minutes, Mike asked, "Do any of you have any questions? Or, for that matter, do you have any item you think should be added to either list?"

No one suggested any additional items or offered any comments.

"All right, since it's after eleven o'clock, rather than get into another discussion now, I suggest we break for lunch. We can pick up our agenda when we return."

"I think I know where you're taking us for lunch, dear," Lillian announced.

"And which place would that be, Miss Know-It-All?" Harold asked.

"We're going to Joe Muir's Restaurant, of course," she announced knowingly.

"I wouldn't take such a fine group to any place less prestigious, my dear."

"Oysters on the half shell and all the trimmings?" Marilyn asked.

"Exactly, young lady," Harold promised.

"You have my vote, Judge," Joe Yager agreed. "Lead the way."

***

The group returned from lunch around one thirty and went to the coffee room for fresh refills. On the way back, Mike's receptionist gave him a telephone message.

"Retired FBI agent Gordon Shanklin wants you to call him at exactly two p.m. Evidently, he is not at his Dallas law office, so you are to use this phone number."

"Thanks, Pat," Mike said as he took the note. "But would you please place the call. I think the agent would feel more comfortable if he heard your voice first."

"I'd be happy to, Mr. Burke."

"Thanks. I'll be with Harold in the conference room."

Sure enough, a minute or two after two o'clock, the intercom on the conference table lit up and Mike heard a buzzing sound. He knew the call was for him.

"We're on, Harold," he said, and pressed the flashing button to connect with the caller.

"Good afternoon, Mr. Shanklin. This is former FBI agent Burke, and I am joined on the other line by former Congressman Ryan. Thank you for calling back."

Without recognizing Mike's sarcasm or returning the greeting, Shanklin simply started to talk.

"I'm not very comfortable revealing too much to you at this time. Despite your current connection to a member of Congress, I don't know really you, so, I can't trust you. Much of my law practice depends upon my government contacts. I do not wish to see those relationships jeopardized."

"Being a practicing lawyer myself, I can understand that, Mr. Shanklin," Mike assured him.

"I don't give a rat's ass what you understand, Burke," Shanklin snapped. "But I will suggest that you check out the CIA Director of Counterintelligence, a fellow named Angleton. He discovered that Robert Kennedy was passing highly secret CIA briefing material to the Soviets. I recall that he decided to do something about it. What you find may be useful to your investigation.

"Another fellow you might want to look at was the Assistant Director of the CIA's Clandestine Directorate of Operations. The man was called 'The Crow.' A third fellow you will find interesting is Vedder B. Driscoll. He was linked to the Defense Intelligence Agency.

"All these men shared an alarm with the Kennedy agenda and the president's cozy relationship with the Soviets and Castro. They discovered that there were other people in the administration who were seriously alarmed, too."

"Thank you for that information," Mike told him. "Can you verify that there were several wire taped conversations between Mafia leaders which strongly suggested there was a mob contract out on Kennedy's life?"

"That's real fire you're playing with, Burke," Shanklin responded. "Some pretty powerful Mafia figures met an untimely and violent end just before they were to testify before the recent House Select Committee on Assassinations. Think about it. You may wish to put your family in harm's way nosing around the Mafia role in this. But, I'm not."

Harold spoke for the first time. "So, you want me to tell Congresswoman Boggs that this is your response to her personal request for help on this investigation?"

"Ryan," Shanklin snapped. "I don't give a damn what you tell the gentle lady from Louisiana. I've opened the door for you to a treasure trove of information. It's up to you to get off your lazy ass and make something of it. I'll not hold your hand. You can tell Boggs that, too."

The line went dead.

***

Mike chuckled as he put the receiver back on the phone base.

"I guess former Agent Shanklin failed the rookie agent's class in common courtesy."

"Arrogant son-of-a-bitch," Harold muttered, not under his breath.

"Now, dear," Lillian cautioned. "Didn't he give you some good leads?"

"Yes, he did, dear," Harold admitted to his wife. "But he was such a condescending ass. It's hard to credit him for it."

Mike wanted to move on. "We ought to ask Lindy to call our insider friend, George. The information Shanklin provided us is probably beyond the reach of our research. In all the reading I've done, I've never even come across a reference to Angleton, the 'Crow' or a Driscoll. Have you heard anything about them, Harold?"

"Not a single reference," Harold responded. "But I think our informant George would know about them if there is anything to know."

Without comment, Harold picked up the phone in front of him and got an outside line. In short order, Mable from the Congresswoman's office in Washington had asked and received a confirmation from Boggs. She would try to arrange another meeting for them with George.

"Excuse the interruption, everyone," Harold said. "It's over. Now can we get back to our other work?"

"Easy, dear," Lillian cautioned. "There are no enemies at this table. So, please don't act like Agent Shanklin toward us."

"I think that's a gotcha', Judge," Mike chuckled.

Harold had to smile too. "You're right Lillian," he admitted. "I'm sorry everyone. Now, can we get back to work?"

Joe, who had been sitting quietly, offered a suggestion.

"Mike, I've read the Edward Luttwak material you gave us describing a coup d'état. Having done that, every time you talk about people who opposed the Kennedy agenda, I keep trying to fit them all into my vision of a coup.

"So, I'd like to talk some about the elements of a coup. It would help me," he went on, "if we sort of set up a framework to help those who read this report better understand these folks, their motives and actions. Then, everyone might better see how Kennedy's opponents potentially fit into the bigger picture of a true coup d'état."

"How would you suggest we start that discussion, Joe?" Mike asked.

"By first clearly reminding the reader that,

"If two or more individuals agreed to take action for the purpose of killing President Kennedy, and at least one of them took action in the furtherance of that plan and it resulted in the murder of the president, he would have been killed as a result of a conspiracy.

"In your report for the House Judiciary Committee submitted twelve years ago, you clearly proved the existence of a conspiracy. You concluded then: "*There was more than one assassin involved in the killing of President Kennedy on November twenty-second, 1963.*"

"Then, just last year, the House Select Committee on Assassinations agreed with your conclusion when they concluded that: "*On the basis of evidence presented to it, President Kennedy was probably assassinated as a result of a conspiracy.*"

"Now we must ask if that conspiracy was part of a coup d'état. It seems to me we must remind the readers of your report that a coup d'état is always a conspiracy, but a conspiracy is not always a coup d'état."

"Why should that distinction be of interest to us, Joe?" Marilyn asked.

Joe Yager was quick to respond. "All we have on the table at this point is that there was a conspiracy to kill President Kennedy. Both the FBI Report of December 1963 and the Warren Commission Report of September 1964 had it wrong. It was not just the act of one lone assassin. That has been proven.

"But just because the success of the conspiracy resulted in a change of government, it doesn't mean it was a cleverly planned and concealed action to achieve that change of government. We have yet to prove that."

Harold interjected. "So, that's why you want to look at the elements of a coup d'état in light of what happened in Dallas on November twenty-second, 1963 and in the days following?"

"Exactly," Joe stated emphatically. "It's like that old saying about a duck."

"You mean if it walks like a duck and quacks like a duck and looks like a duck, it probably is a duck?"

"You got it, Lillian," Joe told her.

Harold began. "As I recall from Luttwak's book, *Coup d'État: A Practical Handbook*, conspirators must be provided the opportunity and means to carry out their plan.

"Earlier in 1963, the president had a motorcade scheduled in Chicago and another in Miami. Both were canceled due to security issues. A motorcade in Tampa, Florida was severely altered because of security concerns, too. Planned motorcades in each of four Texas cities, all with tall buildings, would seem to have provided the next possible opportunities to shoot the president."

Marilyn asked, "So, you're saying that the downtown Tampa motorcade was changed so much that it took away the opportunity to shoot the president?"

"That's correct," Harold confirmed.

Marilyn continued, "So, to create the proper opportunity, it was important to the success of the conspirators' plan that similar security measures not be taken in one of the Texas cities?"

"Correct again, Marilyn," Joe said.

"Was there any other condition that would be needed, aside from lax security?" Lillian asked.

"Things like, the route taken by the president's limo past tall downtown buildings, and the speed at which the vehicle traveled during the parade, would have a bearing on any plan to murder the president."

"You're saying that the slower the vehicle traveled past tall buildings, the greater the probability that skilled shooters would be able to successfully kill the president, right?"

"Well put, Marilyn," Mike answered. "You're correct, of course."

Marilyn continued. "Crap! If I can figure that out, why wouldn't trained people whose job is to protect our leaders know that, too?"

"They knew that, but on November twenty-second, 1963 they fell down on the job," Mike told everyone.

"So, the parades in San Antonio, Houston and Fort Worth were evidently well secured. That left Dallas as the last chance."

"It would seem so, Mike."

"Since the assassination succeeded in Dallas, we can conclude the Secret Service people failed to do so there," Joe stated.

"I assume a bunch of them lost their jobs over it," Lillian said.

Harold said, "We'll get into the lax security of the Dallas visit in the final report. But to answer you, Lillian, no one lost his position or was even reprimanded."

"That's enough to pee off a saint," Marilyn spat.

"The next element is, 'means,'" Mike added.

"How does 'means' differ from 'opportunity?'" Lillian asked.

"Not much," Harold informed his wife. "Actually, we could have been talking about means a moment ago when we discussed the motorcade's speed, tall buildings and such."

"In addition, Lillian," Mike added, "Luttwak insists that to be successful, the plan must be executed quickly from the moment of the killing to the transfer of power."

"Before we leave this point, let's look at the timeline of events in Dallas on November twenty-second," Joe suggested.

"President Kennedy received a fatal shot to the head at approximately twelve twenty-five local time. He was rushed to Parkland Hospital and declared officially dead at one o'clock local time. Lyndon Johnson was taken to Love Field and given the oath of office aboard Air Force One at three o'clock.

"That same afternoon, Lee Harvey Oswald was arrested just seventy minutes after Kennedy was shot. It was announced by Dallas County District Attorney Henry Wade later the same day that the president had been the victim of a conspiracy. But shortly after Oswald had been killed, Wade declared that Oswald was the killer of President John Kennedy.

"So, the world was told that a suspect had been arrested for the killing of President Kennedy at about the same time the new president was sworn in."

"Right," Mike said. "Then the evidence needed to be controlled. Toward that end, the body of the murdered president was taken from Parkland Hospital at gunpoint by Secret Service agents, thus preventing the legally required autopsy from being performed in Texas. They also took his clothing. All of this happened by the time the vice president was sworn in at three o'clock.

"So, the initial requirements for a successfully carried out coup were accomplished: the target killed, a killer identified and apprehended quickly, a plausible successor put in place of the murdered head of state and the critical evidence controlled. Did I cover that stage completely, Harold?"

"I think so, Mike," Harold said. "The second requirement is to obtain the support of the key elites in the government power structure before any opposition develops. Toward that end, while on the flight to Washington, the new president was on the phone to Kennedy's cabinet members and other government elites.

"In that latter group, LBJ contacted FBI Director Hoover, Chairman of the Joint Chiefs of Staff General Maxwell Taylor, and the director of the CIA, John McCone. All of them agreed to stay on in the new administration for the time being. Even Kennedy's inner circle of aides agreed to stay on.

"This not only assured the public and the federal bureaucracy that the new president had the support of Kennedy's people, but gave the new regime time to solidify its control and put its agenda in place.

"While the new president was in the air traveling back to Washington, John F. Kennedy's office was ordered cleared out to allow Johnson to occupy it on Saturday. Jacqueline Kennedy would move out of the White House eleven days later.

"When the plane landed in Washington, Johnson would make a statement over national television with Mrs. Kennedy at his side."

Joe added, "It appeared to the nation that an acceptable, if sad, transition had taken place."

"Exactly," Marilyn said.

"I remember those events as though they happened yesterday," Lillian said. "I was heartbroken, of course, but I felt that the transition was proper; didn't you all?"

"Yes, I agree, Lillian," Joe said. "All that was needed then was to fix blame for the killing on someone who was outside of our government."

"Right, Joe," Mike said. "Carrying that further, we also needed our most respected law enforcement people, the FBI, to verify that finding."

"Hoover's FBI did just that," Mike continued his review. "Even before Air Force One carrying the new president had landed in Washington late on Friday, November twenty-second, the FBI took control of all available evidence.

"And, within forty-eight hours of the assassination, the accused shooter was killed on national television.

"Then, within two weeks of the assassination and the death of the accused, a formal FBI report was leaked to the press confirming that Oswald was the shooter and had acted alone. Case closed."

Harold added, "Still, many of my colleagues in Congress wanted to open investigations of their own. To prevent that, acting United States Attorney General Nicholas Katzenbach urged the president to appoint a blue ribbon panel commission to conduct a formal investigation. President Johnson did, thus preempting Congress and the Texas authorities from doing so.

"And from that point on FBI agents in Dallas were instructed to drop the investigation of all leads in the Oswald case and to stop cooperating with Dallas law enforcement people on the case. After all, the assassin had been arrested and was dead. The case had been solved.

"Even the investigation by the appointed Warren Commission had to depend upon the FBI for most all of its information. Most of the forensic evidence had been quickly collected by the Secret Service or the FBI. The body had been spirited out of Dallas before any proper autopsy had been performed. Once at Bethesda Hospital, a severely limited autopsy of sorts was conducted by military personnel and a national audience saw John Kennedy's body buried in Arlington Cemetery.

"The Argentine Mauser rifle found at the Book Depository by Dallas law enforcement people disappeared. Instead, an Italian rifle was declared the one used to kill President Kennedy. The only bullet in evidence was a nearly pristine shell found at Parkland Hospital in Dallas on a gurney.

"The president's limo parked outside of Parkland Hospital was washed down in Dallas by Secret Service agents driven to Love Field and immediately flown to a garage in Washington. While it was there, the blood stained carpet was replaced. From there a President Johnson staff member ordered it sent to a Ford Motor

Company facility for the replacement of the windshield that had a bullet hole and a complete makeover of the rest of the vehicle."

"So," Marilyn concluded, "you are saying that not only was all the forensic evidence scooped up by the Secret Service and the FBI, but the bullets that struck the president in Dallas are still hidden in his body."

"That's correct," Mike agreed. "The bullet that entered his throat, as well as the one that hit him in the back, were never recovered from his body. And the projectile that hit him in the head exploded on contact. So, those fragments are still in the body, too."

"It would appear that all evidence of the crime was placed under the control of the FBI. Thereafter, Chief Justice Warren placed a seal on most of the autopsy photographs and President Johnson hid most of the rest by executive order."

"Before we go any further, though," Joe cautioned, "I think we should take a look at Oswald's role in all of this. I remember one of the last things he shouted to reporters as he was walked through Dallas Police headquarters. He said he was a patsy."

"You think he was?" Mike asked.

"Who knows," Joe responded. "I surely don't know for sure. But some things don't add up."

"What doesn't add up, Joe?" Marilyn asked. "Don't you think he was involved in the shooting?"

"Of Officer Tippit, maybe," Joe said. "But how could he have shot Kennedy? Consider this. What we know for sure is that Oswald's boss Roy Truly and Marion Baker, a Dallas police officer, encountered him in the lunchroom on the second floor some ninety seconds after the final shot was fired.

"That means that after firing the third shot Oswald was supposed to have taken the time to chamber a round in his rifle, hide the weapon behind some boxes at the opposite side of the sixth floor, move to the nearby stairway, sprint down four flights of stairs, and get a cola out of the Coke machine before being approached by a policeman and his employer. How likely is all that?"

"I remember reading that Chief Justice Warren ran down those stairs from the sixth floor to the lunchroom within ninety seconds. So, how hard could it have been for a much younger guy like Oswald?" Lillian challenged.

"All right," Joe responded. "Let's say he could have done everything I said he did and still made it to the lunchroom in time to be seen by his boss and the policeman. The elevators were not working; one was under repair and the door to the second elevator was open on a different floor and therefore was not available to anyone on the sixth floor.

"So, Oswald had to use the stairs. How then, do you explain that two fellow employees, who were on the fourth-floor landing during this same period of time, never saw Oswald coming down the stairs?"

"Are you sure about this, Joe?" Marilyn asked.

"Afraid so, ladies," Joe assured them. "Victoria Adams and Sandra Styles were using the stairway after the last shot was fired. They swore that they didn't see anyone come down that stairway. Their testimony was simply ignored."

"Why weren't their sworn statements given more attention?" Marilyn asked.

Harold said, "Some contend that, because their testimony didn't fit the conclusion already reached their sworn statements were ignored or distorted. For a coup d'état to be successful it is necessary to identify and convict the assassin quickly, remember.

"So, in the case of the Kennedy assassination the door had to be closed quickly on even a suspicion that there were others involved. A quick investigation would assure the public that the assassination was the act of a lone gunman, not a conspiracy.

"Possibly that is why President Johnson called Parkland Hospital, and by identifying himself, got the switchboard operator to get him through to Dr. Clark. Clark was in an operating room working to save Oswald's life. The president asked him if Oswald had given a deathbed confession.

"But if Oswald was not the lone assassin then, who did the shooting? Conspirators could not allow the public to wonder about this. Nor could they allow a long and drawn-out investigation during which they might lose control of the story. On the contrary, the murder had to be solved quickly.

"Immediately after the assassination, Dallas District Attorney Henry Wade declared the killing a result of a conspiracy involving multiple assassins. But two days later, right after Oswald was killed, he declared Oswald to be the lone killer of the president.

"Mrs. Carolyn Walther was standing across the street from the Book Depository on November twenty-second. She reported that she saw a man in a sixth floor window pointing a rifle at the motorcade. She described the man aiming the rifle as having blond hair and wearing a white shirt. A second man, she said, was standing alongside him. She gave her testimony to the Dallas authorities. But she was never called by the Warren Commission nor was her sworn statement investigated.

"In a telephone conversation with Secret Service Agent Forest Sorrels ten hours after the assassination, Secret Service agent Jerry Behn in Washington said:

"It's a plot," Behn said.

"Of course," Sorrels agreed.

"But later, Behn told the Oral History folks at the JFK Library in 1976 that the Warren Commission got it right; single shooter and no conspiracy.

"I remember Prouty telling us about all the changes in the story, Harold," Mike said. "But there were still some doubts expressed. Five days after the assassination, in a front page editorial, the editor of the New York Times apologized to his readers for having called Oswald the president's assassin before it had been satisfactorily proven," Mike reported.

"Wait a minute," Lillian insisted. "I also remember the Warren Commission announcing that Oswald's fingerprints were on the mail-order weapon that was used to kill the president."

"That is what they first reported to us, Lillian," Harold said. "It was later admitted that none of Oswald's fingerprints were on the rifle; only his palm print, on the underside of the barrel itself. In addition, the paraffin test the Dallas police administered on his skin showed no residue on his cheek, when there should have been if he'd fired a rifle."

Mike added, "Concerning that Italian-made Mannlicher-Carcano rifle, several local law enforcement people who were familiar with weapons swore they found an Argentine Mauser rifle on November twenty-second, hidden on the sixth floor of the Book Depository, not an Italian-made rifle.

"District Attorney Wade held up the Mauser they found that day for all to see at a press conference held the same afternoon. That Argentine Mauser soon mysteriously disappeared and Oswald's Italian-made rifle took its place as the murder weapon.

"Another sticky point," Mike continued. "In their final report the Warren Commission stated that the Washington autopsy showed the kill shot to the president's head was caused by a high velocity bullet which was designed to shatter on impact. What they didn't reveal was that the Italian-made rifle Oswald was supposed to have used could not fire a high velocity bullet."

"When the bullets were taken out of Kennedy's body during the official autopsy wouldn't that mix-up have been discovered?" Lillian asked.

"Yes it could have been, dear," Harold agreed. "But there was no such autopsy. Texas law required such an examination in gunshot deaths. But the Secret Service guys took the president's body at gunpoint from Parkland Hospital before the legally required autopsy could be performed there.

"Later that night, during an autopsy of sorts performed at Washington's Bethesda Hospital, one bullet was retrieved from the president's coffin. It was immediately given to Admiral Burkley, who was present in the room. He gave it to an FBI agent who was also present at the scene. That agent gave the admiral a signed receipt for it. Unfortunately, that bullet was never seen again."

"Other than that," Mike added, "there was a bullet found on a gurney at Parkland Hospital. The man who found it there claimed it was from the gurney used for President Kennedy. Arlen Specter needed it to have come from Governor Connally's gurney, thus supporting his 'magic bullet' theory. The Commission members ignored the fact that the bullet which hit the governor's body left most of it in fragments still in his body.

"In either case, it has been dubbed the 'pristine bullet,' because it shows almost no sign of having hit anything or leaving any fragments behind. It was claimed to have been fired from the Italian-made Mannlicher-Carcano rifle supposedly owned by Oswald.

"The doctors who worked on Connally said that they left whatever remained of the bullet in his leg. So, we'll never really know the weapon from which it was fired, either."

"Isn't all this monkey business called impeding justice or something?" Lillian asked.

"I think you mean obstruction of justice, Lillian," Harold told his wife.

"Yes. That's exactly what I meant."

Joe spoke up at this point. "Just so you all know," he said, "the report you and Marilyn wrote back in 1967 proved that Oswald didn't act alone; the killing of Kennedy was a conspiracy which involved more than one assassin."

"Joe's right," Mike said. "Let's not get hung up on whether or not Oswald fired at the president on November twenty-second, 1963. He could very well have been part of the conspiracy after all."

"Right, Mike," Joe stated. "When I think of your report, I'm reminded of the quote you used from a St. Louis Post article of December first, 1963, written by Richard Dudman."

"The question that suggests itself is: How could the President have been shot in the front from the back?"

"Following that line of reasoning, all you proved in your earlier report was that more than one assassin had to have been involved; you didn't get into who might have been the assassins or why Kennedy was the target of assassins."

"That's right, Joe," Marilyn assured everyone. "That was all we were asked to do."

"I didn't mean my comment as a criticism, Marylyn. It was just a statement of fact."

"No offense was taken, Joseph."

***

"I suggest we move on to a discussion of the nature of a coup d'état," Joe suggested.

"First, let's list where we stand on identifying evidence of a coup.

1. President Kennedy's motorcade was required to use a route in Dallas that violated both basic security considerations and established Secret Service protocol. It placed JFK in a kill zone. (Thus, was opportunity established.)

2. The President of the United States was killed while traveling in that danger zone.

3. Contrary to established security protocol, the vice president traveled in the same parade as the president. So, he was on hand and was available to assume the presidency on the spot within two hours of Kennedy's death. The entire world saw

the photo of Johnson taking an unnecessary oath of office (He was already president of the United States as soon as JFK was declared dead) in the presence of President Kennedy's widow. (This established legitimacy in the public mind.)

4. On the day of the assassination, the dead president's body, all other forensic evidence as well as tape recordings of doctors giving early wound directionality evidence was taken out of Dallas by the Secret Service within hours of the assassination. (Control the evidence.)

5. A suspect was arrested within seventy minutes of the shooting. Within twenty four hours he was declared guilty as the sole assassin. (Establish blame on someone from outside of the government.)

6. A quorum of the Kennedy cabinet was in the air traveling to Japan and thus could not oppose or question the transfer of power. Likewise, the large number of federal employees subject to the cabinet leader's orders was temporarily cut off from their leadership and thus rendered powerless to oppose or even question the transfer of authority to Lyndon Johnson. (Gain the support of government elites and the bureaucracy for the new leadership.)"

Joe continued. "In addition, there were other factors which would lead an impartial investigator to believe it was a coup d'état, such as:

1. Potential opposition from government elites was avoided by the new president when he sent signals that the Kennedy agenda would be scrapped or ignored, and the status quo circa 1960 restored.

2. Within hours of the assassination, every member of the Kennedy cabinet agreed to serve in the new administration.

3. The new president moved into the Oval Office within twenty-four hours of the assassination.

4. The arrested suspect was murdered within forty-eight hours of his capture.

5. All evidence of a conspiracy was immediately controlled by federal government officials.

6. To preclude any other investigation of the crime, a prestigious panel was named to control the investigation and evidence of the assassination.

"Did I overlook anything?" Joe asked.

"I don't think so," Harold told everyone. "Does anyone else think of something we missed?"

Marilyn said, "I think somewhere we ought to go down the list of Kennedy's foreign policy agenda and domestic policy initiatives that were going to be either ignored or rescinded.

"That sounds sensible," Mike said. "But we have to first see if the assassination and the events of the following few days thereafter justify calling it a coup d'état."

Joe suggested, "Let's use Luttwak's study as a guide. He suggests in his book, *The Elements of a Coup d'État*,' Joe continued, "that a coup is initiated from within the state itself and must be guided by two principal considerations:

The need to seize the chain of command of the state quickly from the political leadership it wishes to replace, and;

The need to use this chain of command to quickly consolidate its own power and position within the state."

Joe continued. "Both of these elements were achieved with the swearing in of Lyndon Johnson on Air Force One at Love Field in Dallas the afternoon of November twenty-second, 1963 and by his subsequent actions," Joe contended.

"We have already seen that the Kennedy agenda promised to establish a new status quo, which in the opinion of the elites in the administration would seriously threaten national security. It was also an agenda opposed by corporate America, the international banking system elites and criminal elements in the United States."

"To thwart this agenda and return to the status quo of 1960, it was decided by the leaders representing these factions in America that the only way to prevent Kennedy of winning a second term was to assassinate him. Once that decision was made, an opportunity was sought to accomplish this act in 1963.

Opportunity/Means

1. The president scheduled campaign trips to several major cities in the fall of 1963: Chicago, Miami and Tampa. Each involved a motorcade.

2. The president was also urged to schedule a campaign trip in the fall of 1963 to Texas, a state that was arguably crucial to his reelection. During that trip he was

committed to speeches in four cities and to be in a motorcade through each of those cities: Houston, Fort Worth, San Antonio and Dallas.

3. The site for the president's luncheon speech in Dallas was a matter of debate.

a. The president's advance man Jerry Bruno wanted the Woman's Building, Governor Connally wanted the Trade Mart for the president's luncheon speech.

b. The Secret Service said neither route to the two sites would be a security problem.

c. To please the Texas governor, he was allowed to choose the site. The Trade Mart site was chosen. It required that the parade route turn off Main to Houston Street and then turn on to Elm Street and drive past the Book Depository Building.

4. This route required that the presidential limo slow to less than eleven miles per hour in order to make each of the two sharp turns.

5. Dallas Chief of Police Curry drove Secret Service advance man Forrest Sorrels, who approved the route, and Secret Service agent Winston Lawson, who was in charge of the parade itself, on a test drive over the proposed parade route. Experiencing the sharp turns required and seeing the over twenty thousand windows in the multi-story buildings along the route, Agent Lawson commented at that time: *"Hell, we'd be sitting ducks here."* (William Manchester: *The Death of a President*)

6. Members of the Warren Commission and the members of the House Select Committee on Assassinations agreed on one thing. They both concluded that Secret Service security measures were very lax in Dallas and therefore contributed to the success of the Kennedy assassination.

a. On November 22 at Love Field, Secret Service agent Lawson made adjustments to the parade security of President Kennedy:

1. General McHugh, the president's military advisor, usually rode in the front seat between the driver and the Secret Service agent in charge. Agent Lawson moved the general to a vehicle in the rear of the motorcade.

2. The Dallas Police Department offered six motorcycle escorts to flank the presidential vehicle, as had been provided for the motorcades in the other Texas cities. Agent Lawson reduced that protection to two motorcycle policemen and stationed them at the rear of that vehicle. An additional two motorcycles were

stationed at the rear of the motorcade, too far away to be of any assistance should trouble arise at the front of the parade where the president's limo was placed.

a. The press vehicle usually was placed in front or right behind the presidential limousine so members of the press could film and photograph the event. In Dallas on November 22, it was moved to an isolated position at the end of the motorcade and was thus unable to properly record the parade.

b. At Love Field Agent Rogers was in charge of agents in the motorcade. He ordered agents away from their customary positions on the rear bumper and alongside the president's vehicle, thus leaving it exposed.

7. According to Secret Service protocol, when sharp turns are necessary during a motorcade, the street corner involved must be secured.

a. Neither the corner at Houston and Main nor the corner at Houston and Elm was secured.

8. When multi-storied buildings flank a motorcade route, all windows were required to be closed and under observation during a motorcade.

a. Windows along the parade route in Dallas on November 22 were not required to be closed during the motorcade.

b. Windows along the parade route in Dallas on November 22 were not under observation during the parade.

9. When an area like Dealey Plaza's Grassy Knoll flanks a motorcade route, the area is supposed to be secured and policed by security personnel.

a. According to Agent Lawson's Warren Commission testimony, the Grassy Knoll was not secured. No Secret Service agents were assigned to it because Lawson said he had all available agents in the motorcade.

10. When a motorcade must pass under an overpass such as the one on the Dallas parade route, protocol required that it must be cleared of people and policed by security personnel. Instead,

a. The overpass on Elm Street was crowded with onlookers during the parade.

b. It was not secured by law enforcement personnel.

11. During any presidential visit, it was customary to use all available law enforcement and security personnel available to secure the safety of the president.

a. The Dallas FBI station chief offered the assistance of all forty-plus agents to the Secret Service to help secure the president's visit. The offer was refused on the grounds that the additional personnel were not needed.

b. The Dallas County Sheriff was told that additional personnel were not needed to secure the parade route for the president's visit. As a result, a group of over one hundred deputies stood along the parade route, just watching the motorcade pass by. Not one of these trained persons was asked to scan for open windows of buildings along the route.

c. The Dallas Police were told to end their security duties at the corner of Houston and Main, and that the Secret Service would take it from there.

d. Army Counterintelligence units were available at Fort Sam Houston in Texas. These were the 316th Field Detachment and the 112th Military Intelligence Groups. The personnel of these units were offered to assist in assuring the security of the president for the Dallas parade. The Secret Service refused their assistance.

In testimony before the Warren Commission, Agent Lawson replied to a question of why building windows along the parade route were not closed and under observation during the motorcade:

"It was not customary that we would do that for such a motorcade."

12. During a motorcade the standard speed of forty miles per hour was required by Secret Service protocol.

But, because of the sharp turn required of each vehicle in the motorcade from Main onto Houston, the president's limo had to slow to eleven miles per hour. Within several hundred yards another sharp turn was required, this time on to Elm Street from Houston. This meant that the vehicle had to slow once again to less than eleven miles per hour as it passed the unsecured six-story Book Depository Building."

"Is that pretty much it, Joe?" Harold asked.

"I think so," he responded. "If your girls can get that typed up and copied, Mike, we can review it the next time we meet."

"I think so, Joe," Mike assured him.

"So," Lillian added, "the opportunity to kill the president appears to have been assured. Once this was accomplished, you're saying that the means would not have been difficult to bring to that location?"

"Exactly, Lillian," Joe said.

Washington, D.C.

Once again Harold and Mike met their insider in a Willard Hotel conference room.

"Congresswoman Boggs suggested that your request was critical. Have you discovered something only I can help you with?" George said.

"We think so, George," Mike responded. "In all the reading Harold and I have done in the last month, and even in our report for the House Judiciary back in 1967, we have never come across even a passing comment or reference about an assassination operation put together by James J. Angleton, the CIA Director of Counterintelligence. Did one exist? And if so, what can you tell us about it?"

"People from various department of the administration began to meet and share their concerns about Kennedy and his agenda," George began.

"When did this group begin to meet?" Harold asked.

"Members of the administration in every department of the federal government met and still meet all the time to discuss the president's agenda, in light of domestic and foreign policy matters," George responded. "There was nothing unusual about that; only the purpose of this particular group was different."

Harold asked. "I had heard that some unnamed government people were concerned about Kennedy's sex life. Was that what motivated them?"

"Not from a moral perspective," George said. "It's true that after the Truman and Eisenhower years, they held a somewhat puritanical expectation for a president of the United States. But in this case, what actually troubled them was the potential for leaks of sensitive information to the women Kennedy met with."

"Is that all that motivated them, then?"

"Actually, Mr. Burke," George said. "The impetus for the gathering was over a much more serious matter than what the president did with his private parts or the pillow talk that might have been involved. What drove these men to meet was the traitorous activity they felt was going on in the Oval Office by the President of the United States.

"At this point, gentlemen, let me pause to explain something," George said. "Issues we have discussed and information I have given you during our previous meetings have been recorded and made available to my superiors."

"What the hell!" Burke exclaimed, pounding his palm on the table. "Next, are you going to tell us that our rooms here at the Willard are bugged too?" Mike was remembering the conversations he and Marilyn shared during their lovemaking.

"Yes, they are; so are your phones," George revealed. "At least those in Washington are tapped."

"Damn it to hell!" Burke said.

George went on. "When are you two going to realize that your investigation touches on very explosive issues? And, that there are still some important people in and out of Washington who could be seriously hurt by possible revelations. Even the budgets of entire government departments could be compromised as well. I hinted at this sensitivity when your wives were in town a few weeks ago."

Harold remained outwardly calm and just stared at George.

"Where do we go from here, George?" he asked quietly.

"As I told you the last time we met, Congressman," George responded, "I can leave and end our conversations, or you can control your emotions and we can continue. It's your call, Congressman."

Harold was quick to respond. "I'm not leaving and I hope you don't either. What about you, Mike?"

"In for a penny, in for a pound," Mike snapped. "What the hell; I'm not leaving either."

"Till now, I've told you nothing that has not been reported in the conspiracy press or known among assassination researchers. The operation you are asking me about now, however, is a different kettle of fish.

"I believe that you are reading into this Angleton thing more than is warranted."

"Would you tell us that even if your colleagues were not listening in?" Mike asked angrily.

"I can only tell you what I know to be true. You asked me here today to verify or deny something. I can't help it if you don't like my answer, Mr. Burke."

"So, what is this business of traitorous activity in the Oval Office?" Harold asked.

"John Kennedy believed the people over at Defense misled him during his campaign for the presidency. He felt they continued to do so in order to convince him to authorize the Bay of Pigs invasion. To compound his distrust, he believed the information and analysis provided by the CIA and State had proven unreliable right up to and including the Cuban Missile Crisis, the Berlin confrontation and the discussions preceding the Nuclear Test Ban Treaty issue.

"So, Kennedy decided to go around the whole lot a' them."

"How did he manage that, and with whom?" Mike asked.

"You might remember we talked about the contact Kennedy made with Soviet Premier Khrushchev during the Cuban Missile Crisis. His press secretary Pierre Salinger gave personal messages from Kennedy to a KGB agent assigned to the Soviet embassy in Washington. That agent sent them directly to Khrushchev.

"Kennedy simply continued using that method," George continued.

"It appeared that James J. Angleton the Chief of the CIA's Counterintelligence Department received regular information from a mole he had in the Soviet government. On one occasion he received information from that mole that turned out to be a copy of a highly secret CIA briefing paper. It was actually a Daily Intelligence Report. This convinced Angleton that he had a mole in the CIA leaking information to the Soviets."

"How possible was that?" Harold asked.

"In the fierce 1963 atmosphere of the Cold War it is not only possible, it was likely. At least Angleton thought so."

"What did he discover?"

"Despite conducting a serious internal examination, Angleton was unable to discover any leak within the CIA," George reported. "A solution was suggested by Robert Crowley, one of Angleton's colleagues. He suggested adding a unique addendum or code to each of the daily briefing papers given out. Thus, when the

Soviet mole sent Angleton information in the future, the source could be identified."

"I assume it worked," Harold said.

"In December 1962, Angleton identified the person who leaked the briefing papers," George revealed. "It was Bobby Kennedy, the Attorney General."

"Which meant the president was authorizing his brother to give our enemies, the Soviets, highly sensitive information, I assume?" Mike concluded.

"Exactly," George said. "Angleton's trap had determined that President Kennedy was the one committing a treasonous act."

"Since the President didn't trust the CIA, maybe he was using the Soviets to verify the intelligence the CIA and the Department of Defense people gave him."

"You could look at it that way, Mr. Burke. But Angleton and his colleagues still considered what the president was doing to be treasonous. Phone taps on the phones of the Attorney General revealed conversations with Soviet contacts, too."

Harold Ryan took the conversation to the next obvious level.

"Was it at this time that Angleton brought in others who were also alarmed with the Kennedy agenda?" he asked.

"It would seem so, Congressman," George admitted. "Angleton pulled together a group representing the FBI, the Joint Chiefs, State, Defense and the office of the vice president. He apprised them of the situation and sought advice on how to stop it."

"Even the vice president was informed?" Burke asked.

"My information reveals that Abe Fortas was involved, so, I assume Vice President Johnson knew about the problem and the agenda discussed by the group Angleton formed."

"Hoover too, it would appear?"

"William Sullivan attended meetings. I am sure he would not have if Hoover had not authorized it."

"Did anyone have a sit down with the president, cautioning him about the danger of sharing top secret documents with the Soviets?" Burke asked.

"Not that I am aware of."

"What did all those who knew of this problem and attended these meetings decide to do about it?" Harold asked.

"To my knowledge," George revealed, "it was decided to modify the briefings given the president so as to not reveal sensitive information."

"Wow!" Mike exclaimed. "To have the President of the United States cut off from intelligence from his own CIA, Defense and State Departments is stunning."

"A bit of history might help, Mr. Burke," George offered. "In 1941, just before the attack on Pearl Harbor, Army and Navy Intelligence stopped giving President Roosevelt accurate reports because they didn't trust the people in his inner circle of advisors.

"I'm not suggesting that it's right to withhold sensitive information from our chief of state only that it has been done before. Kennedy wasn't the first president who wasn't trusted with sensitive material."

"Remember, Harold," Mike said, "Colonel Prouty told us that in 1963 JFK received one set of briefings on the situation in Vietnam, and LBJ a different one."

"So," Harold responded, "that might explain why the president and his inner circle of advisors received an optimistic appraisal of what was going on in Vietnam while the vice president and the Joint Chiefs were receiving quite the opposite information; presumably less optimistic."

"That's exactly what happened, Congressman. The president and his people received doctored briefings."

"Was any other action initiated by this group?" Mike asked.

"Not that I know of, Mr. Burke."

"Prouty told us about doctored reports on conditions in Vietnam. What about reports dealing with other foreign policy matters? Were they doctored too?"

"I can't answer for State, but if they came from the CIA or Defense, they were modified. Beginning in 1963, reports only contained information which would be of little use to the Soviets or contained misinformation the CIA wished them to have."

"Amazing," Harold said.

"What were they to do, gentlemen? They decided that impeachment was impractical and a leak to the press would be counterproductive because of Kennedy's popularity."

"They didn't decide to kill him then?"

"I suppose that would seem to be an option. But I don't have any solid information that would lead one to believe they chose to do that."

"Based on what you do know, though," Mike asked, "do you think those who were involved in Angleton's group would have stood by and done nothing even if they were aware of an assassination plot?"

"Mr. Burke," George began to reply, "most of the men involved in this had service records going back to World War II. Some had been OSS back then; some in the armed service. Others had been on the front lines, working for the United States in opposition to worldwide Soviet expansion. They were patriots of the first order. As for me, I came on board during the Korean War.

"In 1961, along comes John Kennedy," George continued. "He was a New England liberal who seemed to be getting cozy with our enemies. He had refused to grab victory at the Bay of Pigs, he had backed down over the insertion of missiles into Cuba, he had shown weakness in Laos, he was reducing the defense budget, he was threatening to dismantle our intelligence gathering agency, and now he was giving away our secrets to the Soviet Union. Shouldn't they have been alarmed?"

"So, this group had nothing to do with the assassination of President Kennedy?" Harold repeated.

"Not that I'm aware of, Congressman," George asserted. "But look at the two lists of President Kennedy's actions I gave you the last time we were together. His agenda alarmed more than just the national security people we've been talking about.

"The issues he addressed on the domestic front alone were threatening enough to the status quo to earn him a lot of opposition; even suggestions of assassination. Surely you're aware of threats from the Mafia.

"How about the angry Cuban exiles whose sons he abandoned on the beach in Cuba? Kennedy made some serious enemies in the banking community because he was hell bent on destroying the Federal Reserve. He had used the power of his office to force Big Steel to roll back their prices, despite our so-called free market economy. He was determined to reduce the defense budget by an annual amount that would have seriously challenged the nation's economy.

"And he alarmed many with his support for the racial agenda of school integration and the forced acceptance of Negroes in all walks of American life.

"Seems to me, gentlemen," George continued, "that Kennedy's agenda earned opposition from most every quarter of America's elites."

"Still, he was so popular with the voters that most everyone predicted his reelection in November 1964," Mike reminded the others.

"I believe that his expected reelection was what was most frightened those who opposed his agenda," George said emphatically. "With another four years in office he might have successfully implemented many deep changes and made them permanent. He was certain to try."

"That is what leads me to think," Harold interrupted, "the men who attended Angleton's meetings certainly had the means to stop Kennedy from being reelected if they chose to use them. All they needed was the opportunity."

"George," Mike asked. "You have told me that you have always given us straight answers. Right?"

"Correct, Mr. Burke," George said, smiling.

"Assume for a moment that you were involved in Angleton's high level meetings. The group had concluded that Kennedy's reelection was virtually assured. With that in mind you considered the future security of the United States seriously threatened. However reluctantly, would you not have supported a coup d'état?"

"I certainly would have, Mr. Burke."

"Can we assume that the men who made up Angleton's group believed, as you do, that Kennedy was a danger to the country?" Mike went on.

"That is a safe assumption, Mr. Burke," George responded.

"Surely then, they would have supported a coup d'état, too."

George took a deep breath and said, "I have already told you I have no firm information about Angleton's group being involved in the assassination of John Kennedy. But there were rumors which I have not shared with you."

"Why didn't you share them with us, George?" Harold asked.

"Because they were just that, Congressman, rumors. And I had promised you two that whatever I told you would be factual."

"Would you share those rumors with us now?" Mike asked.

There was silence in the conference room. All three men waited for someone else to talk.

George spoke first. "I will do so, Mr. Burke," George said. "Just remember that I do not have documentation to back up any of this; I cannot prove any of what I am about to tell you. With that understood, do you want me to proceed?"

Harold immediately said. "Yes, please proceed."

"Mr. Burke?" George asked.

"I understand the limitation you just put on what you are about to tell us. I still would like you to proceed."

"All right," George began. "Let me begin at the beginning. After James Angleton discovered that the president was passing sensitive information to the Soviets through his brother, the Attorney General, he contacted key people he knew at State, Defense, the FBI and the Defense Intelligence Agency.

"Thereafter, a representative from each of these centers of authority began to meet. The primary topic was how to stop this leak in the short run and the implementation of Kennedy's peace agenda in the long ruin.

"The members first agreed that Kennedy was likely to be reelected in 1964. And, they decided that his removal from office by impeachment was very unlikely. So, it was only at this point that the topic of assassination surfaced.

"Keep in mind that what I'm telling you is straight from the rumor mill. It was water-cooler talk at best."

"Rumor or not, George," Mike quipped. "You have my attention just the same."

"All right," George continued. "Where was I? Oh yes, how might removal by killing be accomplished was discussed next. One by one, the methods were reviewed and discarded like sabotaging Air Force One or poison added to his daily injections. The only method that seemed to hold up to their examination was shooting Kennedy with a high-powered rifle during a motorcade.

"None of those in the discussion group were willing to be directly involved in such an attempt. But the CIA had experience using Mafia assassins in their efforts to effect regime change in one place or another; like their attempts on Castro's life.

"So, Angleton contacted Sam Giancana, the organized crime Don in Chicago. Their discussion resulted in the contracting of three hit men from Corsica to kill Kennedy. These professional hit men were brought into the United States through Canada by way of Detroit in the late summer or early fall of 1963.

"It was that summer when the Texas governor and Vice President Johnson convinced JFK at a meeting in Corpus Christi, Texas that he needed to schedule a visit to Texas sometime that fall. There were other big city visits for him to make: in Chicago, Miami and Tampa. All presented chances to carry out the contract.

Harold asked, "With exposure in all those places, why was Dallas chosen to attempt the assassination?"

"The way I heard it, Congressman," George revealed, "it just turned out that way. A hit in Chicago was blown when word got out of the planned attack on the president. Miami and Tampa were not suitable opportunities for the same reason. With a four-city tour planned for Texas, Dallas seemed the ideal opportunity."

"Did you ever hear why it turned out that way?" Mike asked.

"It appears, Mr. Burke," George told him, "when the members of Angleton's group checked their files for contacts in Texas, a sometime CIA operative and Russian expatriate named George De Mohrenschildt. He identified an American who had recently returned from Russia, Lee Harvey Oswald. This man had been living with his Russian wife and child in Fort Worth, but had just moved to an apartment in Dallas.

"This De Mohrenschildt reported that a Mrs. Paine, another member of the Russian community in Dallas and a close friend of Marina Oswald, told Lee Oswald about a job opening at the Texas School Depository Building. He was subsequently interviewed and started working there on October fifteenth. He worked in their warehouse building located on Elm Street in Dallas."

"It appears, George, you're suggesting that a plan was then put in place to involve Oswald in an assassination attempt," Harold said.

"It would appear so," George agreed. "But remember, Mr. Burke, I don't know if any of this is true.

"Oswald was then turned over to a CIA operative whose code name was Maurice Bishop," George continued.

Harold added, "One of the investigators for the House Select Committee on Assassinations told us that one of his Cuban exile contacts, Antonio Veciana, saw Oswald and Bishop together in the fall of 1963 in New Orleans."

"That would have fit the timeline too, Congressman," George said.

"Wasn't Bishop's real name David Atlee Phillips?" Harold asked.

"These fellows used all sorts of aliases. So, it's hard for me to accurately pin that down. You could be right, though," George responded.

"One more thing," Mike said. "Would it have been possible for someone at the CIA to have printed agent identification badges, passes and such for the president's Secret Service detail at the time of the Kennedy assassination?"

"It would have been possible, Mr. Burke. They had that capability. In fact I believe a high ranking CIA employee, Dr. Sidney Gottlieb a poison expert actually, was head of the chemical division of the Technical Services Staff. He was called the 'Dirty Trickster.' His unit had the capability of printing badges and passes.

"I do know, for a fact though, that the Secret Service resumed printing their own credentials shortly after the Kennedy assassination.

"I regret to say that I've stayed as long as I dare. I hope I've been of some help"

The men stood as George made his way to the door of the conference room.

Harold asked. "Do you know of man in the CIA organization known as 'The Crow'?"

George stopped and asked a question of his own. "Why do you ask, Congressman?"

"It's just a name we were given by one of our contacts. He said this fellow might have had something to do with the assassination; behind the scenes of course."

"Mr. Robert Turnbull Crowley is the man's full name. He is the very powerful Director for Operations for the CIA," George said. "He could then and still can be behind anything he chooses."

"Was he involved?" Harold persisted.

"Mr. Crowley helped Angleton ferret out the source of those leaks to the Soviet Union. Whether or not he was involved beyond that I don't know. He had the means to facilitate most anything he chose, including assassination; he still does.

"Is there anything else, gentlemen?" George asked. Receiving no response, he left the room.

***

"Phew!" Mike exclaimed. "What do you think of that?"

"Pretty amazing," Harold responded. "I think the most startling thing he told us was that he firmly believes high ranking members of the CIA had the power to orchestrate an assassination of most anybody in the world they chose to eliminate; and that they still can.

"And all the while they would do that believing they were patriots, just protecting our country. Do you have any thoughts about how we might use what he told us, Mike?"

"I think we incorporate what he told us as a possibility," Mike responded. "After all, this is a private report for Congresswoman Boggs. She must know we're not going to come up with court-ready proof. She wants to know about motive and where it points. We've discovered plenty of motives for her."

"We do have that," Harold agreed.

"And, Harold," Mike said "what George told us points directly at people who had motive to kill the president and cause to celebrate his death of along with both his foreign policy and domestic agendas."

"Did what George told us pass your smell test, Mike?" Harold chuckled.

"Sure did," Mike insisted.

"Well, my friend," Harold concluded. "I don't know about you, but in my immediate future, I smell a cocktail and a good steak."

"What? No nap, Judge?"

"Don't get smart with me, kiddo. A man has to have his priorities straight. Right now it's a drink and a good steak. I'll just hit the sack early tonight."

Congresswoman Boggs' Office

Secret Service agent Winston Lawson entered the office at 9 A.M. sharp to keep his appointment with Harold Ryan.

A receptionist greeted him and asked. "Can I get you a coffee, sir?"

"That would be appreciated," he responded. "A dash of cream and two sugars, please."

"Not a problem."

With his coffee in hand he was shown into a conference room. Harold rose to greet his guest.

"Good morning Mr. Lawson," Harold said as they shook hands. "It is good of you to give me some of your time."

"I am happy to assist Congresswoman Boggs. She has been a friend of the Secret Service, as was her husband before her," he told Ryan. "So, how can I help you, Congressman?"

"Allow me to establish a few facts first, all right?"

"Fine."

"You had a hand in picking the route the motorcade took to the Trade Mart?"

"I was asked by Mr. Bruno if we could protect the president should the Trade Mart be chosen for his luncheon speech."

"And, you reported?"

"I told the decision makers that the Secret Service could ensure the president's safety on the route that we would have to take in order to reach the Trade Mark luncheon site within the time desired."

"I'll take that as a 'yes' answer. All right?" Harold said.

"If you wish," Lawson answered.

"Were you and the Dallas station chief Winston Sorrels driven over this route by Sherriff Curry before the decision was made to use the Trade Mart?"

"Yes, we were."

"It has been reported that you told Agent Sorrels at that time,

"*Hell, we'd be sitting ducks here.*'"

"Having made this assessment how could you have told the decision makers that President Kennedy would be safe if this route was chosen for the motorcade?"

"I don't recall saying anything of the sort," Lawson claimed.

"So, William Manchester in his book, *Killing of a President,* didn't quote you accurately?"

"I didn't say that."

"Hells bells Agent Lawson," Harold almost shouted. "Either you were quoted correctly or not. Which is it?"

Lawson paused for a moment. "I don't recall saying that about the route to the Trade Mart."

"Were you also responsible for the security arrangements of the motorcade?"

"Yes, I was."

"During your appearance before the Warren Commission you were asked why all the windows of the buildings along the route weren't closed, the overpass cleared of people and the Grassy Knoll secured. Is that true?"

"Yes, I was."

"I'm confused by your answers, Mr. Lawson."

"How so Congressman?"

"I have read that you responded to the questions on this matter in two ways. First you said that you were shorthanded. But then I read that you also told the Commission that such security measures were not customary. Which was it?"

"Actually, it was both," Lawson responded. "I was asked if there were Secret Service men on the Grassy Knoll as reported by several witnesses. I told the Commission that I did not have enough agents for that, they were all assigned to the motorcade.

"In response to a question about Secret Service protocol regarding open windows along a presidential motorcade, I said it was not customary for us to require that all windows be closed and under observation during any such parade."

"So, the six agents riding with Agent Roberts on the car following the president's vehicle could not have been spared?"

"I don't remember. That was a long time ago."

"When the president was in Miami earlier in the month of November, an assassination alert caused Captain Charles Sapp of Miami's Intelligence Bureau's assassination team to become involved. Word was that someone with a high powered rifle and scope would attempt to kill President Kennedy from a window in one of the tall buildings along the motorcade route. Captain Sapp said he notified both the FBI and the Secret Service of this threat on November 9th. Were you aware of this earlier threat?"

"No, I wasn't." Lawson insisted.

"How do you explain the testimony of Secret Service agent Mike Howard? He was in charge of security for the Fort Worth motorcade on November 21. He said that he made sure all windows along the parade route were closed and under observation."

"Was he just being a 'nervous Nellie,' Agent Lawson?

"You'll have to ask him, Congressman."

"Well Mr. Lawson, I did just that," Harold snapped. "Howard did not comment on the excuse you gave for not securing the parade route in Dallas. He did say though that he used local police and sheriff's deputies to augment his crew of agents.

"During the Eisenhower days, Colonel Prouty told us he had helped make the arrangements for several presidential visits to cities in this country and abroad. Parades were involved in many of those visits. He told us that it was protocol to ensure that all windows along the parade route were closed and under observation during motorcades. Has Secret Service protocol changed since then, or was the colonel lying?"

"All I know is," Lawson responded testily, "I did not have sufficient personnel to do all of that for the Dallas parade."

"If you were so shorthanded, why did you tell FBI Agent Shanklin, Director of the Dallas FBI office, that you didn't need the forty-plus FBI agents to help you secure the motorcade when he offered them?"

"I don't recall him offering us help or my telling him anything of the sort."

"He testified to the Warren Commission that you did."

"Well, he's mistaken."

"The Dallas County Sheriff testified to the Warren Commission that he had over one hundred deputies just standing in front of his office building watching the parade because you informed him that you didn't need the help of his deputies for security assignments."

"Now, why would I turn down the help of trained deputies when I was short-handed?"

"That is what I would like to know, Mr. Lawson. Why would you do that? These men gave sworn statements to the effect that their help was refused by you. Were they all lying?"

"I have no idea what was in their testimony."

"Agent Lawson," Ryan pressed. "Is it proper security to allow a vehicle carrying the President of the United States to pass under an unsecured street viaduct?

Lawson slumped in his chair. "No, it isn't," he admitted.

"Then why was the president's limo allowed to drive toward the viaduct over Elm Street when it was full of people watching the motorcade come toward them?"

"I didn't have sufficient security personnel to clear and secure that overpass, that's why," Lawson insisted.

"I remind you that an overpass in Fort Worth had been cleared and secured by security personnel just the day before. How did Agent Howard have enough security personnel and you didn't?"

"Ask Howard, Mr. Ryan."

"That won't cut it Lawson," Ryan slapped his open hand on the table. "Agent Howard in Fort Worth and the agents in charge at Houston and San Antonio all used local law enforcement personnel to augment their crew of Secret Service agents. You refused help.

"They all accepted help from the locals. You did not. We have proof that you were offered considerable help but you refused it. Why did you refuse help?"

"That was too long ago for me to remember." Lawson replied weakly

"Why did you move the police motorcycle escorts from traveling alongside the president's vehicle to the rear of his vehicle?"

"I moved them because the president requested they be moved to give the crowd a better view of him and the first lady. Also, he didn't like the noise."

"Are you aware that his aides and other Secret Service agent shave testified that he gave no such instructions? On the contrary, he repeatedly told them he trusted his Secret Service detail to do what they felt was necessary to protect him; that he wouldn't and didn't interfere in any way.

"Photographs of the Fort Worth motorcade of November 21 clearly showed motorcycle policemen riding alongside the presidential limousine. So, it was only in Dallas that President Kennedy wanted the motorcycle policemen moved to the rear?"

"It would seem so," Lawson protested.

Ryan continued to press. "You also moved his military aide, General McHugh from his normal position in the middle of the front seat to a position in the rear of the motorcade. Why did you do that?"

"Again, the president requested that I move his aide to give the public a better view of him."

"And again," Ryan snapped, "you must know that Kennedy's aides deny that he did or would have done that. He didn't in the other November motorcades, why Dallas."

"They weren't present at Love Field. I was."

"Of course, you were, Agent Lawson. Much to the Kennedy family's regret." Ryan said sarcastically.

"One more thing about the motorcade, Agent Lawson," Ryan said. "It was normal for the press flatbed trailer to be placed either right ahead or immediately behind the president's limo so they could photograph and film the event.

"In the Dallas motorcade, you placed their vehicle and trailer at the rear of the motorcade. Why did you make it impossible for the press to film or photograph the president and the crowd as they normally did?"

"You're implying there was something sinister involved in how I placed the press people. It was nothing of the sort. Actually, it was just one of those decisions a man in my position had to make; and I made it," Lawson insisted.

"I suppose you're aware that both the members of the Warren Commission and the members of the House Select Committee on Assassinations concluded that you did not do a proper job on November twenty-second, 1963; that you failed in your responsibility to protect the president of the United States."

"Yes, I am," Lawson admitted. "Your point being, Congressman?"

"My point being, Agent Lawson, is that after careful examination both investigating bodies judged all your excuses to be far from adequate to explain your failure that day.

"My point being is that history will mark you as the man who placed the president of the United States in a kill zone and then stripped him of all normal security. You will be remembered as the man who President John F. Kennedy trusted. You will be remembered, Agent Lawson, as the man who betrayed that trust.

"By the way, since you failed to protect President Kennedy, have you been asked by your superiors to supervise the security of any high-ranking federal or foreign official since November twenty-second, 1963?"

"I have been assigned other duties, Congressman," Lawson said testily.

Ryan smiled and said, "I'm not surprised, Agent Lawson." Then Ryan stood and opened the conference room door.

"Thank you for coming in today."

Ryan stood by the open door. He did not offer to shake Lawson's hand as the Secret Service agent left the room

***

Meanwhile, Mike Burke was in St. Petersburg, Florida to interview former Secret Service agent Roy Kellerman.

Burke had arrived too late in the afternoon to fly back to Washington. So, he had taken a room at the Vinoy Hotel in downtown St. Petersburg. The retired agent had agreed to meet him there for drinks and supper.

Mike was waiting in the hotel lobby. At the agreed upon time a hotel desk clerk approached and told him.

"Your guest is here, Mr. Burke."

Mike stood and greeted Roy Kellerman.

"Good evening Mr. Kellerman. Thank you for meeting me."

"It's my pleasure, Mr. Burke. It is a special treat to meet you for supper at this fine hotel. It is definitely not within my retirement budget."

"You are quite welcome," Mike said. "You can thank Congresswoman Boggs, who is funding this investigation. She's paying the tab for both of us."

"I'll remember to send her a thank-you card."

"Why don't we chat some over a cocktail before we order dinner?"

"That sounds good to me. Lead the way, Mr. Burke."

Once they were seated and a drink delivered to each of them, Mike asked, "You were in charge of the Kennedy presidential limousine detail, as I recall."

"Yes, I was. It was my first time in that role. I replaced Jerry Behn, who stayed in D.C. for this trip. I guess he needed a break from all the traveling the Kennedy detail had been doing that month."

"In that role, you would give orders to your fellow Secret Service agent, who drove the vehicle?"

"Yes, that would be part of my duties."

"There was usually someone riding between the driver and the agent in charge on other motorcades. Why wasn't there someone seated in that position during the Dallas parade?"

"I don't know, Mr. Burke," he answered. "Agent Lawson moved the president's military aide, General McHugh, from that position to somewhere in the rear of the motorcade. I heard him tell the general that the president wanted more exposure to the public."

"Is that the reason Lawson moved the motorcycle policemen from traveling alongside the vehicle to its rear?"

"That's what I was told."

"Why was that done in Dallas and not the motorcades in the other three Texas cities?"

"Agent Lawson gave the same reason, 'The president had requested they be moved because of the noise and because he wanted the crowd to have a better look at him and the first lady.'"

"Are you aware that since that time there has been a good deal of testimony that President Kennedy made no such request?"

"Yes, I have read that."

"Did you notice that the press vehicle normally ahead of or right behind the president's vehicle was also moved to the rear of the motorcade?"

"I was aware of that, Mr. Burke. But it didn't really register with me as something unusual."

"Agent Emory Roberts was in charge of the follow-up car," Burke continued. "He had six agents under his command. Why did he tell the agents he supervised not to take their normal positions on the rear of President Kennedy's vehicle?"

"I noticed that. But I don't know why he waved them off their normal positions."

"When interviewed by the Warren Commission people, he told them the president requested it."

Kellerman smiled. "I must admit Roberts' order didn't make any sense to me. Agents rode on the rear of the presidential limo all the time. When they did, they were not obstructing anyone's view of President Kennedy. So, I never did understand that change in procedure."

"It has been noticed that agent Roberts received a promotion to become a member of President Johnson's office staff shortly after the assassination. Do you find that strange?"

Kellerman paused a moment collecting his thoughts. "Are you suggesting that Roberts was rewarded for exposing President Kennedy to rifle fire from the rear?"

"I'm not suggesting anything; just stating the facts. After all, the FBI Report and the Warren Commission both stated that all the shots hitting the president came from the rear."

"Yes, that's what both reports concluded," Kellerman agreed.

"So, wouldn't it have been more difficult for a shooter to hit the president from the rear if Secret Service agents had been positioned on the rear bumper as they had been on earlier motorcades?"

"That's the purpose of positioning men there, Mr. Burke," Kellerman said.

A waiter approached. "Mr. Burke," he said, "your table is ready for you and your guest."

Burke interrupted their conversation.

"We can get back to our talk after we order."

Both men took their drinks and followed the waiter to a table.

"Looking at this menu," Kellerman said. "I see the Vinoy is featuring several delicious looking seafood entrees. "While you're in this area I suggest the grouper or the scallops. Both are gathered in the Bay area and are usually very good."

"Thanks," Mike said. "I'm from the Chesapeake area so I'm well acquainted with scallops. Grouper is new to me, so, I'll try that tonight."

"I'm sure you'll like it. I get seafood all the time, so, I think I'll have the T-bone steak."

Orders were placed and the two men returned to their conversation.

"Mr. Kellerman," Mike began.

"Please call my Roy, Mr. Burke."

"Fine, if you call me Mike," Burke urged. "Am I correct to believe your duties in the presidential vehicle included directing the driver as well as protecting the president riding behind you?"

"Both of those are pretty basic responsibilities."

"I read the testimony you gave the Warren Commission. You told the interviewer that you heard the president say, 'My God, I'm hit.' Is that correct, Roy?"

"Yes," Kellerman responded. "That is exactly what I heard him say."

"What did you do when you heard him say that?"

"I turned to look at him."

"Was that when he was seen to have raised his arms and placed his hands at his throat?"

"Yes, it was."

"A few cars back, on film taken that day show your colleague, Agent Youngblood, to be moving on top of the vice president by then. Why weren't you seen to be even rising from your seat to move toward the president?"

"After I took a look at the president, I turned back and told my driver, Bill Greer, 'We've been hit. Let's get out of line.'"

"But Greer put his foot on the brake instead, didn't he?"

"Yes, he did. Much later, I saw the Zapruder film, and the vehicle's tail lights brighten just before the kill shot hit the president's head. I can't understand why Greer slowed the vehicle. Maybe he didn't believe me.

"He later claimed to the Warren Commission people that he didn't apply the brake. But had Bill accelerated the vehicle when I shouted at him to do so, President Kennedy might still be alive today.

"Like I told that writer, Mr. Manchester, before accelerating the limo as I ordered, I saw Bill look back over his shoulder at the president.

"By that time though, two more shots were heard in quick succession, and it was too late. So, I concentrated on getting us to the hospital."

"At Parkland Hospital you had the vehicle hosed down," Mike reminded him. "Why did you do that?"

"Agent Emory Roberts told me to have it done."

"Was Roberts your superior?" Burke asked. "I thought Lawson was in charge of the agents in the motorcade."

"Technically he was, Mike. But in the confusion of the aftermath those lines were blurred. I just accepted his direction and did it. In retrospect, I know I shouldn't have touched that vehicle."

"Were you ordered to have the vehicle transported to the garage in Washington?"

"Yes, I was, sort of. I had a phone conversation with my boss, Jerry Behn, who was in Washington. We decided to take the limousine out of Dallas to Love Field, where the transport plane was parked. From there, we flew it to Andrews Air Base and from there to our garage on Twenty-second Street in Washington."

"Roy," Mike asked, "two Dallas motorcycle patrolmen observed a bullet hole in the limousine windshield when it was parked at Parkland Hospital. Did you see that hole, too?"

"Yes, there was a pencil sized hole in the windshield."

"I read a report by Charles Taylor about that windshield," Burke said.

"Yes, Mike," Kellerman said. "Chuck was on security duty in the Washington garage and wrote a report about his inspection of the limo."

"Right," Mike said. "He wrote that he examined a small hole just left of center in the windshield. There was nothing about that in the Warren Commission Report. What ever happened to that windshield?"

"After it got to our garage in D.C., the windshield and the bloody carpet were both replaced."

"Didn't that hole suggest a bullet came from the front?"

"I didn't examine it closely enough to tell. I'm pretty sure that forensic people could have determined if that hole came as a result of bullet hitting the windshield from the rear or the front of the vehicle. That's not my field, though."

Burke told Kellerman, "In the courtrooms I'm used to working in, replacing that windshield would be considered tampering with evidence and possibly obstruction of justice."

"All I know, Mike, is that someone from the White House ordered it replaced and the car cleaned up before we sent it to Ford Motor Company in Wixom, Michigan."

"What about the president's body? Why did you forcibly remove it from Parkland Hospital?"

"After President Kennedy was proclaimed dead, Roberts and Youngblood rushed Vice President Johnson out of the hospital. Johnson said he didn't want to leave Dallas without Mrs. Kennedy. He said that he would wait for her at Love Field.

"So, on the way out of the building Roberts ordered that Mrs. Kennedy not be left behind, but instead taken as soon as possible to Air Force One, waiting at Love Field. Our problem was, she wouldn't leave without her husband's body.

"Everyone was scared that the killing was part of a larger plot possibly involving the killing of the Vice President too. So, in that atmosphere, taking his body was the only way to get her to leave and thus to protect Johnson.

"When the Texas people objected to our removal of President Kennedy's body and tried to interfere, I drew my service revolver and threatened to shoot them if they tried to stop us."

"You also took the president's clothing; why?"

"It seemed like it was part of him, ya' know. So, I grabbed it too. Later I took it to the White House residence where I thought it belonged.

"It seemed like the thing to do, that was all."

"My information is that you stayed with the body until the autopsy was completed at Bethesda Hospital and during the embalming as well."

"Yes, I did. One strange thing I remember happened at the autopsy."

"What was that?"

"I was standing alongside one of the doctors, a Colonel Pierre Finck, when he examined the president's body for wounds. There was an entry wound below the president's right shoulder. The Colonel was inserting a probe when I said to him, *"Colonel, where did it (the bullet) go?"*

He responded, *"There are no lanes for an outlet of this entry in this man's shoulder."*

"Is that the same bullet that supposedly exited the president's throat and wounded Governor Connally?"

"One and the same, Mike," Kellerman said. "I told all of this to the people who interviewed me for the Warren Commission. How they could move that bullet over and up to come out the President's throat and then wound the Governor too, is beyond me."

"Me too, Roy," Mike agreed.

"Who ordered you to send President Kennedy's limo to Ford Motor?"

"We got a call from Bill Moyers, one of Johnson's aides."

"You do know, Roy," Mike reminded Kellerman, "that the House Select Committee on Assassinations said some harsh things about your performance in Dallas."

"I'm well aware of that, Mike," Kellerman admitted. "I have replayed events of that day a thousand times over in my mind. I'm not alone. It haunted Bill Greer so badly he had to take a medical retirement due to bleeding ulcers.

"What I wouldn't give to have those six seconds in Dallas back."

"One last question, Roy," Mike proposed.

"Sure. What is it?"

"Do you have any idea why all the normal motorcade security was absent in Dallas that day?"

Kellerman replied. "I flew into Fort Worth on November twenty-first," Kellerman told Mike. "I landed about eleven thirty that night and reported to Love Field around seven thirty the next morning. Agent Lawson was in charge there and was directing the line-up for the motorcade headed to Dallas.

"I heard him move the press people to the rear of the parade, the motorcycle policemen from alongside our vehicle to the rear bumper. He also took General McHugh out of his normal front seat position between me and my driver, Bill Greer. Each of these moves was unusual for a Kennedy motorcade."

"I heard that Agent Rogers ordered agents off their usual rear bumper riding position on the limo, too."

"In retrospect, Mike, I suppose those actions would appear to have stripped the president of his normal protection and completely exposed him to attack."

"Well ya'," Mike snapped. "Of course, it did. Why do you think Lawson and Rogers did this?"

"I see where you're going with this, Mike. But I can't believe either of them were part of a conspiracy to kill the president."

"Look at it from my perspective, Roy," Mike asked. "Lawson chose a route that both Sorrels and Sheriff Curry said made the president a sitting duck; their words, not mine.

"Then, the agent in charge of the parade, Lawson, stripped the president of all normal motorcade security. He also refused security help from local law enforcement and the FBI despite his testimony that he was shorthanded. What does that suggest?"

"It does seem suspicious, doesn't it?" Kellerman agreed.

Mike went on, "And then, after the first shot was fired, your order to Bill Greer to get out of there was ignored. Instead, he stepped on the vehicle's brake. As for yourself, you sat stone still, never moving to protect the president after you heard him exclaim that he was hit.

"How can these actions or lack of them be ignored?"

Kellerman sat quietly just looking down into his lap.

"That's what haunts me to this day," he finally whispered.

"Roy," Mike told his guest. "Your punishment is to live with that guilt."

After several moments Mike broke the silence at the table.

"Waiter, can I have the check please."

Washington, D.C.

The phone was ringing in a Willard Hotel room.

Harold Ryan picked up the phone. "Good afternoon," he said.

"Did I wake you, Judge?" Mike asked.

"I guess," Ryan asked somewhat groggy. "What time is it anyway?"

"It is three-thirty," Mike told him. "I've been sitting around for an hour just waiting. I didn't want to disturb your nap too early, don't ya' know."

"Good boy," Harold said. "I take it you just got in from Florida."

"Right," Mike told him. "My plane got in a couple of hours ago. Want to meet for a cocktail downstairs around four?"

"That sounds good. That'll give me time for a shower, too."

"See ya' then." Mike hung up the phone and called home.

Harper Woods

Marilyn Burke picked up the phone.

"The Burke residence," she said. "How can I help you?"

"Hi sweetheart," Mike began. "How ya' doing?"

"Fine," she answered, finding a chair to sit on. "How're you doing?"

"Just got back from St. Petersburg," Mike reported. "While I was there, I had a good interview with Roy Kellerman. I'm going to meet with Harold in a few for a drink at four and some supper after that."

"What a life you lead, Burke," Marilyn teased. "You caught me putting my feet up for the first time all day."

"What has kept you so busy?" Mike asked his wife.

"Fulfilling my wifely responsibilities is all."

"Like what?"

"I did wash this morning; had lunch with Cathy Yager and Lillian. We brought Cathy up to date on the report. Then I shopped for some new towels at the Eastland Mall. When I got home, I fixed a meat loaf. Then you called."

"Meat loaf!" Mike almost shouted into the phone. "That's my favorite. How could you fix meatloaf when I'm out of town?"

"If you're done throwing a hissy-fit, I'll tell you," Marilyn chuckled. "Are you calmed down now, little boy?"

"I'm calm."

"As we speak, my meat loaf is in the freezer preparing to wait until the master of the house returns."

"Oh," Mike said, thoroughly deflated.

"I'm waiting to hear an apology, buster."

"I'm sorry for my outburst. I lost my head for a moment," Mike said somberly.

"Not very enthusiastic, but I'll take it. When are you getting home?"

"Harold and I have one more interview to conduct. Then we plan to check in with the Congresswoman and get a plane out of here sometime late tomorrow or the next day at the very latest."

"Sounds good," Marilyn said. "The kids will be happy to see you."

"And what about their mother?" Mike asked. "Will she be happy to see their father, too?"

"Depends upon how thankful he is for my meat loaf dinner awaiting his arrival. I've gotten to like sleeping alone without someone snoring next to me. Undisturbed sleep is kind a' nice."

"You have definitely been left alone far too long," Mike responded. "I may get a flight and be home tonight."

"Promises, promises. All I get are promises. See you in a couple of days, big shot."

"Great. Love you." Mike said.

"Me too," Marilyn said in parting.

The Willard Hotel

Harold was waiting for Mike in the hotel lounge.

"I see you have your Manhattan already," Mike said, taking a stool next to his former boss.

"Of course," Harold responded. "I had no idea how long you were going to be on the phone so I went ahead. How's the family?"

"Everyone seems fine. Marilyn fixed a meat loaf to celebrate my arrival home. So, all is well with the Burke family."

"Tell me about your interview in St. Petersburg."

Mike reviewed his conversation with Roy Kellerman at the Vinoy Hotel. "He never did come up with an answer for why he did not make a move to protect JFK after the first shot."

"Strange that Agent Youngblood was on top of the vice president almost before the echo of the first shot had faded. Kellerman's not hard of hearing, is he?

"He didn't seem so to me."

"What was his opinion of Greer's virtually stopping the car after the first shot?"

"He couldn't understand it," Mike told Harold. "Kellerman was assigned to be in charge of the vehicle. It was his job to direct Greer, the driver. Greer's reaction to Kellerman's shouting, '*We've been hit.*' And the following Kellerman command, '*Let's get out of here.*' was not obeyed. Instead, Greer stepped on the brake of the vehicle."

"Do you think either of them was involved somehow?"

"I can't imagine," Mike responded. "Both of them and Lawson were desk bound after all the hubbub died down; no reward there. We checked their finances, and didn't find anything. Only agents Rogers and Youngblood received promotions from Johnson."

"How did your interview with Lawson go, Judge?"

"I didn't discover anything new either, Mike. Lawson was evasive about stripping the presidential limousine of protection and gave no credible reason for having done so."

"He obviously did not follow the usual Secret Service motorcade security procedures," Mike said.

"We're in agreement with the Warren Commission and the Select Committee on that conclusion."

"Maybe we'll get something out of our interview with Greer tomorrow," Mike suggested.

"We'll see."

Boggs' Washington Office

It was almost ten in the morning. Ryan and Burke were in the conference room waiting to talk with Bill Greer. He had retired in 1966 because of a severe stomach ulcer that grew worse after the Kennedy assassination. In 1973 he moved his residence to Waynesville, North Carolina.

At exactly ten o'clock the phone intercom in the conference room buzzed. Mike answered.

"Mr. Burke," Mable said. "I have Mr. Greer on the phone; line two."

"Thanks Mable," Mike said and punched the blinking button on the phone's base.

"Good morning, Mr. Greer," Mike began. "I'm Mike Burke with Congressman Ryan, who is on the other line. Thank you for visiting with us today."

"You're welcome, Mr. Burke," Greer responded. "I've admired the way Mrs. Boggs has followed in her husband's footsteps. So, I am happy to accept her invitation and help in your investigation."

"May I begin with a basic question, Mr. Greer?" Harold said.

"Of course Congressman. Ask away."

"At the time you were driving for President Kennedy, did you have a hearing impairment of any kind?"

"Not at all," Greer responded. "All agents have an annual physical, especially those of us who were assigned to the presidential detail. I had passed mine that very fall with flying colors."

"Possibly the senior agent in the vehicle, Roy Kellerman, didn't shout loud enough for you to hear him order you to accelerate the vehicle out of line?"

"No sir," Greer answered quickly. "I heard him clearly and did as he ordered."

"But first, you put your foot on the brake and turned to look at the president before you followed his order did you not?"

"I don't recall touching the brake," Greer insisted. "Before I could accelerate the vehicle, the president was hit two more times. I remember hearing the sound of the second and third shots in rapid succession."

"You don't remember turning to look back at President Kennedy before you accelerated the vehicle, either?"

"No, I don't. It all happened so fast, then the acceleration; like one motion."

"Have you ever seen the Zapruder film, Mr. Greer?" Harold asked.

"I think the lawyers showed it to me when I testified for the Warren Commission people."

"And you don't remember seeing the limo's tail lights come on, and the vehicle slowing almost to a dead stop after the first shot hit the president?"

"No, I don't."

Then another voice came on the line. "Gentlemen, I'm Mr. Greer's son, Richard. My father is not well, as you probably know. This questioning has made him very agitated. His ulcers have probably acted up again. I'm afraid he can't continue."

"If you don't mind, we have to end the call."

"Certainly Richard, we understand. We're sorry if this has upset your father," Burke told the son.

"Please give him our thanks," Harold added. The line went dead.

The two men sat and just looked at one another.

"Well," Mike reminded his partner. "We didn't expect to gain much from talking with Greer. But talk about selective memory. Whew!"

"Right," Harold agreed. "That's probably the only way he can live with what he did that day in Dallas."

*

The intercom on the phone buzzed once again.

Mike picked up the receiver and engaged the line. "Burke here," he said.

Mable was on the line. "Mr. Burke," she said, "Congresswoman Boggs is ready for you and Congressman Ryan, if you are."

"We're on our way, Mable."

The two men entered the Congresswoman's office and walked toward her desk.

"Please, have a seat," Boggs said. "What do you have for me?"

Harold began. "We've wrapped up our final interview, Lindy. So, we wanted to get you up to date before we returned home and wrote up the report."

"That's good news," she responded. "I was beginning to worry that you had gotten to like the Willard Hotel so much I was never going to be rid of you."

"That hotel is good, I must admit," Mike told her. 'But as Dorothy said in the movie, 'The Wizard of Oz,' there's no place like home.'"

"My bookkeeper will be pleased to hear that, Mike. Kidding aside, gentlemen, how do you feel about the report?"

Harold responded first. "We haven't put all the pieces together yet, Lindy. But we can give you a couple of definite maybes to tide you over until we put it all in a report."

"For starters," Mike told her. "We think it is highly doubtful that Oswald was one of the shooters."

"Whew!" Boggs exclaimed. "That's a stunner. I hope you can back that up."

"Another probable is that we believe a true coup d'état was in operation on November twenty-second, 1963."

"Holy mackerel!" Boggs said. "I'm glad I'm sitting down. Any more revelations like that?"

"Sure," Burke said. "How about, 'we also think that President Johnson and J. Edgar Hoover were guilty of obstruction of justice, right along with several members of the Warren Commission, a future president among them?'"

"You guys are killing me here," Boggs taunted. "You come in here all ready to leave town and you drop these on me. My Lord in heaven; and you two expect me to wait here in Washington while you take your sweet time to put all this in a report?

"Are you going to tell me you can identify the shooters, too?"

"Afraid we're not, Lindy," Harold told her, chuckling.

"Don't you start up with that chuckling, Harold Ryan," Boggs challenged. "I'm about ready to break my own rule and have a drink right here in the office, right now, thank you very much.

"I hope you can back up these probable conclusions of yours. I won't have you leaving me up the creek without a paddle on such a thing. You hear me, Harold?"

"I hear you loudly and clearly, Lindy," Harold promised. "Nothing will be in our report we cannot support. That's a promise."

"I'll hold you to it, my friend; you too, Mr. Michael J. Burke."

"Yes, ma'am," Burke assured her. "You will not be embarrassed in any way with our report."

***

On the plane to Michigan Mike Burke asked Harold, "Did we go too far with what we told Boggs?"

"Maybe," Harold said. "But, I believe we'll put together a report that will stand up to a good courtroom cross-examination. Do you agree with me that we can do that, Mike?"

"On some conclusions that we've already reached, yes; on other conclusions, we might be a bit shaky. But all in all, we'll not embarrass the Congresswoman. What do you think?"

"I agree with what you just said," Harold assured his partner. "Now I'm going to take a nap."

"You do that, Judge," Mike urged his former boss. "I'll wake you when we get close to home."

Harper Woods

"Was that meal super, or what?" Mike said. "Can't beat your mother's meat loaf, can you girls?"

"Not even all those fancy meals at the Willard Hotel in Washington?" his daughter Jackie teased.

"Not even close," Mike insisted.

"You say that about all of mom's cooking," Ann reminded her father.

"Ya' got me there Annie," Mike agreed. "I've never had a bad home-cooked meal. But your mom's meat loaf happens to be my favorite."

"Mine too, actually," Susan confessed. "One of these days you'll have to try my meat loaf, Dad. I think it's pretty close to Mom's."

"Music to my ears Sue," Mike told his eldest daughter. "Get the calendar Mom. Let's schedule the unveiling of Susan's meat loaf right now."

"While you guys are looking for a date for the big event, I've got to get over to the Andersons to baby sit," Ann told them as she picked up her plate and headed for the kitchen.

"I have to leave, too," Jackie said. "The sweet shop is open late on Fridays. There'll probably be a line-up by the time I get there. Drop me off on your way to the Andersons, will you, Ann?"

"Sure," Ann assured her younger sister. "If you hustle it up, that is."

"It seems that you're always in such a hurry," Jackie told her sister. "I'd love it to have another car around here."

Jackie's mother said, "You can take our car, Jackie. We're not going anywhere. Besides, it will save us having to pick you up later."

Within five minutes all their children were gone and the house was quiet.

"Join me for coffee in the TV room, sweetheart?"

"That sounds good to me," Marilyn told her husband. "Pour your own, will you? I'll fix mine after I use the lavatory."

Shortly, they were sitting side by side.

"It can't get any better than this, my dear," Mike mused.

"It depends," Marilyn answered.

"On what?" Mike asked.

"It depends on whether or not you're done with traveling for this Kennedy report Congresswoman Boggs has paid you to prepare."

"So, you did miss me; snoring an' all?"

"Sorta , I guess," Marilyn admitted, smiling. "The girls sure did, as busy as they are."

Mike slid closer to his wife. "Missed me, eh? That's nice to hear. I know I missed snuggling with my wife."

"Is that all, just snuggling?"

Mike began to unbutton his wife's blouse. Soon he had slipped his hand under her bra while he unsnapped it from behind with the other.

"You're still pretty good with those warm hands of yours, I see."

"Haven't lost my touch?"

Marilyn's breathing increased. "Not hardly." She gasped and leaned closer to her husband.

"Don't you want to talk about your trip and the Boggs Report?" Marilyn teased as she settled into her husband's arms.

"Not hardly," Mike told her.

Kissing his wife ended all further conversation. Mike and Marilyn spent the rest of the evening in their bedroom.

Detroit Office

It was ten o'clock Monday morning and everyone was seated at the conference table. Cathy Yager was able to make this meeting as well.

"Is everyone ready?" Harold asked.

Hearing no negative response he said, "Let's get started, then."

Joe Yager began. "While you two were gallivanting around the country last week, I went over the minutes of our last meeting. I think those notes of our discussion and the information you two provided pretty well supports the notion that we're dealing with a classic coup d'état. But before we approve those minutes, are there any comments?"

Mike proposed they tackle several categories of discussion. "Before we act on Joe's suggestion, I think we need to address topics such as:

Was obstruction of justice involved in the aftermath of the assassination?

If so, was anyone from the Johnson administration involved in obstructing the investigation or tampering with evidence?

Were any members of the Warren Commission involved in obstruction?

Is it probable that Oswald was not one of the shooters?

Is it likely that Secret Service agents acted on their own when they clearly denied Kennedy proper security in Dallas on November twenty-second, 1963?

Why were three members and the chairman of the Commission so determined to deny the existence of a conspiracy to kill President Kennedy?"

Harold was the first to react. "Before we decide to include all of this into our report in some way, I suggest we discuss each one, first."

"I agree," Mike said. "Any other comments before we start?"

"I have a question," Lillian said. "Before we start any discussion, I'd like to know just what constitutes obstruction of justice."

"Good question, dear," Harold told his wife. "Assume a crime has been committed. You happen by and pick up something from the crime scene. It could be most anything. But you innocently pick up something. Whatever its value to the investigation of the crime, it is still part of the crime scene. By picking up whatever you did, you interfered with the investigation of the crime. That's obstruction."

Marilyn added, "We know that the president's body was forcibly taken from Parkland Hospital before a legally required autopsy was performed. That's gotta be obstruction, eh, judge?"

"Right, that's big time obstruction, Marilyn. No question about it."

Joe added, "The presidential limo was washed down by Secret Service agents while it was parked at Parkland Hospital. Was that obstruction of justice, too?"

Mike responded this time, "Yes it was, Joe. That vehicle was part of the crime scene. Those agents were destroying evidence. And when one of them drove the limo away from the hospital to Love Field he was removing potential evidence, so that also was obstructing justice.

"Once the vehicle was flown back to its Washington garage, the bloodstained carpet was removed and the windshield with the bullet hole in it was replaced. Whoever ordered that done was committing a crime by destroying evidence and thus obstructing justice. Agent Kellerman told me that someone from Johnson's staff ordered it done."

"He had any idea who it was?" Joe asked.

"He said it might have been Bill Moyers," Mike said. "But he wasn't positive."

"Actually, Kellerman removed evidence from Parkland Hospital, too," Mike told everyone.

"What did he take?"

"He took Kennedy's clothing, which he later turned over to the White House residence staff."

"Was that obstructing justice?" Lillian asked.

"Definitely it was, Lillian," Harold answered.

Mike continued. "Then, the vehicle was flown to the Ford factory in Willow Run, Michigan where it was completely refurbished. All of this happened on the orders of someone in the White House.

"What about testimony?" Cathy Yager asked. "If testimony is changed is that a criminal act, Judge?"

"Yes, it is, Cathy," Harold told him. "Do you have anything specific in mind?"

"In the reading material you've provided as well as in your first report for the House Judiciary Committee, there were references to witnesses who claimed their testimony to FBI agents was altered."

"Well, Cathy," Harold responded, "if that could be proven, such an act would be an obstruction of justice and thus a criminal offense."

"What about withholding information that resulted in a crime?" Joe asked.

"What's the context, Joe?" Mike asked.

"According to information you received during your recent interviews, the FBI knew of credible threats from important Mafia persons on the life of President Kennedy. If that information was not shared with the proper authorities, wouldn't that be criminal?"

By way of answering, Mike said, "The threats made by Mafia figures were obtained by the FBI via wiretaps and through informants who were present when these threats were made. It appears, then, that the FBI knew well in advance of the assassination that an attempt would be made on the life of John Kennedy before the 1964 presidential election. So, to answer your question, knowing of a planned attempt on the life of the president, and doing nothing with the information, would be criminal."

"Remember," Marilyn reminded everyone, "Hoover had been told by the Kennedys that he would be forced to retire at age seventy-four, the mandatory retirement age for federal employees. So, he had a stake in the game."

"I think we all remember, too," Harold added, "that once he was president, Lyndon Johnson announced that J. Edgar Hoover could stay on as director of the FBI for as long as he wished."

"I don't suppose there was any connection," Mike commented to no one in particular.

"Withholding information in a criminal investigation is a crime, isn't it?" Cathy wondered.

"Yes, it is," Harold confirmed. "What information are you referring to?"

"I don't have any specifics in mind, Harold," she responded. "But I do recall that the House Select Committee on Assassinations declared in their final report that the CIA and the FBI both withheld important pertinent information from the Warren Commission. If this House committee discovered enough to warrant such a conclusion, wouldn't that mean that someone in both of these important departments of our government was criminally guilty?"

"Yes, it would, Cathy."

"Well that's enough to piss off a saint," Marilyn complained.

"You certainly have a way with words, dear," Mike told his wife.

"Are you suggesting that my anger is misplaced?" Marilyn snapped back.

"Not at all," Mike soothed. "But there was no way in Hades anyone back then would have suggested diving into that hornet's nest by accusing the CIA or the FBI of obstruction. Remember, the objective of the FBI and later the Warren Commission investigation was to verify that a single shooter had committed the crime, end all the rumors floating about, and thus close the books on the whole sorry mess, quickly."

"So, according to Epstein in his 1966 book, *Inquest*," Harold added, "the Warren Commission was charged as follows:

'There was thus a dualism of purpose. If the explicit purpose of the Commission was to ascertain and expose the facts, the implicit purpose was to protect the national interest by dispelling rumors.'

"The two purposes were compatible so long as the damaging rumors were untrue. But what if a rumor damaging to the national interest were true? The Commission's explicit purpose would dictate that the rumor be exposed regardless of the consequence, while the Commission's implicit purpose would dictate that the rumor be dispelled regardless of the fact that it was true."

Marilyn asked, "So, Judge. You're saying that the Warren Commission did not necessarily go with the facts wherever those facts led, but decided to discard or accept evidence depending upon what they thought what was in the national interest?"

"Yes, Marilyn. That's exactly what they did."

"Give us an example Judge," Joe asked.

"All right. I'll use the issue of Kennedy's throat wound for instance. At Parkland Hospital, seven doctors and an emergency room nurse saw the throat wound before the tracheotomy was performed. All these experienced emergency room professionals described the pre-tracheotomy wound as one of entry.

"At a press conference that same afternoon Dr. Malcom Perry and Dr. Kent Clark described the throat wound as one of entry. If their observations were correct a second shooter was present in Dealey Plaza on November twenty-second. The same evening as the press conference, Perry received a call from an FBI agent challenging his observation and demanding that he change it in a public statement.

"In March 1964 the chairman of the Commission, Earl Warren called Arlen Specter to his office. Mr. Specter was in charge of the forensics of the crime. He told Specter that they had a problem with the throat wound testimony Dr. Perry had given. He ordered Specter to Dallas that same evening to sort it out. Once there, Specter questioned Dr. Perry.

"Specter asked a hypothetical question. 'Could the throat wound possibly have been an exit wound?' Perry responded that he would have to agree, hypothetically, that the wound could possibly have been an exit wound. But Perry insisted later that the wound had all the characteristics of an entry wound. Other Parkland doctors testified that it was unlikely to have been an exit wound.

"Nevertheless, from that point on, the Commission was content to insist that Kennedy's throat wound was an exit wound."

"Meanwhile, the tape recording of the Perry/Clark press conference of November twenty-second was confiscated by the Secret Service. The FBI publicly told the New York Times, the St. Louis Post Dispatch, the Associated Press and the United Press International that their independently written stories citing the Perry/Clark press conference announcement that Kennedy's throat wound was as an entry wound, were based on a misquote.

"In its December Report the FBI insisted that the president's throat wound was an exit wound. Subsequent media requests to review the tapes of the press conference were denied."

"Commander Humes, who was in charge of the Bethesda Hospital autopsy told the Commission that because of the tracheotomy performed in Parkland Hospital at the site of the president's throat wound, it was not possible for him to judge whether the wound was one of entry or exit. So, the Commission had to explain away the entry wound testimony of the Parkland physicians without help from Humes.

"Another Parkland Hospital emergency physician, Dr. McClelland, told Richard Dudman, a St. Louis Post-Dispatch reporter, that he and his colleges were surprised that the Dallas police insisted that all the shots fired came from behind the president. This doctor told the reporter that: *"(He) and his colleagues at Parkland saw bullet wounds every day, sometimes several a day, and recognized easily the characteristically tiny hole of an entering bullet, in contrast to the larger tearing hole that an exciting bullet would have left."*

"Nevertheless, the Commission concluded: *"Immediately after the assassination, many people reached erroneous conclusions about the source of the shots because of Dr. Perry's observations to the press... Dr. Perry stated merely that it was 'possible' that the neck wound was one of entry."*

"So," Lillian observed, "in order to protect the conclusion that all the shots fired came from behind the president and the to support the single- shooter theory, the Commission had to dispel the 'rumor' that there was an entry wound to the president's throat, instead of dealing with the truth."

"Now you've got it, dear," Ryan told his wife.

"Consider the Warren Commission as the prosecution. Had this particular argument about the source of a decedent's wounds been argued in my courtroom, a decent lawyer would have exposed the position of the prosecution as unsupportable. I would have ruled in favor of the defendant over the objection of the prosecution."

"Just to be clear, Judge. You would have thrown out the Warren Commission's conclusion that no wound was caused by a shot from the front of the president; that all wounds were caused by shots fired from behind him?" Joe asked.

"Absolutely, Joe," Harold responded without hesitation. "The Commission had no foundation for the conclusion they stated in their September 1964 Report.

"On the other hand, the defense had a considerable amount of support for their position that at least one shot that struck the president was fired from the front."

Mike interrupted by saying, "What the Judge just said does not mean that Oswald or somebody else did not shoot President Kennedy from behind, though."

At this point Joe asked. "If you are finished with that point, can I ask another question about obstruction, Harold?"

"What is your question?"

"What about locking up all the documents for a zillion years?" Joe asked. "Doesn't that amount to obstruction too, Judge Ryan?"

Mike chuckled at Joe's zillion year reference. "I think the records are to be released in year 2039, Joe."

"I'll be long gone by then, Michael," Joe responded. "Might as well be a zillion years." Everyone laughed at this.

"That action seems to fit the legal definition of obstruction to me, Joseph," Harold agreed. "But remember there was no Freedom of Information Act back then. Even after it was enacted, it took Congress fifteen years to open a limited re-examination of the assassination and its aftermath by creating the House Select Committee on Assassinations. Locking documents away for the sake of national security was alive and well in those days."

"Also," Joe went on, "number three on this list of yours, Mike, suggests to me that you think members of the Warren Commission were guilty of obstruction. How do you figure that?"

"When we interviewed Arlen Specter for the House report, he told us that Congressman Ford altered evidence."

"You're talking about the man who was recently President of the United States, aren't you, Mike?" Cathy asked. "What in heaven's name did he do to obstruct justice?"

"Specter told us that Ford changed an illustration in the final Commission report which showed the entry wound on the president's back. He moved the wound up several inches closer to the neck. He did this, Specter said, to reinforce the single-bullet theory he supported.

"This was clearly contrary to eyewitness at the Bethesda Hospital autopsy testimony showing where the back wound actually was: five-and-one-half inches down from the collar line and two inches to the right of the spine."

"So, Congressman Ford altered evidence to serve a conclusion he favored?" Marilyn asked.

"Unless Specter lied," Harold assured her, "that is exactly what Ford did."

"But that's a criminal offense, isn't it?" Marilyn asked.

"In my courtroom, it would be," Harold confirmed.

"And the other members of the Warren Commission knew he altered evidence, didn't they?" Joe surmised.

"They had to, Joe," Mike said. "There was a three-three split on the Commission over whether or not the back wound exited through the throat. The issue was thoroughly argued. Three members would not support that conclusion.

"Congressman Ford argued in support of the throat exit wound theory. So, they all had to be aware when Ford arbitrarily changed the location of the entry wound on the president's back. The Congressman said later that he made the changes to clarify the issue for anyone reading the report."

"While we're on the subject of Warren Commission members, why were they so determined to deny the existence of a conspiracy?" Lillian asked.

Mike offered an explanation. "In a memo he wrote, J. Edgar Hoover said that Johnson felt it important to reassure the nation that the assassination was not in any way a political act, but rather the act of a lone gunman who was outside of government entirely.

"There were also two other interrelated reasons that were apparent at the time. The first of these was expressed by President Johnson when he recruited Earl Warren to serve as chairman of the Commission. He told Warren that an investigation by a blue-ribbon commission, chaired by the Chief Justice of the United States Supreme Court would dispel false rumors and calm public uneasiness over the assassination.

"He emphasized in his attempt to recruit Warren that a report by such a highly respected commission supporting the December 1963 FBI report, stating that a lone gunman was responsible for all the shots fired, would help dispel growing rumors of Cuban or Soviet involvement from gaining traction and possibly causing a nuclear war.

"The second reason was that a national election was just around the corner. It was important to President Johnson that doubts about the Kennedy assassination not become a campaign issue. To avoid that, it was imperative that the highly respected Chief Justice of the United States Supreme Court and the members of this blue-ribbon panel endorse the lone gunman theory. This would put to rest rumors of a conspiracy with multiple gunmen of unknown origin before the fall 1964 election.

"Evidence of a conspiracy could open the door to wild speculation and possibly lead to international trouble and potentially corrupt an orderly election in the fall presidential election."

"It appears to me, then," Marilyn concluded, "that any evidence calling into question the lone gunman conclusion had to be discredited."

"That brings us back to obstruction of justice issue," Joe reminded everyone.

"Maybe it does," Harold said. "But some things the Commission ignored were probably not obstruction. For example, several hundred witnesses to the assassination were interviewed. Ninety of them were asked if they had an opinion about where the shots came from. Of this number fifty-eight identified the Grassy Knoll and thirty-two said they thought shots came from the School Book Depository building.

"Thirteen of those interviewed were railroad employees watching the motorcade from the overpass. All of them testified that shots came from the Grassy Knoll. Eight of that number said they saw smoke coming from behind the shrubs and wooden fence located there."

Mike added, "Back in 1967, I interviewed several people who were standing on the Grassy Knoll watching the parade. They all said that shots were fired from behind them. Even a number of trained policemen testified to that as well."

"Despite this," Mike concluded. "The September twenty-fourth, 1964 Warren Commission Report stated very clearly that: *The shots that killed President Kennedy and wounded Governor Connally were fired from the sixth-floor window at the southeast corner of the Texas School Depository.*"

"So," Joe said, "case closed on any conspiracy involving more than one shooter."

"Regarding that lone shooter, Joe," Lillian asked, "the first time we met here you or Mike said something about Oswald might not have been on the sixth floor that day. Can we go over that again?"

Mike continued. "While Joe's checking his notes on that subject, Lillian, let me bring up a few problems with Oswald being the lone shooter. First, he was discovered drinking a soda some ninety seconds after the shooting on the second floor lunch room by his boss and a police officer. Second, two employees who were standing on the fourth floor landing testified that no one had gone past them down the stairs right after the shooting. The two elevators in the building were not available for anyone's use then either."

Joe entered the conversation then. "I've found the notes I made during that conversation, Lillian. We raised the same question then: We decided then that after Oswald fired his weapon for the third time, he had to have chambered a fresh round, gone to the other side of the sixth floor and hidden the weapon behind some boxes before he went down the stairs to the second-floor lunchroom. We asked the same question about the ladies on the staircase. You remember that discussion now?"

"Yes, I do. Thank you, Joe."

"So, what is your question?" Joe asked.

"Since the FBI and the Commission named him as the lone shooter, is it safe to assume that question was answered?"

"I'm afraid not, Lillian," Mike told her. "Specter told us back in '67, when we interviewed him for our Hose Judiciary Committee Report, that once Earl Warren himself had hurried down those same stairs to the lunch room from the sixth floor of the Book Depository Building within 90 seconds, it was assumed that Oswald did too."

"But what of the two witnesses on the staircase who never saw Oswald?" Lillian asked.

"Their testimony was not taken seriously."

"And the fact that the Dallas police reported that Oswald's paraffin test failed to show nitrate residue on his cheek from firing a rifle. How was that resolved?" Lillian continued.

Mike told her, "It was assumed to have been a poorly administered test and therefore not a trustworthy result."

***

"All right everyone," Harold announced, "we've shown that obstruction of justice was committed in the aftermath of the assassination."

"Right," Mike chimed in. "We've also shown there was a continuing effort by the Warren Commission to support the single-shooter conclusion at the expense of evidence to the contrary."

Marilyn added quickly, "Don't forget that there is a serious question about Oswald's involvement as well."

"Right, Marilyn," Harold continued. "But now, let's get down to the most important question that remains."

"What would that one question be, Marilyn?" Mike asked.

"Why was John Kennedy assassinated?"

"My Lord, Marilyn, take your pick," Joe chuckled. "In the one thousand days of the Kennedy administration he had managed to upset virtually all the elites in government and the private sector."

"We could start with all the national security people in his own administration, Marilyn pointed out. "He forced Allan Dulles to retire as Director of the CIA and began his promised dismantling of that agency. That sure earned the anger of the hierarchy in the CIA."

"Harold," Lillian asked. "Didn't you say that Lyndon Johnson told a reporter after he left office that he believed the CIA was behind the assassination."

"Yes, I did," Harold responded. "He also was interviewed by Leo Janos, a friend and writer. In the July 1973 issue of the Atlantic Monthly, Janos says that LBJ told him: "'The assassination in Dallas had been part of a conspiracy.' He also told his friend, 'I never believed that Oswald acted alone.'"

"Remember folks," Mike added. "In October 1963, JFK also ordered the evacuation of all United States personnel, including the thousands of CIA operatives out of Vietnam by the end of 1965. And with a 1962 executive order, he cut the CIA out of the military intelligence and covert activity loop entirely. According to General Taylor, JFK was serious about breaking up that agency during his second term."

"I can just imagine their outrage when they discovered Kennedy was secretly sharing top secret intelligence with the Soviets and ordered NASA to share space program technology with them too," Mike concluded.

"That wasn't the only group of elites he angered." Joe reminded everyone. "In 1962 he used dollars from the defense budget and threats of Internal Revenue investigations to force Big Steel to roll back their price increase.

"Their anger was shared by the international banking community," Harold continued. "In 1963 Kennedy ordered the Treasury Department to print several billions of dollars backed by silver. This would have destroyed the Federal Reserve, reduced the national debt and deprived international bankers who controlled the Fed of millions of dollars in tax-free income."

"Mike," Joe asked, "didn't you tell us that Johnson ordered the Treasury Department people to stop printing silver certificates?"

"Yes, he did. Not long after he took office, in fact."

"Harold, how does Big Oil fit into all of this?" Cathy Yager asked.

"JFK had promised to reduce or eliminates the oil depletion tax credit big oil had enjoyed for over thirty years. In the last budget he submitted to Congress he included a suggestion that they do just that: eliminate the oil depletion allowance. Everyone knew that Johnson had long favored the continuation of that tax loophole for his Texas supporters. By the way, it is still allowed by our tax code."

"You guys have been sort a' quiet about J. Edgar Hoover. Didn't he hate the Kennedys?" Marilyn asked.

"According to his biographers and the recent tell all by Hoover's Deputy, William Sullivan," Mike answered. "Hoover had a deep hatred for them. It was only made worse when Bobby Kennedy stepped in as Hoover's boss. That event took away Hoover's long-standing direct access to whomever was president. Then Bobby really upset the great man by installing a phone line directly to the director's desk. RFK used it to summon Hoover to his office whenever he wished.

"It was reliably reported that as soon as he heard of JFK's death he ripped the phone cord connection out of the wall.

"Anyway, JFK had informed Hoover that he would have to retire by 1964 at the latest when he had reached the federally mandated retirement age. But President Johnson announced publicly that Hoover could stay on as long as he liked."

"Would that have had anything to do with keeping all the Mafia threat information on JFK's life from the Attorney General and other law enforcement people?" Lillian asked.

"We don't know that," Harold said.

"Speaking of the Mafia," she continued. "I thought their Chicago organization had helped Kennedy win the electoral votes of Illinois in 1960."

Harold told her, "The story has been told that Joe Kennedy, John's father, had connections with the Chicago Mafia going back to his bootlegging days of prohibition. According to the same story, Joe asked for their help during the primary race against Humphrey in West Virginia. It was rumored that the Chicago Mafia Don, Sam Giancana, raised money for that primary campaign.

"In the November election, so the story goes, the Chicago Mafia supposedly delivered one hundred thousand votes for Kennedy to help him win all the Illinois electoral votes."

"So, in 1963, they wanted him dead?" she asked puzzled. "What changed?"

"Bobby Kennedy changed them, that's what," Mike told her.

Harold picked up the explanation.

"After he became Attorney General," Harold began, "Bobby Kennedy established a federal task force for the express purpose of destroying organized crime in our country. The Mafia leaders who had helped John Kennedy win election felt betrayed. Appeals from people close to the Kennedy brothers for Bobby to lay off fell on deaf ears. Instead the campaign against them only intensified; successfully, I might add. Then, death threats against the president were heard through wiretaps and reports by informants."

"So, it was the Mafia who killed John Kennedy?" Lillian asked.

"Mike and I have not uncovered any proof of that, dear," Harold told her. Threats made by leaders of organized crime were made. But there is no proof that they did what they said they would do."

"But the man they threatened to kill was assassinated just as they promised," Lillian snapped. "That means nothing?"

Mike added. "It's interesting that Sam Giancana, the Mafia Don in Chicago, and Santos Trafficante Jr., the Mafia Don in Tampa and Miami, were both killed days before they were to testify before the House Select Committee on Assassinations. Only Carlos Marcello, the Don in New Orleans who also made threats, is still alive."

"Are you saying," Joe asked. "That pursuing information about Mafia involvement is a dead end?"

"Afraid so, Joe," Harold admitted. "Unless Marcello fesses up to the killing, all we have are the wiretap recordings and a few sworn statements from people who witnessed the threats being made."

"To top that off, most of the men who made the threats are dead," Harold added.

"If there was any proof, I believe the House Select Committee would have unearthed it," Mike concluded.

"All right everyone, aren't we about ready to put a report together?" Joe asked.

"I think so," Mike said. "What do you think, Harold?"

"We've probably done all we can today. Lillian and I are going out of town for a few days. We've agreed to babysit with some grandkids while their parents go on a business trip. You could meet while we're gone if you like."

"I agree that we're done for today," Mike said. "While you and Lillian are gone, why don't Marilyn and I put something together and run it by Joe and Cathy?"

"Give us a call, Mike," Joe said.

"Knock yourselves out," Harold urged. "We'll all go over it when we get back."

Harper Woods

It was a lovely fall evening, and the Yagers, with their hosts the Burkes had finished a light supper and were enjoying a cup of coffee on the back porch.

"This screened-in porch we had built last spring was a super investment," Marilyn told her guests. "I can't count the number of evenings we've spent out here."

'I especially like the privacy of your back yard, Marilyn." Cathy Yager said.

"So do I, Cathy. Mike put in privet hedges when we moved here from Maryland. He keeps them trimmed, so they have thickened quite a bit and sort of screen out the world from the yard."

"I didn't know you had a green thumb, Mike," Joe commented. "Where did that come from?"

"I have no idea, Joe," Mike said. "I just like to putz around the yard. I'm not so sure it's a green thumb as much as you can hardly kill privet hedges. It seems that the more you whack at' em the more they grow. Sort of a no brainer, seems ta' me."

"Have you given any more thought to putting together a draft of your report?" Joe asked.

"As a matter of fact, Marilyn and I did just that the other day," Mike told his friend. "I had the girls at the office type it out and make us some copies. Why don't we review the draft we came up with?"

Once the four of them were seated around the dining room table, Mike passed out copies of the draft report.

"Before we get started, can I get anyone some coffee or a glass of wine?" he asked.

Everyone declined refreshments and instead began to read the draft report.

Report for Congresswoman Lindy Boggs

An Examination of the Motivation for the Assassination of John Kennedy

Prepared In 1979 by:

Harold Ryan

Michael J. Burke

Page 2:

Statement of the House Select Committee on Assassinations

September 15, 1978

"We believe, and the facts strongly suggest that President John F. Kennedy was assassinated as the direct result of a conspiracy, although the persons responsible for such an act cannot be identified."

Congresswoman Lindy Boggs

"The House Select Committee on Assassinations is to be applauded for their tireless work. However, it is unfortunate that the committee members stopped short of looking into why President Kennedy was murdered. By not doing that, they temporarily closed the door on possibly discovering who might have been involved in the conspiracy to murder the President of the United States."

Charge

"So, it is my intention to take that investigative step and open that door." – July 19, 1979

Page 3:

The House Select Committee members chose to restrict their investigation to whether or not President Kennedy was killed as the result of a conspiracy. This committee concluded that the killing was not accomplished by one man. Instead, they announced that there probably was a conspiracy involving more than one shooter. In 1967, for the House Judiciary Committee, we conducted a review of the evidence considered by the both the FBI and the Warren Commission. Like the House Select Committee, we came to the conclusion that the assassination of John F. Kennedy was the result of a conspiracy.

Now, twelve years later, Congresswoman Boggs charged us to look at motives which might lead us to discover who was involved in that conspiracy and possible coup d'état. Sep. 1979

Harold Ryan

Michael J. Burke

Page 4:

Index

Pre-assassination Status Quo in the United States

National Security Challenges

Domestic Policies Challenging the Existing Status Quo.

Kennedy's 1963 Decisions of Importance.

Lyndon Johnson's Dilemma.

Dilemma Facing Agenda Opponents

Options Available to Kennedy Opponents

Defeat Kennedy in the November Election of 1964.

Impeachment.

Die in Office.

Page 5

Page 7

"Let every nation know, whether it wishes us well or ill, that we shall pay any price, bear any burden, meet any hardship, support any friend, oppose any foe to assure the survival and the success of liberty."

— John F. Kennedy: Inaugural Address, January 20, 1961

Page 8

Pre-Assassination Status Quo in the United States:

During the presidential campaign of 1960, the Democratic Party candidate, Senator John F. Kennedy presented himself to the voters as a Cold War hawk and a moderate on domestic issues.

By Election Day in November the only issue before the public seemed to be whether or not to place another four years of the Eisenhower agenda in the hands of his vice president, Richard M. Nixon, or in those of the young newcomer from Massachusetts, Senator John F. Kennedy.

During that election campaign, the first televised debate in history was held. Senator Kennedy and Vice President Nixon presented no serious policy differences. Both men reinforced their Cold War hawk positions. But to the TV audience, the vice president came across as nervous and unsure of himself. Meanwhile, his opponent came across as vibrant, confident and reassuring.

Kennedy won.

It would be several months before he would be called upon to match his Cold War campaign rhetoric with action.

Page 9

National Security Challenges:

Bay of Pigs Invasion

Prior to the election, President Eisenhower authorized Vice President Nixon to work with the CIA and the Defense Department in an effort to overthrow the Castro regime in Cuba. Nixon's Democratic challenger was apprised of the planning before the election was held in November.

When Kennedy won the election, he was brought up to date on the effort to overthrow Castro. He allowed the project to go forward. In March 1961, he was assured by his CIA advisors that an invasion by US trained Cubans would be met with an uprising of the Cuban people. In short, the Castro regime would be overthrown and replaced with one friendly to the United States.

Immediately prior to the invasion the new president and his advisors tinkered with the arrangements for the invasion, and at the last minute canceled air strikes against Castro's small air fleet. As a result, Castro's forces successfully stopped the invasion force on the beach. Kennedy was asked by his military leaders to support the stalled invasion with United States military assets then ready just off the coast of Cuba.

Page 10

Kennedy refused to authorize such support. The invasion failed. Then, much to the international embarrassment of the United States, over one thousand invaders were captured. Kennedy was furious. He told members of his inner circle: *"The Bay of Pigs has taught me a number of things. One is not to trust generals or the CIA...."*

The reaction of the administration's Cold War hawks was immediate and predictable. The CIA leadership responsible for the project felt Kennedy had first weakened the chances for success of the very project he had approved and then betrayed the Cubans to whom we had promised support. The military believed Kennedy weak and had had failed his first leadership test.

Kennedy was angry with his advisors. He believed he had been misinformed and misled by both the CIA and the military. In fact, he came to believe they had set him up to invade Cuba with all the strength of the United States, not just give covert support to a Cuban invasion of their homeland and the overthrow of the Castro regime.

Kennedy's firing of General Charles Cabell, Deputy Director of the CIA, and Richard M. Bissell, CIA planner of the Bay of Pigs invasion, sent shock waves through the security community of the administration; and sent a message:

Page 11

"Watch your back, because you can't trust Kennedy and the bunch around him. If things go wrong those New England liberals will blame you."

— Vienna Conference with Khrushchev, June 1961

Two months after the Bay of Pigs embarrassment, President Kennedy met with the Soviet Union's premier, Nikita Khrushchev.

The handsome president of the United States and his beautiful French-speaking wife Jacqueline captured the attention and admiration of Europeans.

That success did not extend to the private meetings in Vienna. On the contrary, the Soviet premier was so forceful and rough, the young American president resorted to injections of amphetamines before meetings and tranquilizers afterward. It was reported later that Khrushchev privately told his people that he considered Kennedy weak and shallow.

National Security Action Memorandums, 55, 56 and, 57: June 1961.

Following on the heels of his threat remark to *"break the CIA into a thousand pieces,"* Kennedy issued three memoranda in June 1961. By issuing them, Kennedy removed the CIA from all Cold War operations and limited that agency to its sole role, under law, the coordination of intelligence.

With these memoranda Kennedy announced to the chairman of the Joint Chiefs of Staff, General Lyman Lemnitzer, that he considered the JCS responsible for our responses within the context of the Cold War as though it were a Hot War. That meant the JCS was in charge of all covert activity associated with the Cold War too.

According to these memoranda the JCS would decide what involvement the CIA would have, if any, in covert activities. He also established a Defense Intelligence Agency to collect and analyze intelligence, unfiltered for the president to replace the CIA in that regard.

Colonel L. Fletcher Prouty was the briefing officer for these memoranda to General Lemnitzer, Chairman of the Joint Chiefs. Lemmitzer told Prouty to file the memoranda away. The general did not intend to take any action on them.

The president's opening effort to rein in the CIA was being quietly ignored. President Kennedy learned it would take time and personnel changes to push his reorganization further.

Toward that end, the CIA Director Allan Dulles was gone by Thanksgiving and by the end of 1961, General Lemnitzer had been sent to head up NATO in Europe. He was replaced by General Maxwell Taylor, who had helped author the three memoranda for Kennedy.

Page 13

Nuclear Strike Recommendation

In July 1961, JCS Chairman General Lemnitzer recommended that the president take advantage of our missile and nuclear advantage and authorize a preemptive nuclear strike against the Soviet Union. Kennedy denied the request with some harsh words, amazed that his generals would even consider inflicting the estimated 140 million Soviet and thirty million American casualties during such an exchange of nuclear weapons.

Increase Vietnam Presence Recommendation

A second proposal from the Joint Chiefs was to allow large increase of troops in Vietnam. This was also denied in July 1961.

Berlin Crises

In August of 1961, the Soviets threatened access to Berlin. The Joint Chiefs suggested using nukes in response. Kennedy denied that option and instead relied on a brigade of ground troops and negotiation. Russia backed off but constructed the 'Berlin Wall.'

Members of the administration's hawks considered Kennedy's lack of action as backing down to the Soviets. They were joined in their disapproval by people from the State Department and from the retired Secretary of State, Dean Acheson, as another show of Kennedy's weakness and the lack of a consistent foreign policy.

Anti-Castro Campaign

Smarting from the failure of the Bay of Pigs and irritated by the rhetoric coming out of Havana and broadcast to the world, Kennedy authorized an anti-Castro buildup within the United States. During the summer of 1961 the president assured the Cuban community in America that he would give them whatever resources they needed to weaken and hopefully overthrow the Castro regime. Toward that end, Kennedy authorized an aggressive campaign to destroy the Cuban economy.

Overseen by Attorney General Robert Kennedy, many CIA agents and large amounts of money were allocated to train and equip exiled Cubans. Training centers in Florida the size of large cities were built. Millions were spent to support Cuban business enterprises in the state as well. Raids on Cuban ports and shipping were supported. It was decided to put as much pressure as possible on Cuba's economy short of invasion.

Even during the buildup, President Kennedy cautioned during a Miami speech that, *"There will not be an American solution to every world problem."*

Page 15

Despite such public pronouncements to the contrary, Kennedy had had begun to repair his standing as a Cold War hawk; at least within the Cuban community and the CIA. Doubts within the security community were cast again when he forced Allan Dulles to retire in the fall and exiled General Lemnitzer to Europe.

Laos Coalition Government Negotiated by Kennedy

Concern was once again fueled when the President rejected a covert military solution to the guerrilla war in Laos. He insisted on a negotiated solution which was achieved in April 1962 with the establishment of a coalition government. With this move national security hawks saw Kennedy backing down from a fight once again. They believed that he was assuring the successful march of Socialist/Communist governments in the Far East. Once again President Kennedy denied his Cold War hawks the opportunity to confront our enemies, the Communists. Instead, he insisted on accommodation, not on winning.

The TFX Fighter Plane Contract

Also, that spring, the award of the largest defense contract in history was announced. Back in 1960, that selection by the Source Selection Board was ready to be made to the Boeing Aircraft Company.

With the Kennedy administration new to the process and the addition of 2.5 billion dollars of Navy money to the original

Page 16

four-billion-dollar contract, it was sent back by Secretary of Defense McNamara for further review.

The political implications of the award began to emerge. Looking to the next presidential election it was decided to spend the money

within politically marginal counties of the United States. Kennedy directed Secretary of Labor Arthur Goldberg to establish a task force to compare the political impact of the contract if Boeing Aircraft got it, or if General Dynamics got the award. The political comparison showed that General Dynamics/Grumman, would yield the greater political gain for the Democratic Party.

So, despite the Source Selection Board again recommending Boeing Aircraft, Secretary McNamara announced that General Dynamics/Grumman would be awarded the entire contract. The military/industrial community was turned upside/down for reasons that had had nothing to do with what was best for the military. Instead, for the Kennedys, it had become more important to consider the political impact such awards could have on Election Day, and in depressed communities. The Kennedy political agenda had changed things for their own political advantage.

The Nuclear Test Ban Treaty and Disarmament: September 1962

During the Eisenhower administration talks with the Soviet Union over disarmament had stalled over the issue of on-site inspections.

Page 17

In 1962, the Soviet premier signaled for a resumption of those talks. Kennedy wanted to address a ban on atmospheric nuclear testing first. With that in mind, Great Britain, the United States and the Soviet Union resumed negotiations.

While the talks were going on, the JCS recommended that the United States resume testing in the atmosphere.

President Kennedy refused, fearing such an action would disrupt the talks and even cause another round of testing to begin.

The Nuclear Test Ban Treaty was accepted by the Senate of the United States by a vote of ninety-six to four in September 1962.

The Cuban Missile Crisis

In October 1962, American intelligence picked up information from their Cuban contacts that the Russians were installing in Cuba, medium- range missiles capable of carrying nuclear warheads. The Kennedy administration refused to believe this, because they had been assured by the Soviets that no such think was taking place. Pressure from Senator Keating and others in the United States Senate caused Kennedy to allow one U-2 reconnaissance overflight. Photographs taken revealed construction sites for the installation of such missiles.

Photographs revealed that the Russians had been lying. An international crisis developed. The JCS urged Kennedy to bomb the sites and take this opportunity to invade Cuba as well. The president refused both recommendations in favor of negotiations.

Page 18

There was no hot line then but a backdoor link was established between Kennedy and Khrushchev. Both countries seemed close to a devastating exchange of nuclear weapons.

The two leaders settled the issue diplomatically. Kennedy was hailed around the world as the great peace maker. It seemed that the Soviet Union had suffered a severe setback. Secretary of State Dean Rusk said that the leaders of the two nations were eyeball to eyeball, and the other fellow blinked.

It was true that the Soviets had agreed to remove their missiles, aircraft and personnel from Cuba. This was a clear victory for the Kennedy administration.

But, in exchange, the American president had agreed to remove our missiles from Turkey. More significantly, he had agreed to never invade Cuba or support groups attempting to overthrow the Communist regime on that island. The latter two provisions had serious repercussions in the United States.

Air Force General LeMay told President Kennedy that he believed the settlement was the worst defeat the United States had ever suffered.

Administration support for the anti-Castro campaign ended. In fact, the very people who had been encouraged and financed to attack and weaken the Castro regime, were suddenly cut off from support and in many cases arrested if they continued their efforts.

Page 19

Domestic Fallout Following the Missile Crisis Settlement

The Cuban exile community felt betrayed. And, the CIA leadership now firmly believed Kennedy would sacrifice others to political expediency and would not stand behind his promises.

In short President Kennedy and his people could no longer be trusted. He had shown that he would abandon friends to accommodate our enemies.

President Kennedy had become identified as the enemy.

"We couldn't allow another cripple in the White House."

— Allan Dulles to reporter Tom Sinsen: April 1964

"Well, we took care of that son of a bitch, didn't we?"

— CIA agent David Morales: 1964

"In my judgement, the CIA was involved in the murder of the President."

— Senator Schweiker Chairman of Church Committee 1977

Secret Communication with Khrushchev

President Kennedy no longer trusted his own people at the State Department to accurately communicate his wishes to Soviet Premier

Page 20

Khrushchev. So, he continued using the back-door communication system they had employed during the Cuban Missile Crises.

Domestic Issues of Significance 19610-1962

The above discussion of international and national security issues is not to say President Kennedy had no domestic agenda of significance or faced opposition to that agenda. On the contrary, during the first two years of his administration he took several actions which attracted the opposition of elites in the private marketplace too.

Oil Depletion Tax Credit

During the 1960 election campaign then Senator Kennedy downplayed his opposition to the oil depletion tax credit. This particular credit had a long history in the Internal Revenue Tax Code. It was staunchly defended by the oil lobby whose cause was supported by House Speaker Sam Rayburn and the Leader of the United States Senate Lyndon B Johnson. Just the same, JFK included a reduction of that credit in his last budget submitted to Congress just prior to his death. The new president did not support the reduction or elimination of that tax benefit.

Page 21

J. Edgar Hoover: Director of the FBI

In April 1961, Hoover was informed by Robert Kennedy that he would be expected to retire from federal employment when he reached the mandatory retirement age. A close friend of Lyndon Johnson, Hoover was known to hate the Kennedy family, especially Robert Kennedy.

"I hope someone shoots and kills that son of a bitch."

— Clyde Tolson: FBI Assistant Director, about RFK.

War on Organized Crime

Robert Kennedy was no sooner confirmed as Attorney General when he launched a new war on Organized Crime. The Mafia and some labor leaders were placed under aggressive investigation and prosecuted.

By the summer of 1962 the FBI heard Mafia leaders on wire taps and from informants that they were going to take the life of the president before he had a chance to be re-elected.

"Kennedy's not going to make it to the election. He's going to be hit."

— Carlos Trafficante: Miami, 1962.

Page 22

Civil Rights for African Americans

The early Kennedy administration supported expansion of Civil Rights for African-Americans. JFK was criticized by black leaders for not moving fast enough and opposed by those who thought he was moving too fast.

He used Federal Marshals and National Guard troops to support integration in Southern schools. His drive for the acceptance of black people in public places of business was well known as was his support of the 'Freedom Riders 'and other civil right activists pressing for the expansion of rights for African Americans and for integration.

Fight with Big Steel

In April 1962, the largest steel companies raised prices after the JFK administration had restrained labor's wage demands in the expectation that steel prices would remain as they were.

Kennedy responded by using defense contract money to reward the smaller steel companies and he threatened the larger ones with IRS investigations. Prices were rolled back. It was obvious to big business that Kennedy would use the power of the federal government to intimidate and support labor.

Page 23

Kennedy's 1963 Issues of Importance

Continuing to change the status quo 1960, Kennedy pressed ahead with his domestic and foreign policy agendas. In early 1963, the Kennedy administration took several significant domestic economic steps, made one major national security decision and another political move all of which, some analysts say, sealed his fate.

266   The Kennedy Assassination

Défense Spending

In April 1962, Secretary McNamara had shocked the military/industrial elites when he decided to award the six-billion-dollar fighter plane contract on the basis of political impact not military appropriateness.

President Kennedy went further and attacked the defense budget. He believed the United States far better prepared than the Russians, and he was unwilling to increase the national debt of three billion dollars. So, he instead p reduced defense spending by 10% annually

One year later, his Deputy, Roswell Gilpatrick, gave a speech entitled, 'The Impact of the Changing Defense Program on the US Economy.' In that speech, he touched on the adjustments the domestic economy will have to make in the face of reduced defense spending. He also suggested that in the future, the defense budget would be used to bolster

Page 24

depressed communities. He insisted that the United States could afford disarmament.

The Kennedy administration's 'Planning for Peace' initiative was another blockbuster shoe dropped by John F. Kennedy.

In the month of April, the administration had also announced it would reduce defense spending by ten percent each year for five years.

The national security elites and the defense industry community were staggered at this prospect.

In addition, Secretary McNamara announced the closing of fifty-two military bases in the continental United States and another twenty-one bases abroad. Such contraction of the military had not been experienced since the conclusion of World War II.

Intelligence Information Shared with the Soviets

In November 1962, James Angleton the CIA Director of Counterintelligence discovered leaks of sensitive intelligence documents to the Soviets. A subsequent investigation showed that the leaks came from the Oval Office.

Page 25

It was at this point that intelligence briefings for the President were modified to contain little information considered sensitive.

Angleton also organized discussions with officials at the highest level of the Kennedy administration to discuss the problem. Various steps were considered to prevent President Kennedy winning a second four year term in the White House.

As of this writing no firm evidence has surfaced to suggest that Angleton's group was involved in the assassination. There have been some who thought otherwise.

"In my judgement, the CIA was involved in the murder of the President."

— Senator Schweiker: Chairman of the Church Committee.

"CIA rogues and big oil were involved in the assassination of President Kennedy."

— Lyndon B. Johnson: Dallas 1972

"Well, we took care of that son of a bitch, didn't we?"

— David Morales: CIA Operative 1964.

Page 26

Kennedy signed NSAM 11110 in June 1963

With this order, Kennedy went after the Federal Reserve System. His executive order directed the Secretary of the Treasury to print four billion dollars' worth of silver certificates in two- and five-dollar dominations. Backed by United States silver reserves such an effort would make it unnecessary to borrow funds from the Federal Reserve System. Once in full operation the silver certificates would end dependence on the Federal Reserve.

Wholly apart from the Federal government the privately owned Federal Reserve System prints paper money on demand and lends it to the United States government at interest. This had been the practice since 1913 and was the source of the United States federal debt and immense profits for the stockholders of the Federal Reserve System at the expense of the American taxpayer.

Eight international banking families owned all the stock in the Federal Reserve. Earnings from the Federal Reserve System they owned was received all tax-free.

By issuing this order, Kennedy had followed the constitution and created interest free government money based upon the country's silver reserve.

Page 27

"The high office of the president has been used to foment a plot to destroy the American's freedom and before I leave office, I must inform the citizen of this plight."

— Kennedy at Columbia University: November 12, 1963

In April 1963, President Kennedy began backdoor communications with Fidel Castro.

Unwilling to trust communicating a discussion of normalizing relations through his State Department personnel, John Kennedy began to send messages to Cuba's Fidel Castro via trusted visitors and members of his United Nations staff.

His use of this method was known by our national security personnel. The exact content of his messages was largely unknown. But the topic of the discussion was suspected and strongly opposed by our military and by the Cold War hawks of the State Department and CIA.

In a November 1963 speech in Miami, President Kennedy said that normalized relations with Cuba were possible if Castro returned basic freedoms to his people and stopped being an agent of international communism in the hemisphere.

Page 28

Desirability of Peace, April 1963

President Kennedy made it very clear that he rejected the military solution to Cold War Challenges. On the contrary, he was going down the path of accommodation and détente.

This speech set the stage of what was to come.

Sharing Space with the Soviet Union. May 1963 Speech to UN

In May 1961, President Kennedy challenged the nation to join him in a race to place a man on the moon ahead of the Soviets. His call was met with great support and a great amount of money was dedicated to its achievement. NASA employed nine thousand people at the time of his suggestion. By September 1963, that number had grown to thirty thousand.

In his 1963 speech to the UN, Kennedy offered to abandon the race to put a man on the moon in favor of sharing space with the Soviet Union.

As a first step he offered to share our technology. He followed this speech with NSAM 271, ordering NASA officials to initiate contacts with their Soviet counterparts and begin the process of working with them. He told NASA Director James Webb to report progress to him by 12-15-1963.

Page 29

This proposal and the executive order was met with widespread opposition among the elites of the United States private sector and the national security hawks of his own administration.

But Kennedy moved forward and even directed the CIA to share their files of UFO information as well.

Vietnam Policy

"I don't think that, unless a greater effort is made by the South Vietnamese government to win popular support, that the war can be won out there."

— JFK to Walter Cronkite, April 1963.

In May of 1963 the Secretary of Defense ordered General Harkins to devise a plan for turning over full responsibility for the war effort to the South Vietnamese.

So, the Pentagon and the CIA were warned of Kennedy's intention to withdraw United States personnel as soon as was practical.

When General Maxwell Taylor and Secretary of Defense Robert McNamara returned from a Vietnam visit in the fall of 1963, they assured the president that the South Vietnamese government

Page 30

would be able to assume greater responsibility for the war; that things were going much better there. They assured him: "*It should be possible to withdraw the bulk of United States personnel by that time. [12-31-65]*" Report to JFK October 5, 1963.

Based upon their assessment, Kennedy approved an Accelerated Withdrawal Program and issued NSAM 263 on October 11, 1963.

In this memorandum Kennedy ordered the immediate reduction of one thousand American personnel by 12-31-1963.

In addition, he ordered the complete withdrawal of all American personnel by 12-31-1965.

But JFK cautioned his aides that he would not be able to fully withdraw from Vietnam until after the election of 1964.

"*So, we had better make damned sure I am re-elected.*" Comment to Kenny O'Donnell April 1963.

In the face of arguments made by those people in his administration who believed in a military solution to the Civil War in Vietnam, Kennedy told Roger Hilsman, one of his foreign policy advisors:

"*The Bay of Pigs has taught me a number of things. One is not to trust generals or the CIA, and second is that if the American people do not want to use American troops to remove a Communist regime ninety miles away from our coast, how can I ask them to use troops to remove a Communist regime nine thousand miles away?*"

Lyndon Johnson's Dilemma

In 1960, Senator Lyndon Baines Johnson was considered the second most powerful political figure in the United States. As Senator Majority Leader he followed Richard Nixon, the Vice President, in line for the presidency.

Some thought that by 1960 he exercised more power than President Eisenhower. He certainly thought he did. When the junior senator from Massachusetts declared himself a candidate seeking the Democratic Party's nomination for president, Johnson decided to seek it, too.

That convention contest was won by Senator John F. Kennedy. Friends of Johnson's like FBI Director J. Edgar Hoover and oil billionaire E. L. Hunt convinced the nominee and his father that it would be prudent to have Senator Lyndon Johnson as his running mate. Some say that they used evidence of JFK's legendary history of carousing as blackmail.

Whatever argument was used, the Kennedy-Johnson ticket was forged and it sought to win the November 1960 presidential election.

As the story goes, with some help from the Chicago Mafia, the electoral votes of Illinois went to Kennedy.

Way to the south, the Johnson machine in Texas managed to produce enough votes to win that state's electoral votes as well.

On the evening of the inauguration, Clare Booth Luce was riding with the new vice president, traveling from one inaugural ball to another. She asked Johnson why he had accepted the nomination. He told her: *"Clare, I looked it up; one out of every four presidents has died in office. I'm a gamblin' man darlin', and this is the only chance I got."*

Somewhere along the way, while Johnson served in the Congress, he accumulated a lot of money along with the political power. It was very unlikely it came from frugally saving his federal salary. But no one seriously questioned the source of his wealth until his close aide Bobby Baker was indicted on charges of corruption.

In 1963, Vice President Johnson told his old friend House Speaker John McCormick, *"John, that son of a bitch [Bobby Baker] is going to ruin me. If that [expletive]) talks, I'm gonna' land in jail. "*

The Congressional committee investigating corruption was putting pressure on Baker and others to do just that; talk. *Life* magazine was expected to come out with an exposé in December 1963 that contained damaging information about the vice president. When asked at a press conference if he would in any way interfere with that congressional investigation that might implicate his vice president, Kennedy said he would not interfere in any way. Johnson was on his own.

On the day before he left for Texas President Kennedy talked with his long-time secretary, Mrs. Evelyn Lincoln. She reports that he told her about the Baker scandal and of LBJ's deep involvement with Baker in it. He told her he planned to drop Johnson as his running mate. She related that he said, "*I will need a running mate in sixty-four, a man who believes as I do. At this time I'm thinking about Governor Terry Sanford of North Carolina. But it will not be Lyndon.*"

Even if the developing scandal had not ruined Lyndon Johnson, being dropped from the ticket would have ended his political career and most likely his dream of becoming president too.

President Kennedy was still alive as the investigations went forward in Washington. In fact, testimony was received on November twenty-second, 1963 concerning kickbacks an insurance agent claimed that he had paid Lyndon Johnson when he still was a Senator. Time was running out for Lyndon Johnson.

Under assault, in November, he retreated to his Texas ranch.

Also on November twenty-second, former Vice President Nixon was in Dallas. He was attending a Pepsi Cola bottlers' meeting. While there he was interviewed by a reporter from United Press International on the coming 1964 presidential election and the problem facing Lyndon Johnson.

"*Johnson is getting to be a political liability in both the North and the South.* I think the Democrats will *choose someone who can help the Democratic ticket.*"

The Situation as of November 1963

By the end of October 1963, it was obvious that President Kennedy was moving the United States away from Cold War confrontation with the communist world.

"*There is not an American solution to every world problem.*"

— JFK

He chose to achieve the goal of peace through negotiation rather than through military action. Therefore, he set a path of accommodation in hope of achieving détente with our Cold War enemies. Thus, he had abandoned a near twenty year goal of winning the Cold War.

The impact of reductions in military spending and his memorandum ordering all personnel out of Vietnam earned serious opposition from the military/industrial elites as well at the national security hawks of the CIA and the State Department.

And now, the president wanted to share our space technology secrets with our Cold War enemies. When his sharing of sensitive intelligence information with these enemies became known it was greeted at best with dismay and at worst with cries of 'traitor.' The question asked was:

Could the nation's security and domestic economy survive a Kennedy re-election and another four years?

Harper Woods

Mike and his wife had left the Yagers' to read the draft they had prepared.

"Give us a holler' when you're ready to go over it."

It was almost an hour until Joe appeared in the Burke family room.

"Whew!" Joe said. "I think we're ready, guys."

Seated around the table, Joe was first to speak.

"You two did a super job of organizing all the information you and Harold collected. I think your format allowed you to pull together all the various threads together in an understandable manner." Joe said.

Cathy agreed. "Not having been a party to all the discussions, research and interviews I must say I now feel better prepared to discuss the forces arrayed against the Kennedy Agenda. Some things seem missing though."

"What would that be, Cathy?" Marilyn asked.

"Aren't you going to address the possible involvement of the vice-president, the FBI, the mafia or elites of the military/industrial complex?" Cathy answered. "Basically, it seems to me you should address just who stood to gain from the assassination, too."

At this point, Joe jumped added his assessment. "I think once you lay out what Cathy is talking about you can logically jump into the issue of whether or not the conspiracy was a coup d'état."

"Right," Cathy concluded. "That would make sense to me as first time reader of the report.

"Somewhere in all of this I believe it essential to address the obstruction of justice issue as well." Joe added.

"Phew," Mike exclaimed. "You two really dug into this."

"Well, ya', Joe snapped. "Isn't that what you wanted us to do?"

"Absolutely," Mike responded. "Sorry, I wasn't trying to be critical of your comments. Actually, you two have pointed directly at some key stuff that should be in the report. Don't you agree, Marilyn?"

"Excuse me," Marilyn said. "I'm busy here taking notes. But, yes. Your comments lead us right into the next section of the report and then to our conclusion, the last section.

"If you two are up to another couple of hours of editing and proofing, Mike and I can have that last part of the report in your hands in say, two days? What do you think Mike?" Marilyn asked her husband.

"Sounds good to me," Mike answered. "How about it you two? Are you up to another session?"

Cathy answered, "I think so. Don't you agree, Joe?"

"Sounds like a plan to me," Joe responded. "Now, before we leave, how about a game of spoons?"

"Only if you restrain yourself, Joe," Cathy told her husband. "The last time we played you practically knocked me off my chair grabbing a spoon away from me."

"No guarantees my dear," Joe chuckled. "We Belgian's always strive to win don't ya' know, whatever the costs. No pussyfooting around for us."

"Whatever. But I'll not be responsible for treating you with kid gloves either, big shot.

"First, let me finish up our serious business, Mike. Could you drop off the next draft of the 'Report' Friday night on the way home from your office? Then you two come over Saturday around three for a couple hours of editing and discussion. Afterwards, we can run off to the Golden Buddha for Chinese."

"I think we can meet the Friday deadline," Mike answered. "Are you all aboard on that, Marilyn?"

"Yes, I am, Mike," she responded quickly. "Do you think Harold and Lillian will be back by then?"

"They might," Mike told everyone, "If they are, fine. They can join us Saturday. But, let's go ahead in either case." I'll drop off a copy of our next draft at their house the same time I deliver yours Cathy."

"Now," Joe clapped his hands together. "Get out the cards and spoons, Marilyn. I feel lucky tonight."

"Spare me the bravado." Cathy said laughing at her husband's excited anticipation. "Prepare for battle my Belgian superman."

Harper Woods

The following morning, Mike and Marilyn were up early as usual. Ann and Jackie were sleeping in and Susan was at the dental office, working. Mike was at staying at home today going over the 'Report' with Marilyn.

"We have two days to get this final section done if we're going to have it typed up and to the Yagers by Friday evening." Marilyn reminded her husband.

"You're right," Mike agreed. "Let's start with the obstruction of justice allegations we discussed last week."

"No," she suggested, "I think we should start with the set-up in Dallas. It seems more logical to me that we talk about the kill zone President Kennedy was placed in by the Secret Service before we get to the aftermath with its evidence of tampering and obstruction."

"That makes sense," Mike agreed. We can start there."

Page 32

The Dallas Set-Up

In the Warren Commission Report it is suggested that Lee Harvey Oswald obtained a job at the Book Depository Building in order to be in position to murder President Kennedy as he rode by the building during the Dallas motorcade.

However, Oswald applied for and obtained his job with that company in mid-October.

But, the parade route using Elm Street forcing the motorcade to drive past the Book Depository Building wasn't chosen until mid-November.

In the fighting for control of the Texas Democratic Party between the liberal U.S. Senator Yarlborough's faction and the conservative Governor Connally's faction, it was Connally's turn to pick the November 22 lunch site.

He chose the Trade Mart which required the motorcade to use Houston and Elm Streets. This forced the president's vehicle to reduce speed as it turned on to Elm and drive past the Book Depository Building on that street.

When Sheriff Bill Decker, Secret Service agents Sorrels and Lawson drove this part of the route, Sorrels said:

Page 33

"Hell. We'd be sitting ducks here."

Just the same, President Kennedy's aide, Kenny O'Donnell was told by Lawson that either the route via Elm Street to the Trade Mart or the one using Main Street to the Women's Center would be a security problem for the motorcade. The Secret Service could secure either route properly.

With that green light from the president's Secret Service detail, Governor Connally's choice of the Trade Mart was accepted.

Security Arrangements in Dallas

Long-standing Secret Service protocols required that all the windows in buildings along a motorcade route be closed and placed under observation until the motorcade had passed.

For the motorcades in Houston, San Antonio and Ft. Worth this protocol was followed. In Dallas on November twenty-second, 1963, it was not followed.

Testifying for the Warren Commission Secret Service agent Lawson who was in charge of security for the president's visit said that he did not have enough men to see to it that all windows along the parade route were closed and under observation.

Page 34

But the head of the FBI office in Dallas, agent Shanklin, testified that he had offered his forty-plus agents to assist the Secret Service and was refused because Lawson said his agents had it covered.

And, Sheriff Decker had well over one hundred deputies standing out in front of his headquarters on Houston Street watching the parade go by. He was told that his assistance was not needed.

At Love Field several unusual steps were taken which weakened security for the president.

Four motorcycle Sheriff Deputies were provided to travel alongside the president's vehicle. Lawson moved two to the rear of the motorcade and two to the rear finders of the president's vehicle.

Lawson testified that he moved them because:

President Kennedy didn't like the noise they made so close to his vehicle.

The president said the motorcycles interfered with his exposure to the crowd.

Lawson moved General McHugh from his front seat position in the president's vehicle. He was assigned instead to a vehicle in the rear of the motorcade.

Page 35

The media vehicle was also moved to the rear of the motorcade. It was normally either in front of the president's vehicle or right behind it in order to film and photograph the event up close.

Agent Rogers in charge of the seven agents in the follow-up car removed all agents under his direction from riding on the side and rear of the president's vehicle.

Page 36

The Assassination

The Shots

With the president's vehicle moving at only ten miles per hour on to Elm Street, the first shot hit the president in the throat.

The second shot hit the president in the back.

Because of the brace Kennedy wore around his torso, he did not slump over, but continued to sit upright.

Agent Kellerman did not move to protect the President at any time after the first shot. Instead he ordered Agent Greer, the drive, to accelerate and get the vehicle out of there.

Agent Greer did not accelerate when ordered. Instead, he put his foot on the brake and looked back at the president. Only after the third shot to the president's head was Greer seen on film to accelerate the vehicle.

Harper Woods

"So," Mike began, "If we say that obstruction is doing anything that impedes or cripples the investigation into the assassination is obstruction. Where does that take us?"

"For starters," Marilyn began. "Someone had to order the body of the slain president removed from the hospital before an autopsy could be performed there. So the Secret Service took it out of the jurisdiction where the crime was committed. The same goes for the president's vehicle and clothing."

"Who had the clout and authority to do that?"

"Secret Service agent Kellerman did all three," Mike said. "He admitted to me that he did. But who ordered him to do it is the question. He told me he just thought it was the right thing to do in the case of the body and clothing. As for the vehicle, he said someone from LBJ's staff ordered it flown to Detroit from D.C."

"And that was all ok?" Marilyn asked. "No charges were filed? No reprimand issued? No one was fired?"

"None of the above." Mike told her.

"The same day, tape and video of the press conference given by two Parkland hospital doctors, Clark and Perry were seized by Secret Service agents. The tapes have been sealed in the National Archives. Who ordered them seized? Why were they kept from the public until 2039?

"We don't know the answers to those questions," Mike told his wife. "We do know that in each case we've mentioned, the crime of obstruction was committed by federal employees."

"At the autopsy performed at Bethesda Hospital in Washington, D.C., evidence turned up missing there too," Mike reminded Marilyn.

"The bullet found in the casket used to transport the president's body was given to Admiral Burkley. He gave it to one of the FBI agents present and even got a signed receipt for it. That bullet then turned up missing. Photographs and x-rays of President Kennedy's body have also gone missing. So, now we have two more instances of obstruction," Harold told everyone.

"But who do we say ordered it done?" Marilyn asked.

"We can't because we don't know." Mike insisted.

"Lieutenant Command Bill Pitzer was the photographer during the Bethesda Hospital autopsy. The story goes: he kept a set of photographs at home. He was killed in 1966 under mysterious circumstances," Mike revealed.

"Back in Texas," Mike said, "the German Mauser rifle found on the sixth floor of the Book Depository Building, and at first identified as the murder weapon by the Dallas County District Attorney, was somehow lost. After Oswald was arrested, the Italian rifle owned by him became the murder weapon."

"But according to the Bethesda Hospital autopsy, doctors found that the shot to the president's head left particles of the bullet that killed him in the brain matter. Only a high velocity bullet can explode on contact like that one did. The Italian made Mannlicher-Carcano rifle identified as the murder weapon cannot fire high velocity shells," Marilyn reminded her husband.

"Correct. But, that's probably not obstruction," Mike said. "More likely, that's just sloppy investigative work."

"It was also a convenient oversight which allowed the Commissioners to blame Oswald as the lone shooter who used the Italian made rifle he owned," Marilyn said, shaking her head.

"Let's list all these acts of obstruction in our report format," Mike suggested.

Page 37

Aftermath of the Assassination

Dallas/ Parkland Hospital / Love Field

Presidential vehicle (the crime scene) was hosed down by Secret Service agents at Parkland Hospital, destroying evidence. Obstruction.

President Kennedy's body and clothing was forcibly taken from the hospital over the objections of Dallas County coroner. Obstruction.

Presidential vehicle (the crime scene) was driven to Love Field and then flown to Washington, D.C. Obstruction.

Press conference held by Doctors Clark and Perry was taped. All tapes were confiscate by Secret Service. Obstruction.

Doctor Perry was contacted by an FBI agent on 11-22-63 and told to change his testimony about the wound at Kennedy's throat. He urged the doctor to say it was an exit wound not an entrance would as described in hospital paperwork and at the press conference held that afternoon. Obstruction.

Secret Service agents confiscated Abraham Zapruder's film of the assassination. They did not share it with Dallas officials but took it out of that jurisdiction. Obstruction.

Page 38

The Argentine Mauser rifle found on the sixth floor of the Book Depository Building disappeared. An Italian Mannlicher-Carcano rifle surfaced and was declared the murder weapon. Obstruction.

Washington, D.C.

The president's vehicle was driven from Andrews Field to its Washington garage. There it was cleaned and the carpet replaced. Obstruction.

Then, it was flown to Ford Motor company in River Rouge, MI. There the windshield was replaced by George Whitaker's team and ordered destroyed. The vehicle was then sent to away for a complete do-over. Obstruction.

Bullet found lose in the Kennedy casket at Bethesda Hospital was turned over to the FBI and then lost by them. Obstruction.

Photographs and x-rays taken from the autopsy performed at Bethesda Hospital and ordered sealed from the public. Obstruction.

President Kennedy's clothing was taken from the autopsy room and was given to Mrs. Kennedy. Obstruction.

Page 39

Warren Commission

Earl Warren ordered all autopsy photographs and x-rays sealed and placed in the National Archives. Obstruction.

Congressman G. Ford, a member of the Commission, altered language describing the wound to President Kennedy's back. The Commission language was: "*A bullet had entered his back at a point slightly above the shoulder and to the right of the spine.*"

Congressman Ford changed that to read: *A bullet had entered the base of the back of his neck slightly to the right of the spine.*"

Ford said he changed this wording to clarify it for the reader. In fact, the wound was almost six inches below the collar of the president's shirt and two inches to the right of the spine and entered the president at a forty-five-degree angle. This was obstruction too.

Page 40

Responsibility for Obstruction of Justice

Given the authority standing of the officials who removed and/or destroyed crime scene evidence it would appear that:

Federal officials with greater authority ordered the illegal acts of obstruction.

Secret Service and FBI agents did not have the authority to do what they did without authorization from superiors. We must assume they acted at the direction of their superiors.

Therefore, the acts of obstruction committed by Secret Service and FBI agents was so immediate and so thorough they defy the possibility that the acts were randomly performed by agents acting in an unsupervised manner.

Page 41

Could the Assassination Have Been a Coup d'État?

Based on somewhat questionable acoustical analysis in 1979, the House Select Committee on Assassinations concluded that the Kennedy assassination was probably a conspiracy.

Based on Daeley Plaza eyewitnesses, reenactment testimony and emergency room records of Parkland Hospital a study completed for the House Judiciary Committee in 1967came to the same conclusion.

If it was a conspiracy, it could not have been the random act of a crazed killer. On the contrary, it would have been an organized and coordinated act of two or more assassins. But was it a coup d'état?

Simply put, a coup d'état is a seizure of the state apparatus to displace control of the government from its current leader and the current agenda and to be replaced with a new leader espousing a different agenda.

To be successful, a coup d'état must:

Be accomplished quickly.

Leadership must be transferred quickly and appear legitimate.

The assassin must be identified, arrested and killed quickly.

The assassin must not be from within the government.

The story must be believable and supportable.

All evidence of the crime must be gathered and controlled by the leaders of the coup.

The new leader must acquire the support of key government elites immediately.

The bureaucracy must be assured of legitimacy and continuity by their leaders.

Is that what happened at Daeley Plaza on November twenty-second, 1963?

The President of the United States was murdered that day in Dallas, Texas.

Contrary to long standing security protocol, his successor, Lyndon B. Johnson, was in the same motorcade and thus on the scene to take over the government, immediately.

Within hours, a man was arrested and accused of the crime. Within forty eight hours the accused was assassinated.

Within hours all of the crime scene evidence was removed from Dallas and placed under the control of the FBI in Washington, D.C.

Within hours, a complete story about the assassin was created and published. Any contrary evidence was suppressed or ignored.

Within twenty-four hours, the new president gained the support of the former president's cabinet and staff.

To avoid uncontrolled investigations, the new president appointed a blue-ribbon panel to investigate the assassination.

Over the next few months, all the murdered president's agenda initiatives were wither reversed or simply ignored.

St. Clair Shores

The Ryans had come home a day earlier than planned. So, the Burkes and the Yagers met at their house Saturday afternoon. Mike had put a copy of the draft report by their back door, inside the screen, on Friday. It seemed that everyone was ready to critique the draft.

"Well," Mike asked. "How are the babysitters?"

"You will discover one day, my friend, that it is exhausting. Let me just say, as much as I love my grandkids, I was so happy to leave for home yesterday I can't tell you. I am still exhausted."

Lillian hugged him and added, "Actually, he was pretty good with the kids this week. He took them on daily walks to the nearby community pool and ball field."

"Don't tell me you gave up your naps?" Mike teased.

Lilian answered. "Harold didn't get a nap per se. But when I joined him at the poolside, I watched the kids and he napped in a lounge chair.

"At night, when he would read to them, I found him a couple of times asleep with them."

"Well sure," Harold protested. "After all it was after their eight o'clock bed-time; mine too."

"You should have seen him making pancakes or macaroni and cheese. The kids love it."

"I have some skills around the kitchen, you know. I'm not just a big-shot judge. But, I must confess, those kids wore me out every day. I'm happy to be home."

"I hate to interrupt, but how about we get you two back in the saddle here and go over this draft 'report' Mike and I put together?" Marilyn suggested.

"After a week of answering the 'why' question five million times from my three inquisitive grandkids, I'm ready, Marilyn," Harold said.

"I assume all of you had a chance to go over the report. So does anyone have any comments?"

Joe was the first to respond. "I thought your draft covered things pretty well. I especially liked how you touched on motive, opportunity, and means in the late pages.

"But I think you need to conclude the report with a recommendation of some sort."

"I agree, Joe," Harold said. "With thousands of pages locked away by the Warren Commission, the FBI and President Johnson, I think we should recommend to Congresswoman Boggs that she introduce legislation of some sort opening up that kettle of fish for examination."

Joe added, "Possibly a panel of historians could be gathered to review all the documents and decide which should be released."

"Joseph," his wife asked, "do you mean to suggest that there is information about the assassination that should continue to be hidden from us?"

"Oh-oh," Joe exclaimed. "That tone of voice tells me I'm in trouble."

"Darn right you are, big shot college teacher," Cathy snapped. "What could possibly be so sensitive that the housewives among us in this country couldn't handle it?"

Cathy was clearly outraged. Mike and Harold sat silently, very reluctant to get into this on Joe's behalf.

"I didn't say that, Cath," Joe protested. "I only meant that there might be some documents so sensitive none of us should see them. Oh, crap. I didn't mean that, either."

Harold finally got into the conversation. "This is not an issue that we have before us right now. If we do recommend Congress order such a review of documents, it will be up to Boggs and her colleagues to wrestle with the details.

"How about if we suggest that it does not seem to us that any information about the assassination is so sensitive that the people of this country should be deprived of access?"

"Thank you. I like that language, Harold," Cathy said.

Lillian offered a suggestion. "I felt so much better informed after I read the draft. I appreciate that. I must admit, though, that all the obstruction of justice that was committed by our government people made me angry. The only reason I can fathom for it to have been ordered was that Johnson, the FBI and the CIA somehow had a hand in the assassination."

"Or knew about it being planned and did nothing to stop it," Marilyn added. "Getting back to the report, did you feel comfortable with how we treated the notion that the assassination was part of a coup d'état?"

Joe Yager got back into the conversation. "I liked the way you and Marilyn laid that all out. You made it pretty clear for me that it was a classic coup. But you left it up to the reader of the report to see the connection."

Harold offered another comment. "I can see the need for us to comment on the decision made by at least three members of the Warren Commission to reluctantly agree on the single-shooter conclusion. They did this even in the face of overwhelming evidence that multiple shooters were involved in the assassination and the lack of evidence supporting the single-shooter position."

"Why don't you write that up, Harold," Mike suggested. "We can go over that and the recommendation section Monday at the office."

"All right, I can do that Sunday afternoon."

"After your nap, of course. Eh, Judge?" Mike teased.

"After my nap, of course," Harold answered, not bothered by Mike's teasing.

"Can everyone meet for a final review around ten Monday morning at my office? We should be done with that in time for a nice lunch."

Everyone agreed.

"Will that be our last meal on Congresswoman Boggs?" Marilyn asked.

"It will be your last meal, Marilyn," Harold answered. "Mike and I have to present the report to her in D.C. yet. So we'll have one night and a couple of meals there when we do."

Each couple took their own car to the Golden Buddha Restaurant for dinner.

"Why do you even bother to look at the menu, Michael?" Marilyn asked. "You always get almond chicken."

"You never know when something else on the menu will strike my fancy, my dear. Lightning has been known to strike in strange places, don't ya' know."

"If you say so," Marilyn chuckled.

"By the way, Judge," Mike began, "remember our wager over the possibility of an interview with McNamara? I won that bet, so I think you owe me a drink."

"Holy smoke, you've got the memory of an elephant, Burke," Harold Ryan responded. "I had forgotten all about that."

"You know what they say about old folks, Judge. Short-term memory goes first."

"Thank you very much, smart aleck," Harold snapped. "Just order your damn drink."

"Now boys," Lillian cautioned. "No fighting at the dinner table."

Detroit

The report team gathered in one of the conference rooms to review the final draft of the Boggs report. Harold opened the discussion.

"Before we decide on the entirety of our report, let's take a look at what I wrote yesterday.

"That would be the addition of comments regarding the Warren Commission and the report recommendation?" Joe asked.

"Right, Joe," Harold told him. "That would be on pages 63, 64 and 65 of the draft report."

It didn't take long for everyone to review the additional pages.

"As you can see, I didn't go into all the problems Mike and I had with the two reports. I chose what has been considered the key problem that has plagued both reports since they were published.

"Do you have any additions or deletions, folks?"

There were none.

"If that's the case, we're going to put this baby to bed and send a copy to Congresswoman Boggs for her review. Thanks, everyone for all the time and energy you have put into this."

"How about Carl's Chop House for our final lunch together?" Harold asked.

"That sounds great to me," Cathy Yager said. "I can't remember when we were last there. Can you, Joe?"

"Try never, Cath," Joe responded with a laugh.

Willard Hotel

Two weeks later, Burke and Ryan were sitting at their favorite table in the Willard Hotel dining room. Copies of their report had been delivered to Congresswoman Boggs and they had an appointment with her to review it.

They had flown into D.C. earlier in the afternoon and checked into their favorite hotel. Of course, they made reservations in the hotel dining room, too.

Harold held up his cocktail glass.

"Here's to our enjoyable adventure, Mike."

"Hear, hear, my friend," Mike responded. "It has been fun working with you again."

"Let's not let our friendship drift apart like the last time though," Harold urged his former court clerk. "I know you're busy building a law practice. But that's no excuse for us not having lunch now and then or bringing the four of us together once a month or so."

"You're right, of course, Judge," Mike agreed. "What's your feeling about our report? Any last thoughts, any regrets?"

"Nothing serious, Mike," Harold responded. "But every time I go over it, I think of saying something a little better or adding this or that comment or fact. I can't tell you how many times I wanted to pencil in something. But, enough is enough. I think we put together a pretty good report, one that Boggs can be proud of."

"I think a lot of your opinion, Harold," Mike said. "So to hear you say you're proud of the work we did makes me feel real good. I just hope your friend Boggs agrees with you."

"Not to worry," Harold assured Mike. "She might be a bit shocked at first. But she will love the report. You can take that to the bank."

"Joe and the girls seemed to enjoy working on this, don't you think?" Harold asked.

"I think so," Mike said. "Ya' know, I didn't realize what a sharp gal your Lillian really is. You've been hiding her all these years. What's with that?"

"I never hid her. I just don't recall that she never wanted to get involved with my work. She had the kids and she did some part-time teaching. But it's only been lately that she has shown any interest. I think it's great.

"I believe you and Marilyn as well as the Yagers are part of the reason Lillian enjoyed the experience so much. I know she enjoys being around all of you guys. Coming to D.C. and interviewing Madeleine Brown was a real treat for her, too. So was getting involved in putting together the report.

"It was for Marilyn, too," Mike confided.

"Here's our food," Mike told Harold. "I think I'll have some iced tea with my meal," he told the waiter.

"By the way, Mr. Burke," the waiter said. "the chef ordered some apple sauce for the kitchen when he saw your reservation. He knows how much you like that with your pork chops. Do you want cinnamon with your applesauce, sir?"

"Please thank the chef for me. That was very thoughtful of him, getting the applesauce for me. I love that stuff with my pork chops. You can skip the cinnamon."

"He remembered from the last time you were here, sir. I'll tell him how pleased you are."

Over coffee, Mike asked. "What do you think Boggs will do with our report?"

"I can't imagine, Mike," Harold said. "It would be nice if she followed our recommendation and pushed for the release of documents. Beyond that, I have no clue."

"Right," Mike said. "We'll find out tomorrow when we meet with her. We don't have much to do tonight. How about taking a walk?"

"Sounds good to me," Harold said. "Say, it's a nice evening. Let's go to the Lincoln Memorial first."

Congresswoman Boggs' Office

"Good morning, gentlemen," Lindy Boggs greeted. "If your coffee cups are filled, let us get started."

"I think we're good, Lindy," Harold told her. "Where do you want to start?"

"You two really think the Kennedy assassination was a coup d'état?"

"Yes," Mike stated. "We absolutely think it was. The set-up, the execution and the follow-up were all classic and were perfectly executed. Clearly, the assassination of President Kennedy meets all the criteria of a planned coup."

Boggs continued. "And I suppose part of the follow-up you're talking about is all the obstruction of justice that was going on. According to you two, Secret Service and FBI agents were up to their eyeballs in obstructive activity."

"Lindy, whom would you expect to have taken the body of the dead president at gunpoint, along with his vehicle, confiscated press conference tapes and armature film? And, that's just to mention a few things. All of that was actually done. It's a matter of record, Lindy, not just an accusation by two hicks from Detroit." Harold reminded her.

"So, you're stating that a proper investigation into the crime of the century was prevented by our own federal government?"

"There is no other conclusion possible, Lindy," Harold insisted.

"And on top of that, members of the Warren Commission, J. Edgar Hoover and the CIA all lied to the American people.

"Yes, they did," Mike said. "And that, Congresswoman Boggs, is a matter of record, too. It's not in the report, but Judge Burton Griffin, who was the original legal counsel for the Warren Commission said,

'What is most disturbing to me is that the two agencies of the government that were supposed to be loyal and faithful to us, deliberately misled us.' Judge Burton Griffin, 1977.

"Why would they do that?" Boggs asked.

"It was all part of the effort to carry out a change of leadership and agenda successfully," Harold told her.

"What the hell do you expect me to do with the explosive stuff in your report?" she asked.

"Now you know why the House Select Committee came out with such a lackluster report last year. They got close to the fire and then backed off. But you led me to believe you wanted to dig deeper than your colleagues on that committee were willing to go.

"We did as you asked," Harold reminded her. "Our research was not rocket science. All the information we used is out in the open, available to anyone who wants to see it. Since November 1963, no one has wanted to do that; until you said you did.

"If you expected more whitewash, Lindy, why did you ask us to do this at all?"

"You're right, Harold," Lindy admitted. "I did want to open the door no one else has wanted to be opened. I did want you to lay it all out, once and for all.

"Then I showed your report to President Carter. His staff went out of their minds worrying about the fallout. He simply asked what I wanted from him to shelve the thing; pretend it was never written.

"Former President Ford saw it and practically went through the ceiling. He was so angry I can't describe it. I've never seen him this way. He asked me the same question. What will it take to deep-six this report?"

Mike finally spoke up. "So Congresswoman," he asked, "what are you going to do?"

"My inclination, my fine Irish friend, is to deep-six the report in order to get these two very influential men to support my bill and open up all the assassination files that have been locked away since 1964."

"I think that would be a great idea," Harold assured her. "It would also accomplish one of your primary goals for having us do this report. Namely, give to the people of this nation information that will allow them to better understand what happened and why, back there in Dallas on November 22, 1963."

"What about you, Mr. Burke?" Boggs asked. "Do you think I'm just a chicken to shelve this report and accept their offer of support?"

"Maybe you are," Mike responded. "But I think more will be accomplished when all that hidden information is available to the people of our country. The people may be angry at first, but they will eventually realize that the people in office now should be thanked for releasing all this information Heck, the people might even regain some of their lost trust in our federal government and our leaders."

"That would be worth it, don't you think, Lindy?" Harold asked.

"Yes, I think so too, guys," Boggs responded. "If that would be the result, the taxpayer dollars I spent on hiring you two might be the best money Congress has spent in a long time."

Mike and Harold raised their coffee cups and clicked them together.

"We can drink to that," Harold said.

Harper Woods

Later that fall, the Ryans and Burkes were sitting at the dinner table over cups of coffee.

"I noticed that it is awfully quiet around your house this evening," Lillian asked. "What gives?"

"You're right," Marilyn responded. "It is strangely quiet. Susan is working late at the dentist's office. She's responsible for debt collection now, as well as billing. She's pretty good at it, she says. Ann is in a dorm at Michigan State, just starting her freshman year, and Jackie is working late at Susi's Sweet Shop this evening."

"You're practically empty nesters," Lillian observed. "I went through that issue years ago. Harold hardly noticed, but the place seemed deserted. I had a hard time with it."

"What do you mean, I hardly noticed?" Harold sort of whined. "I noticed. I just didn't mope around about it."

"So, I moped around, did I?" Lillian challenged.

"I didn't say that," Harold insisted. "I was so concerned about you back then, that I didn't let on how lonely I felt too."

"That's so sweet," Marilyn said.

"I don't remember Judge Ryan being sweet," Mike teased. "Were you sweet, Judge? I guess I missed that during the ten years that I clerked for you."

"Thank you, Marilyn," Harold said. "That's very observant of you."

"Oh my goodness," Lillian moaned. "He's got you snowed too, Marilyn?"

"Not really," Marilyn responded with a chuckle. "I just hate to see a grown man cry." Lillian howled with laughter.

Harold changed the subject. "If you two don't mind, can we get back to something important; deciding on a game night?"

"Oh all right, crybaby," Lillian soothed. "So, we're going to have one game night per month. Who is going to be invited besides us?"

"I'd like to have Joe and Cathy as regulars. That would give us six to play games like rummy-cube, sequence, gin or Michigan Rummy."

Marilyn added. "That sounds good. We can rotate around the three homes, dessert and snacks only."

"I think to have a fourth couple every now and then would be fun too," Harold suggested.

"We'll start with the first game night next month at my place. I'll get together with you and Cathy to figure out the best night."

"That's fine, Lillian. I'll take the second month, Cathy the third and so on."

Later that night, Susan and Jackie were home and downstairs watching TV. Marilyn and Mike were in bed upstairs. They had the windows open and were enjoying a nice fall breeze.

That wasn't all they were enjoying. In fact, they were in one another's arms lying on top of the bedclothes. And despite the breeze, they were sweating.

"That was very nice, Mr. Burke," Marilyn told her husband.

"It has been my pleasure, madam. Is there anything else I can do for you?"

"Now that you mention it, there is."

Marilyn led the way to other things.

"Oh, my," Mike exclaimed.

Bibliography

Coup d'État: A Practical Handbook. Author: Edward Luttwak. Penguin Press. Great Britain 1968. 215 pp.

Who Killed Kennedy? Author: Thomas G. Buchanan. G.P. Putnam's Sons Publishing, New York 1964. 207 pp.

Inquest: The Warren Commission and the Establishment of Truth. Author: Edward Jay Epstein. The Viking Press. New York. 1966. 223 pp.

The Secret Team: The CIA and Its Allies in Control of the United States and the World. Author: J. Fletcher Prouty. Skyhorse Publishing. New York. 2011. 572 pp.

Whitewash: The Report on the Warren Report. Author: Harold Weisberg. Skyhorse Publishing. 1965. 224 pp.

The Last Investigation: What Insiders Know About the Assassination of JFK. Author: Gaeton Fonzi. Skyhorse Publishing. 1993. 446 pp.

Treachery In Dallas. Author: Walt Brown. Carroll & Graf Publishers. 1995. 435 pp.

The Death of a President. Author: William Manchester. Harper and Row Publishers. 1967. 710 pp.

Regicide: The Official Assassination of John F. Kennedy. Author: Gregory Douglas. Monte Sano Media Publishers. 2002. 223 pp.

Crime and Cover-up: The CIA, the Mafia, and the Dallas-Watergate Connection. Author: Peter Dale Scott. Open Archive Press. 1977. 84 pp.

The Politics of Escalation in Vietnam. Authors: Peter Schurmann, Peter Dale Scott, & Reginald Zelink. Fawcett Publications. 1966. 160 pp.

Rush to Judgment. Author: Mark Lane. A Fawcett Crest Book. 1966.

The Bureau: My Thirty Years in Hoover's FBI. Author: William Sullivan. W.W. Norton. 1979.

Best Evidence: Disguise and Deception in the Assassination of John F. Kennedy. Author: David S. Lifton. Macmillan Publishing. 1980.

Not in Your Lifetime: Fifty Years on: Weighing the Evidence. Author: Anthony Summers. Open Road Press. 1980.

The Advance Man: An Offbeat Look at What Really Happens in Political Campaigns. Authors Jerry Bruno and Jeff Greenfield. Bantam Books. 1972.

Kennedy and Johnson. Author: Evelyn Lincoln. Holt, Rinehart and Winston 1968.

The Warren Commission Report: Report of the President's Commission on the Assassination of President John F. Kennedy. Barnes and Noble Books. 1964.

Plausible Denial: Was the CIA Involved in the Assassination of JFK? Author: Mark Lane. A Herman Graff Book 1991.

Who's Who in the JFK Assassination: An A-to-Z Encyclopedia. Author: Michael Benson. A Citadel Press Book 1993.

E Books

Coup d'État: author Jerry Knoth

The Park Near the Underpass: author James Charles Schulz

JFK Assassination – 50 Years (On 60 Minutes): author Dr. Frey Hardy

Master Chronology of JFK Assassination: author Walt Brown Ph.D.

LBJ: The Mastermind of the JFK Assassination: author Phillip F. Nelson

The Complete Guide to the 1963 JFK Assassination: Progressive Management Publication.

The Death of a President: November 20-November 25: author: William Manchester. 1965.

The Kennedy Conspiracy: 12 Startling Revelations About the JFK Assassination. Author. Bill Sloan.

Prior Knowledge: America's Decent Into Terrorism and the Resultant Murder of JFK: Author: Tom Swinson.

Oswald: Assassin or Fall Guy? Author: Joachim Joesten. Iconoclassic Books. 1964.

Magazines

Life Magazine Issues:

   November 1963 (Special Issue)

   November 29, 1963

   December 6, 1963

   November 25, 1966

   October 4, 1964

Report on the Assassination of President John F. Kennedy

Prepared in 1967 By:

Michael J. Burke

Harold Ryan

Page 2:

The Charge of the House Judiciary Committee

In a 1966 Harris-Washington Post poll, sixty-seven percent of Americans said they did not believe the single-shooter conclusion announced in both the FBI Report of December 1963, and the Warren Commission Report of September 1964.

In reaction, members of the House Judiciary Committee directed their chairman, Congressman John Conyers, and their minority leader, Congressman Gerald Ford to initiate a study of the evidence surrounding the assassination of President John F. Kennedy.

The question the Committee wished answered first was: Did Oswald Act alone?

To arrive at the answer investigators talked with persons involved in the post-assassination investigations and looked at other bodies of evidence collected for the FBI and Warren Reports.

Page 3:

The report done for the Judiciary Committee deals with:

Directionality: Did all the shots come from behind?

Shots: How many shots were fired?

Shooters: Were all the shots fired by one assassin?

One section of this report will be devoted to each of the above questions. An appendix and notes dealing with the testimony taken will follow.

This will be followed by another section presenting conclusions and recommendations.

Page 4:

Directionality

"The shots that killed President Kennedy and wounded Governor Connally were fired from the sixth-floor window at the southeast corner of the Texas Book Depository."

— Warren Commission Report: Sept. 24, 1964.

However:

"The physicians who attended President Kennedy in the Parkland Hospital Emergency Room identified his throat wound as one of entry." See Appendix A.

"Several physicians at Parkland and others at the scene of the assassination on Elm Street identified the head wound as one inflicted from the front." See Appendix B.

Shots from the front: The Grassy Knoll?

Ken O'Donnell, Special Assistant to JFK, said, "I told the FBI what I had heard (two shots from behind the Grassy Knoll fence), but they said it couldn't have happened that way and that I must have been hearing things. So I testified the way they wanted me to. I just didn't want to stir up more pain and trouble for the family. *Man of the House. By Thomas O'Neill Jr. p. 178.*

Page 5

"As soon as I heard the shots, I turned toward the fence on the Grassy Knoll. Then I got on the car phone and ordered, 'Move all available men out of my office to the railroad yard… and hold everything secure until homicide and other investigators should get there.'" *Dallas County Sheriff J. E. Decker: Warren Commission Report. Sept. 1964; Vol. 6, p 287.*

Motorcycle Officer Bobby Hargis was positioned at the left-rear of the presidential limo. A light breeze was blowing toward him.

"I had got splattered with blood (and) I was just back and left of Mrs. Kennedy..." *Warren Commission Report. Sept. 1964. Vol. 6, p. 247, 248.*

There were thirty-eight witnesses interviewed by Warren Commission investigators. All of them reported that one or more shots came from the direction of the Grassy Knoll, and or suspicious activity in that area.

"In any event, no one present at the time saw anything at all suspicious." Congressman *Gerald Ford: Warren Commission Member. Life Magazine Oct. 2, 1964*

For more testimony see Appendix C.

Page 6

How Many Shots Were Fired?

FBI Report: December 1963. "There were three shots fired. The first shot hit President Kennedy. The second shot hit Governor Connally. The third shot hit the president in the head."

While standing in front of the underpass, James Tague was hit in the face by a piece of cement. This incident was witnessed by Dallas County Deputy Sheriff Walthers and reported to the FBI the same day. The following summer, the FBI verified that a bullet had hit a curb and caused a cement fragment to hit Mr. Tague. *Warren Commission: Vol. 19. p. 502.*

Warren Commission Report: September 20, 1964. "The first shot missed; the second shot hit the president in the back at the base of his neck, exited and then wounded Governor Connally. The third shot hit the president in the back of the head."

However, if we listed only the verified shots fired, the total number of shots exceeds those (three) announced in the FBI Report of December 1963 and the Warren Commission Report of Sept. 1964.

Page 7

Verified Shots Fired

1. One shot hit President Kennedy in the back.

2. A separate shot hit the president in the throat.

3. Still another shot hit a street curb and wounded Mr. Tague on the cheek.

4. Another shot hit the president in the head.

5. A bullet was found by the physicians at Bethesda Naval Hospital during the autopsy and given to Admiral Burkley, who was in the room. He then turned it over to FBI agents present (at Bethesda) who gave him a receipt for the bullet.

6. Another bullet fired was the one the FBI said hit Governor Connally.

7. One might also count the bullet found on a gurney at Parkland Hospital (the nearly pristine bullet).

"The weight of the evidence indicates that there were three shots fired." *Warren Commission Report: Sept. 1964*

Author's Note: Even if one accepts the Warren Commission's "single-bullet theory," it is clear that there were still at least four, if not five, shots fired, not just three.

Page 8

See Appendix D for more information.

Page 9

Were all the shots fired by one assassin?

"There is not one scintilla of proof that there was a conspiracy (more than one assassin), foreign or domestic..." *J. Edgar Hoover Warren Commission: May 14, 1964*

"The assassination of President Kennedy was the work of one man, Lee Harvey Oswald. There is no conspiracy, foreign or domestic." *New York Times: Sept. 27, 1964.*

Abraham Zapruder's film, taken from his position on the Grassy Knoll, clearly shows President Kennedy hit on the right-front of his head. *Life Magazine: page 45, frame 6. Oct. 2, 1964*

"There is no evidence of a second man, or of other shots, or other guns." *Congressman Gerald Ford: Warren Commission member. Life Magazine, October 2, 1964*

Author's Note: If any of the shots were fired from the front or side of the president, there was more than one assassin at Dealey Plaza that November day. Should such have been the case, therefore, the basis of both the FBI Report and the Warren Commission Report would be wrong.

See Appendix E for more information.

Page 10

Appendix A

Throat Wound: Front or Rear Entry?

Author's Note: If any of the shots were fired from the front of the president, there had to be more than one assassin in Dealey Plaza on November 22, 1963.

Dr. Perry: During an 11-22-63 afternoon press conference, he said the throat wound was one of entry. *New York Times November 23, 1963.* After an evening phone call from Secret Service Agent Elmer Moore on Nov. 22, 1963, Dr. Perry changed his story to, could have been an exit wound.

Dr. Crenshaw: Saw the throat wound and considered it one of entry. He was not interviewed by either the FBI or the Warren Commission investigators.

Dr. Carrico: Parkland ER physician. He saw the throat wound and considered it one of entry. He helped Dr. Perry perform the tracheotomy at the site of the throat wound. *Warren Commission Testimony. Vol VI, page 478.*

Page 11

Dr. Clark: Parkland ER physician: He saw a throat wound as an entry wound. *Warren Commission Deposition: Dallas, TX. March 21, 19645.*

Margaret Henchcliffe: Parkland ER Nurse. She described Kennedy's throat wound: "It was just a little bullet hole in the middle of his neck...about as big as the end of my little finger...that looked like an entrance bullet hole..." *Warren Commission Deposition: Dallas, TX. March 21, 1964.*

Page 12

Appendix B

Head Wound: Bullet Exit in Front or Back?

Author's Note: Both the FBI Report of December 1963 and the Warren Commission Report of September 1964 insisted that all the shots were fired from behind President Kennedy. There were witnesses who testified otherwise.

Dr. Clark: He examined JFK at Parkland ER. He reported that the president was hit on the right front (occipital) with an exit wound in the back of the head. *Warren Commission Deposition: March 21, 1964.*

Dr. Perry: He examined JFK at Parkland ER. He said the president was hit on the right with an exit wound in back of the head. *Warren Commission Testimony: Vol. VI, p. 478.*

Dr. McClelland: Examined JFK at Parkland ER. He testified that JFK was hit on the right with exit wound in back of head. *Warren Commission Deposition: Dallas, TX. March 21, 1964.*

Page 13

Dr. Peters: Examined the president at Parkland ER. He saw a "…large defect in the right occipital area…" *Warren Commission Testimony. Vol. VI, p. 478.*

Clinton Hill: Saw head wound at back of JFK's head when protecting Mrs. Kennedy in the limo. *Secret Service Report: November, 30, 1963*

Motorcycle Patrolman Bobby Hargis: Motorcycle and uniform was covered with blood and flesh. *Warren Commission Interview: Dallas, TX April 8, 1964*

Bill & Gayle Newman: They saw a bullet hit JFK on the front-right. *FBI Interview: Dallas, TX, November 24, 1963.*

Abraham Zapruder film: It clearly shows a bullet striking the president's head at the right-front, the skull being blown out and the head forced backward and to the left.

Parkland Hospital ER Nurse Margaret Henchcliffe: She saw a large skull wound on the back of the president's head when she was cleaning his body before it was put into the bronze casket. *Warren Commission Deposition: Dallas, TX. March 21, 1964.*

Page 14

Secret Service Agent Roy Kellerman: He saw a large portion of the back of JFK's skull missing. *Warren Commission Report: Vol. 11, p 124. Testimony: March 9, 1964.*

Secret Service Agent William Greer: He saw a portion of JFK's skull missing at back right of Kennedy's head. *Warren Commission Testimony: Vol. 11, page 124. Testimony: March 9, 1964*

Page 15

Appendix C
Were Any Shots Fired From the Grassy Knoll?

Author's Note: There were thirty-eight witnesses interviewed by the FBI and/or the Warren Commission investigators. All claimed to have heard one or more shots coming from the Grassy Knoll area. None of these claims were considered credible enough to investigate further. The following is a sample of those thirty-eight witnesses. For a complete list, Google Grassy Knoll Witnesses: The JFK Assassination.

Sheriff Decker: Sent his deputies to secure RR and parking area behind the Grassy Knoll area. *Warren Commission Deposition: Dallas, TX. April 16, 1964*

Dallas Chief of Police Curry: Looked to Grassy Knoll upon hearing the first shot.

Bill and Gayle Newman: Watched from Grassy Knoll. Bill Newman testified to FBI that shots came from behind them. *FBI Interview: Dallas, TX. November 24, 1963.*

Seymour Weitzman: Deputy Sheriff. Went to the Grassy Knoll to investigate and was sent away by men showing Secret Service identifications. *Warren Commission Deposition: April 1, 1964.*

Sam Holland: Union Terminal Co. supervisor. He stood with his son by Triple Underpass. He heard four shots and saw puff of smoke on the Grassy Knoll. *Warren Commission Testimony: Dallas, TX. April 8, 1964, 2:20 PM.*

Mary Woodward: A reporter for the Dallas Morning News. Watched the motorcade from Grassy Knoll. She believed that shots came from behind her. *FBI Interview: Dallas, TX. December 6, 1963.*

Page 16

Maggie Brown: A reporter for Dallas Morning News. Watched the motorcade from the Grassy Knoll. She believed that shots came from behind her. *FBI Interview: Dallas, TX. December 6, 1963.*

Ken O'Donnell: Presidential aide was in the motorcade. He believed shots came from Grassy Knoll. *'Man of the House,' by Thomas O'Neill Jr. p. 178.*

U.S. Senator Ralph Yarborough: He was in the motorcade car with Vice President Johnson. An experienced hunter, he told reporters after the assassination, "…you could smell the gunpowder." *James M. Perry: Reporter for the National Observer in Dallas traveling with the press corps on Nov. 22, 1963.*

Page 17

Mrs. Elizabeth Cabell: Wife of Dallas mayor. She rode in the motorcade. She smelled gun smoke coming from the Grassy Knoll. *Warren Commission Deposition: Dallas TX. February 13, 1964.*

Forrest Sorrels: Secret Service: In motorcade's lead car. Testified he thought shots came from the Grassy Knoll. *Warren Commission Deposition: May 7, 1964.*

Dallas patrolman Joe Marshall Smith: Ran to the fence on the Grassy Knoll after the shots. He was told to leave by a man who claimed to be a Secret Service agent. *Warren Commission Deposition: Dallas, TX. July 23, 1964.*

Page 18

Appendix D

Were All the Shots Fired by One Assassin?

Author's Note: If even one of the president's wounds was inflicted from the front, all the shots could not have been fired from the rear of the motorcade. Therefore, there had to have been multiple assassins.

Dr. Clark: Parkland ER said head wound was inflicted on front-right of JFK's head and exited on back. *Warren Commission Deposition: Dallas, TX. March 21, 1964.*

Dr. McClelland: Parkland ER doctor said JFK's skull opening indicated a bullet hit on the front of his head exiting on the back of the skull. *Warren Commission: Dallas, TX. March 21, 1964.*

DPD Sgt. D.V. Harkness: "I saw a group of men at the fence on the Grassy Knoll. I was told to leave by a man who said they were Secret Service." *Warren Commission Deposition: Dallas, TX. April 9, 1964.*

Bill and Gayle Newman: Watched from Grassy Knoll. They told the FBI that they saw JFK hit in head from the front.

Page 19

And, they believed that the shot was fired from behind them. *FBI Interview: Dallas, TX. November 24, 1963.*

Margaret Henchcliffe: Parkland ER Nurse. She saw the president's large wound on the back of his head when cleaning JFK's body prior to its transfer into the bronze casket. *Warren Commission Deposition: Dallas, TX. March 21, 1964.*

Dr. Perry: Parkland ER described the wound on the head as a rear exit wound. *Warren Commission Testimony: Dallas, TX. Vol VI p. 478.*

Sam Holland: Stood on the railroad bridge known as the Triple Underpass at the west end of Dealey Plaza. "I counted four shots..." *Warren Commission: Vol. 6 p. 243. April 8, 1964*

Mary Woodward: Journalist for Dallas Morning News. She wrote for her paper on Nov. 23, 1963, "Suddenly there was a horrible, ear-shattering noise coming from behind us and a little to the right." *Warren Commission Exhibit No. 2084 Vol. 24. P.520.*

Maggie Brown: Reporter for Dallas Morning News. She stood on the Grassy Knoll. She believed the bullets were fired from behind her. *FBI Interview: Dallas, TX. December 6, 1963.*

Page 20

DPD Patrolman Joe Marshall Smith: Headed toward the fence on the Grassy Knoll. He was told to leave by a man who claimed to be Secret Service. *Warren Commission Deposition: Dallas, TX. July 7, 1964.*

Page 21

Appendix E
Were all the shots fired by one assassin?

Frazier, Robert A., FBI Special Agent assigned to the FBI Crime Laboratory in Washington, D.C. He testified that it took him (best time out of three tries) 4.6 seconds to hit a target three times, one hundred yards away with Oswald's Mannli-cher-Carcano rifle. In response to a direct question, Frazier said he would have to add an additional second per shot if he were firing at a moving target (for a total of 6.6 seconds). *Warren Commission. Vol. iii, p. 407.*

Ronald Simmons: Chief of the Infantry Weapons Evaluation Branch of the Ballistics Research Laboratory of the Dept. of the Army.

He recruited three riflemen considered 'expert' by the National Rifle Association. They fired twenty-one shots each at three stationary targets. Only one of the 'experts' hit the target within the WC's time limit of 5.15 seconds. *Warren Commission. Vol. iii, p. 446.*

Page 22

Findings

This investigation has led us to believe that there is substantial evidence that:

There were more than three shots fired in the plot to kill President Kennedy on November 22, 1963.

There were shots fired at President Kennedy from the front as well as from behind.

There was more than one assassin involved in the killing of President Kennedy on November 22, 1963.

Page 23

Recommendation

Therefore, we recommend the House Judiciary Committee support the action suggested in the *Life Magazine* editorial, published on November 25, 1966.

"One conclusion is inescapable: the national interest deserves clear resolution of the doubts. A new investigating body should be set up, perhaps at the initiative of Congress. In a scrupulously objective and unhurried atmosphere, without the pressure to give assurance to a shocked country, it should reexamine the evidence and consider other evidence the Warren Commission failed to evaluate." *Life Magazine. November 25, 1966. P.49b.*

About the Authors

Michael J. Deeb was born and raised in Grand Rapids, Michigan. His undergraduate and graduate educations centered on American Studies. His doctorate was in management. He was an educator for nineteen years, most of which saw him teaching American history and historical research.

His personal life found him as a pre-teen spending time regularly at the public library, reading non-fiction works of history. This passion has continued to this day. Teaching at the college, university and high school levels only increased his passion for such reading and research.

Since 2005, he and his wife have lived in Sun City Center, Florida. In the fall of 2007 he published the first historical novel in the Drieborg Chronicles series, "Duty and Honor." The sequel, "Duty Accomplished" was completed in 2008. "Honor Restored" followed in 2009 and "The Lincoln Assassination" became available in 2010. He wrote and published a prequel, "1860," to this trilogy in 2011 and concluded the series with "The Way West" in 2013.

Currently, Dr. Deeb is working as a Civil War speaker on the ships of the American Cruise Lines. He also gives presentations at libraries, book stores and service clubs. His interests include, bridge, choral singing and walking.

You are welcome to contact him at **civilwarnovels@gmail.com**. His websites are www.civilwarnovels.com and **www.thekennedyassassination.com**.

Robert Lockwood Mills spent most of his life as a Wall Street broker and was an instructor in financial planning for Adelphi University. In middle age he began to focus on historical research and his avocation, writing. Beginning in 1994 he has authored eleven published non-fiction books, including "It Didn't Happen the Way You Think" (Heritage Books 1994), "Stamford: An Illustrated History" (American Historical Press 2002), "The Lindbergh Syndrome: Heroes and Celebrities in a New Gilded Age" (Wheatmark 2005), and most recently, "Conscience of a Conspiracy Theorist" (Algora Publishing 2011), which studied the Kennedy assassination with an emphasis on governmental and media efforts to stigmatize honest skeptics as conspiracy theorists.

His other works consist of six stage plays, two personal biographies, a baseball book (written entirely from memory), and a history of the Darien (Connecticut) Country Club. Mills also authored and directed a docudrama, "The Trail of John Wilkes Booth," which was broadcast by Connecticut Public Radio in 1999.

Mills has been Project Editor for five Reader's Digest Illustrated Trade Books on historical topics, and now does free-lance editing work for local authors. His diverse interests include acting and directing, choral singing, songwriting, satire, and crossword puzzle construction. He is a widower with three grown daughters and four grandchildren, and lives in Florida with his companion and fellow author, Rosemary Clifton.

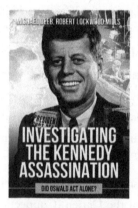

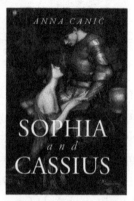

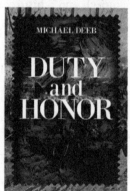
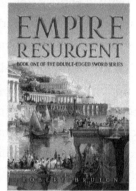